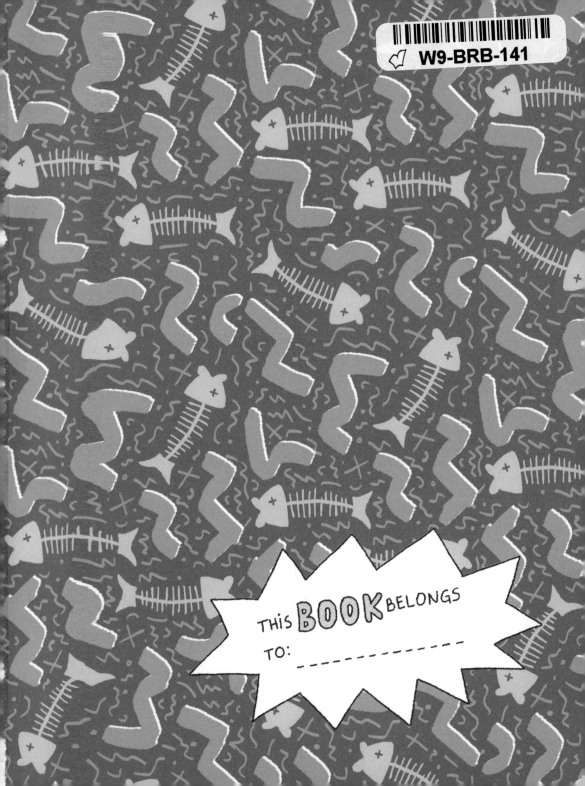

THIS **BOOK** BELONGS TO: _ _ _ _ _ _ _ _ _ _ _ _ _

This is a second edition.
First published in English in 2018 by Flying Eye Books,
an imprint of Nobrow Ltd. 27 Westgate Street, London E8 3RL.

Akissi: Histoires Pimentées, by Marguerite Abouet and Mathieu Sapin
© Gallimard, France, 2014.
Published in agreement with Éditions Gallimard.

Text by Marguerite Abouet 2018. Illustrations by Mathieu Sapin 2018.
Marguerite Abouet and Mathieu Sapin have asserted their right
under the Copyright, Designs and Patents Act, 1988,
to be identified as the Author and Illustrator of this Work.

Translation by Judith Taboy and Marie Bédrune.

Published in the US by Nobrow (US) Inc.
Printed in Poland on FSC® certified paper.

ISBN: 978-1-911171-47-8
Order from www.flyingeyebooks.com

Abouet & Sapin

Akissi

TALES OF MISCHIEF

FLYING EYE BOOKS
LONDON | NEW YORK

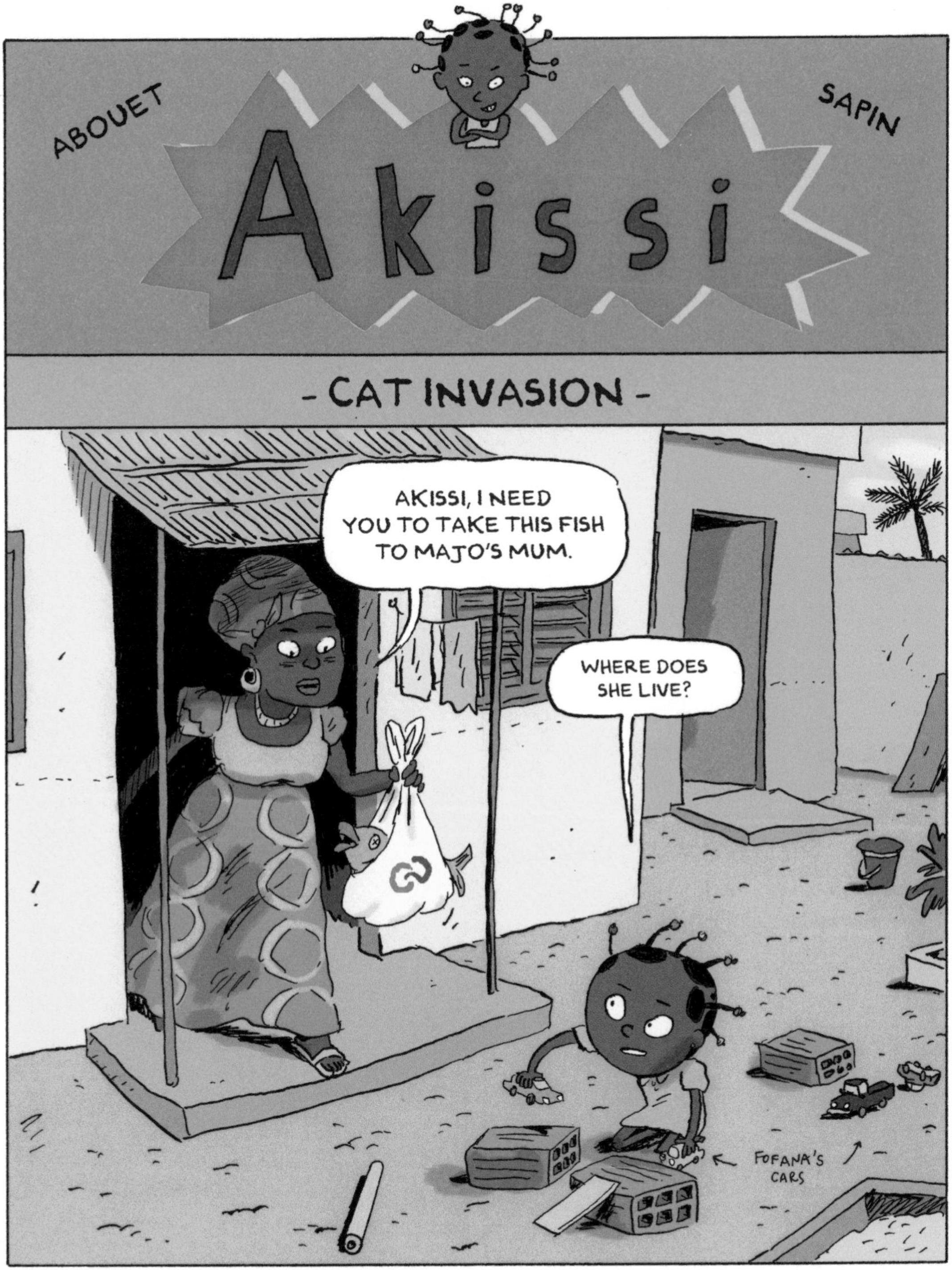
ABOUET
Akissi
SAPIN
- CAT INVASION -
AKISSI, I NEED YOU TO TAKE THIS FISH TO MAJO'S MUM.
WHERE DOES SHE LIVE?
FOFANA'S CARS

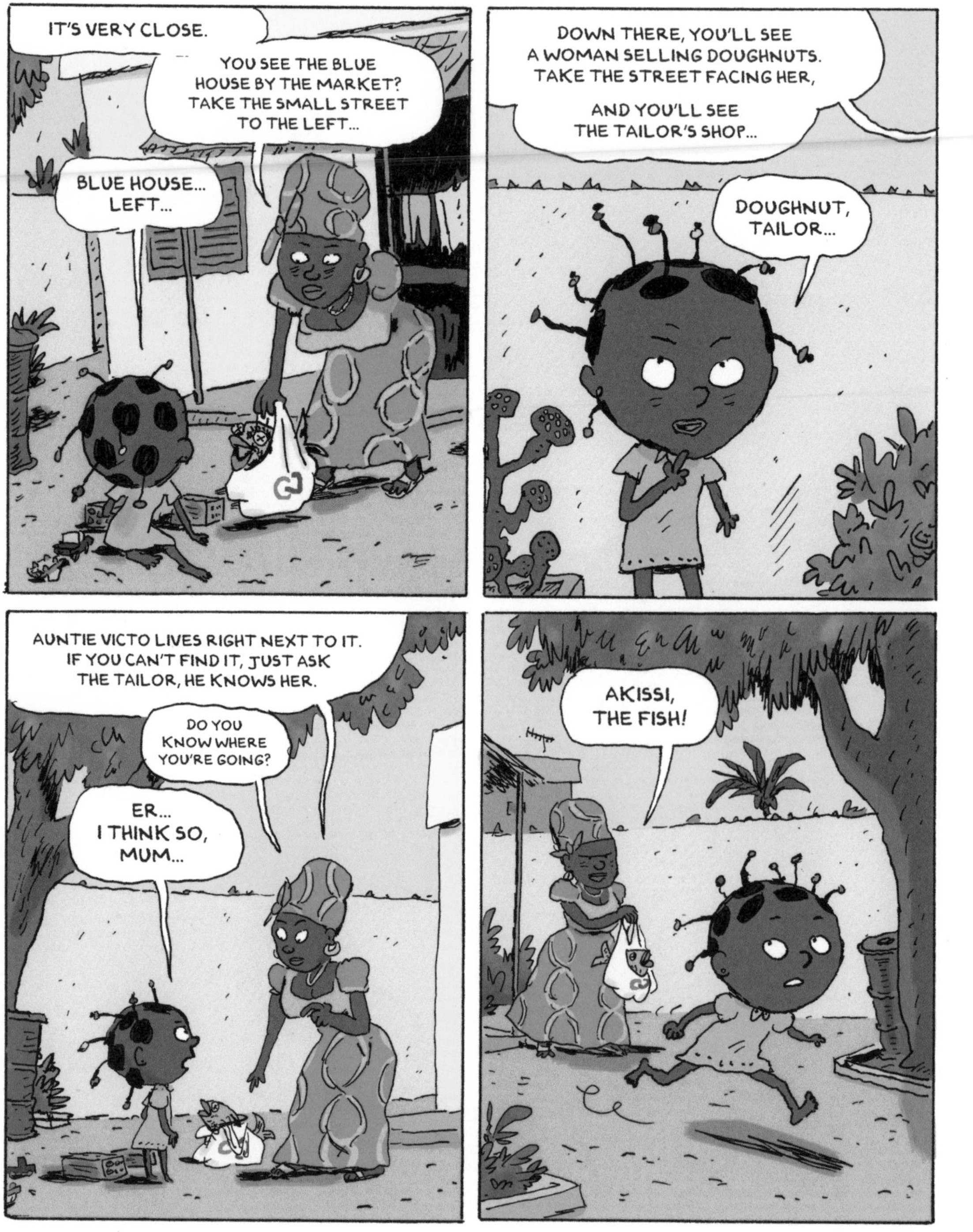
IT'S VERY CLOSE.
YOU SEE THE BLUE HOUSE BY THE MARKET? TAKE THE SMALL STREET TO THE LEFT...
BLUE HOUSE... LEFT...
DOWN THERE, YOU'LL SEE A WOMAN SELLING DOUGHNUTS. TAKE THE STREET FACING HER,
AND YOU'LL SEE THE TAILOR'S SHOP...
DOUGHNUT, TAILOR...
AUNTIE VICTO LIVES RIGHT NEXT TO IT. IF YOU CAN'T FIND IT, JUST ASK THE TAILOR, HE KNOWS HER.
DO YOU KNOW WHERE YOU'RE GOING?
ER... I THINK SO, MUM...
AKISSI, THE FISH!

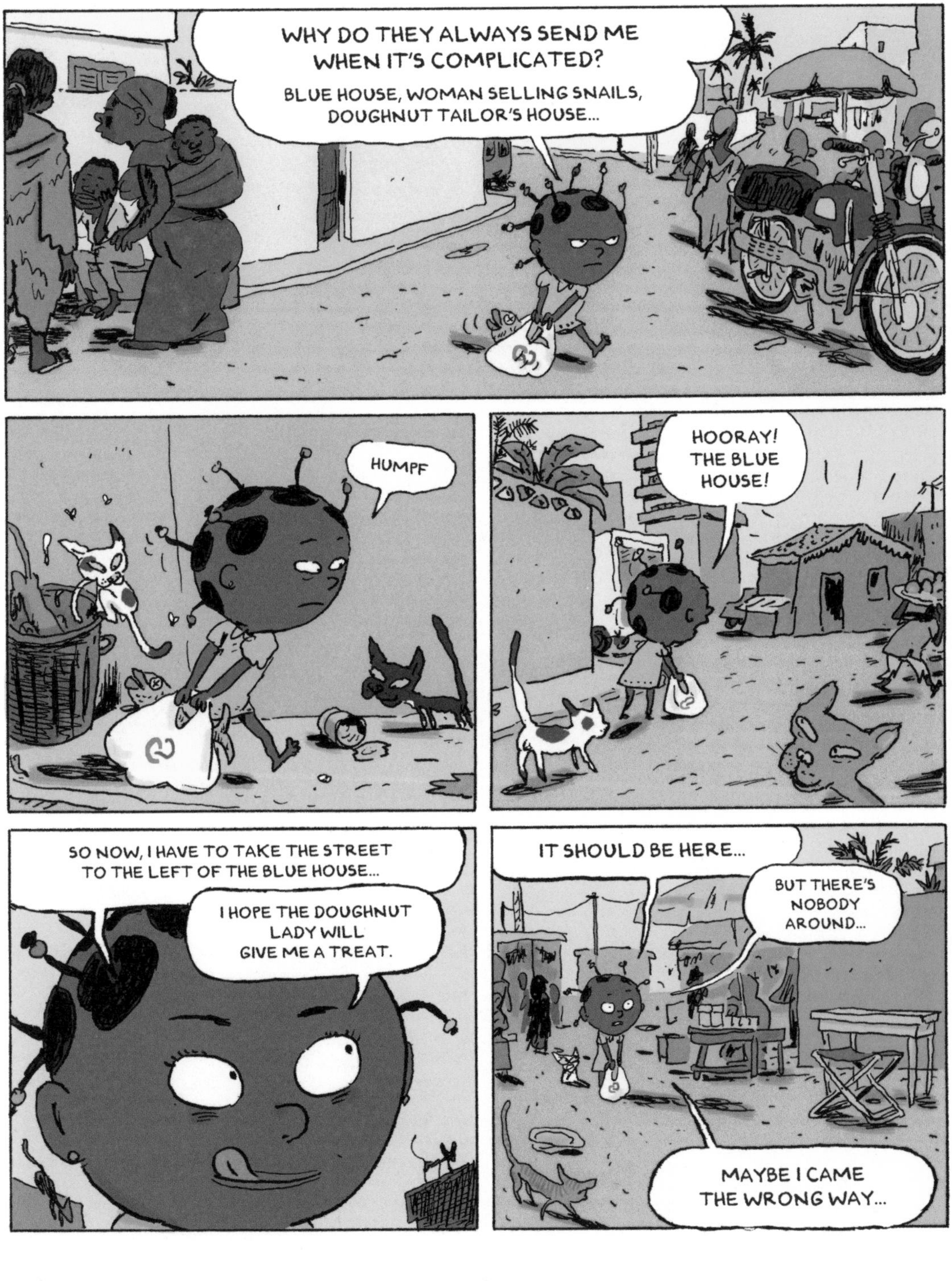
WHY DO THEY ALWAYS SEND ME WHEN IT'S COMPLICATED?
BLUE HOUSE, WOMAN SELLING SNAILS, DOUGHNUT TAILOR'S HOUSE...
HUMPF
HOORAY! THE BLUE HOUSE!
SO NOW, I HAVE TO TAKE THE STREET TO THE LEFT OF THE BLUE HOUSE...
I HOPE THE DOUGHNUT LADY WILL GIVE ME A TREAT.
IT SHOULD BE HERE...
BUT THERE'S NOBODY AROUND...
MAYBE I CAME THE WRONG WAY...

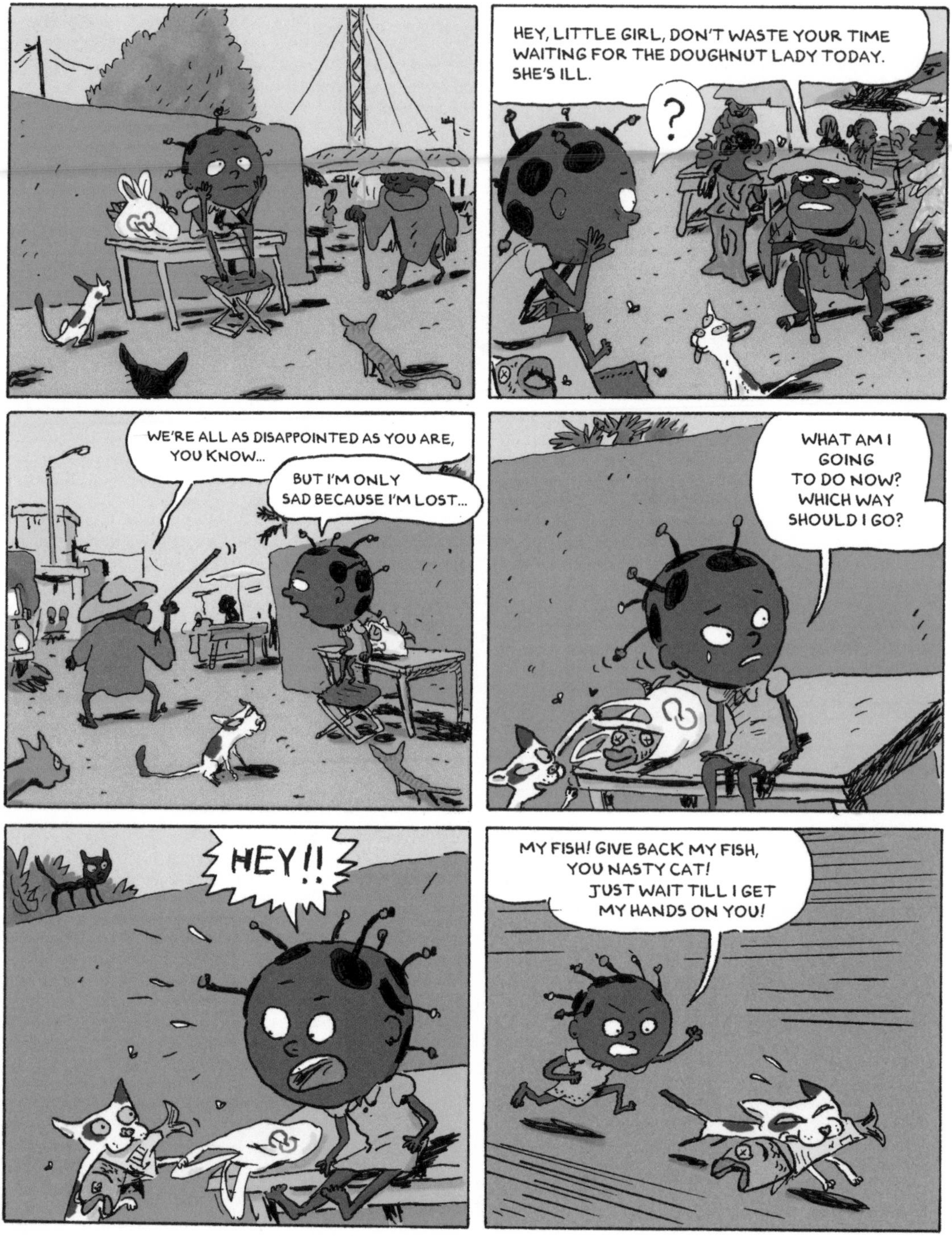
HEY, LITTLE GIRL, DON'T WASTE YOUR TIME WAITING FOR THE DOUGHNUT LADY TODAY. SHE'S ILL.
?
WE'RE ALL AS DISAPPOINTED AS YOU ARE, YOU KNOW...
BUT I'M ONLY SAD BECAUSE I'M LOST...
WHAT AM I GOING TO DO NOW? WHICH WAY SHOULD I GO?
HEY!!
MY FISH! GIVE BACK MY FISH, YOU NASTY CAT! JUST WAIT TILL I GET MY HANDS ON YOU!

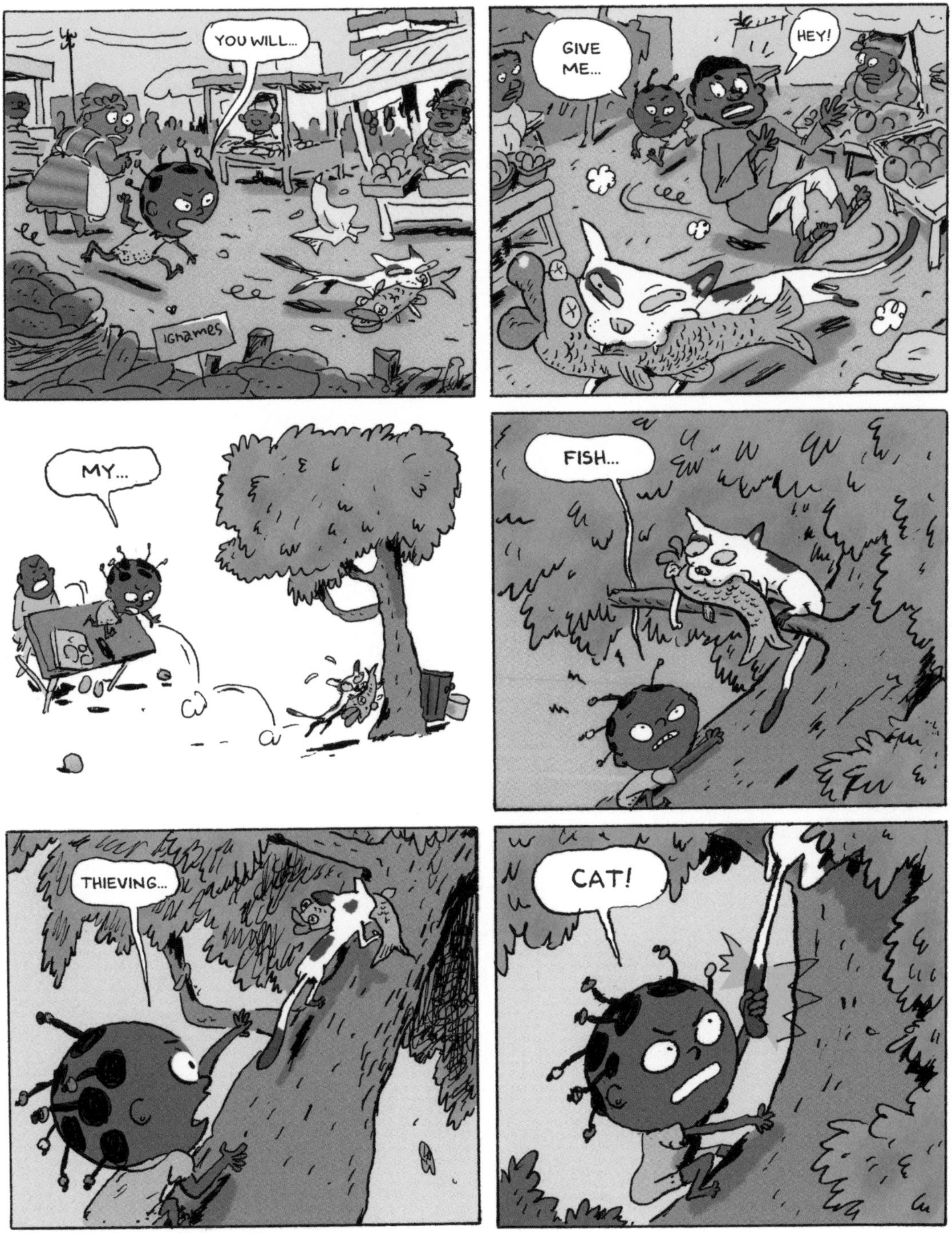
YOU WILL...
Ignames
GIVE ME...
HEY!
MY...
FISH...
THIEVING...
CAT!

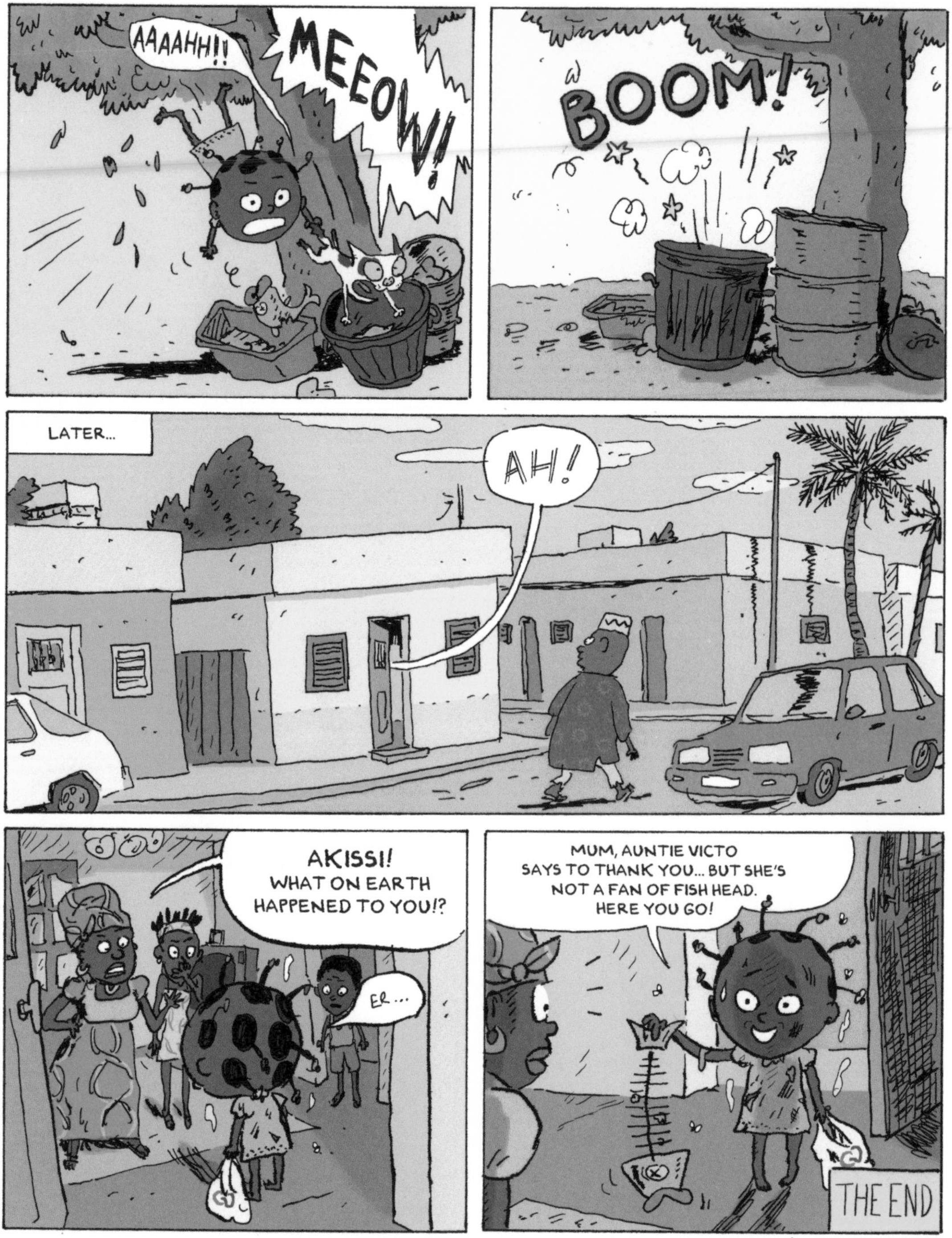
AAAAHH!!
MEEOW!
BOOM!
LATER...
AH!
AKISSI! WHAT ON EARTH HAPPENED TO YOU!?
ER...
MUM, AUNTIE VICTO SAYS TO THANK YOU... BUT SHE'S NOT A FAN OF FISH HEAD. HERE YOU GO!
THE END

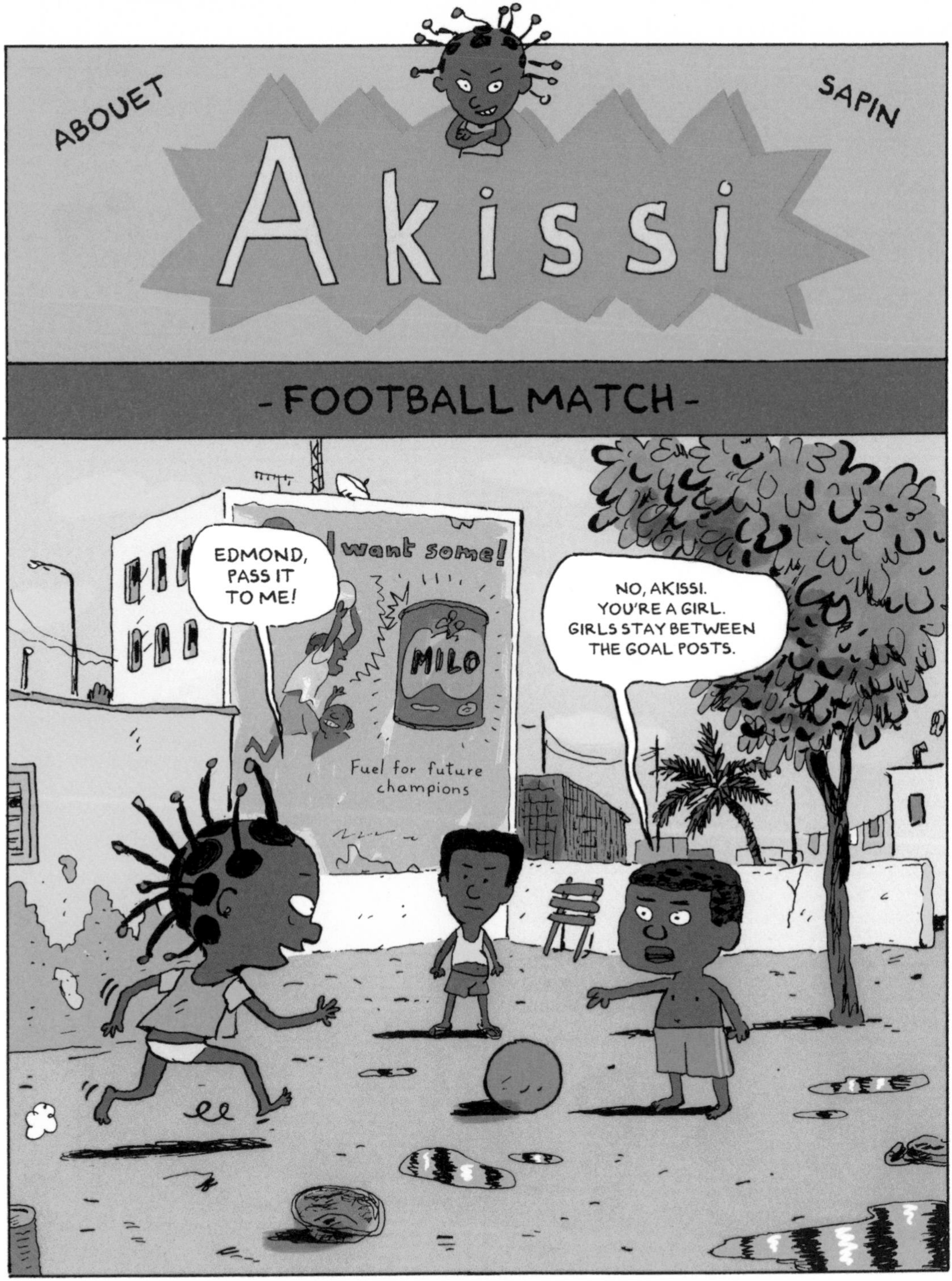
ABOUET
SAPIN
Akissi
- FOOTBALL MATCH -
EDMOND, PASS IT TO ME!
NO, AKISSI. YOU'RE A GIRL. GIRLS STAY BETWEEN THE GOAL POSTS.
I want some!
MILO
Fuel for future champions

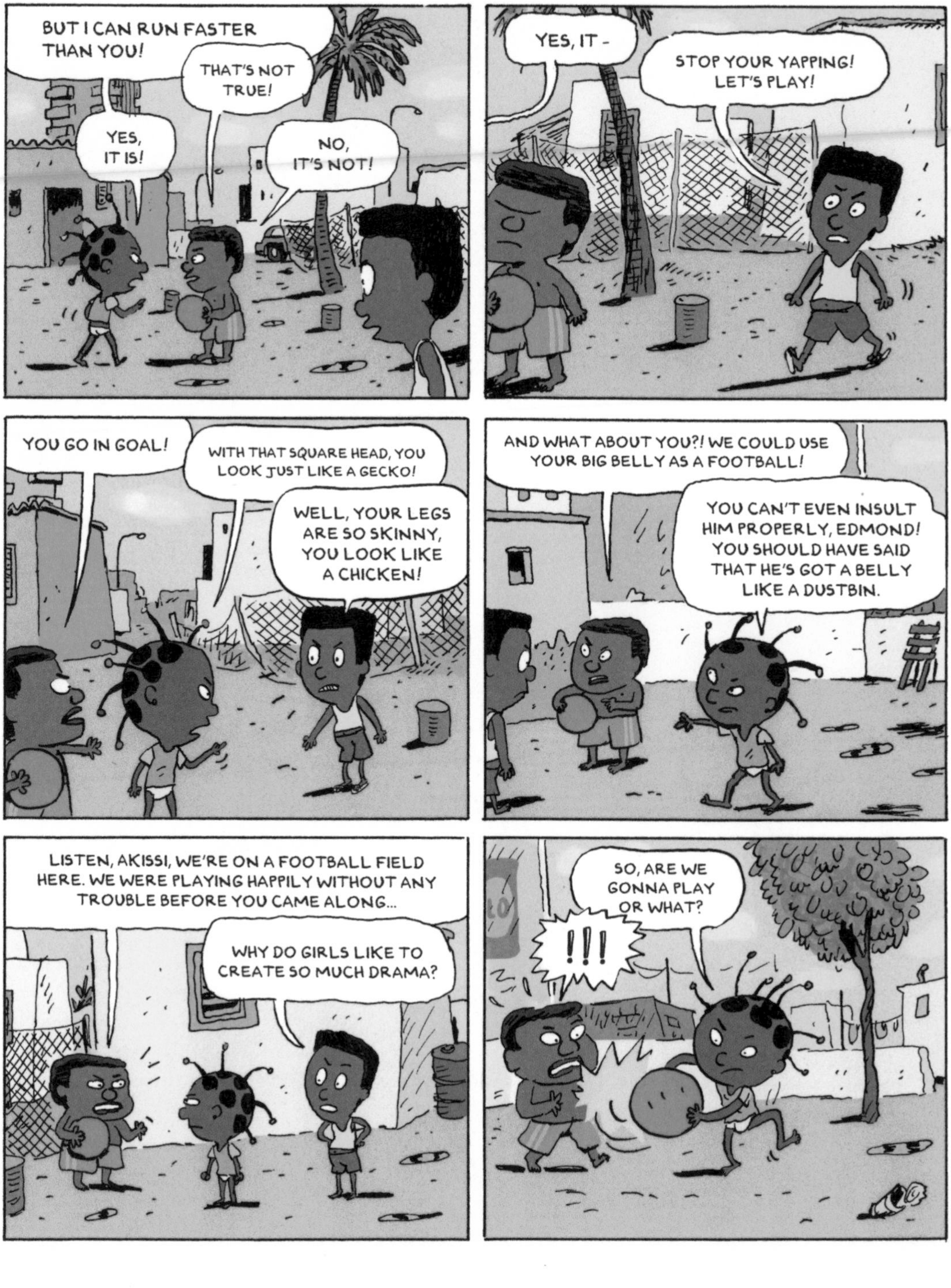
BUT I CAN RUN FASTER THAN YOU!
THAT'S NOT TRUE!
YES, IT IS!
NO, IT'S NOT!
YES, IT -
STOP YOUR YAPPING! LET'S PLAY!
YOU GO IN GOAL!
WITH THAT SQUARE HEAD, YOU LOOK JUST LIKE A GECKO!
WELL, YOUR LEGS ARE SO SKINNY, YOU LOOK LIKE A CHICKEN!
AND WHAT ABOUT YOU?! WE COULD USE YOUR BIG BELLY AS A FOOTBALL!
YOU CAN'T EVEN INSULT HIM PROPERLY, EDMOND! YOU SHOULD HAVE SAID THAT HE'S GOT A BELLY LIKE A DUSTBIN.
LISTEN, AKISSI, WE'RE ON A FOOTBALL FIELD HERE. WE WERE PLAYING HAPPILY WITHOUT ANY TROUBLE BEFORE YOU CAME ALONG...
WHY DO GIRLS LIKE TO CREATE SO MUCH DRAMA?
SO, ARE WE GONNA PLAY OR WHAT?
!!!

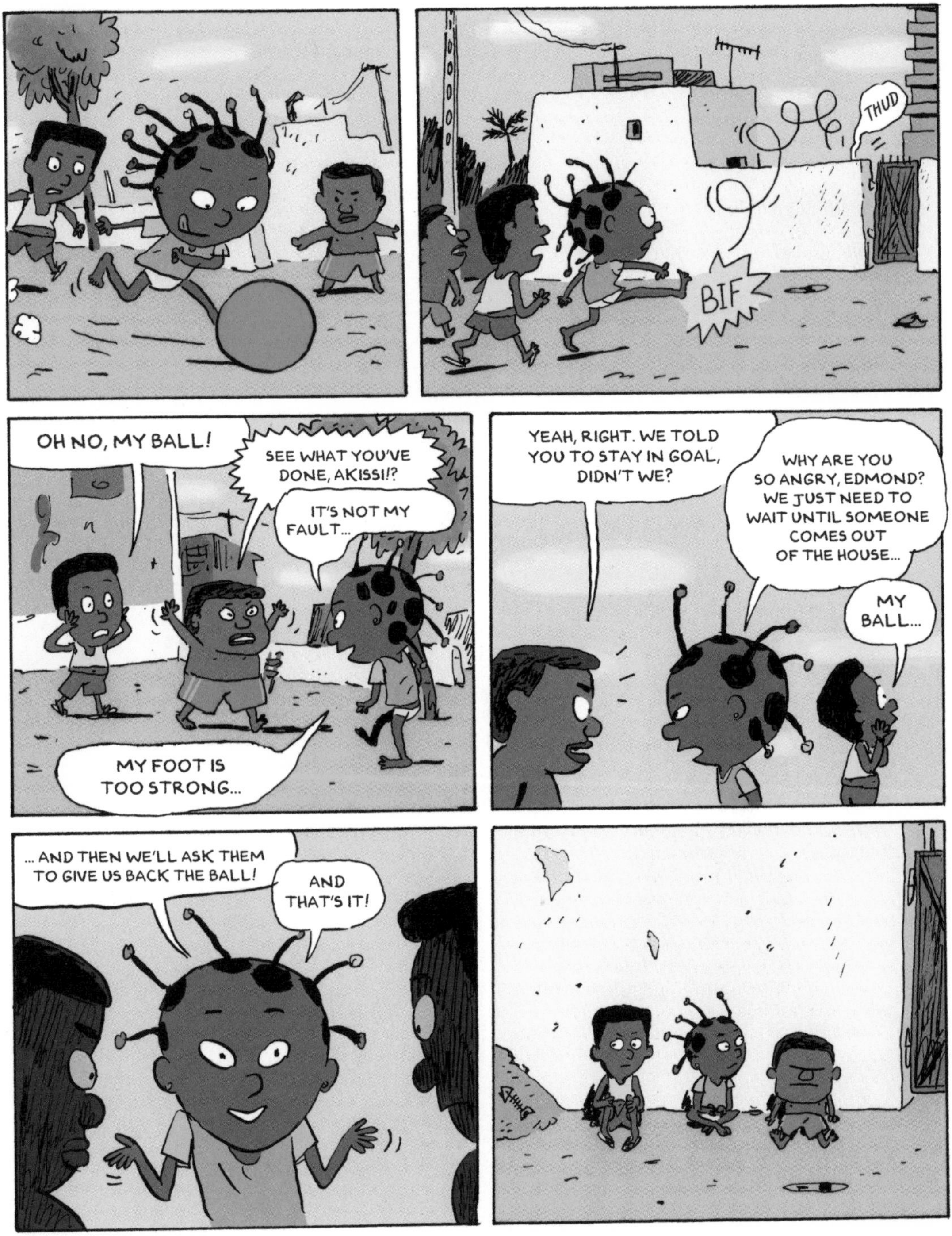
THUD
BIF
OH NO, MY BALL!
SEE WHAT YOU'VE DONE, AKISSI!?
IT'S NOT MY FAULT...
MY FOOT IS TOO STRONG...
YEAH, RIGHT. WE TOLD YOU TO STAY IN GOAL, DIDN'T WE?
WHY ARE YOU SO ANGRY, EDMOND? WE JUST NEED TO WAIT UNTIL SOMEONE COMES OUT OF THE HOUSE...
MY BALL...
... AND THEN WE'LL ASK THEM TO GIVE US BACK THE BALL!
AND THAT'S IT!

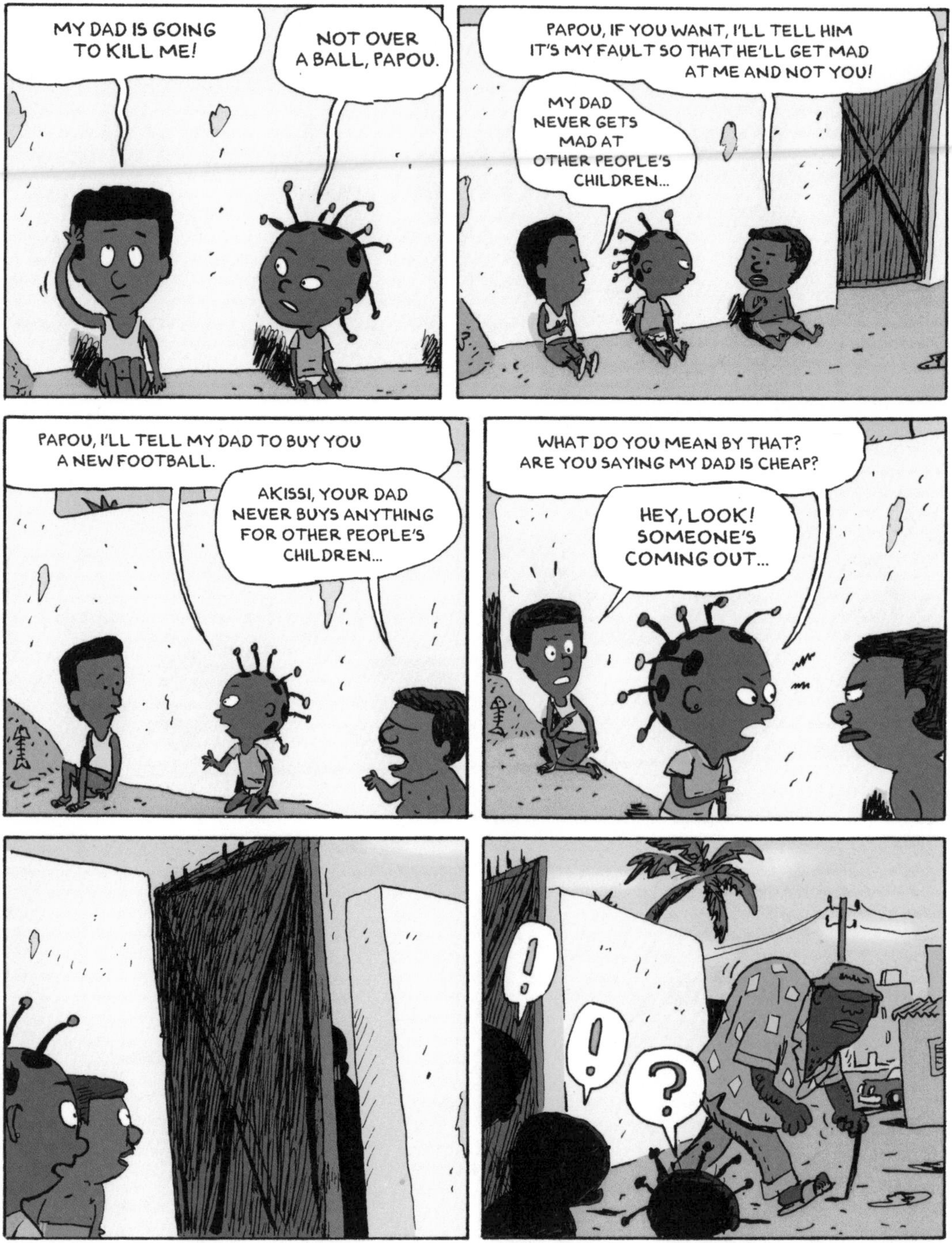
MY DAD IS GOING TO KILL ME!
NOT OVER A BALL, PAPOU.
PAPOU, IF YOU WANT, I'LL TELL HIM IT'S MY FAULT SO THAT HE'LL GET MAD AT ME AND NOT YOU!
MY DAD NEVER GETS MAD AT OTHER PEOPLE'S CHILDREN...
PAPOU, I'LL TELL MY DAD TO BUY YOU A NEW FOOTBALL.
AKISSI, YOUR DAD NEVER BUYS ANYTHING FOR OTHER PEOPLE'S CHILDREN...
WHAT DO YOU MEAN BY THAT? ARE YOU SAYING MY DAD IS CHEAP?
HEY, LOOK! SOMEONE'S COMING OUT...
!
!
?

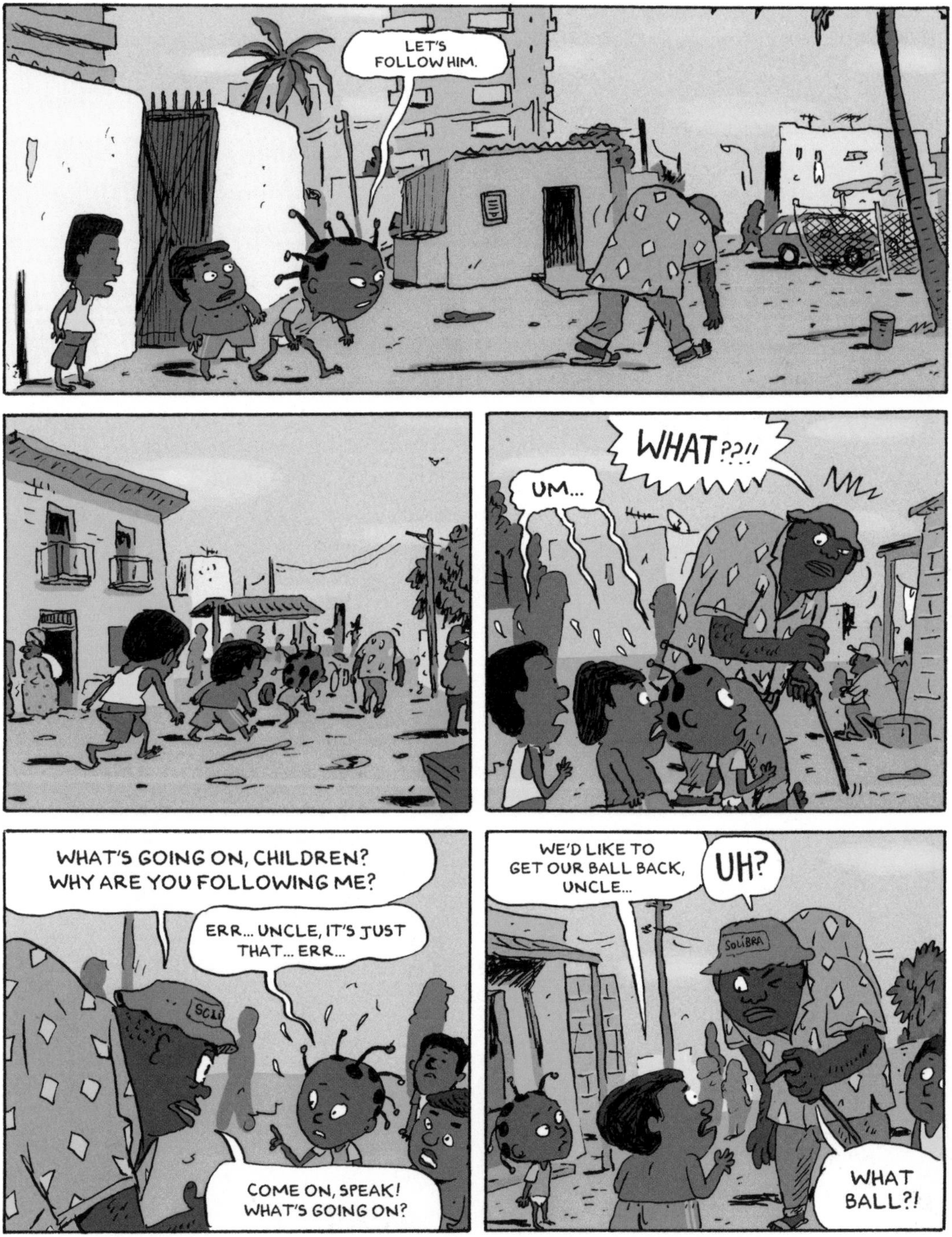
LET'S FOLLOW HIM.
UM...
WHAT??!!
WHAT'S GOING ON, CHILDREN? WHY ARE YOU FOLLOWING ME?
ERR... UNCLE, IT'S JUST THAT... ERR...
COME ON, SPEAK! WHAT'S GOING ON?
WE'D LIKE TO GET OUR BALL BACK, UNCLE...
UH?
SOLIBRA
WHAT BALL?!

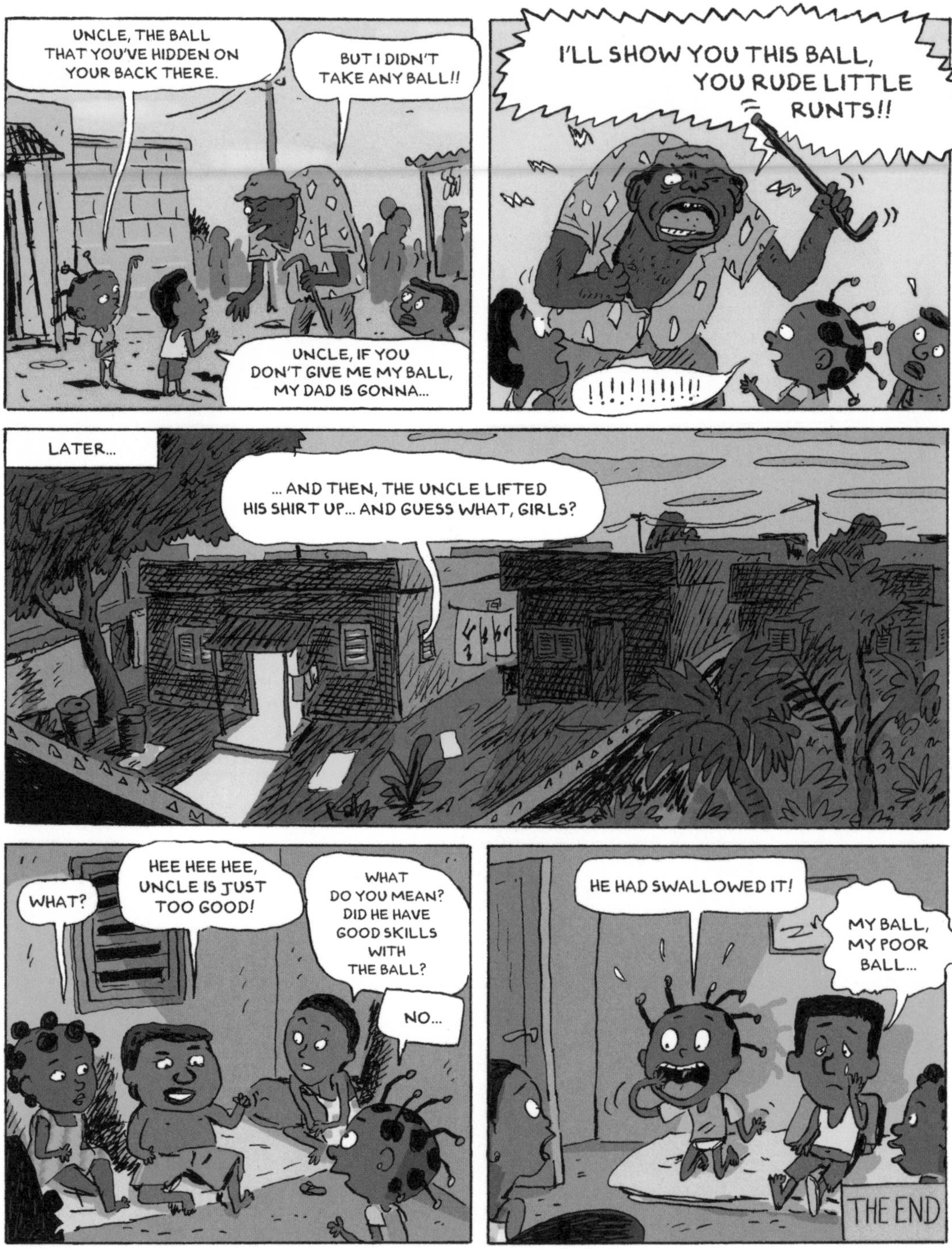
UNCLE, THE BALL THAT YOU'VE HIDDEN ON YOUR BACK THERE.
BUT I DIDN'T TAKE ANY BALL!!
UNCLE, IF YOU DON'T GIVE ME MY BALL, MY DAD IS GONNA...
I'LL SHOW YOU THIS BALL, YOU RUDE LITTLE RUNTS!!
!!!!!!!!!!
LATER...
... AND THEN, THE UNCLE LIFTED HIS SHIRT UP... AND GUESS WHAT, GIRLS?
WHAT?
HEE HEE HEE, UNCLE IS JUST TOO GOOD!
WHAT DO YOU MEAN? DID HE HAVE GOOD SKILLS WITH THE BALL?
NO...
HE HAD SWALLOWED IT!
MY BALL, MY POOR BALL...
THE END

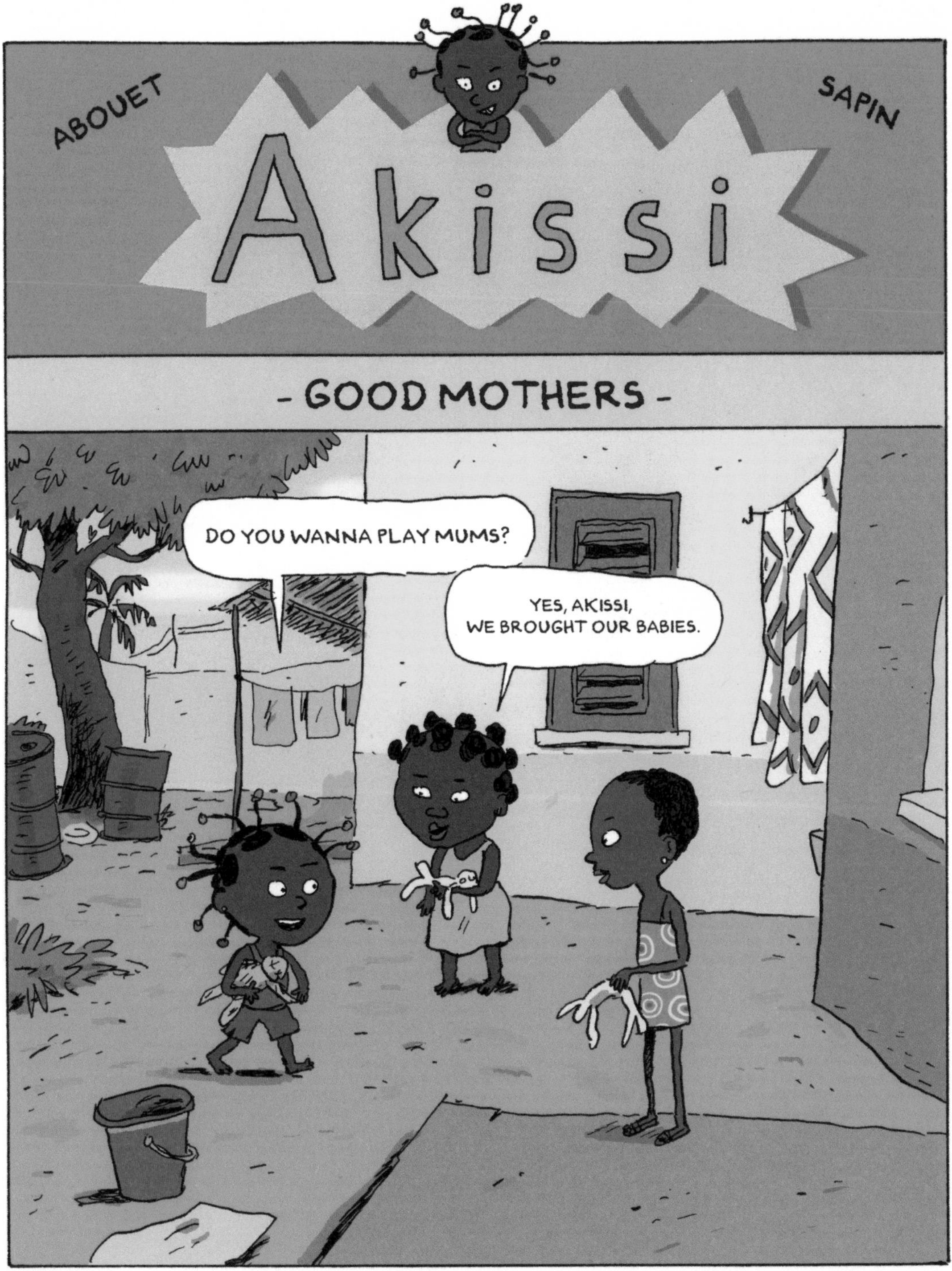
ABOUET
SAPIN
Akissi
- GOOD MOTHERS -
DO YOU WANNA PLAY MUMS?
YES, AKISSI, WE BROUGHT OUR BABIES.

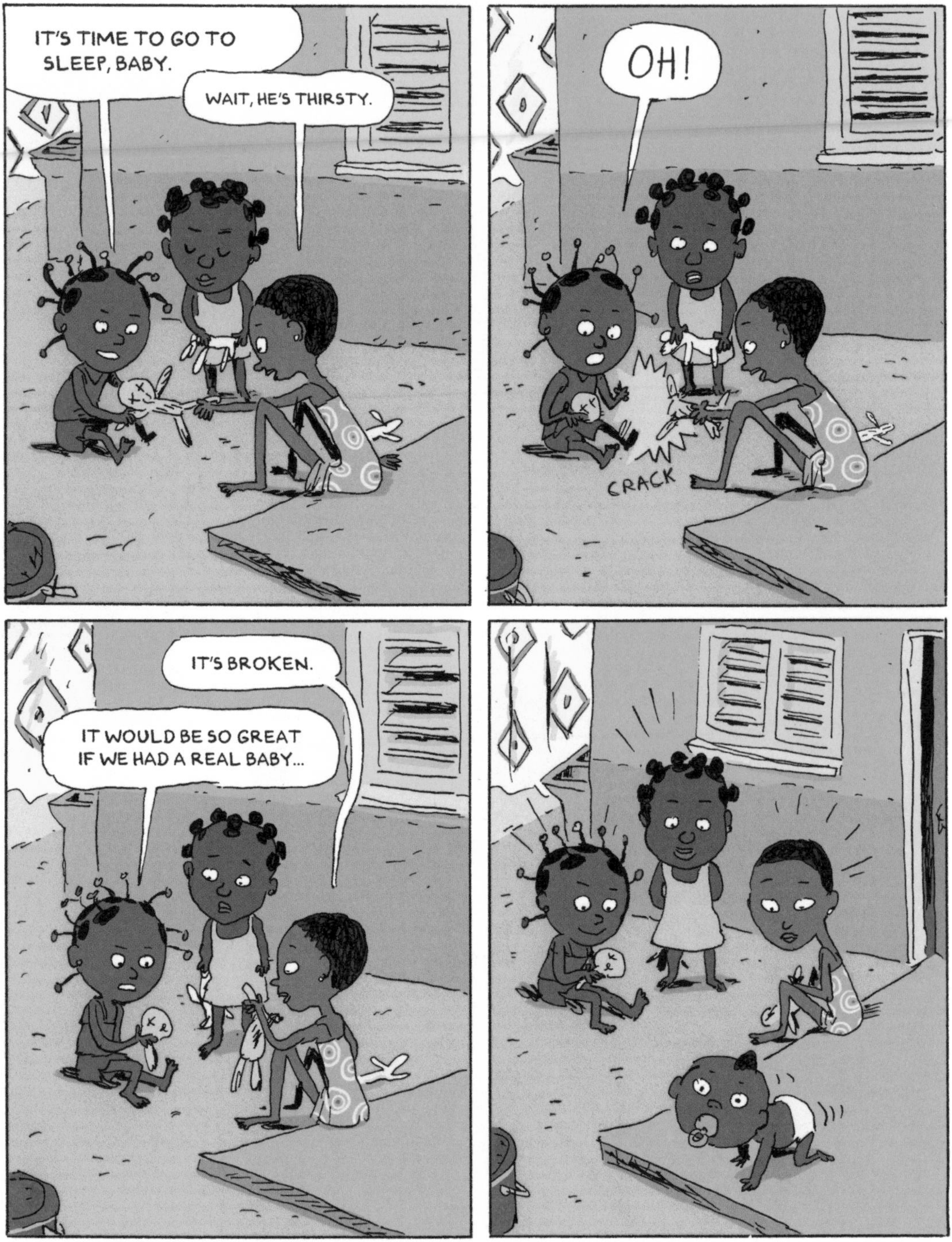
IT'S TIME TO GO TO SLEEP, BABY.
WAIT, HE'S THIRSTY.
OH!
CRACK
IT'S BROKEN.
IT WOULD BE SO GREAT IF WE HAD A REAL BABY...

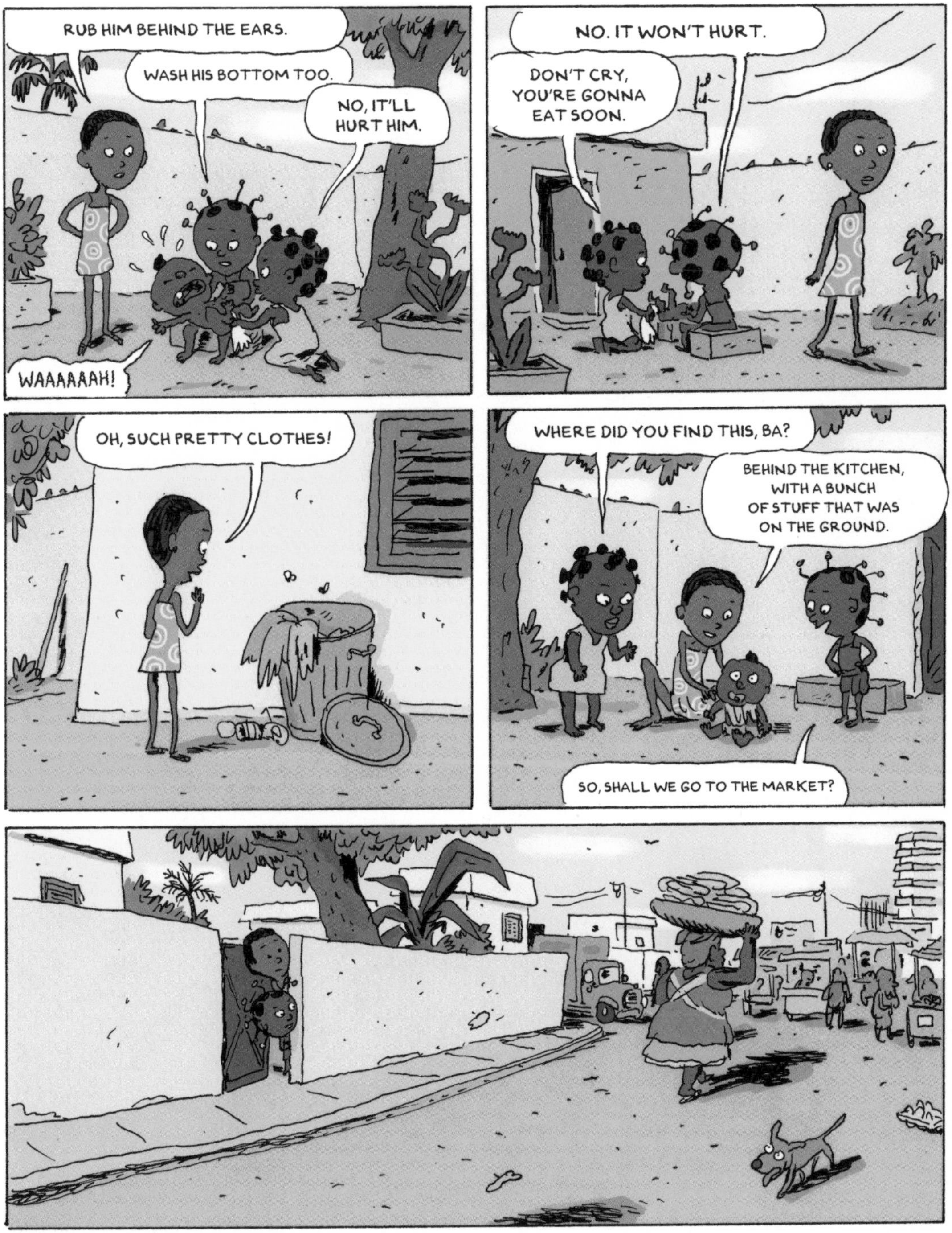
RUB HIM BEHIND THE EARS.
WASH HIS BOTTOM TOO.
NO, IT'LL HURT HIM.
WAAAAAAH!
NO. IT WON'T HURT.
DON'T CRY, YOU'RE GONNA EAT SOON.
OH, SUCH PRETTY CLOTHES!
WHERE DID YOU FIND THIS, BA?
BEHIND THE KITCHEN, WITH A BUNCH OF STUFF THAT WAS ON THE GROUND.
SO, SHALL WE GO TO THE MARKET?

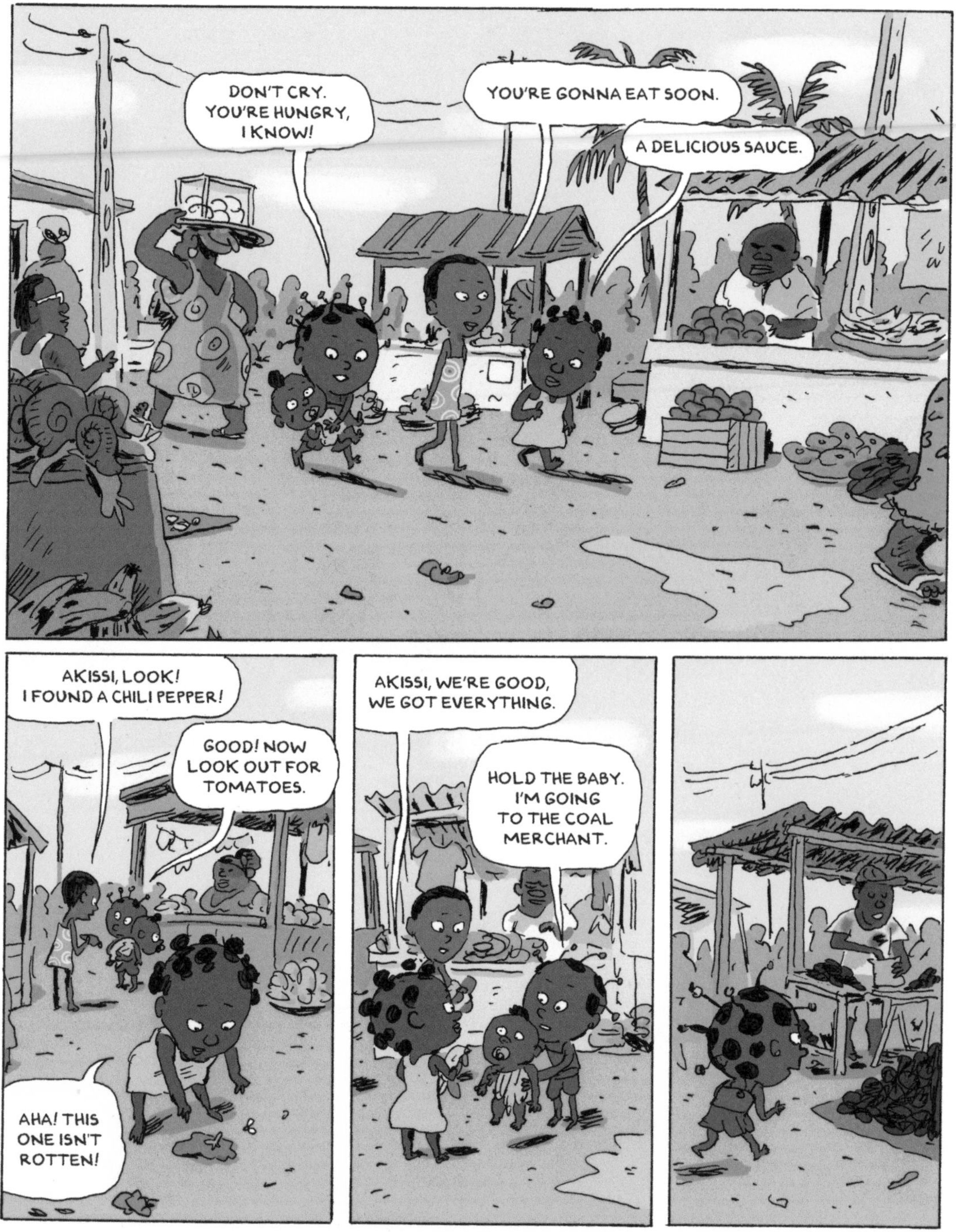
DON'T CRY. YOU'RE HUNGRY, I KNOW!
YOU'RE GONNA EAT SOON.
A DELICIOUS SAUCE.
AKISSI, LOOK! I FOUND A CHILI PEPPER!
GOOD! NOW LOOK OUT FOR TOMATOES.
AHA! THIS ONE ISN'T ROTTEN!
AKISSI, WE'RE GOOD, WE GOT EVERYTHING.
HOLD THE BABY. I'M GOING TO THE COAL MERCHANT.

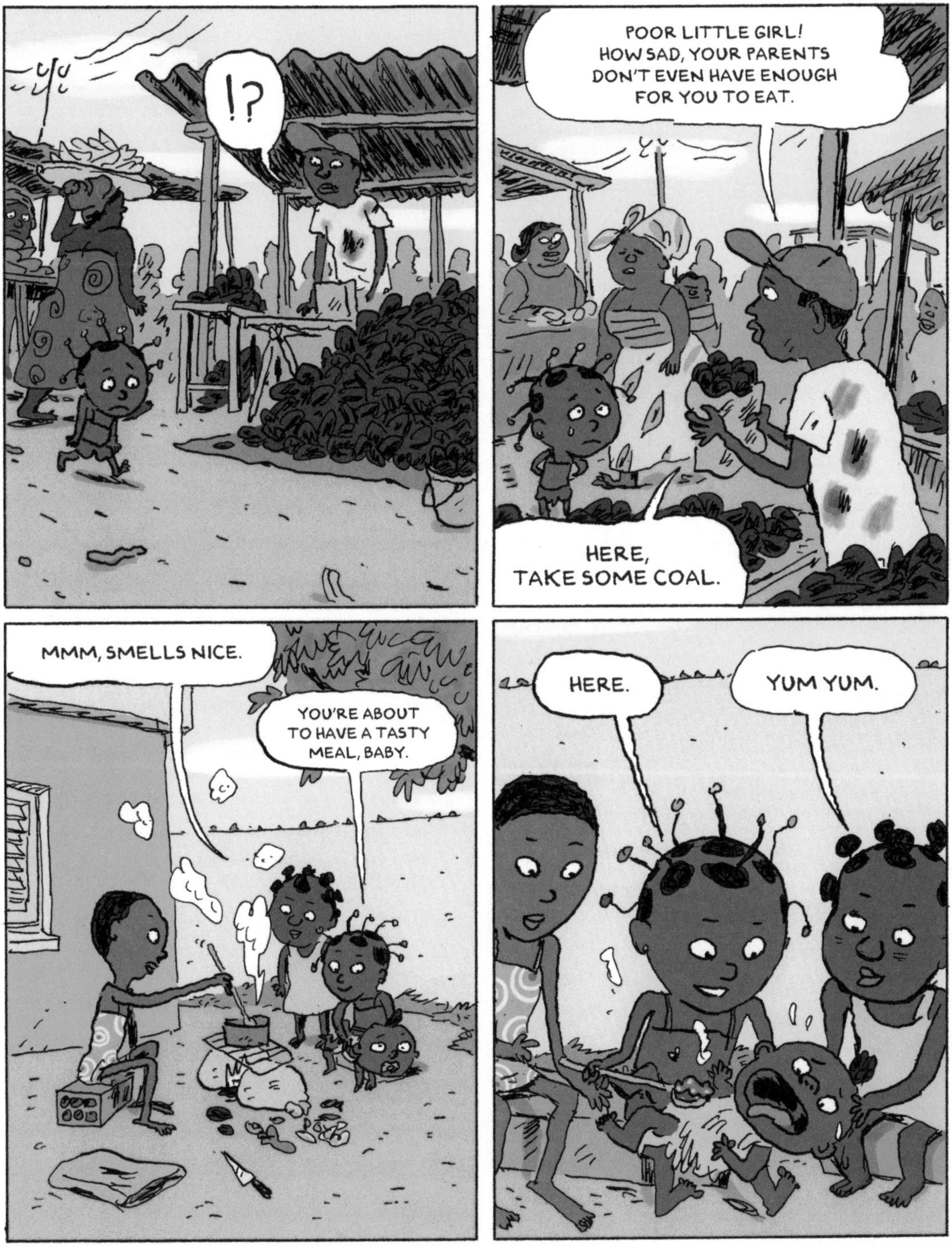
!?
POOR LITTLE GIRL! HOW SAD, YOUR PARENTS DON'T EVEN HAVE ENOUGH FOR YOU TO EAT.
HERE, TAKE SOME COAL.
MMM, SMELLS NICE.
YOU'RE ABOUT TO HAVE A TASTY MEAL, BABY.
HERE.
YUM YUM.

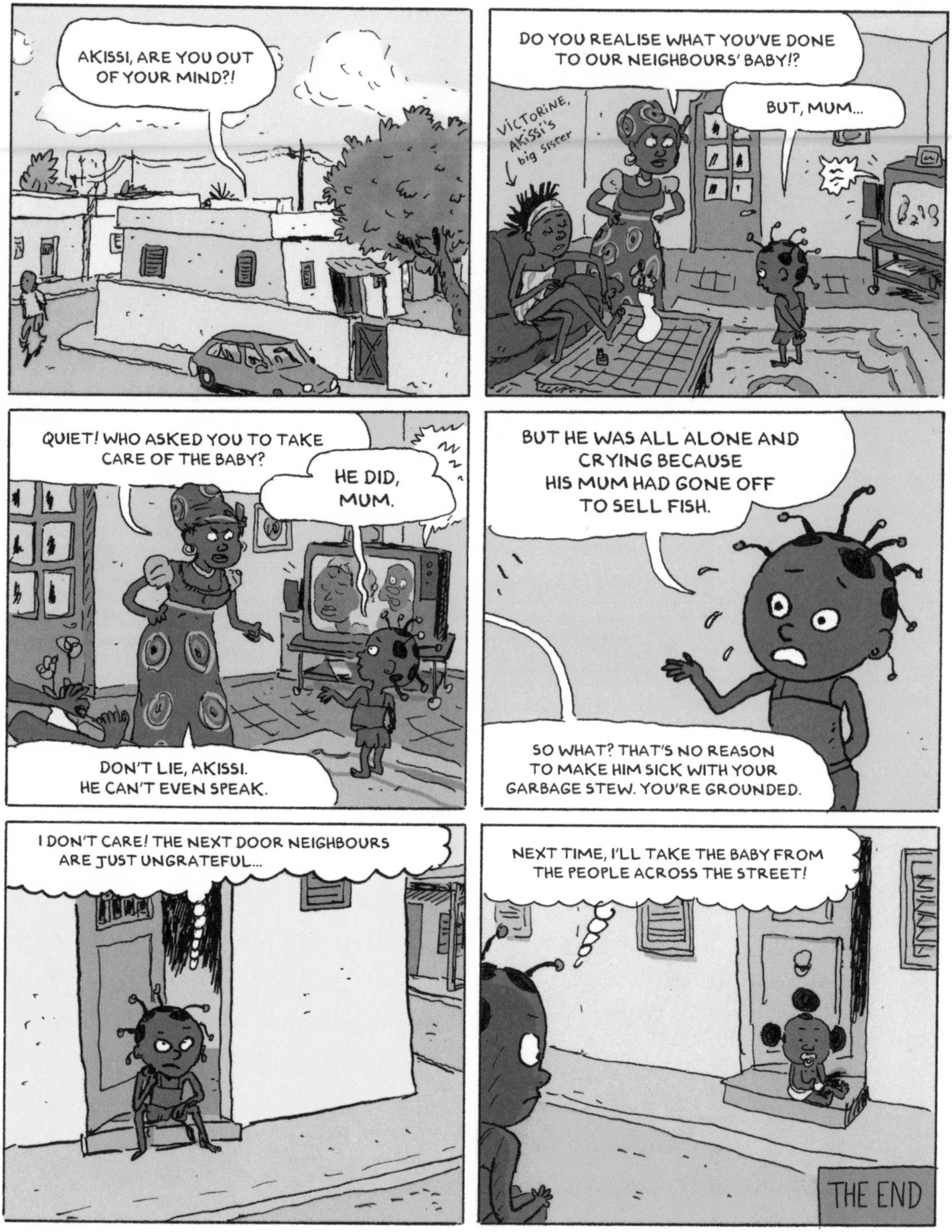
AKISSI, ARE YOU OUT OF YOUR MIND?!
DO YOU REALISE WHAT YOU'VE DONE TO OUR NEIGHBOURS' BABY!?
VICTORINE, AKISSI'S big sister
BUT, MUM...
QUIET! WHO ASKED YOU TO TAKE CARE OF THE BABY?
HE DID, MUM.
DON'T LIE, AKISSI. HE CAN'T EVEN SPEAK.
BUT HE WAS ALL ALONE AND CRYING BECAUSE HIS MUM HAD GONE OFF TO SELL FISH.
SO WHAT? THAT'S NO REASON TO MAKE HIM SICK WITH YOUR GARBAGE STEW. YOU'RE GROUNDED.
I DON'T CARE! THE NEXT DOOR NEIGHBOURS ARE JUST UNGRATEFUL...
NEXT TIME, I'LL TAKE THE BABY FROM THE PEOPLE ACROSS THE STREET!
THE END

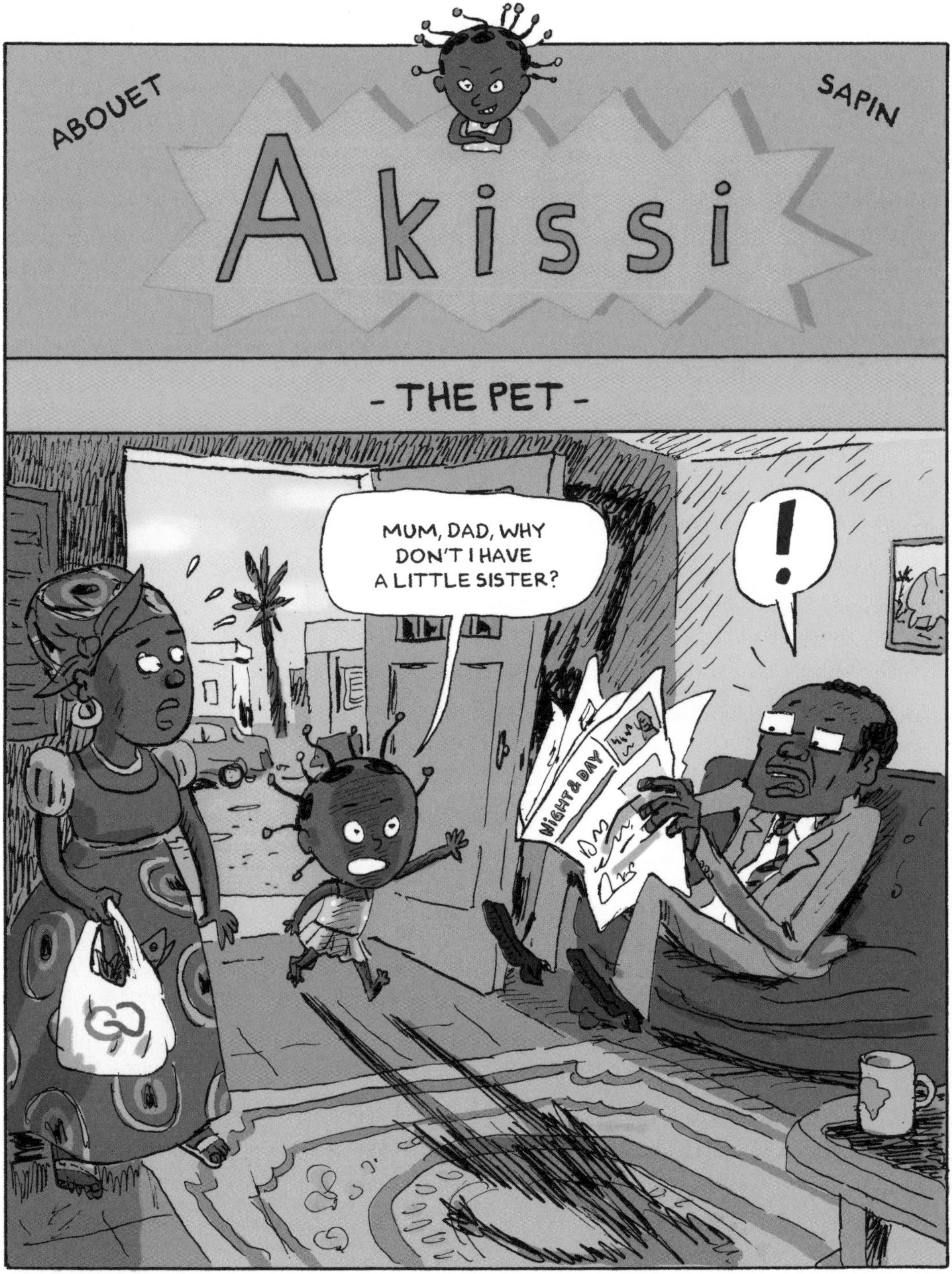
ABOUET
SAPIN
Akissi
- THE PET -
MUM, DAD, WHY DON'T I HAVE A LITTLE SISTER?
!
NIGHT & DAY

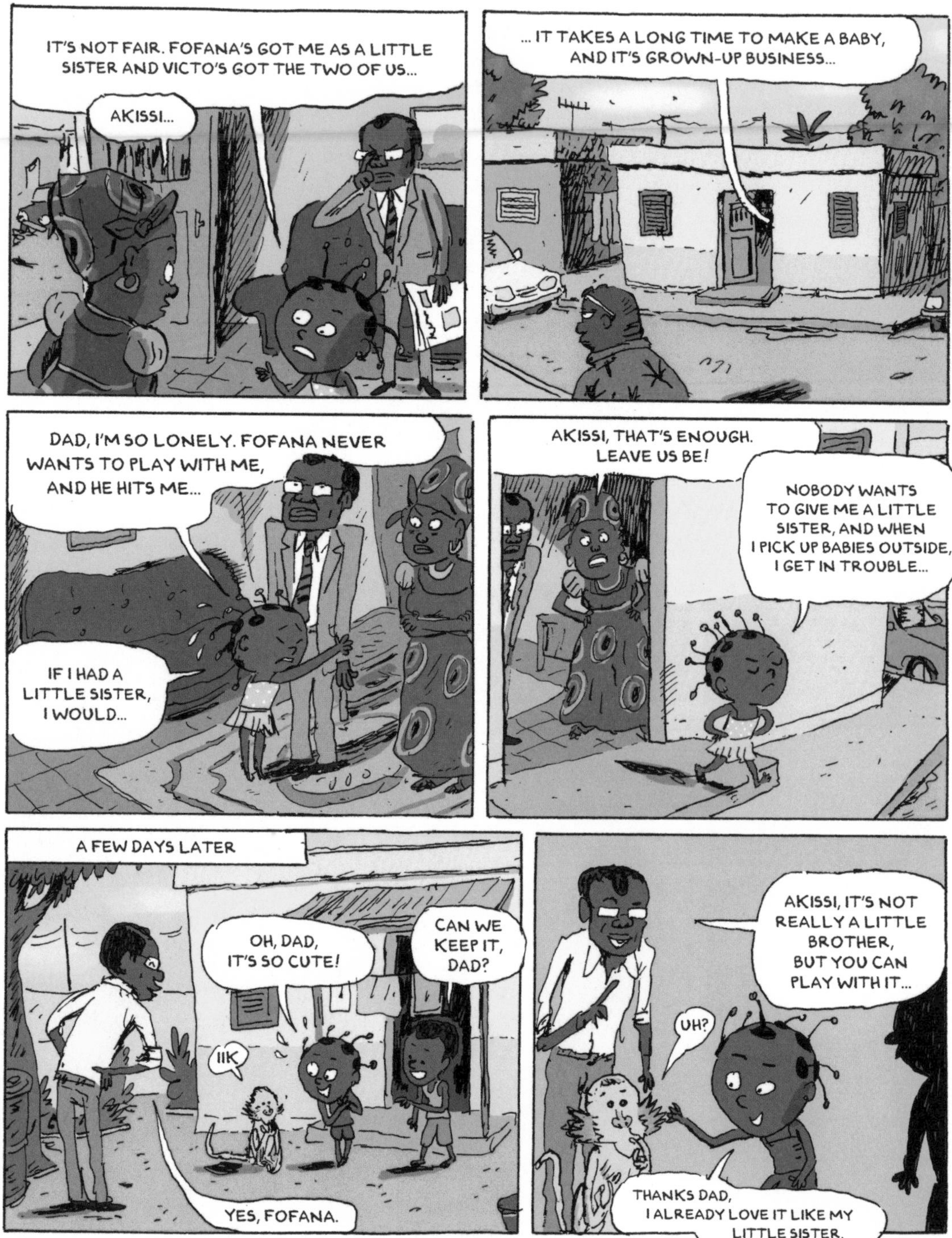
IT'S NOT FAIR. FOFANA'S GOT ME AS A LITTLE SISTER AND VICTO'S GOT THE TWO OF US...
AKISSI...
... IT TAKES A LONG TIME TO MAKE A BABY, AND IT'S GROWN-UP BUSINESS...
DAD, I'M SO LONELY. FOFANA NEVER WANTS TO PLAY WITH ME, AND HE HITS ME...
IF I HAD A LITTLE SISTER, I WOULD...
AKISSI, THAT'S ENOUGH. LEAVE US BE!
NOBODY WANTS TO GIVE ME A LITTLE SISTER, AND WHEN I PICK UP BABIES OUTSIDE, I GET IN TROUBLE...
A FEW DAYS LATER
OH, DAD, IT'S SO CUTE!
CAN WE KEEP IT, DAD?
IIK
YES, FOFANA.
AKISSI, IT'S NOT REALLY A LITTLE BROTHER, BUT YOU CAN PLAY WITH IT...
UH?
THANKS DAD, I ALREADY LOVE IT LIKE MY LITTLE SISTER.

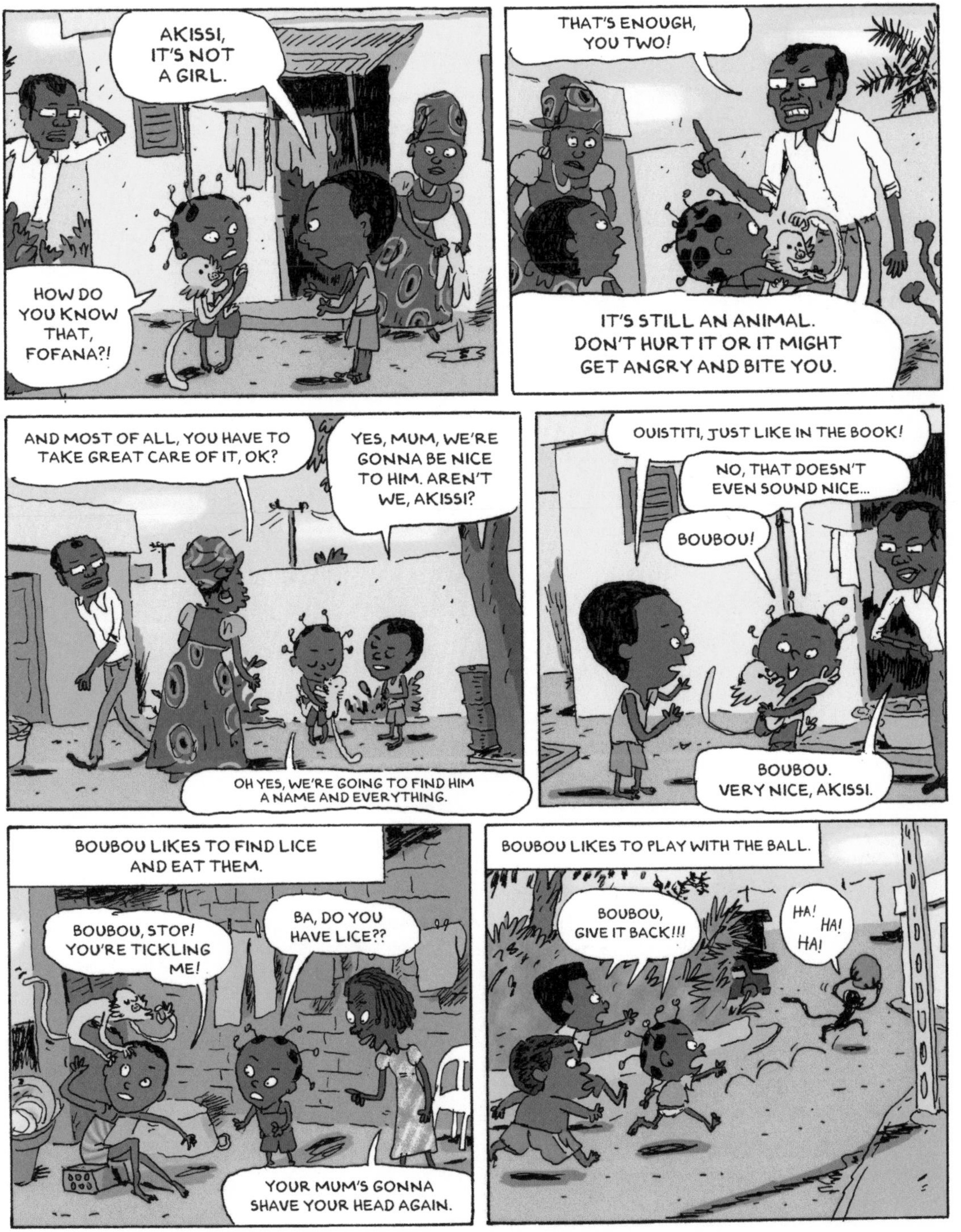
AKISSI, IT'S NOT A GIRL.
HOW DO YOU KNOW THAT, FOFANA?!
THAT'S ENOUGH, YOU TWO!
IT'S STILL AN ANIMAL. DON'T HURT IT OR IT MIGHT GET ANGRY AND BITE YOU.
AND MOST OF ALL, YOU HAVE TO TAKE GREAT CARE OF IT, OK?
YES, MUM, WE'RE GONNA BE NICE TO HIM. AREN'T WE, AKISSI?
OH YES, WE'RE GOING TO FIND HIM A NAME AND EVERYTHING.
OUISTITI, JUST LIKE IN THE BOOK!
NO, THAT DOESN'T EVEN SOUND NICE...
BOUBOU!
BOUBOU. VERY NICE, AKISSI.
BOUBOU LIKES TO FIND LICE AND EAT THEM.
BOUBOU, STOP! YOU'RE TICKLING ME!
BA, DO YOU HAVE LICE??
YOUR MUM'S GONNA SHAVE YOUR HEAD AGAIN.
BOUBOU LIKES TO PLAY WITH THE BALL.
BOUBOU, GIVE IT BACK!!!
HA! HA! HA!

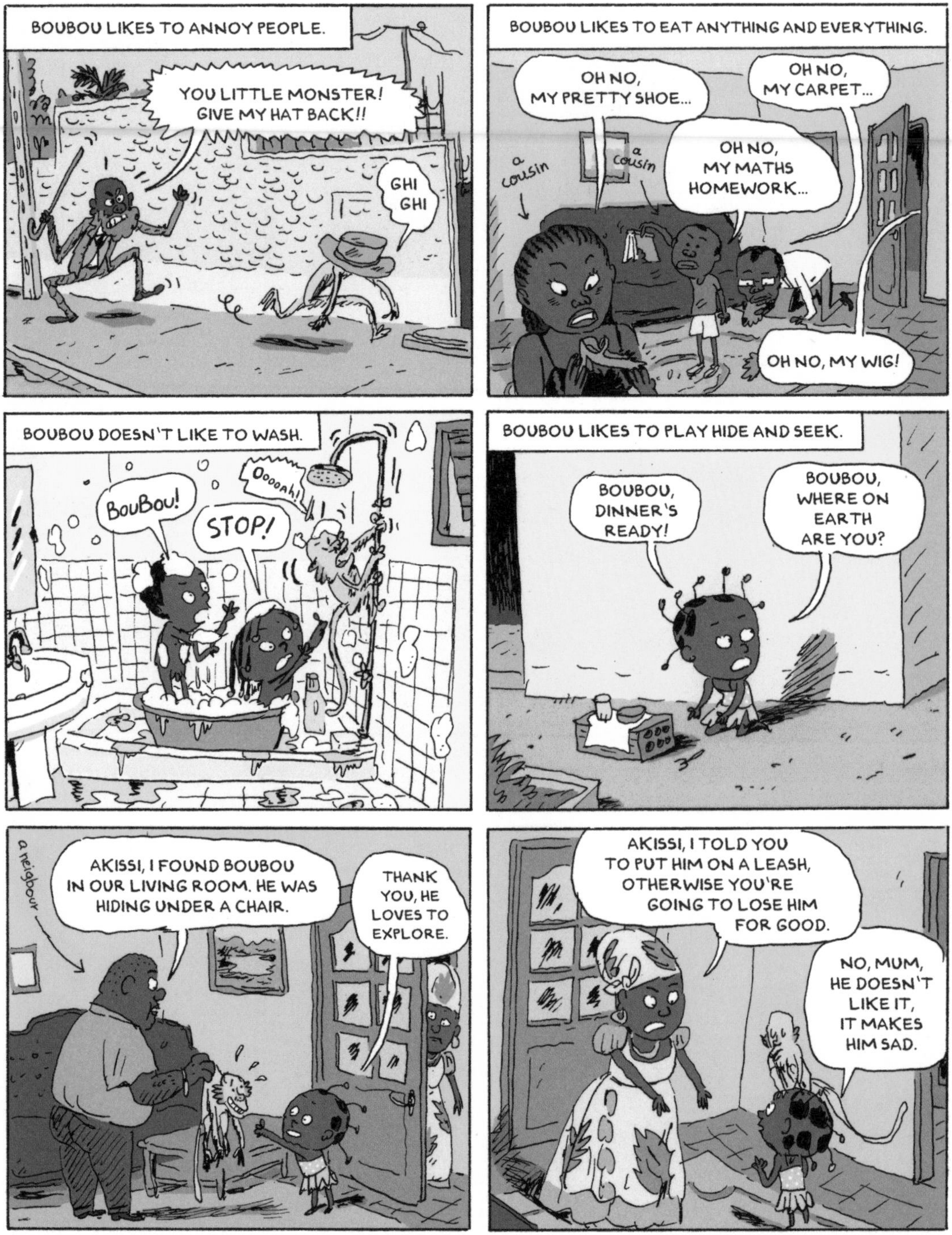
BOUBOU LIKES TO ANNOY PEOPLE.
YOU LITTLE MONSTER! GIVE MY HAT BACK!!
GHI GHI
BOUBOU LIKES TO EAT ANYTHING AND EVERYTHING.
a cousin
a cousin
OH NO, MY PRETTY SHOE...
OH NO, MY CARPET...
OH NO, MY MATHS HOMEWORK...
OH NO, MY WIG!
BOUBOU DOESN'T LIKE TO WASH.
BouBou!
STOP!
Ooooah!
BOUBOU LIKES TO PLAY HIDE AND SEEK.
BOUBOU, DINNER'S READY!
BOUBOU, WHERE ON EARTH ARE YOU?
a neigbour
AKISSI, I FOUND BOUBOU IN OUR LIVING ROOM. HE WAS HIDING UNDER A CHAIR.
THANK YOU, HE LOVES TO EXPLORE.
AKISSI, I TOLD YOU TO PUT HIM ON A LEASH, OTHERWISE YOU'RE GOING TO LOSE HIM FOR GOOD.
NO, MUM, HE DOESN'T LIKE IT, IT MAKES HIM SAD.

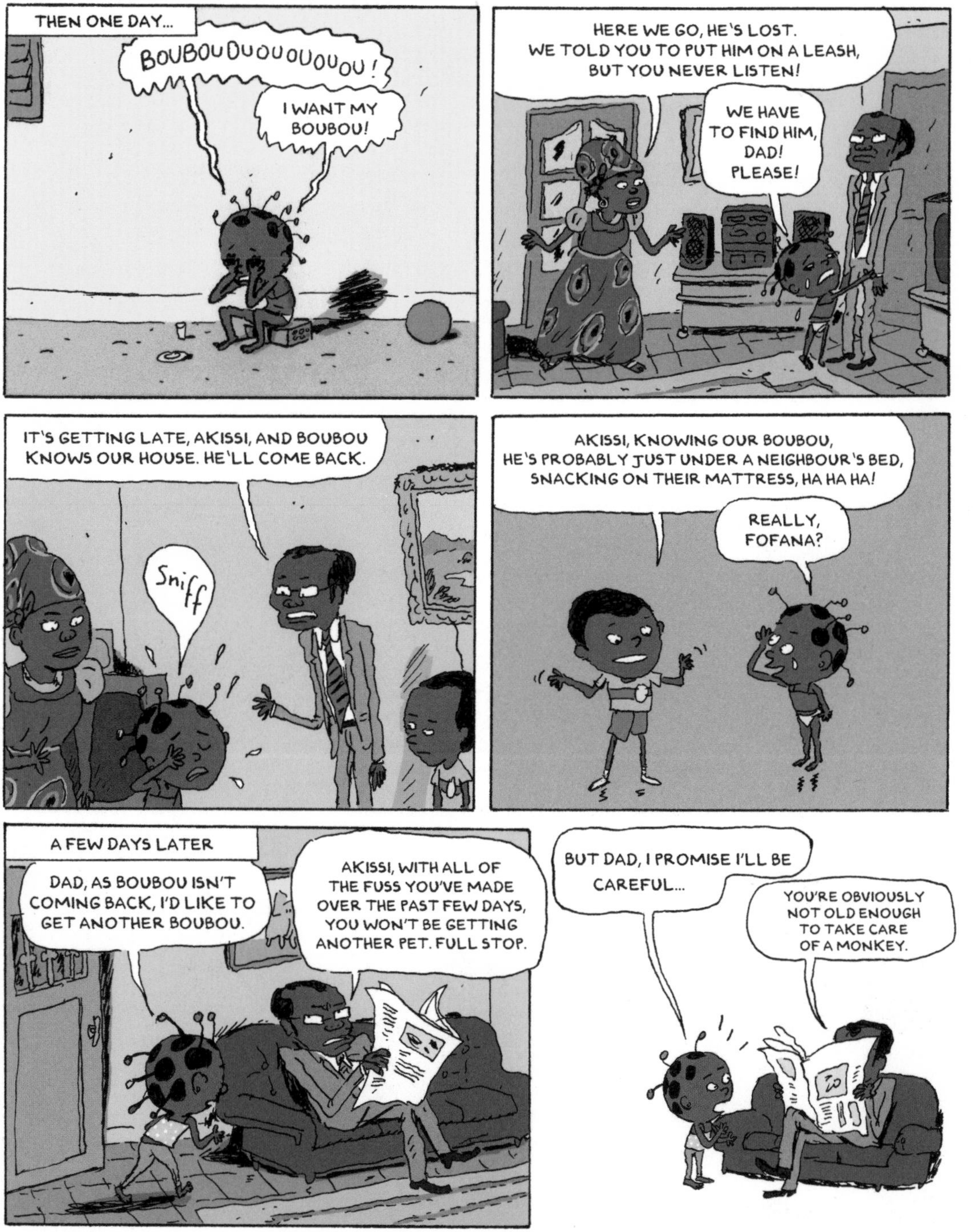
THEN ONE DAY...
BOUBOUOUOUOUOUOUOU!
I WANT MY BOUBOU!
HERE WE GO, HE'S LOST. WE TOLD YOU TO PUT HIM ON A LEASH, BUT YOU NEVER LISTEN!
WE HAVE TO FIND HIM, DAD! PLEASE!
IT'S GETTING LATE, AKISSI, AND BOUBOU KNOWS OUR HOUSE. HE'LL COME BACK.
Sniff
AKISSI, KNOWING OUR BOUBOU, HE'S PROBABLY JUST UNDER A NEIGHBOUR'S BED, SNACKING ON THEIR MATTRESS, HA HA HA!
REALLY, FOFANA?
A FEW DAYS LATER
DAD, AS BOUBOU ISN'T COMING BACK, I'D LIKE TO GET ANOTHER BOUBOU.
AKISSI, WITH ALL OF THE FUSS YOU'VE MADE OVER THE PAST FEW DAYS, YOU WON'T BE GETTING ANOTHER PET. FULL STOP.
BUT DAD, I PROMISE I'LL BE CAREFUL...
YOU'RE OBVIOUSLY NOT OLD ENOUGH TO TAKE CARE OF A MONKEY.

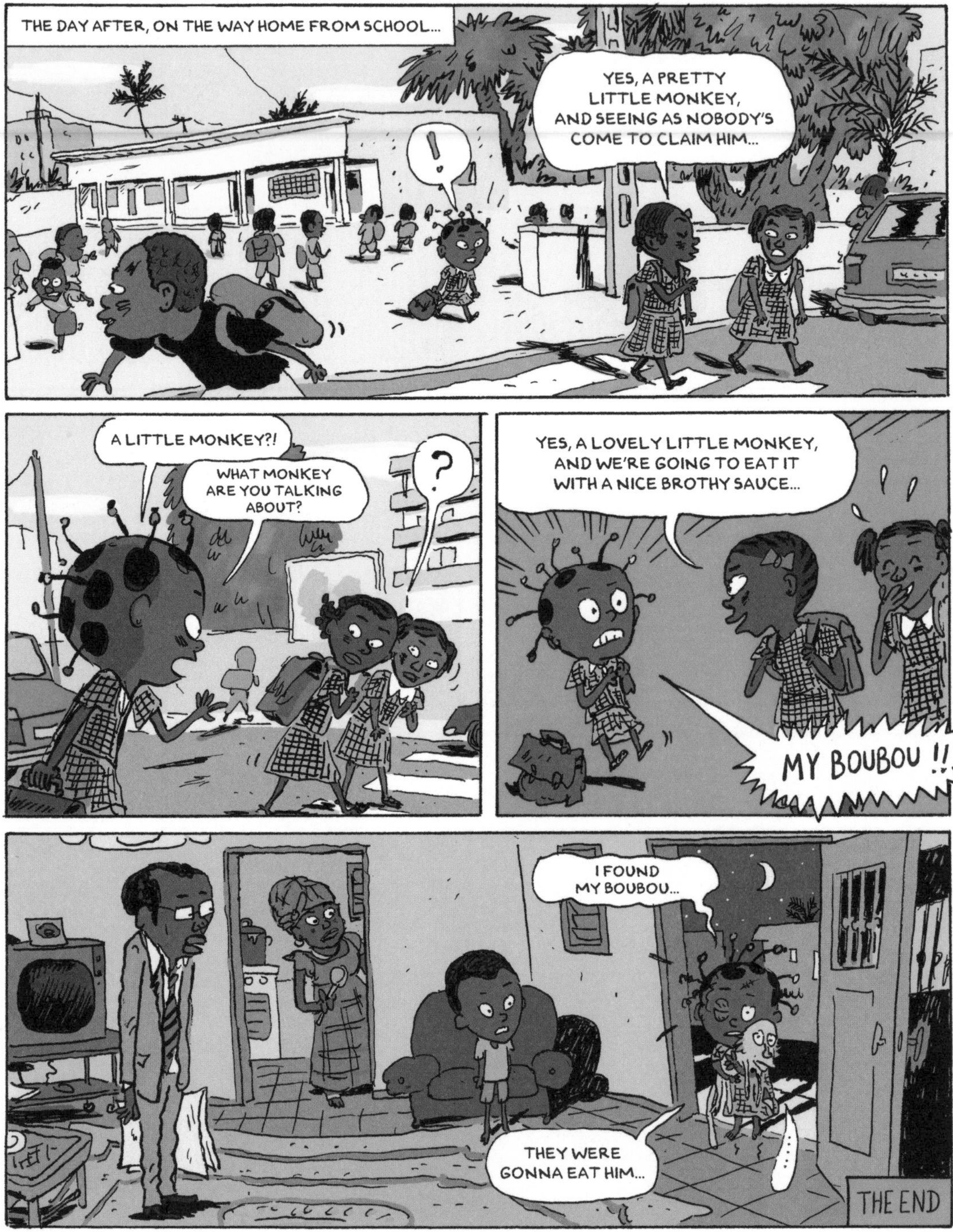
THE DAY AFTER, ON THE WAY HOME FROM SCHOOL...
!
YES, A PRETTY LITTLE MONKEY, AND SEEING AS NOBODY'S COME TO CLAIM HIM...
A LITTLE MONKEY?!
WHAT MONKEY ARE YOU TALKING ABOUT?
?
YES, A LOVELY LITTLE MONKEY, AND WE'RE GOING TO EAT IT WITH A NICE BROTHY SAUCE...
MY BOUBOU !!
I FOUND MY BOUBOU...
THEY WERE GONNA EAT HIM...
THE END

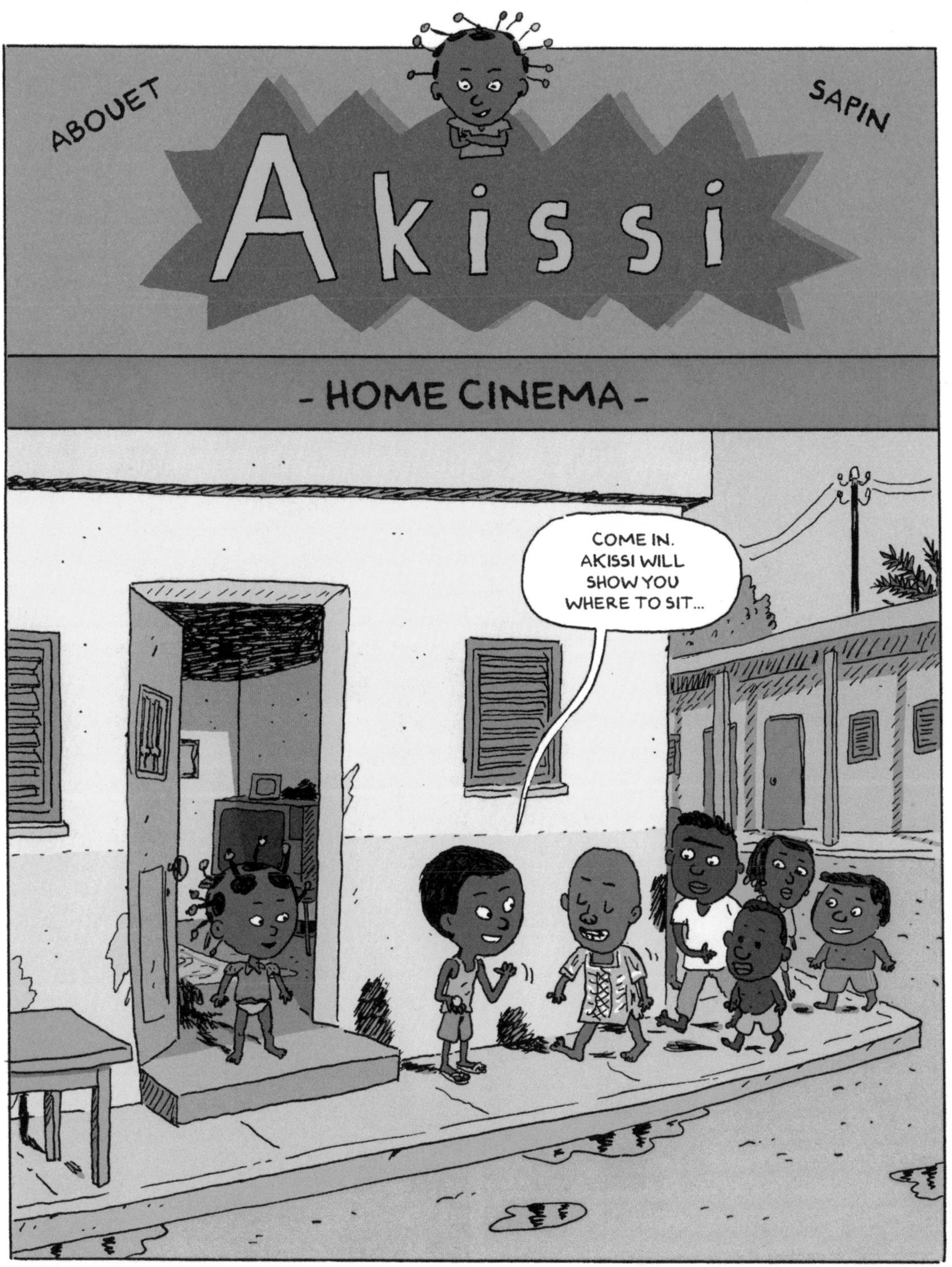
ABOUET
SAPIN
Akissi
- HOME CINEMA -
COME IN. AKISSI WILL SHOW YOU WHERE TO SIT...

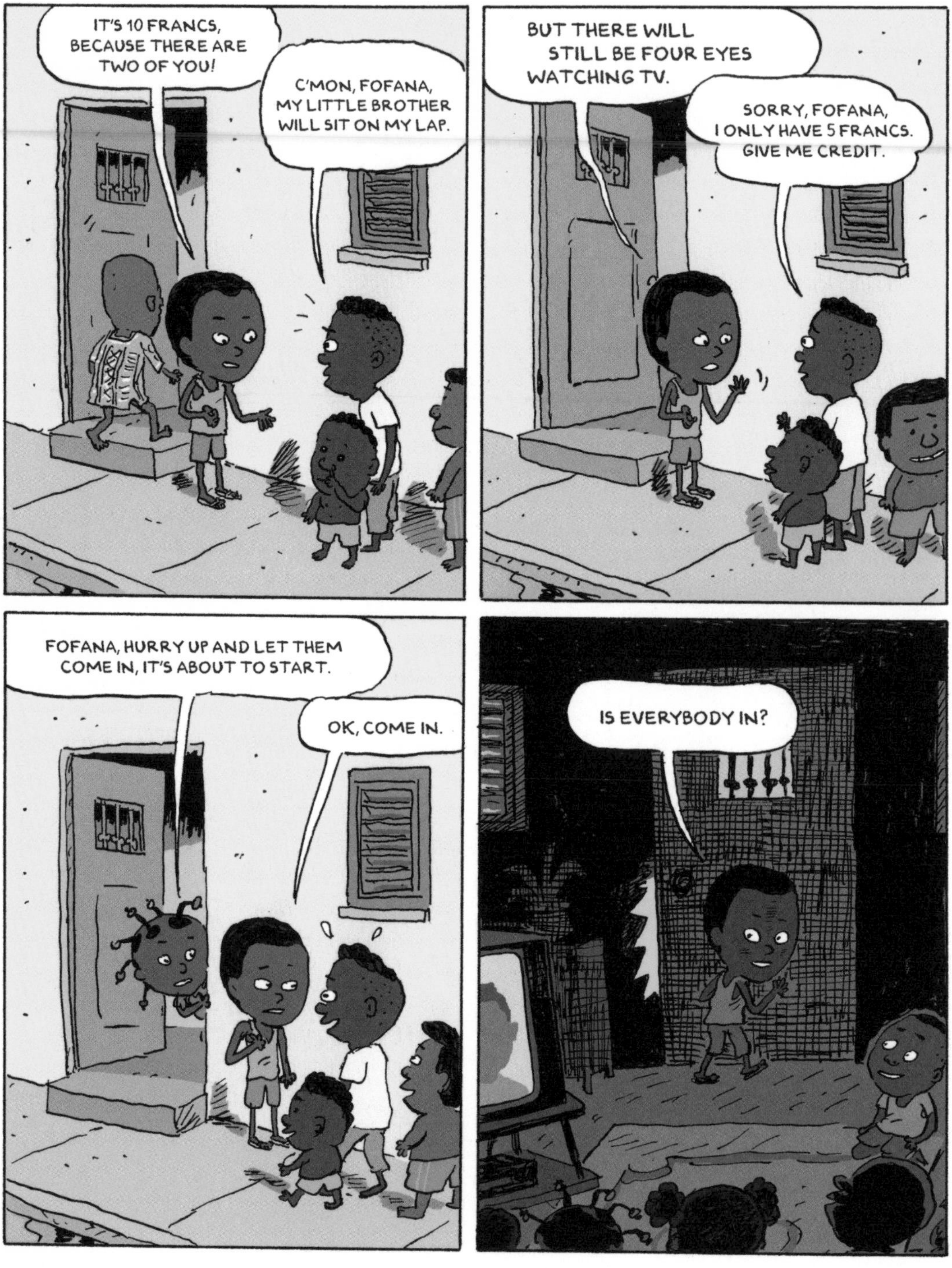
IT'S 10 FRANCS, BECAUSE THERE ARE TWO OF YOU!
C'MON, FOFANA, MY LITTLE BROTHER WILL SIT ON MY LAP.
BUT THERE WILL STILL BE FOUR EYES WATCHING TV.
SORRY, FOFANA, I ONLY HAVE 5 FRANCS. GIVE ME CREDIT.
FOFANA, HURRY UP AND LET THEM COME IN, IT'S ABOUT TO START.
OK, COME IN.
IS EVERYBODY IN?

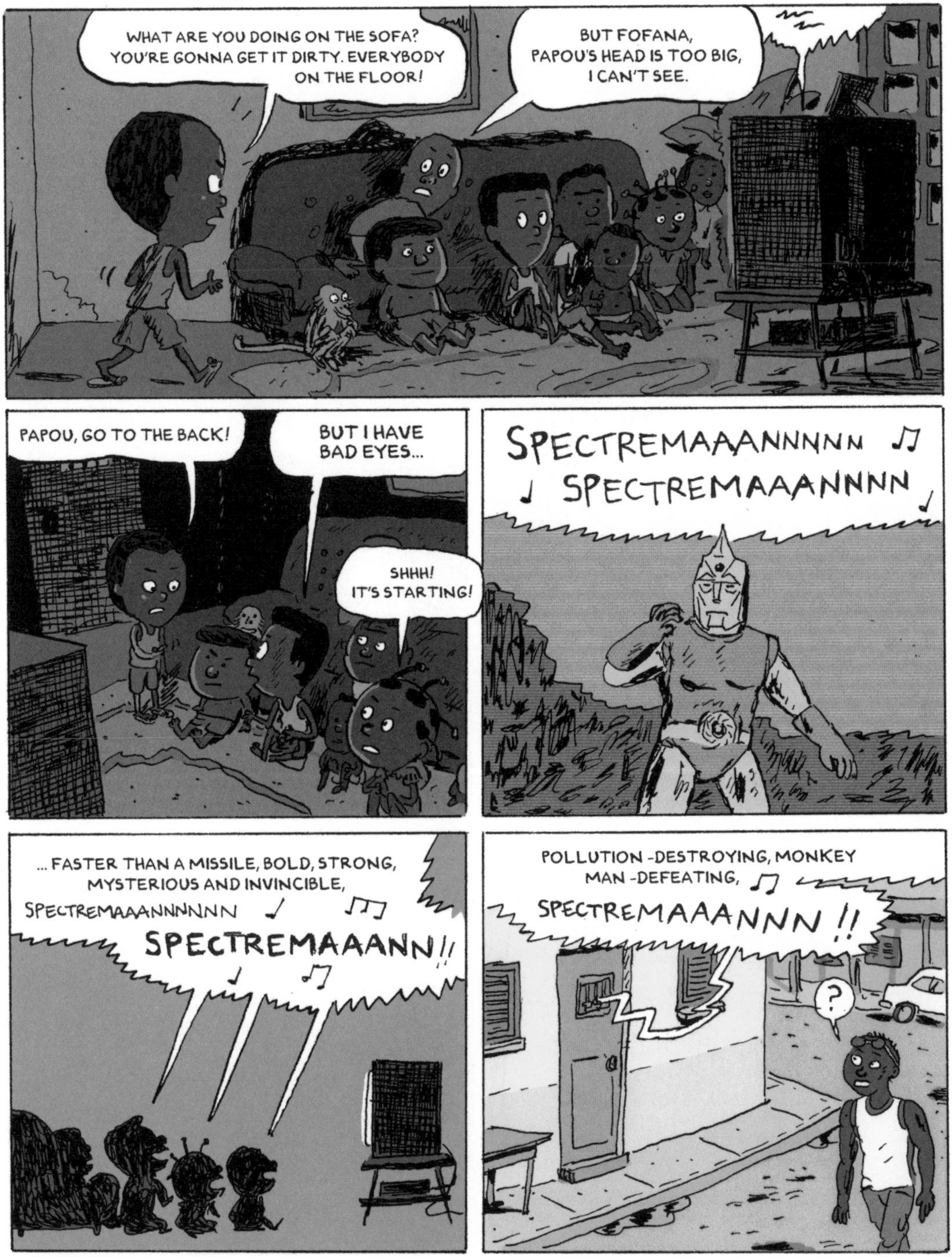
WHAT ARE YOU DOING ON THE SOFA? YOU'RE GONNA GET IT DIRTY. EVERYBODY ON THE FLOOR!
BUT FOFANA, PAPOU'S HEAD IS TOO BIG, I CAN'T SEE.
PAPOU, GO TO THE BACK!
BUT I HAVE BAD EYES...
SHHH! IT'S STARTING!
SPECTREMAAANNNNN
SPECTREMAAANNNN
... FASTER THAN A MISSILE, BOLD, STRONG, MYSTERIOUS AND INVINCIBLE,
SPECTREMAAANNNNNN
SPECTREMAAANN!!
POLLUTION-DESTROYING, MONKEY MAN-DEFEATING,
SPECTREMAAANNN!!
?

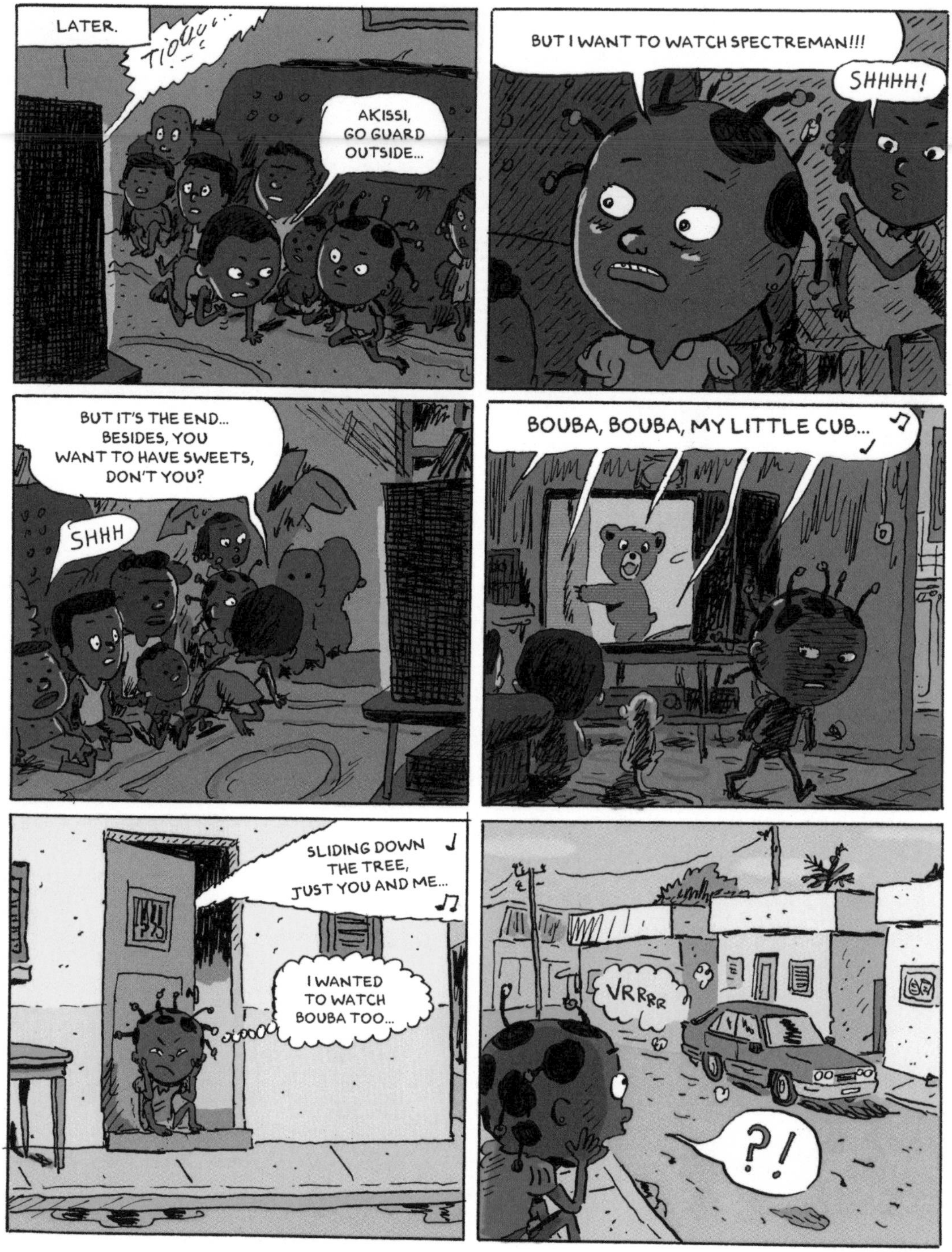
LATER.
TIOUU...
AKISSI, GO GUARD OUTSIDE...
BUT I WANT TO WATCH SPECTREMAN!!!
SHHHH!
BUT IT'S THE END... BESIDES, YOU WANT TO HAVE SWEETS, DON'T YOU?
SHHH
BOUBA, BOUBA, MY LITTLE CUB...
SLIDING DOWN THE TREE, JUST YOU AND ME...
I WANTED TO WATCH BOUBA TOO...
VRRRR
?!

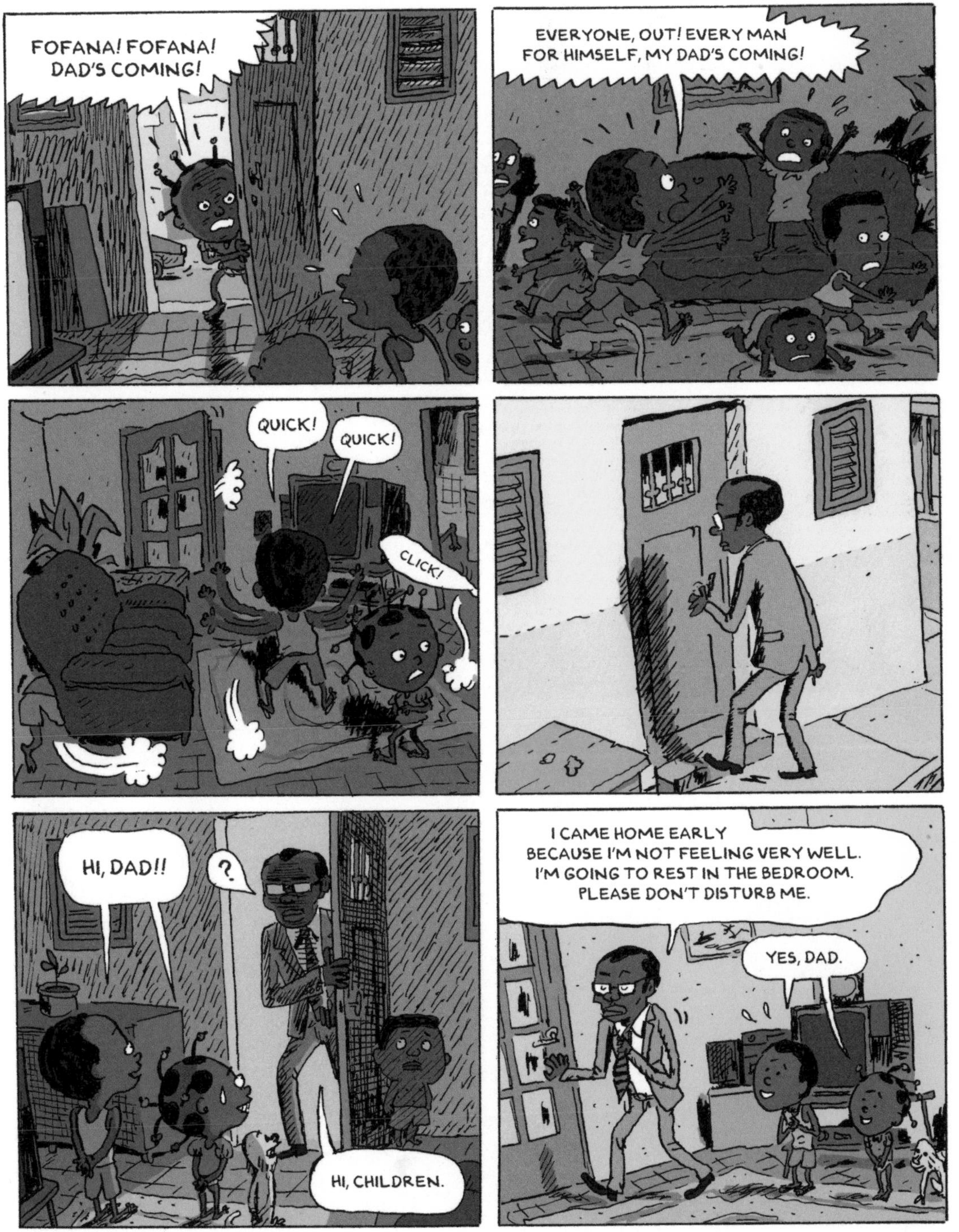
FOFANA! FOFANA! DAD'S COMING!
EVERYONE, OUT! EVERY MAN FOR HIMSELF, MY DAD'S COMING!
QUICK!
QUICK!
CLICK!
HI, DAD!!
?
HI, CHILDREN.
I CAME HOME EARLY BECAUSE I'M NOT FEELING VERY WELL. I'M GOING TO REST IN THE BEDROOM. PLEASE DON'T DISTURB ME.
YES, DAD.

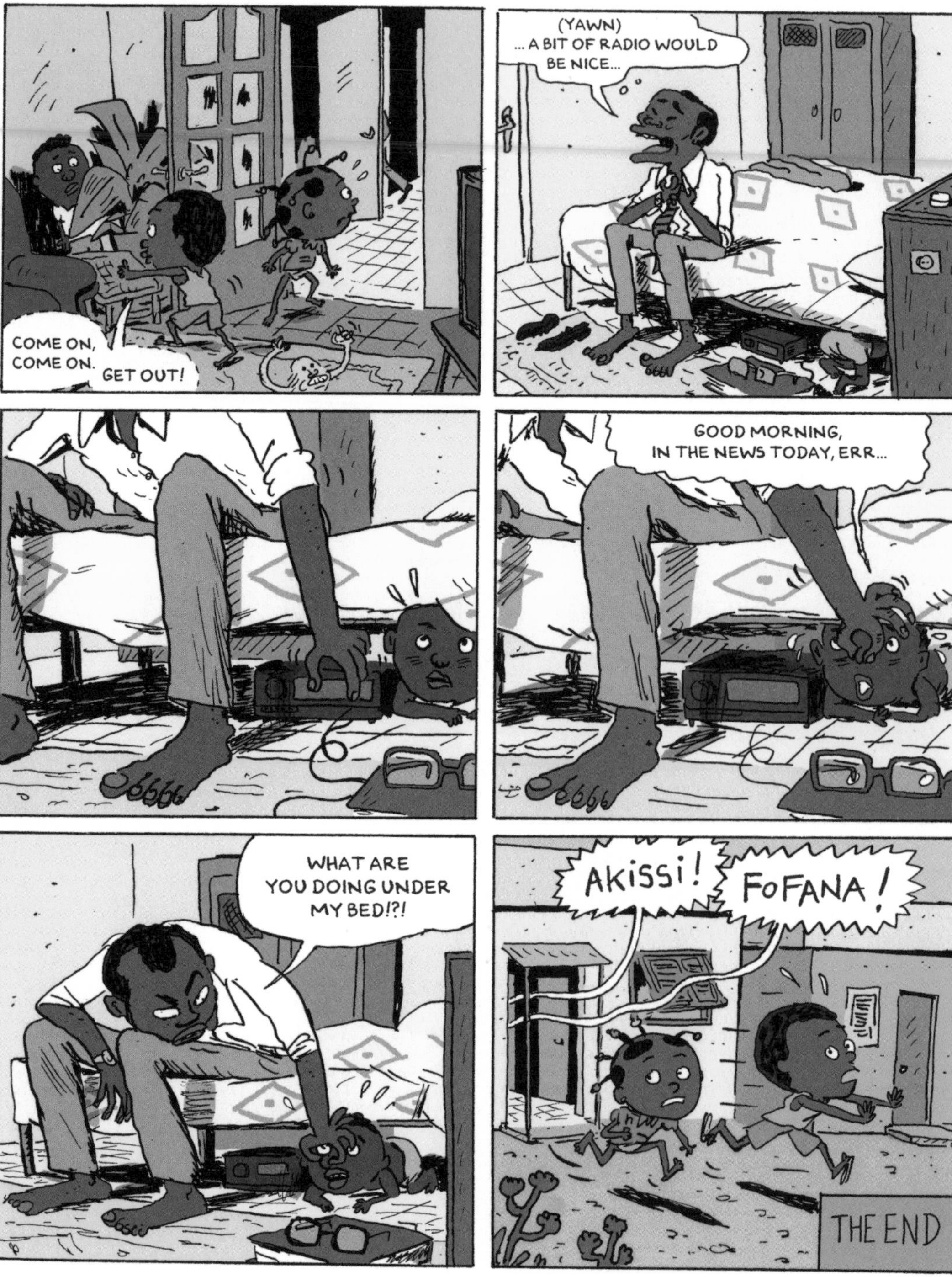
COME ON, COME ON.
GET OUT!
(YAWN) ... A BIT OF RADIO WOULD BE NICE...
GOOD MORNING, IN THE NEWS TODAY, ERR...
WHAT ARE YOU DOING UNDER MY BED!?!
AKISSI!
FOFANA!
THE END

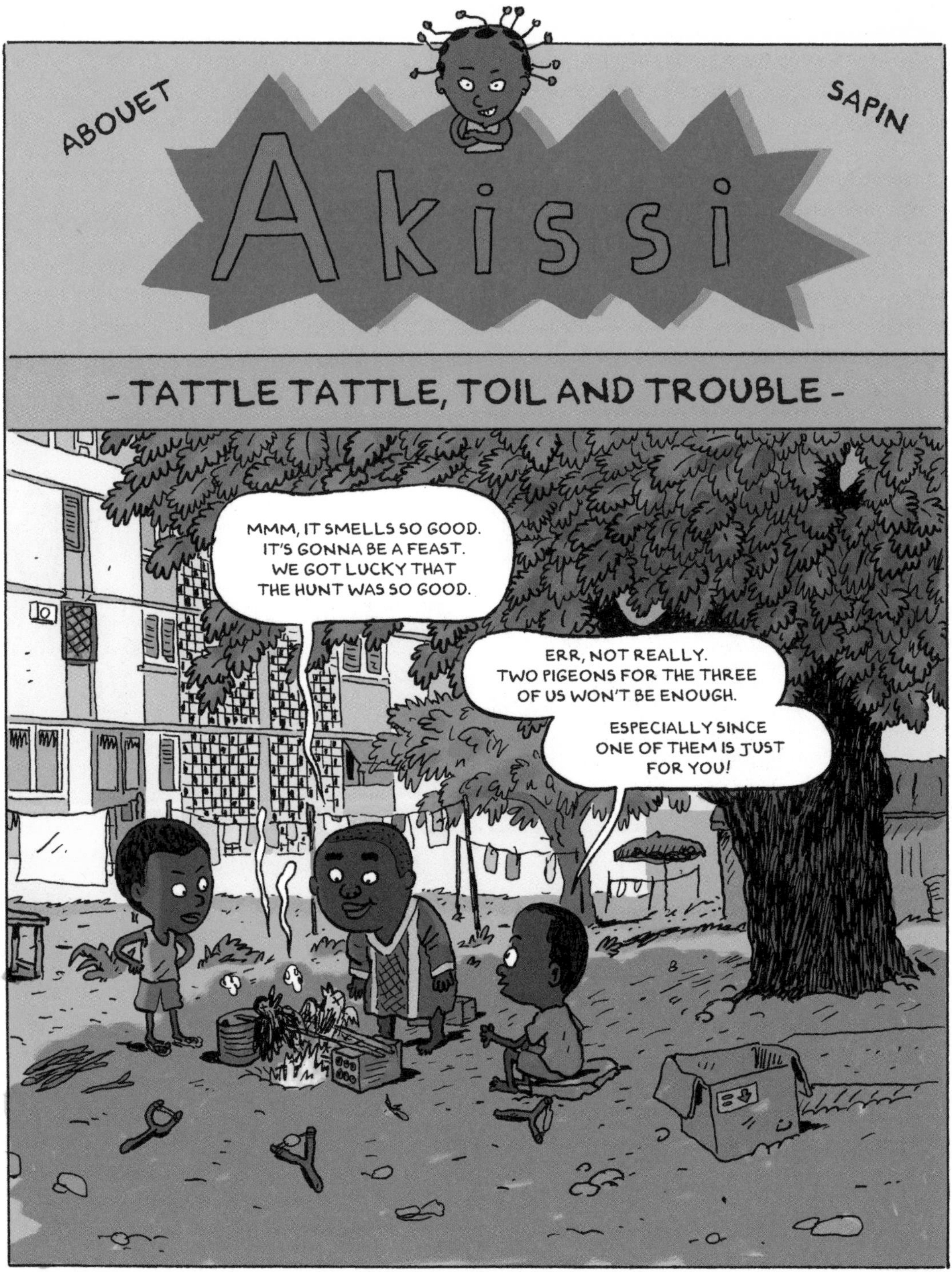
ABOUET
SAPIN
Akissi
- TATTLE TATTLE, TOIL AND TROUBLE -
MMM, IT SMELLS SO GOOD. IT'S GONNA BE A FEAST. WE GOT LUCKY THAT THE HUNT WAS SO GOOD.
ERR, NOT REALLY. TWO PIGEONS FOR THE THREE OF US WON'T BE ENOUGH.
ESPECIALLY SINCE ONE OF THEM IS JUST FOR YOU!

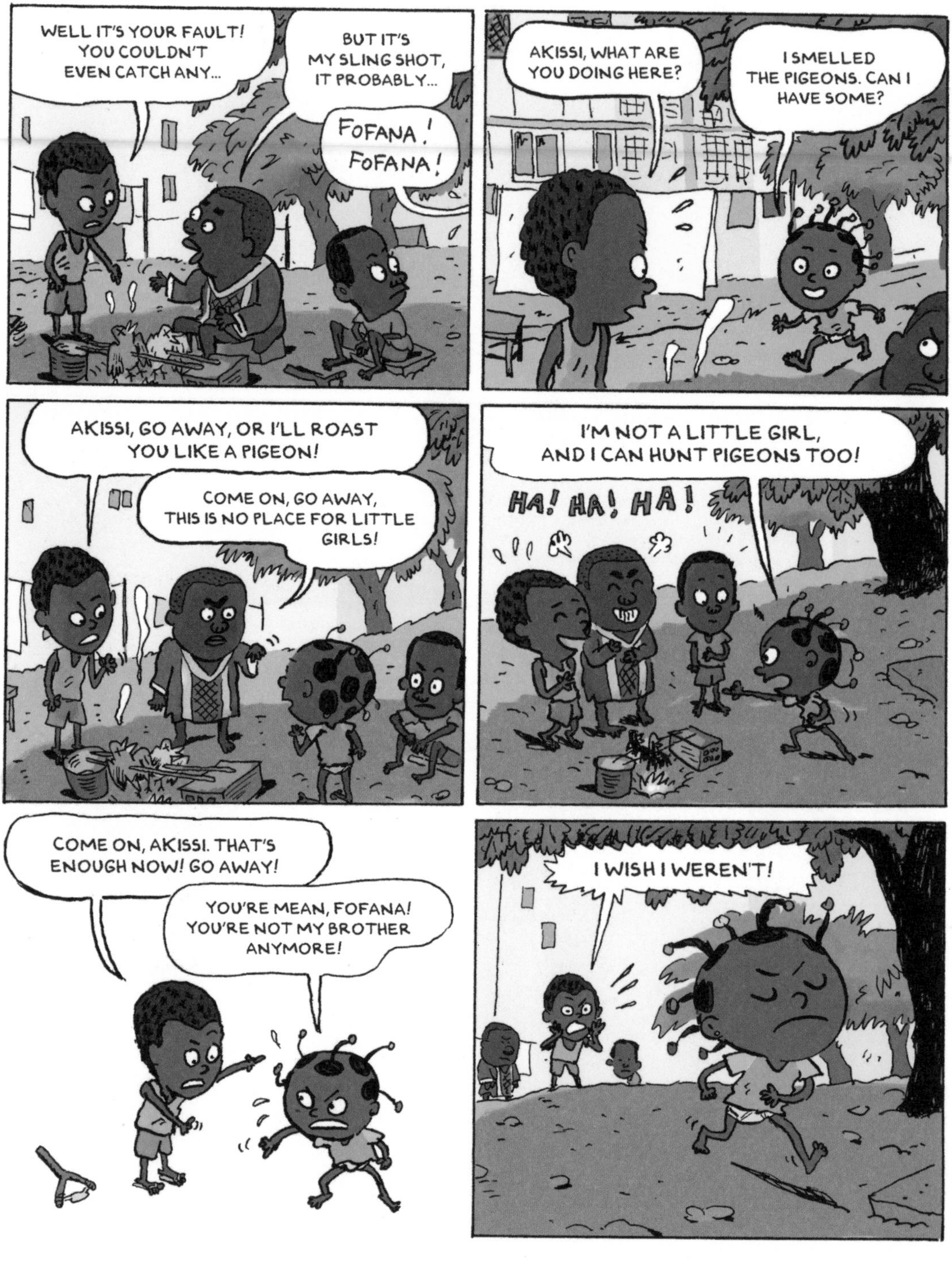
WELL IT'S YOUR FAULT! YOU COULDN'T EVEN CATCH ANY...
BUT IT'S MY SLING SHOT, IT PROBABLY...
FOFANA! FOFANA!
AKISSI, WHAT ARE YOU DOING HERE?
I SMELLED THE PIGEONS. CAN I HAVE SOME?
AKISSI, GO AWAY, OR I'LL ROAST YOU LIKE A PIGEON!
COME ON, GO AWAY, THIS IS NO PLACE FOR LITTLE GIRLS!
I'M NOT A LITTLE GIRL, AND I CAN HUNT PIGEONS TOO!
HA! HA! HA!
COME ON, AKISSI. THAT'S ENOUGH NOW! GO AWAY!
YOU'RE MEAN, FOFANA! YOU'RE NOT MY BROTHER ANYMORE!
I WISH I WEREN'T!

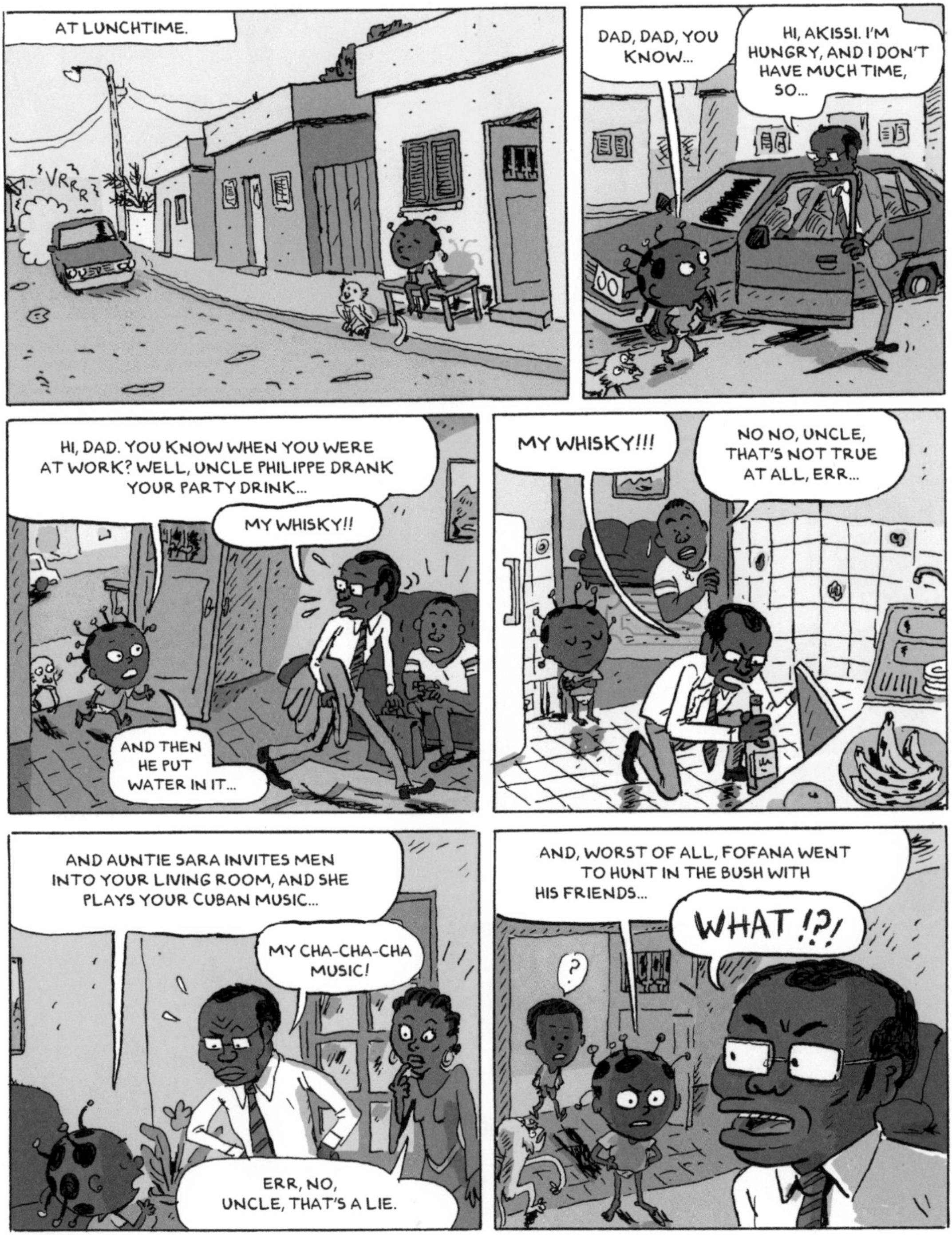
AT LUNCHTIME.
VRRR
DAD, DAD, YOU KNOW...
HI, AKISSI. I'M HUNGRY, AND I DON'T HAVE MUCH TIME, SO...
HI, DAD. YOU KNOW WHEN YOU WERE AT WORK? WELL, UNCLE PHILIPPE DRANK YOUR PARTY DRINK...
MY WHISKY!!
AND THEN HE PUT WATER IN IT...
MY WHISKY!!!
NO NO, UNCLE, THAT'S NOT TRUE AT ALL, ERR...
AND AUNTIE SARA INVITES MEN INTO YOUR LIVING ROOM, AND SHE PLAYS YOUR CUBAN MUSIC...
MY CHA-CHA-CHA MUSIC!
ERR, NO, UNCLE, THAT'S A LIE.
AND, WORST OF ALL, FOFANA WENT TO HUNT IN THE BUSH WITH HIS FRIENDS...
WHAT !?!
?

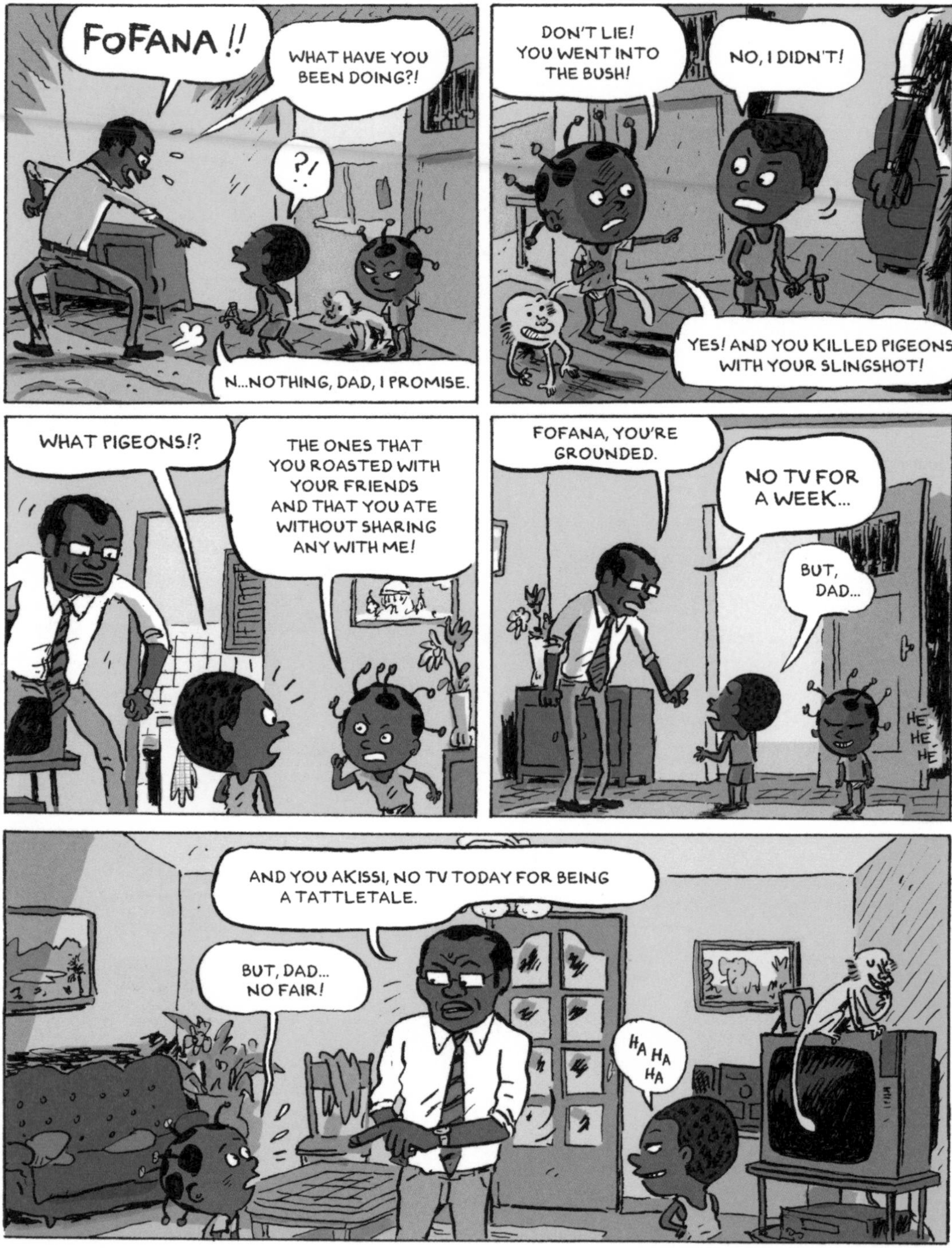
FoFANA !!
WHAT HAVE YOU BEEN DOING?!
?!
N...NOTHING, DAD, I PROMISE.
DON'T LIE! YOU WENT INTO THE BUSH!
NO, I DIDN'T!
YES! AND YOU KILLED PIGEONS WITH YOUR SLINGSHOT!
WHAT PIGEONS!?
THE ONES THAT YOU ROASTED WITH YOUR FRIENDS AND THAT YOU ATE WITHOUT SHARING ANY WITH ME!
FOFANA, YOU'RE GROUNDED.
NO TV FOR A WEEK...
BUT, DAD...
HE HE HE
AND YOU AKISSI, NO TV TODAY FOR BEING A TATTLETALE.
BUT, DAD... NO FAIR!
HA HA HA

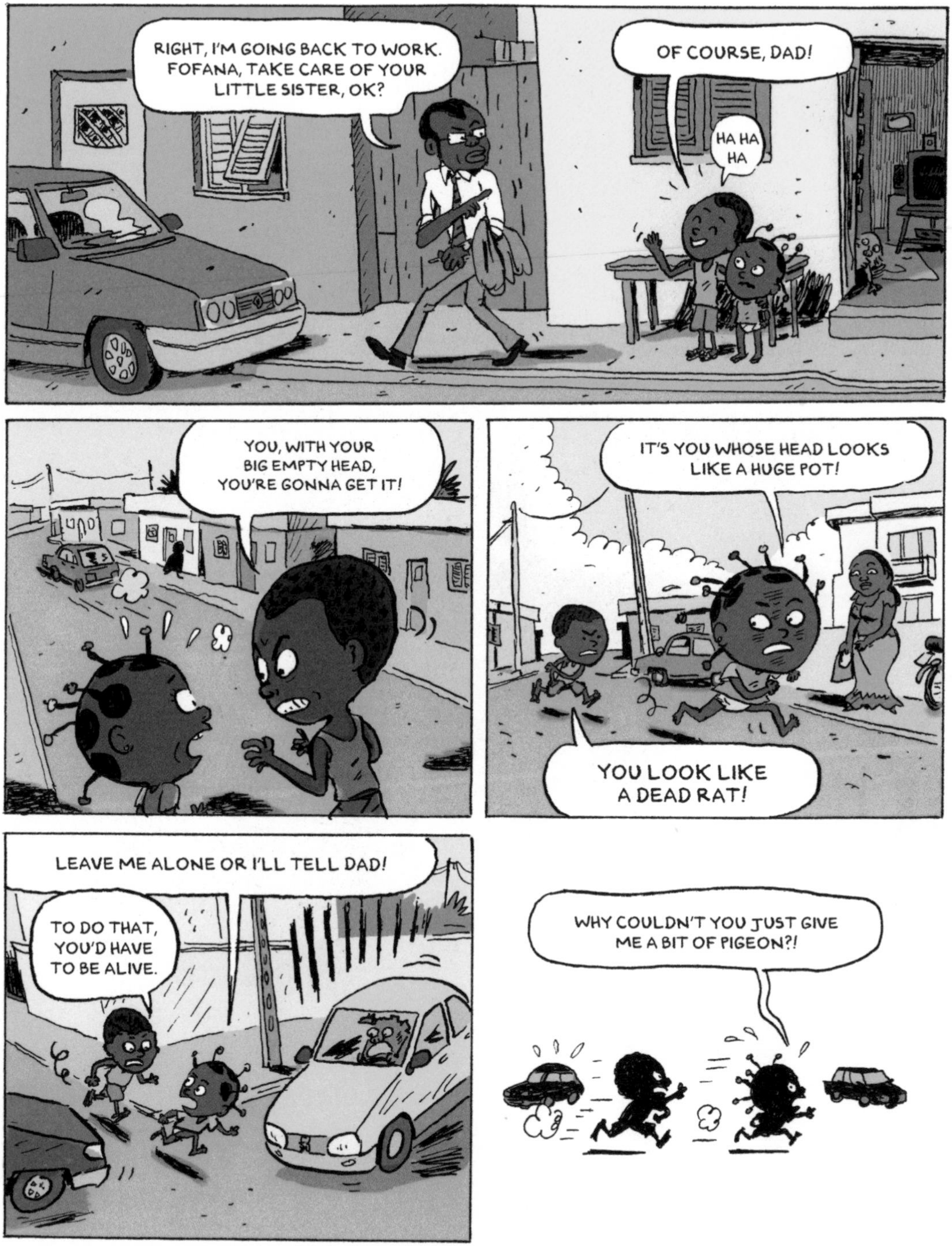
RIGHT, I'M GOING BACK TO WORK. FOFANA, TAKE CARE OF YOUR LITTLE SISTER, OK?
OF COURSE, DAD!
HA HA HA
YOU, WITH YOUR BIG EMPTY HEAD, YOU'RE GONNA GET IT!
IT'S YOU WHOSE HEAD LOOKS LIKE A HUGE POT!
YOU LOOK LIKE A DEAD RAT!
LEAVE ME ALONE OR I'LL TELL DAD!
TO DO THAT, YOU'D HAVE TO BE ALIVE.
WHY COULDN'T YOU JUST GIVE ME A BIT OF PIGEON?!

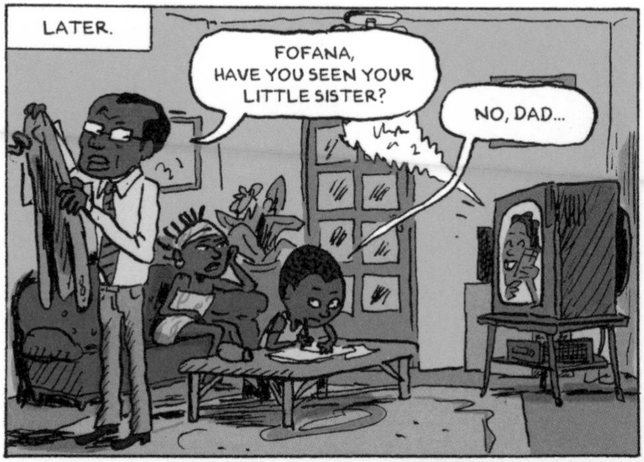
LATER.
FOFANA, HAVE YOU SEEN YOUR LITTLE SISTER?
NO, DAD...

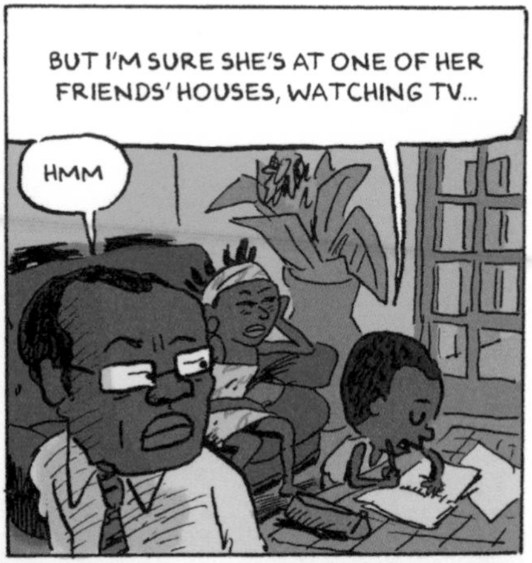
BUT I'M SURE SHE'S AT ONE OF HER FRIENDS' HOUSES, WATCHING TV...
HMM

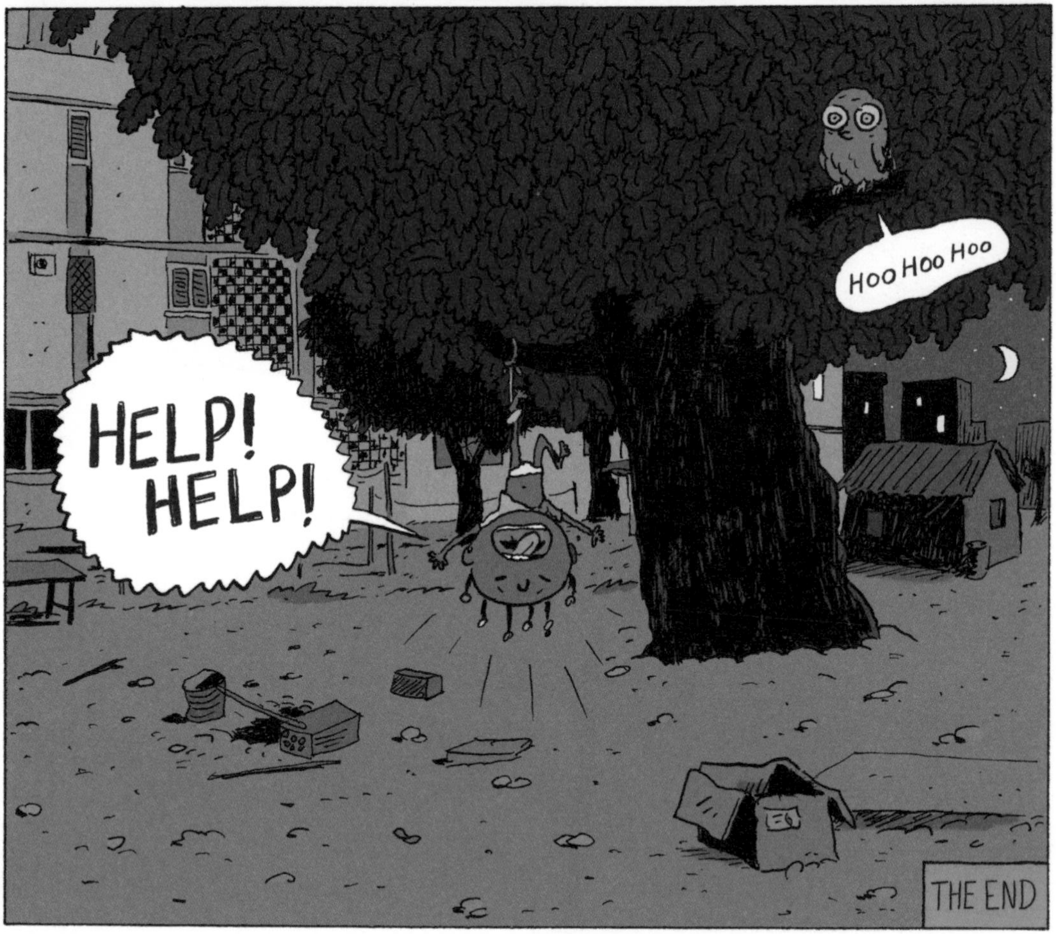
HOO HOO HOO
HELP! HELP!
THE END

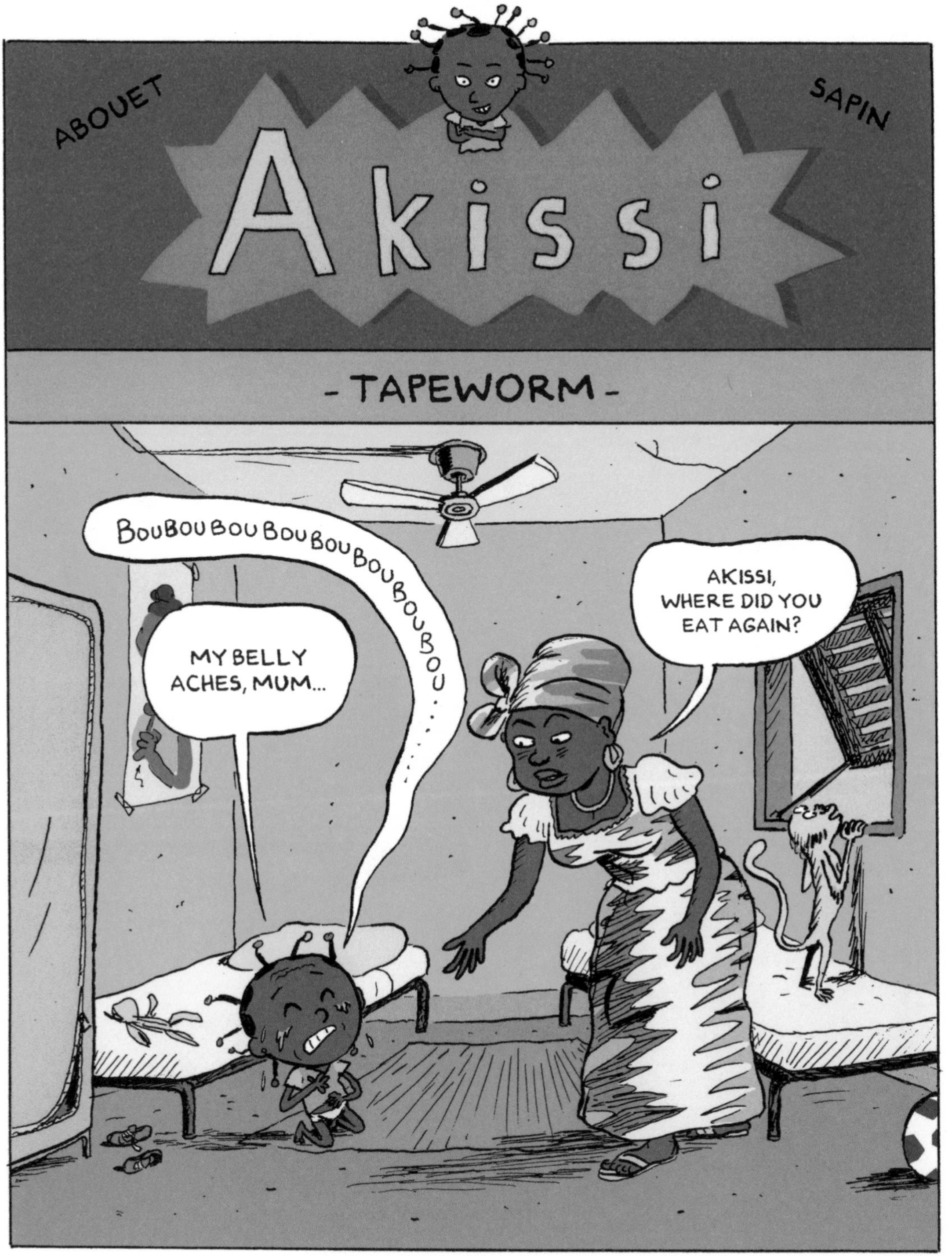
ABOUET
SAPIN
Akissi
- TAPEWORM -
BOUBOUBOUBOUBOUBOUBOUBOUBOU...
MY BELLY ACHES, MUM...
AKISSI, WHERE DID YOU EAT AGAIN?

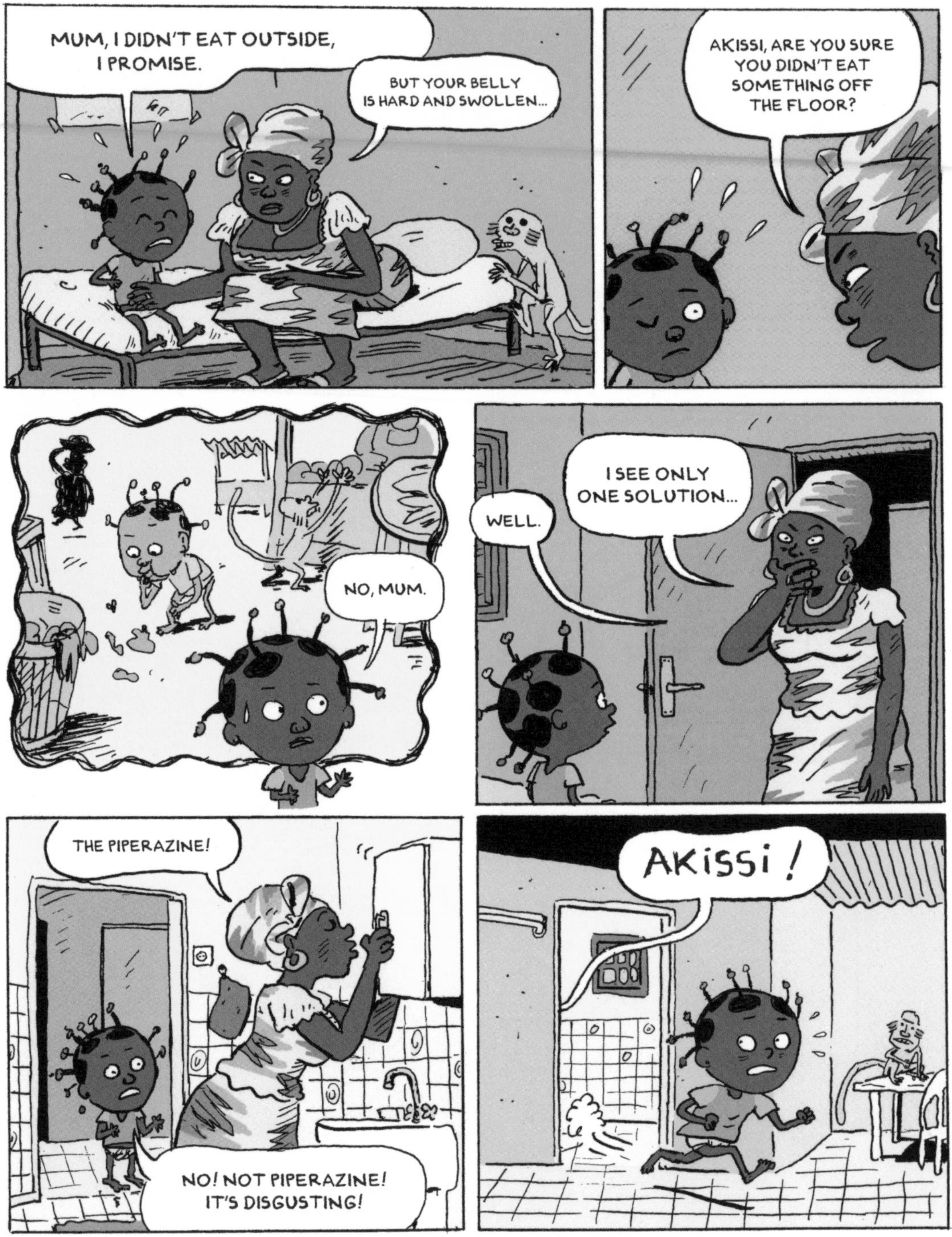
MUM, I DIDN'T EAT OUTSIDE, I PROMISE.
BUT YOUR BELLY IS HARD AND SWOLLEN...
AKISSI, ARE YOU SURE YOU DIDN'T EAT SOMETHING OFF THE FLOOR?
NO, MUM.
WELL.
I SEE ONLY ONE SOLUTION...
THE PIPERAZINE!
NO! NOT PIPERAZINE! IT'S DISGUSTING!
AKISSI !

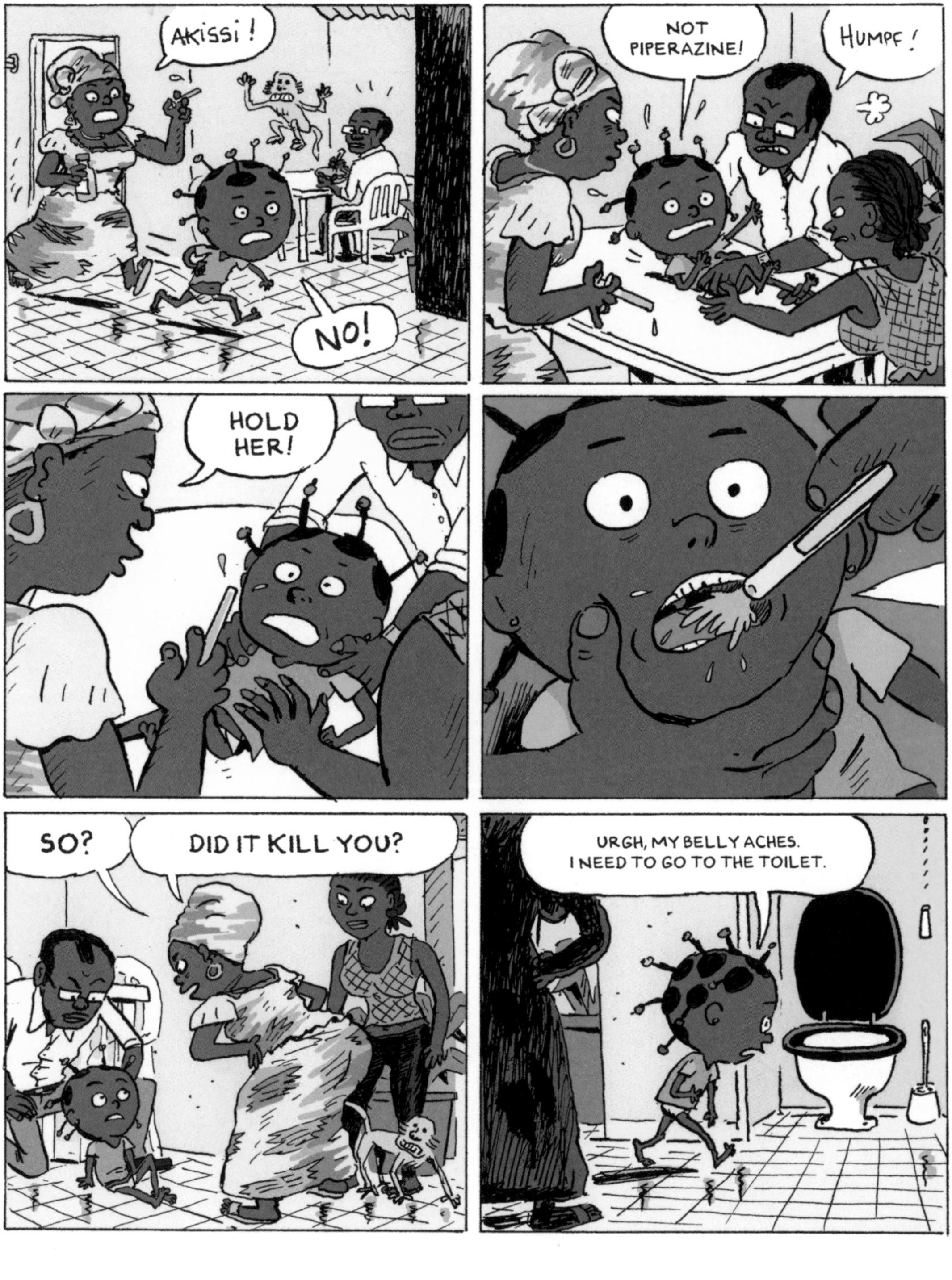
AKISSI!
NO!
NOT PIPERAZINE!
HUMPF!
HOLD HER!
SO?
DID IT KILL YOU?
URGH, MY BELLY ACHES.
I NEED TO GO TO THE TOILET.

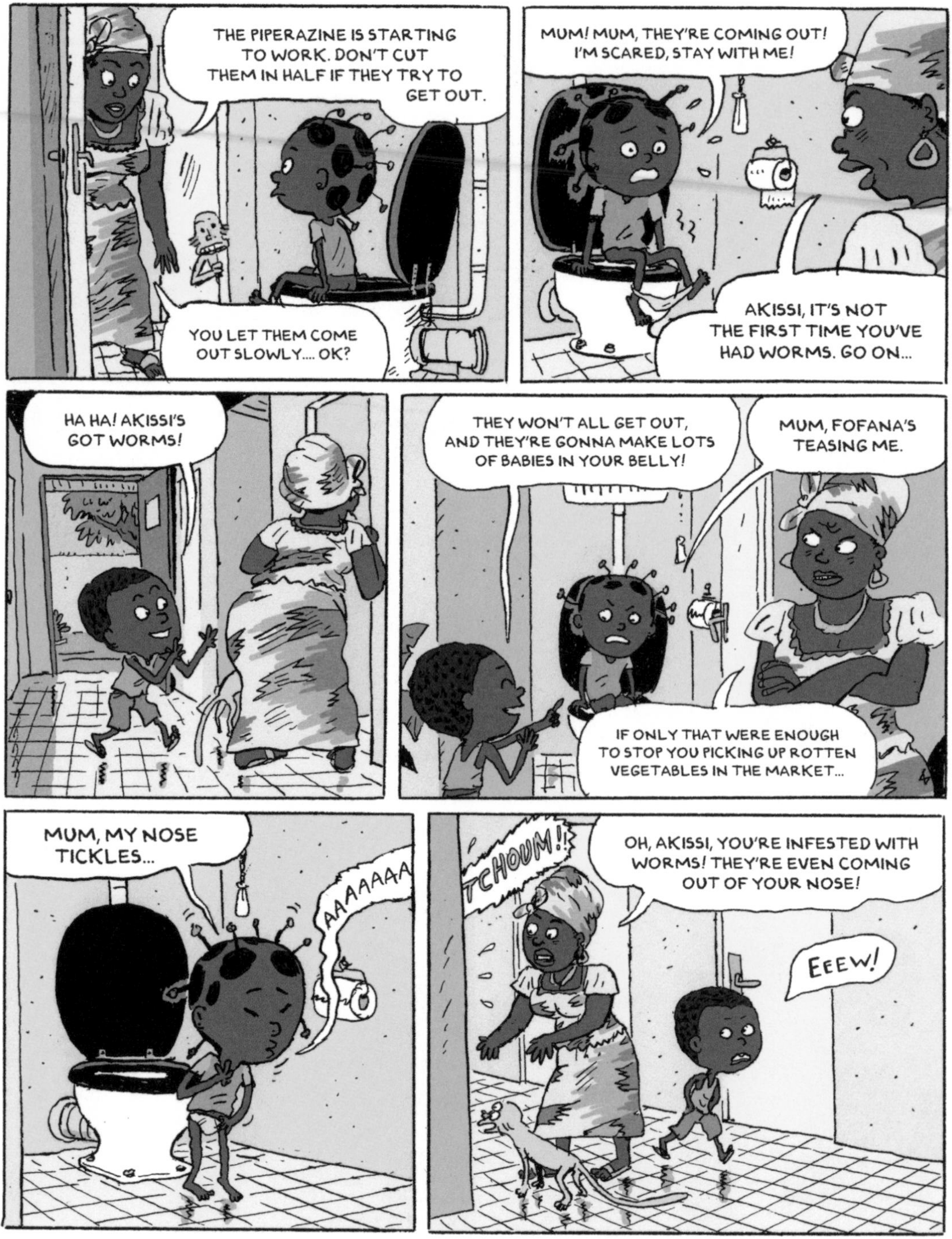
THE PIPERAZINE IS STARTING TO WORK. DON'T CUT THEM IN HALF IF THEY TRY TO GET OUT.
YOU LET THEM COME OUT SLOWLY.... OK?
MUM! MUM, THEY'RE COMING OUT! I'M SCARED, STAY WITH ME!
AKISSI, IT'S NOT THE FIRST TIME YOU'VE HAD WORMS. GO ON...
HA HA! AKISSI'S GOT WORMS!
THEY WON'T ALL GET OUT, AND THEY'RE GONNA MAKE LOTS OF BABIES IN YOUR BELLY!
MUM, FOFANA'S TEASING ME.
IF ONLY THAT WERE ENOUGH TO STOP YOU PICKING UP ROTTEN VEGETABLES IN THE MARKET...
MUM, MY NOSE TICKLES...
AAAAAAA
TCHOUM!
OH, AKISSI, YOU'RE INFESTED WITH WORMS! THEY'RE EVEN COMING OUT OF YOUR NOSE!
EEEW!

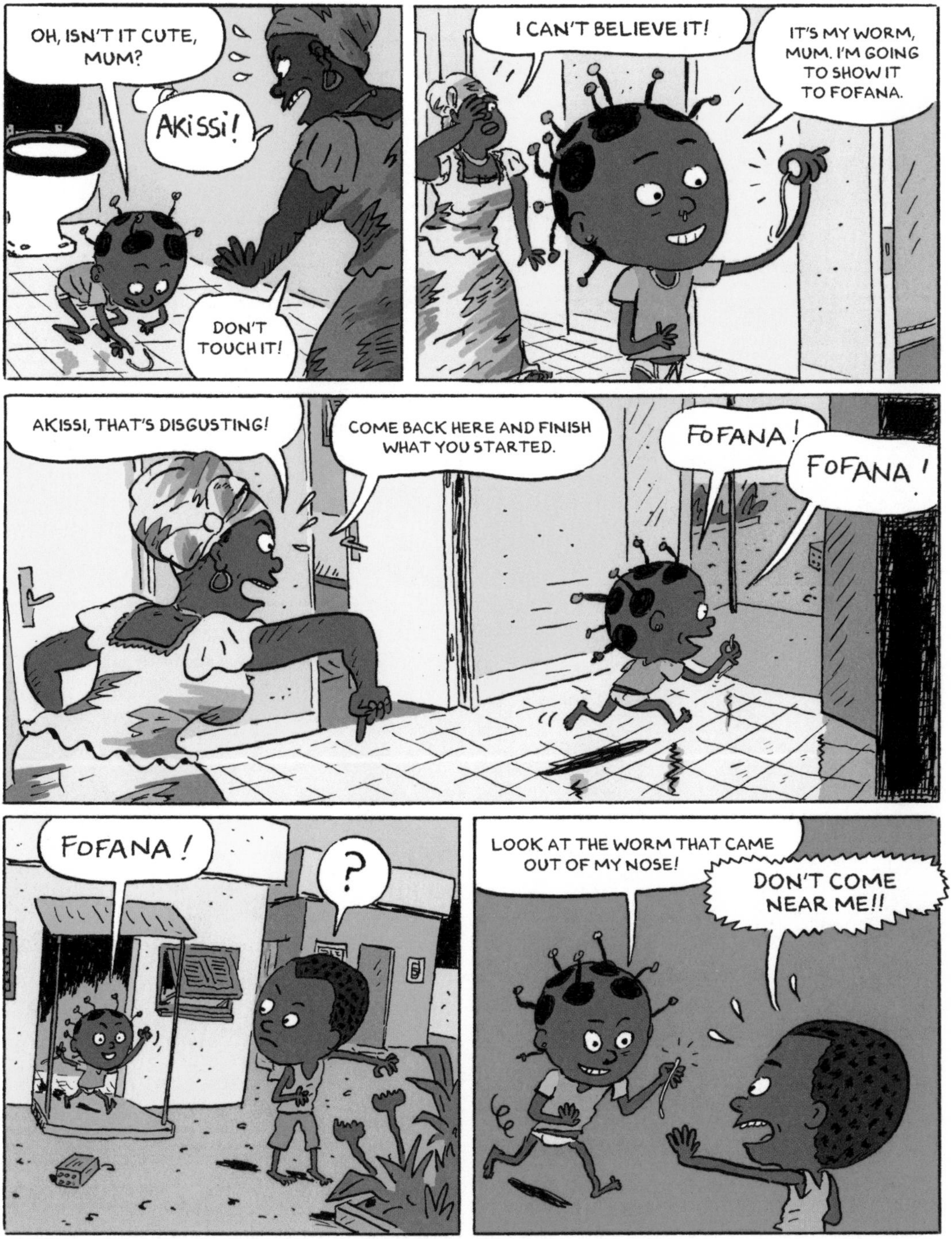

OH, ISN'T IT CUTE, MUM?
AKISSI!
DON'T TOUCH IT!
I CAN'T BELIEVE IT!
IT'S MY WORM, MUM. I'M GOING TO SHOW IT TO FOFANA.
AKISSI, THAT'S DISGUSTING!
COME BACK HERE AND FINISH WHAT YOU STARTED.
FOFANA!
FOFANA!
FOFANA!
?
LOOK AT THE WORM THAT CAME OUT OF MY NOSE!
DON'T COME NEAR ME!!

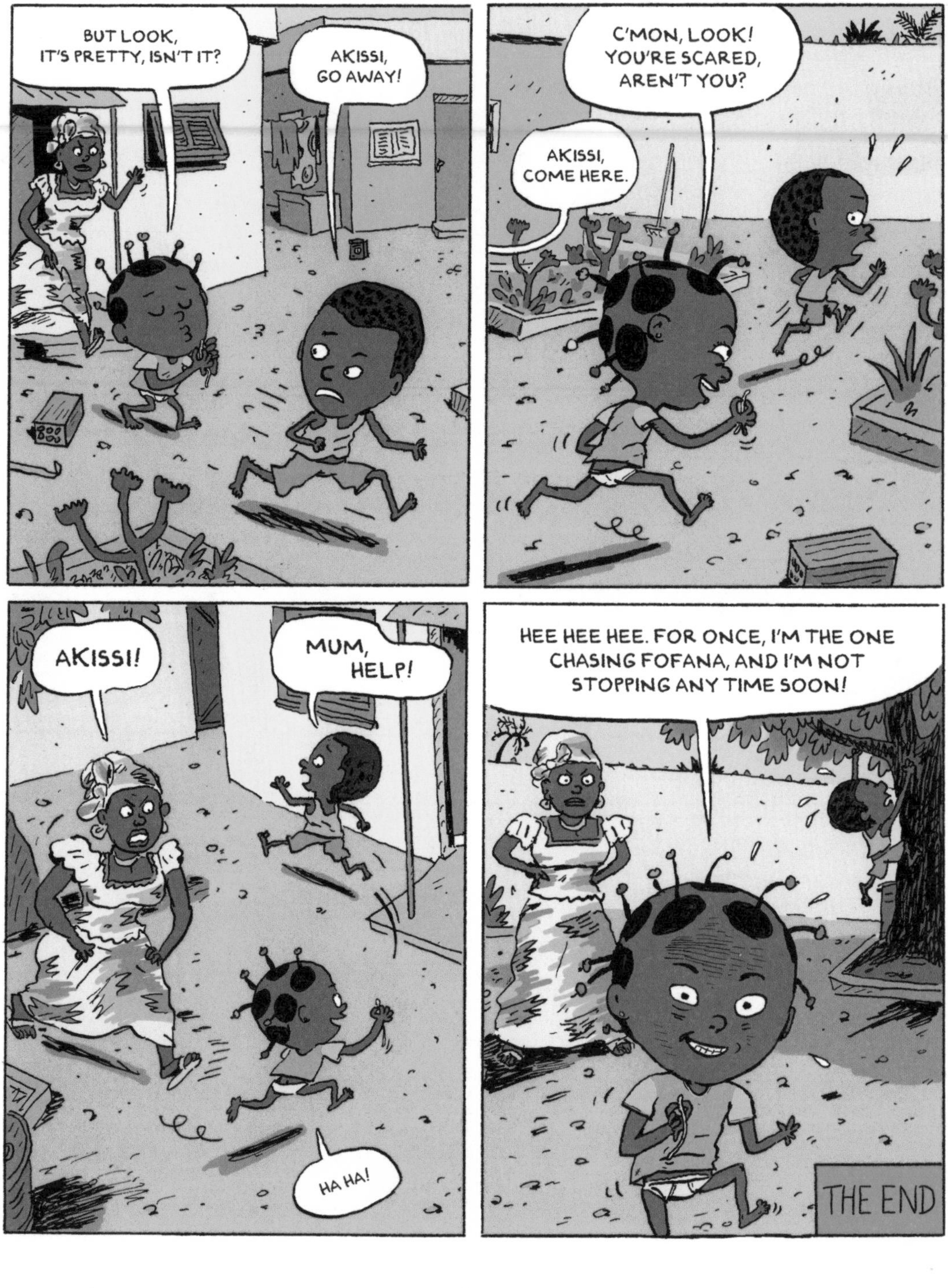
BUT LOOK, IT'S PRETTY, ISN'T IT?
AKISSI, GO AWAY!
C'MON, LOOK! YOU'RE SCARED, AREN'T YOU?
AKISSI, COME HERE.
AKISSI!
MUM, HELP!
HA HA!
HEE HEE HEE. FOR ONCE, I'M THE ONE CHASING FOFANA, AND I'M NOT STOPPING ANY TIME SOON!
THE END

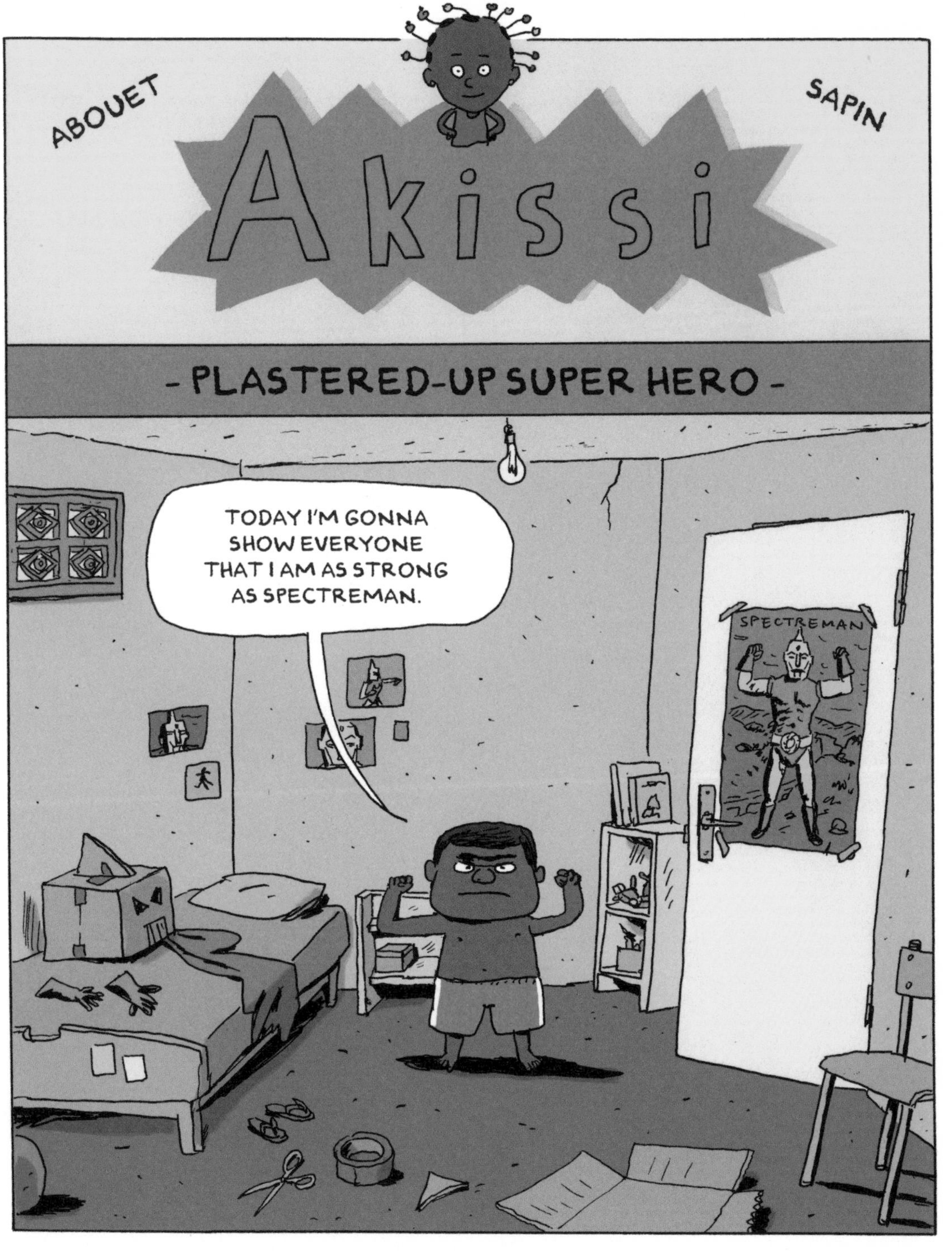
ABOUET
Akissi
SAPIN
- PLASTERED-UP SUPER HERO -
TODAY I'M GONNA SHOW EVERYONE THAT I AM AS STRONG AS SPECTREMAN.
SPECTREMAN

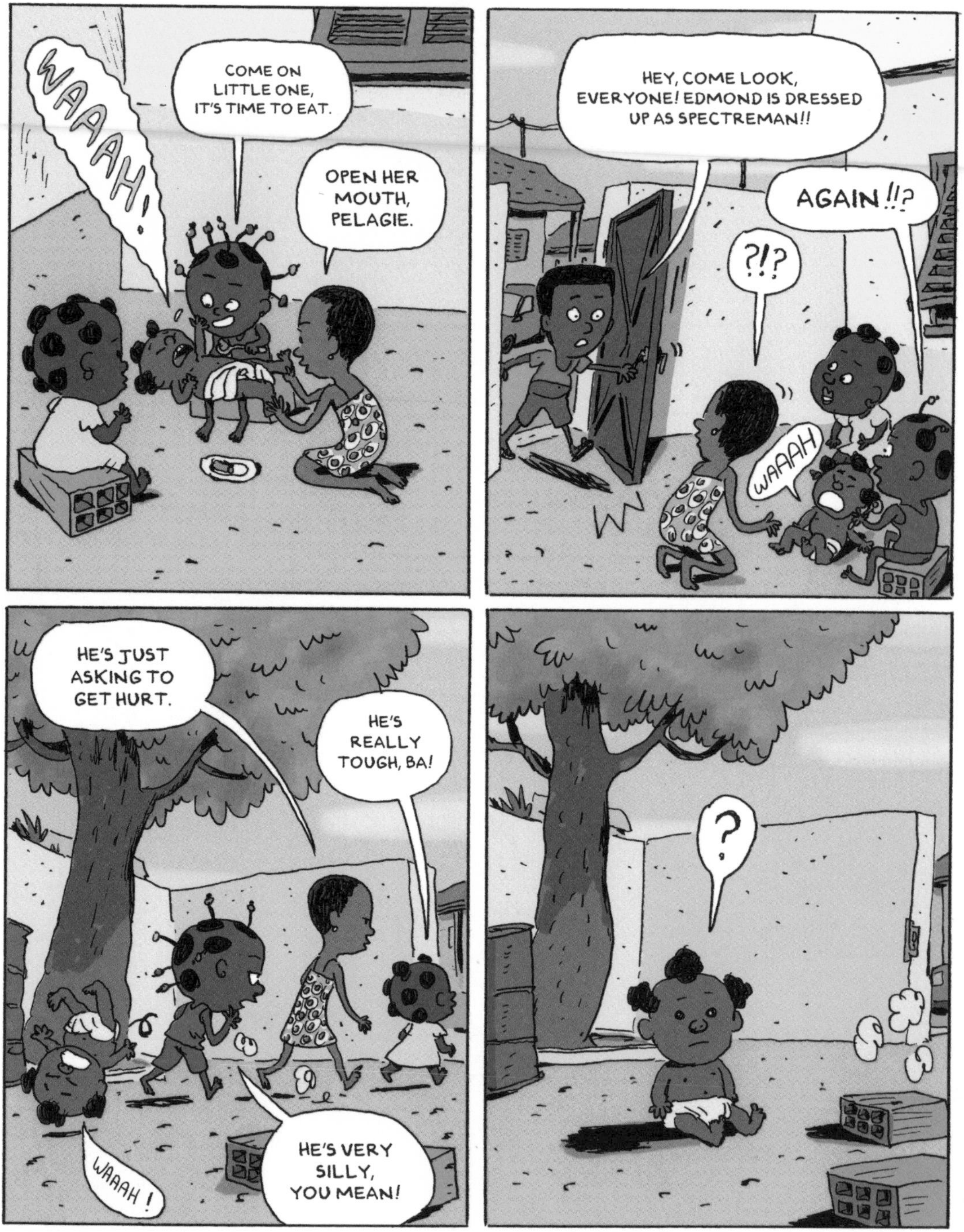
WAAAAH!
COME ON LITTLE ONE, IT'S TIME TO EAT.
OPEN HER MOUTH, PELAGIE.
HEY, COME LOOK, EVERYONE! EDMOND IS DRESSED UP AS SPECTREMAN!!
AGAIN!!?
?!?
WAAAH
HE'S JUST ASKING TO GET HURT.
HE'S REALLY TOUGH, BA!
WAAAH!
HE'S VERY SILLY, YOU MEAN!
?

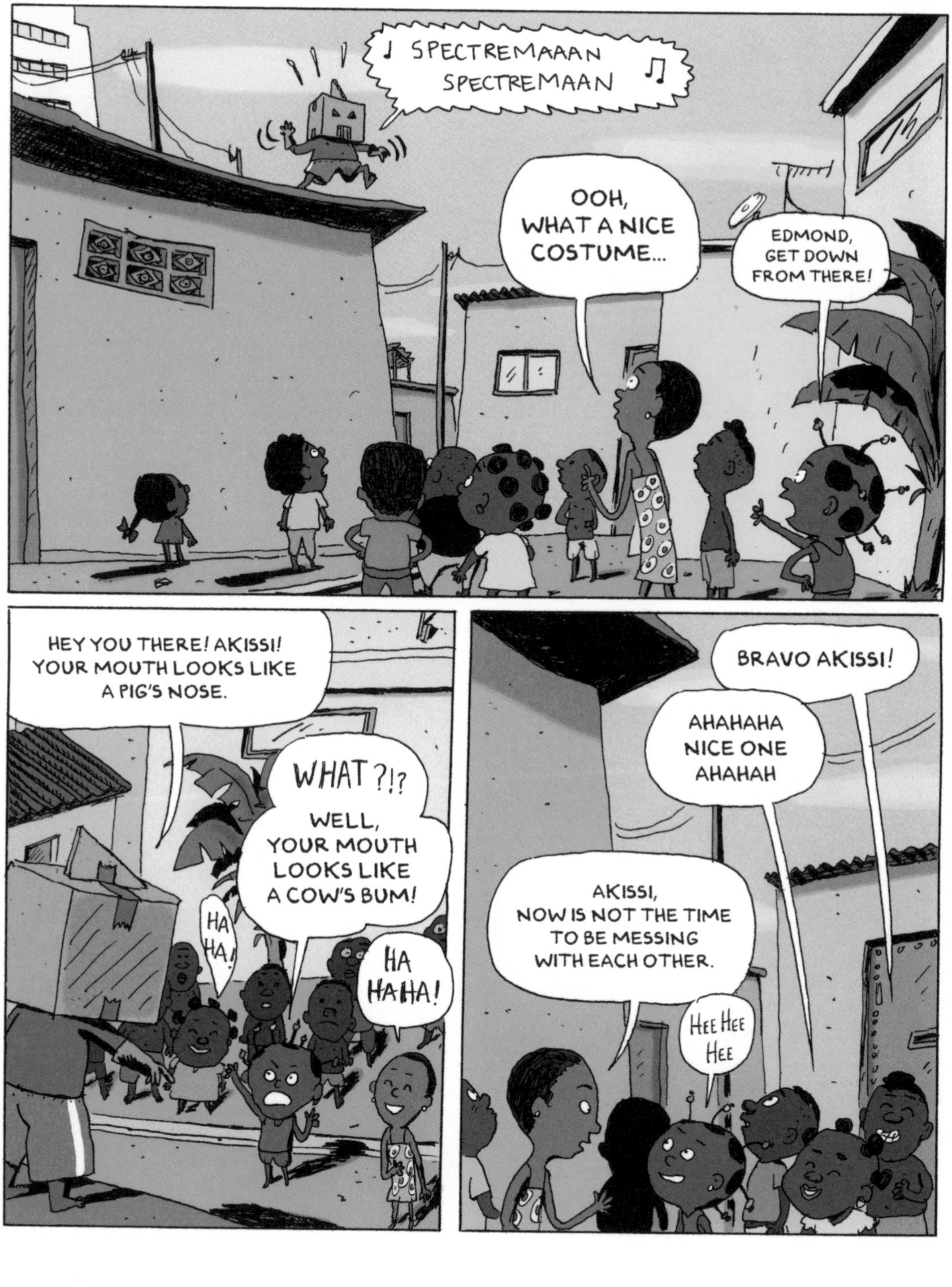
♩ SPECTREMAAAN SPECTREMAAN ♫
OOH, WHAT A NICE COSTUME...
EDMOND, GET DOWN FROM THERE!
HEY YOU THERE! AKISSI! YOUR MOUTH LOOKS LIKE A PIG'S NOSE.
WHAT ?!?
WELL, YOUR MOUTH LOOKS LIKE A COW'S BUM!
HA HA!
HA HAHA!
BRAVO AKISSI!
AHAHAHA NICE ONE AHAHAH
AKISSI, NOW IS NOT THE TIME TO BE MESSING WITH EACH OTHER.
HEE HEE HEE

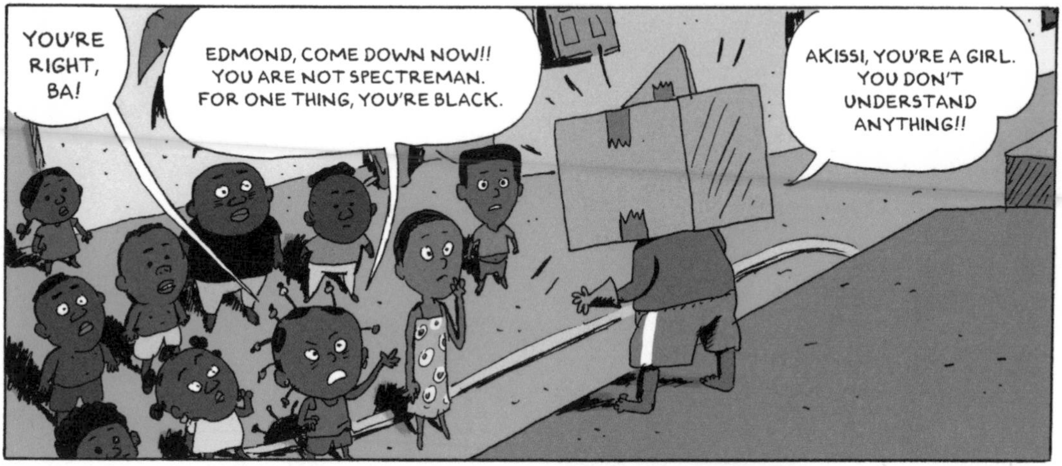
YOU'RE RIGHT, BA!
EDMOND, COME DOWN NOW!! YOU ARE NOT SPECTREMAN. FOR ONE THING, YOU'RE BLACK.
AKISSI, YOU'RE A GIRL. YOU DON'T UNDERSTAND ANYTHING!!

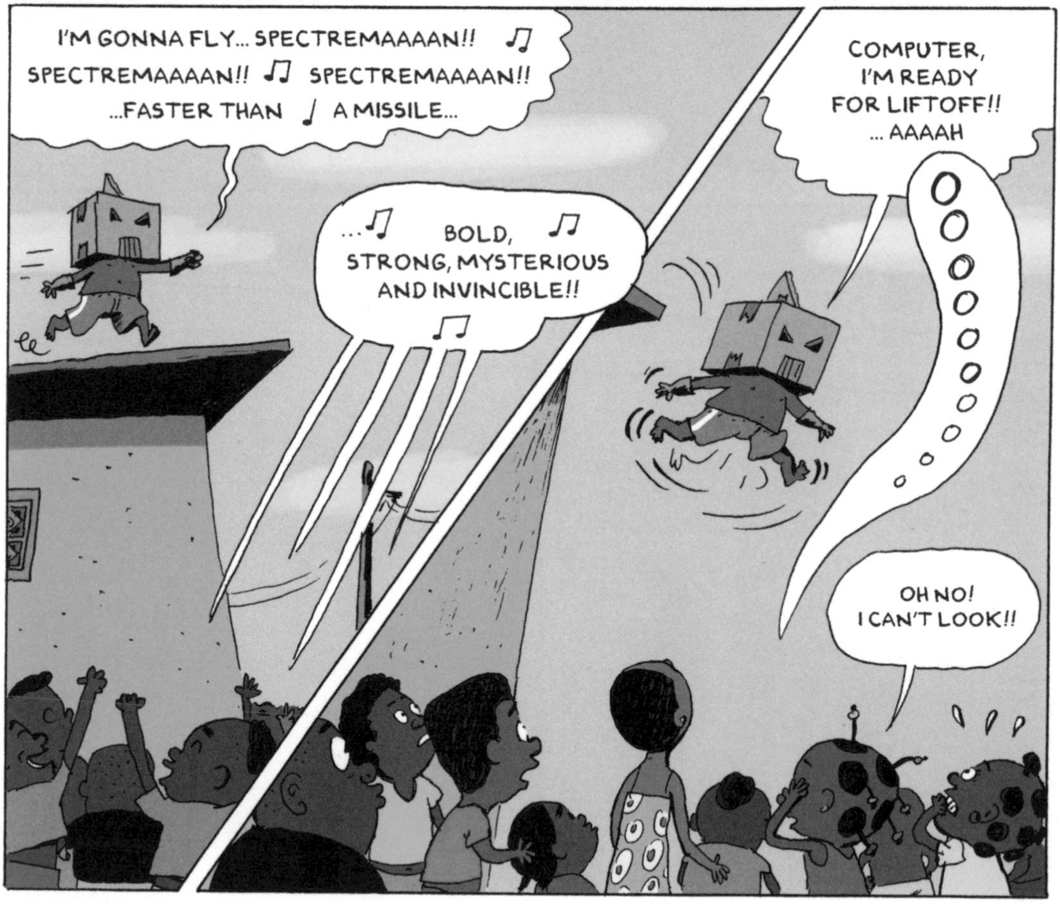
I'M GONNA FLY... SPECTREMAAAAN!! ♫ SPECTREMAAAAN!! ♫ SPECTREMAAAAN!! ...FASTER THAN ♩ A MISSILE...
...♫ BOLD, ♫ STRONG, MYSTERIOUS AND INVINCIBLE!! ♫
COMPUTER, I'M READY FOR LIFTOFF!! ... AAAAH
OOOOOOOOOOOO
OH NO! I CAN'T LOOK!!

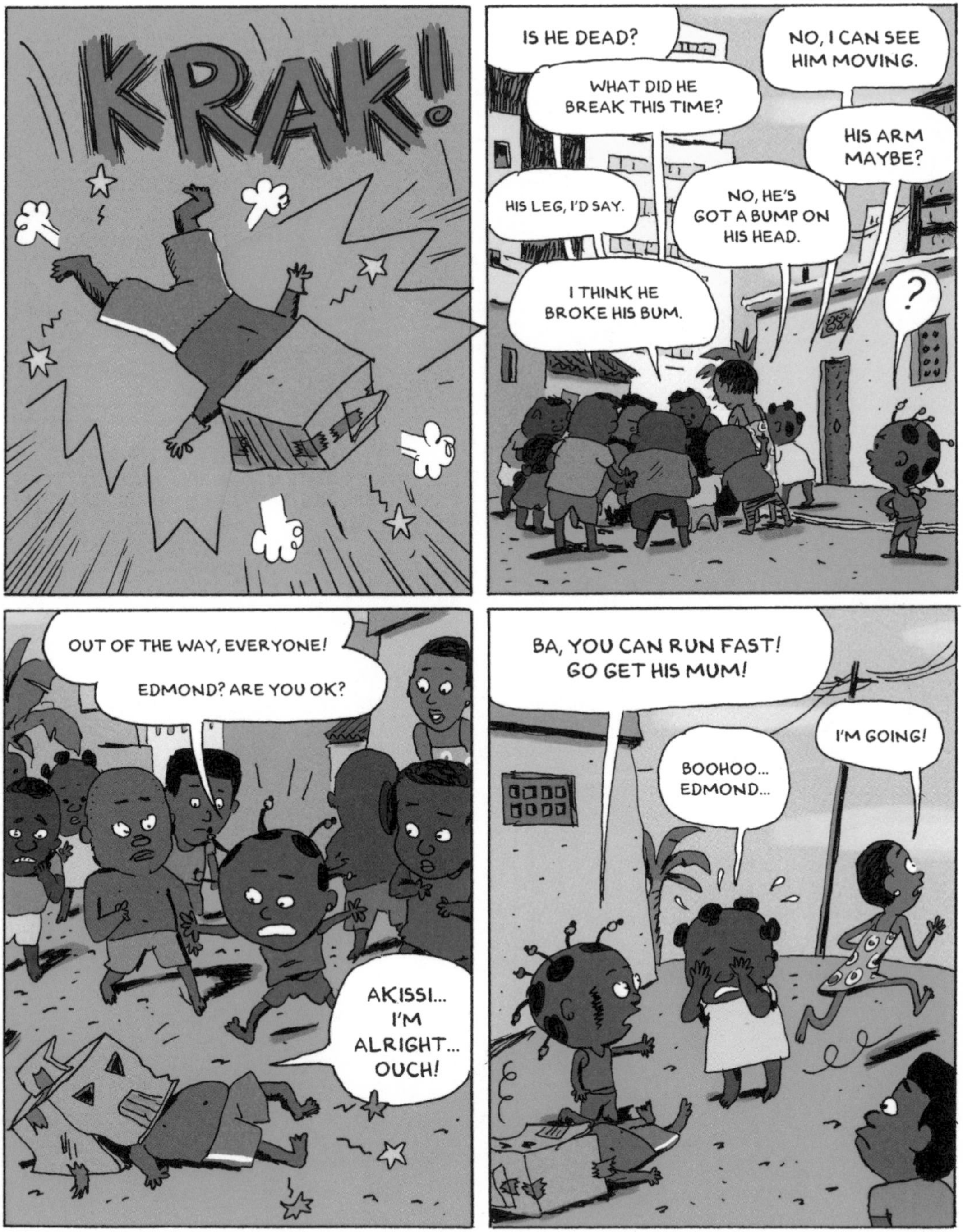
KRAK!
IS HE DEAD?
NO, I CAN SEE HIM MOVING.
WHAT DID HE BREAK THIS TIME?
HIS ARM MAYBE?
HIS LEG, I'D SAY.
NO, HE'S GOT A BUMP ON HIS HEAD.
I THINK HE BROKE HIS BUM.
?
OUT OF THE WAY, EVERYONE!
EDMOND? ARE YOU OK?
AKISSI... I'M ALRIGHT... OUCH!
BA, YOU CAN RUN FAST! GO GET HIS MUM!
BOOHOO... EDMOND...
I'M GOING!

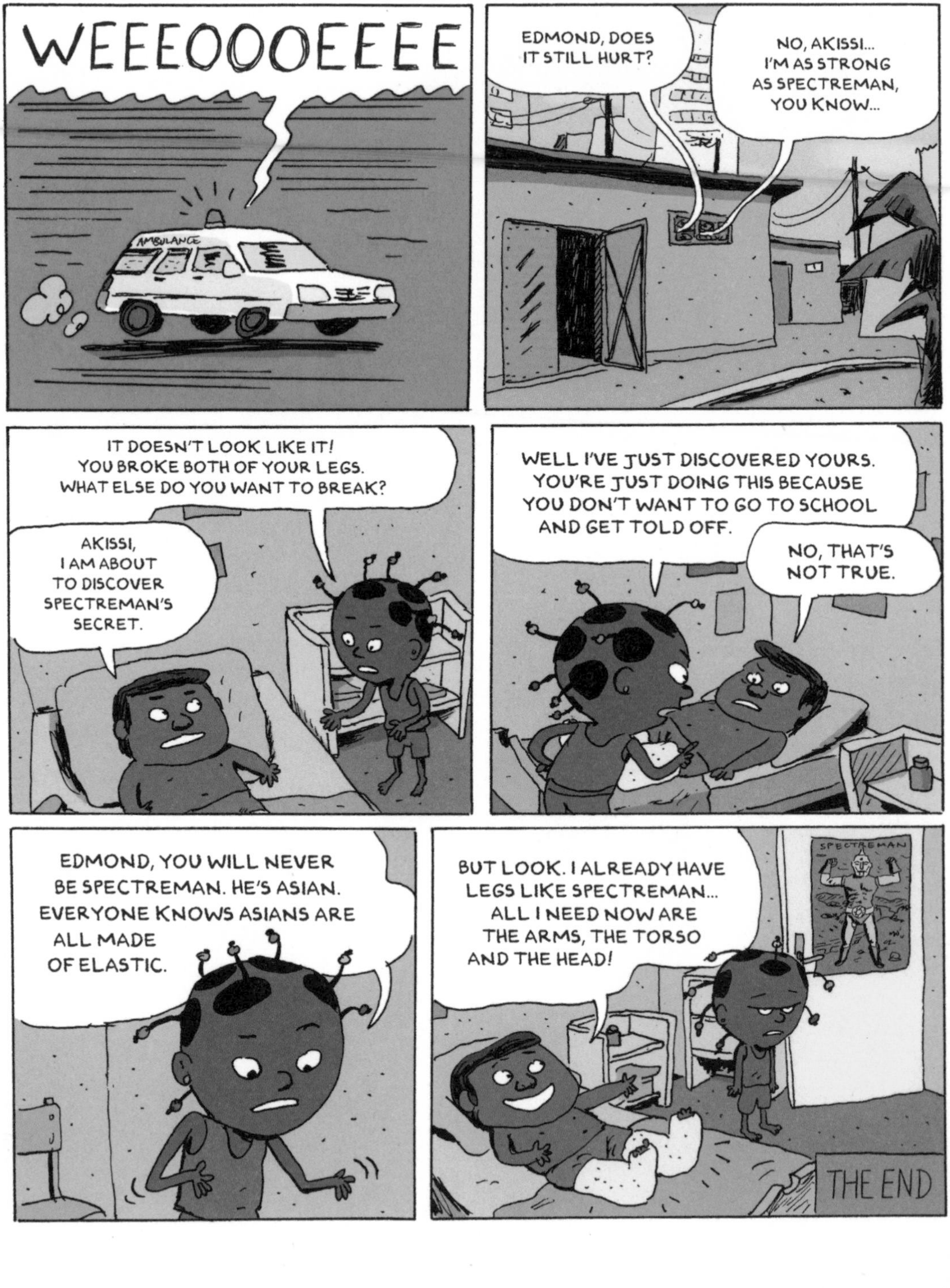
WEEEOOOEEEE
AMBULANCE
EDMOND, DOES IT STILL HURT?
NO, AKISSI... I'M AS STRONG AS SPECTREMAN, YOU KNOW...
IT DOESN'T LOOK LIKE IT! YOU BROKE BOTH OF YOUR LEGS. WHAT ELSE DO YOU WANT TO BREAK?
AKISSI, I AM ABOUT TO DISCOVER SPECTREMAN'S SECRET.
WELL I'VE JUST DISCOVERED YOURS. YOU'RE JUST DOING THIS BECAUSE YOU DON'T WANT TO GO TO SCHOOL AND GET TOLD OFF.
NO, THAT'S NOT TRUE.
EDMOND, YOU WILL NEVER BE SPECTREMAN. HE'S ASIAN. EVERYONE KNOWS ASIANS ARE ALL MADE OF ELASTIC.
BUT LOOK. I ALREADY HAVE LEGS LIKE SPECTREMAN... ALL I NEED NOW ARE THE ARMS, THE TORSO AND THE HEAD!
SPECTREMAN
THE END

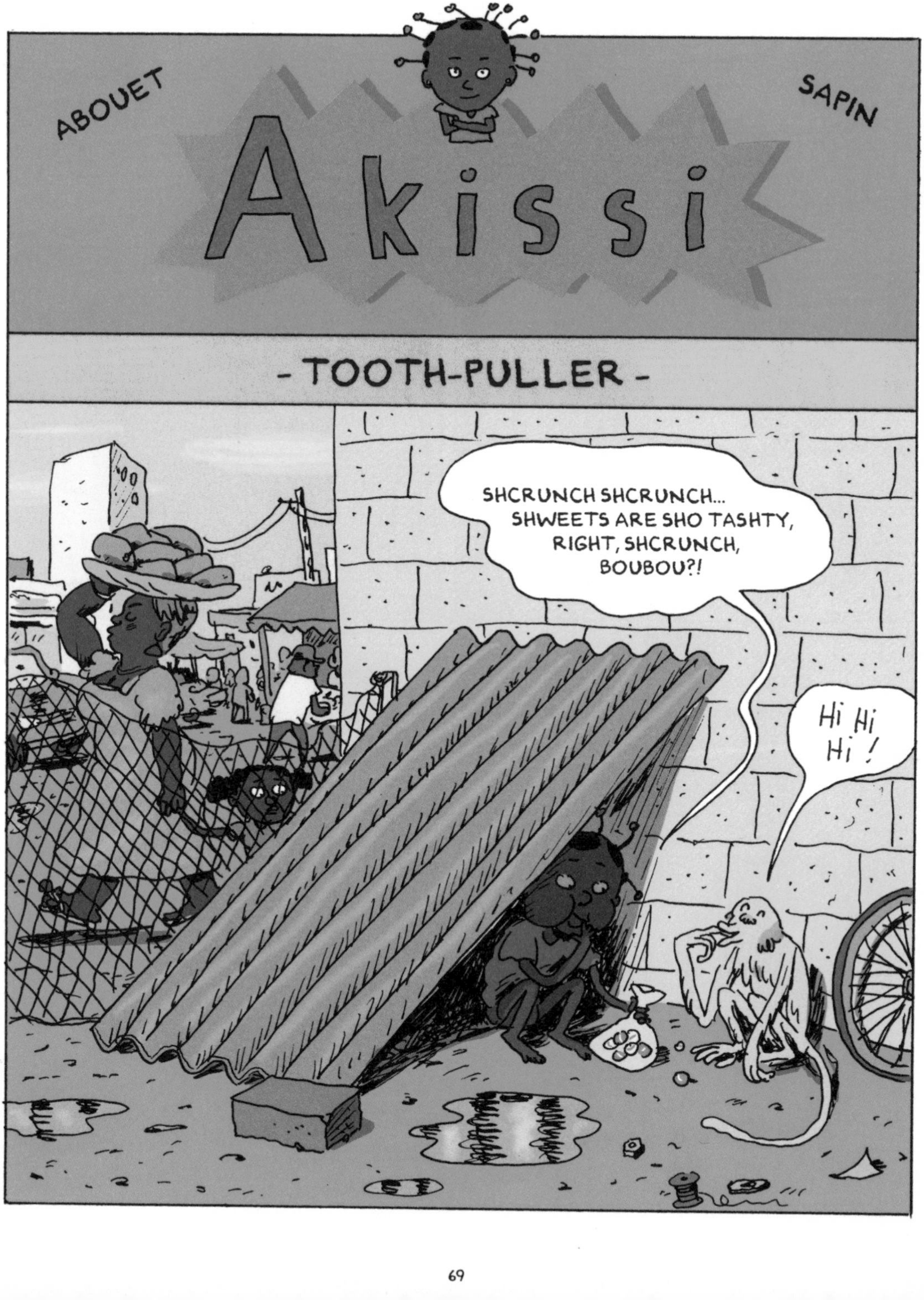
ABOUET
SAPIN
Akissi
- TOOTH-PULLER -
SHCRUNCH SHCRUNCH... SHWEETS ARE SHO TASHTY, RIGHT, SHCRUNCH, BOUBOU?!
Hi Hi Hi !

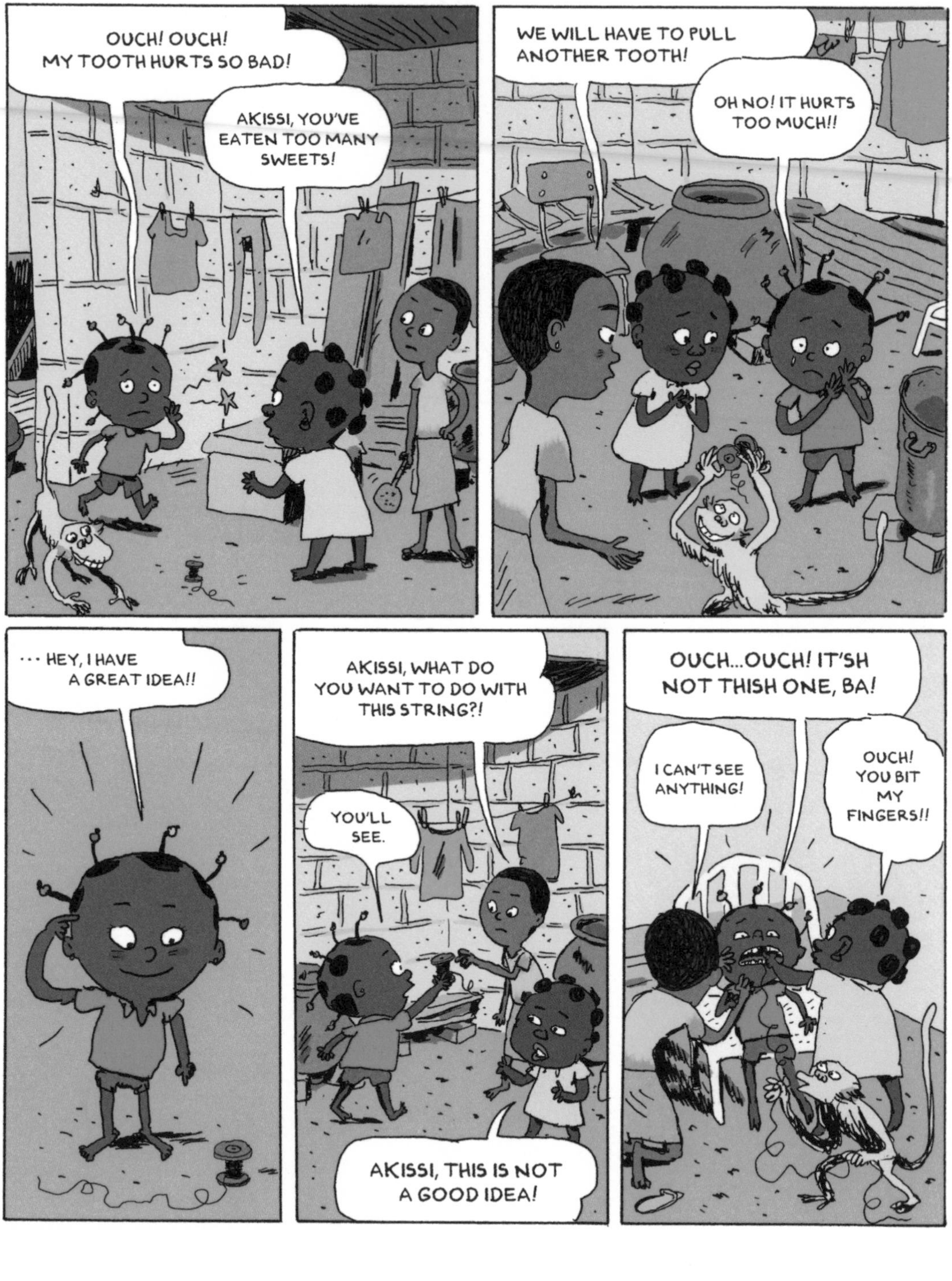
OUCH! OUCH! MY TOOTH HURTS SO BAD!
AKISSI, YOU'VE EATEN TOO MANY SWEETS!
WE WILL HAVE TO PULL ANOTHER TOOTH!
OH NO! IT HURTS TOO MUCH!!
... HEY, I HAVE A GREAT IDEA!!
AKISSI, WHAT DO YOU WANT TO DO WITH THIS STRING?!
YOU'LL SEE.
AKISSI, THIS IS NOT A GOOD IDEA!
OUCH...OUCH! IT'SH NOT THISH ONE, BA!
I CAN'T SEE ANYTHING!
OUCH! YOU BIT MY FINGERS!!

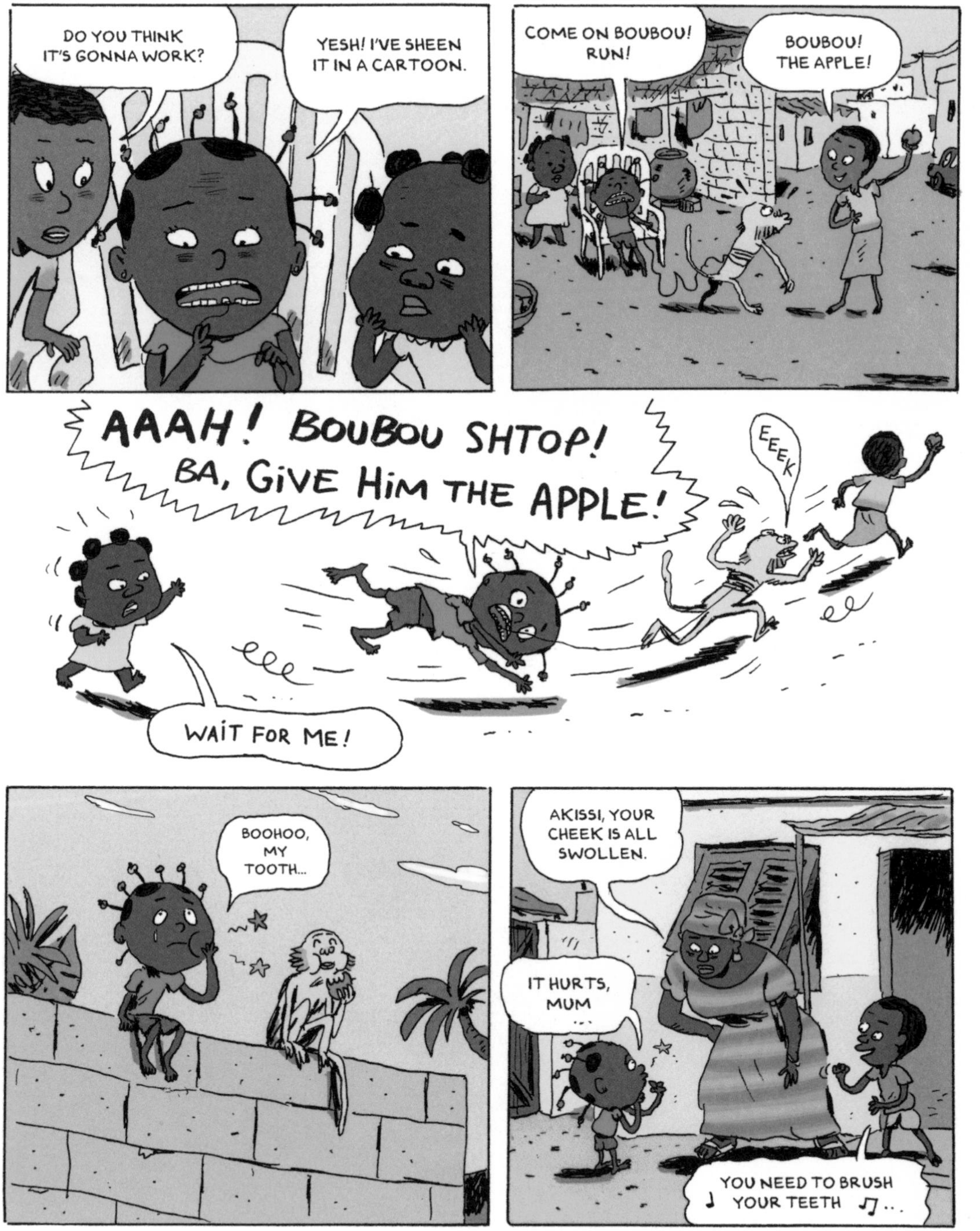
DO YOU THINK IT'S GONNA WORK?
YESH! I'VE SHEEN IT IN A CARTOON.
COME ON BOUBOU! RUN!
BOUBOU! THE APPLE!
AAAH! BOUBOU SHTOP! BA, GIVE HIM THE APPLE!
EEEK
WAIT FOR ME!
BOOHOO, MY TOOTH...
AKISSI, YOUR CHEEK IS ALL SWOLLEN.
IT HURTS, MUM ...
YOU NEED TO BRUSH YOUR TEETH ♪ ♫ ...

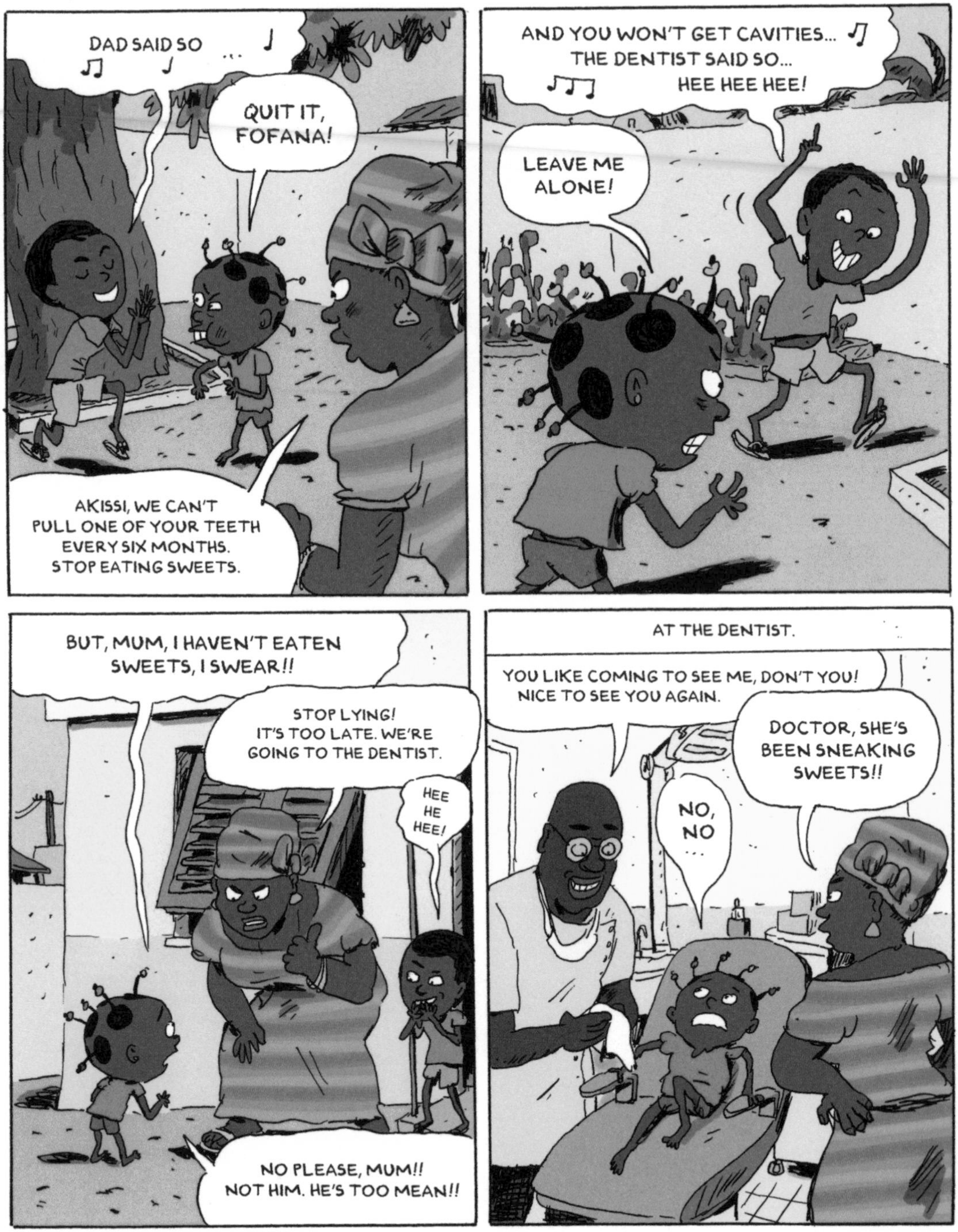
DAD SAID SO ...
QUIT IT, FOFANA!
AKISSI, WE CAN'T PULL ONE OF YOUR TEETH EVERY SIX MONTHS. STOP EATING SWEETS.
AND YOU WON'T GET CAVITIES... THE DENTIST SAID SO... HEE HEE HEE!
LEAVE ME ALONE!
BUT, MUM, I HAVEN'T EATEN SWEETS, I SWEAR!!
STOP LYING! IT'S TOO LATE. WE'RE GOING TO THE DENTIST.
HEE HE HEE!
NO PLEASE, MUM!! NOT HIM. HE'S TOO MEAN!!
AT THE DENTIST.
YOU LIKE COMING TO SEE ME, DON'T YOU! NICE TO SEE YOU AGAIN.
NO, NO ...
DOCTOR, SHE'S BEEN SNEAKING SWEETS!!

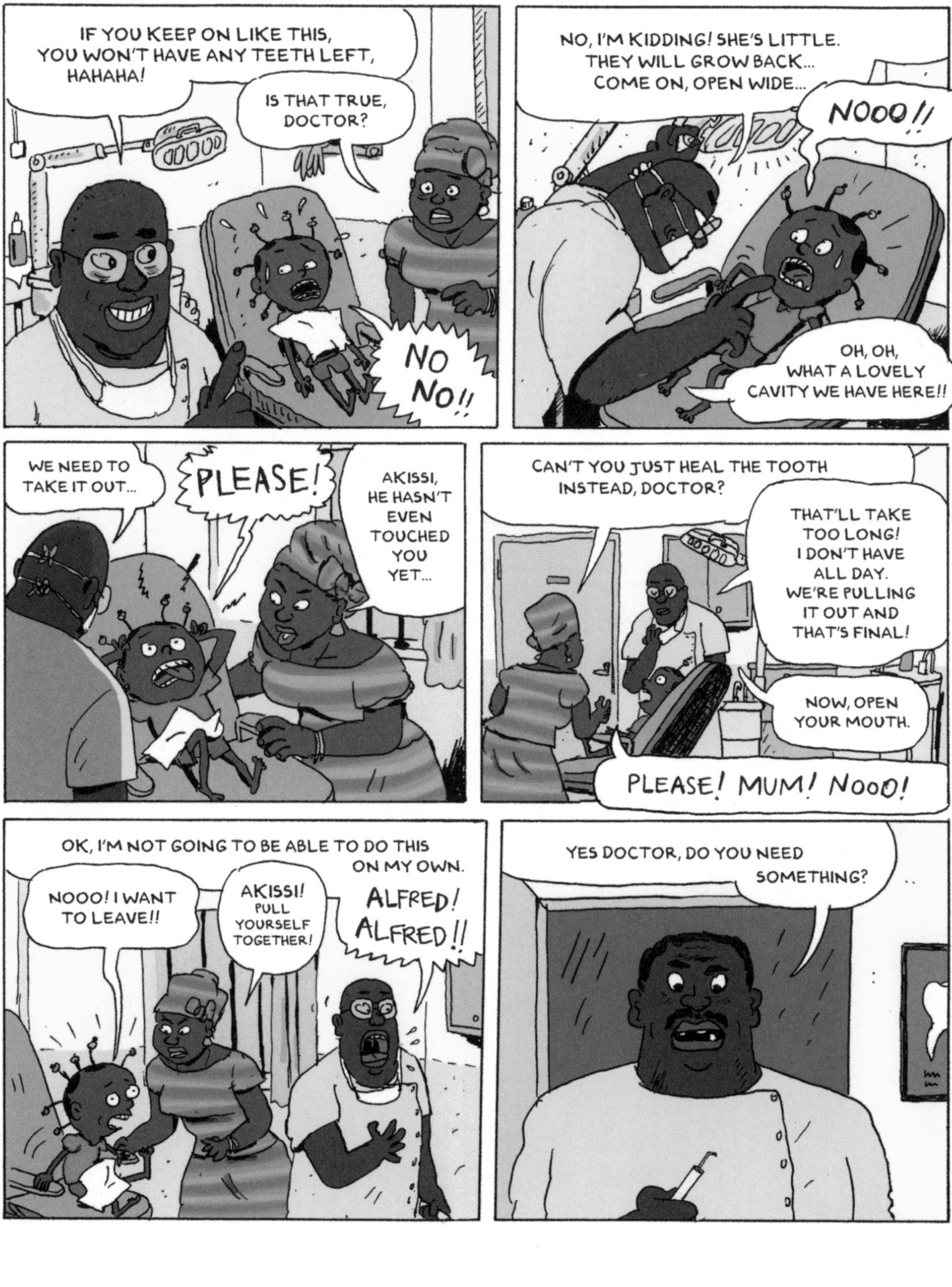
IF YOU KEEP ON LIKE THIS, YOU WON'T HAVE ANY TEETH LEFT, HAHAHA!
IS THAT TRUE, DOCTOR?
NO NO!!
NO, I'M KIDDING! SHE'S LITTLE. THEY WILL GROW BACK... COME ON, OPEN WIDE...
NOOO!!
OH, OH, WHAT A LOVELY CAVITY WE HAVE HERE!!
WE NEED TO TAKE IT OUT...
PLEASE!
AKISSI, HE HASN'T EVEN TOUCHED YOU YET...
CAN'T YOU JUST HEAL THE TOOTH INSTEAD, DOCTOR?
THAT'LL TAKE TOO LONG! I DON'T HAVE ALL DAY. WE'RE PULLING IT OUT AND THAT'S FINAL!
NOW, OPEN YOUR MOUTH.
PLEASE! MUM! NOOO!
OK, I'M NOT GOING TO BE ABLE TO DO THIS ON MY OWN.
NOOO! I WANT TO LEAVE!!
AKISSI! PULL YOURSELF TOGETHER!
ALFRED! ALFRED!!
YES DOCTOR, DO YOU NEED SOMETHING?

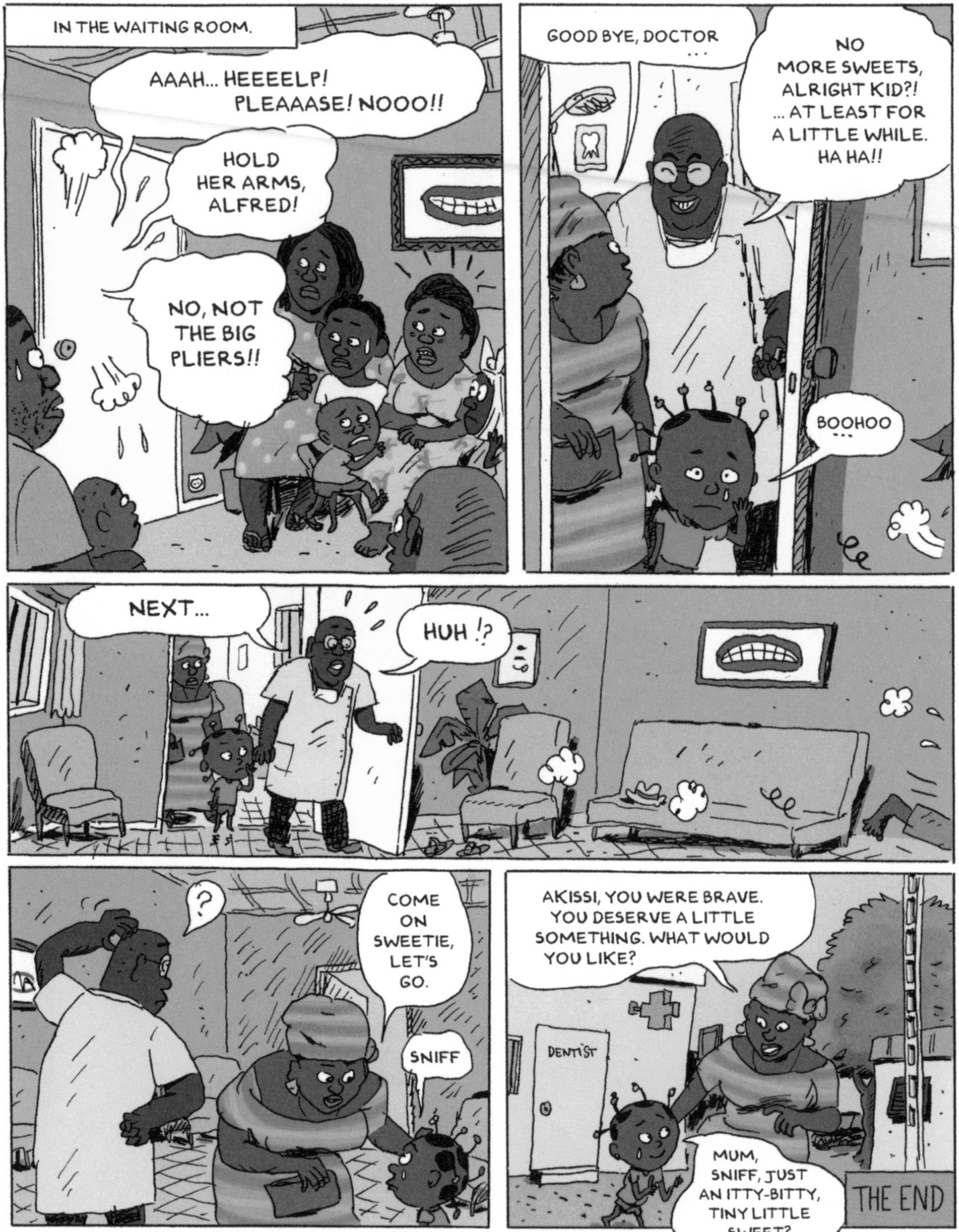
IN THE WAITING ROOM.
AAAH... HEEEELP! PLEAAASE! NOOO!!
HOLD HER ARMS, ALFRED!
NO, NOT THE BIG PLIERS!!
GOOD BYE, DOCTOR ...
NO MORE SWEETS, ALRIGHT KID?! ... AT LEAST FOR A LITTLE WHILE. HA HA!!
BOOHOO ...
NEXT...
HUH !?
?
COME ON SWEETIE, LET'S GO.
SNIFF
AKISSI, YOU WERE BRAVE. YOU DESERVE A LITTLE SOMETHING. WHAT WOULD YOU LIKE?
DENTIST
MUM, SNIFF, JUST AN ITTY-BITTY, TINY LITTLE SWEET?
THE END

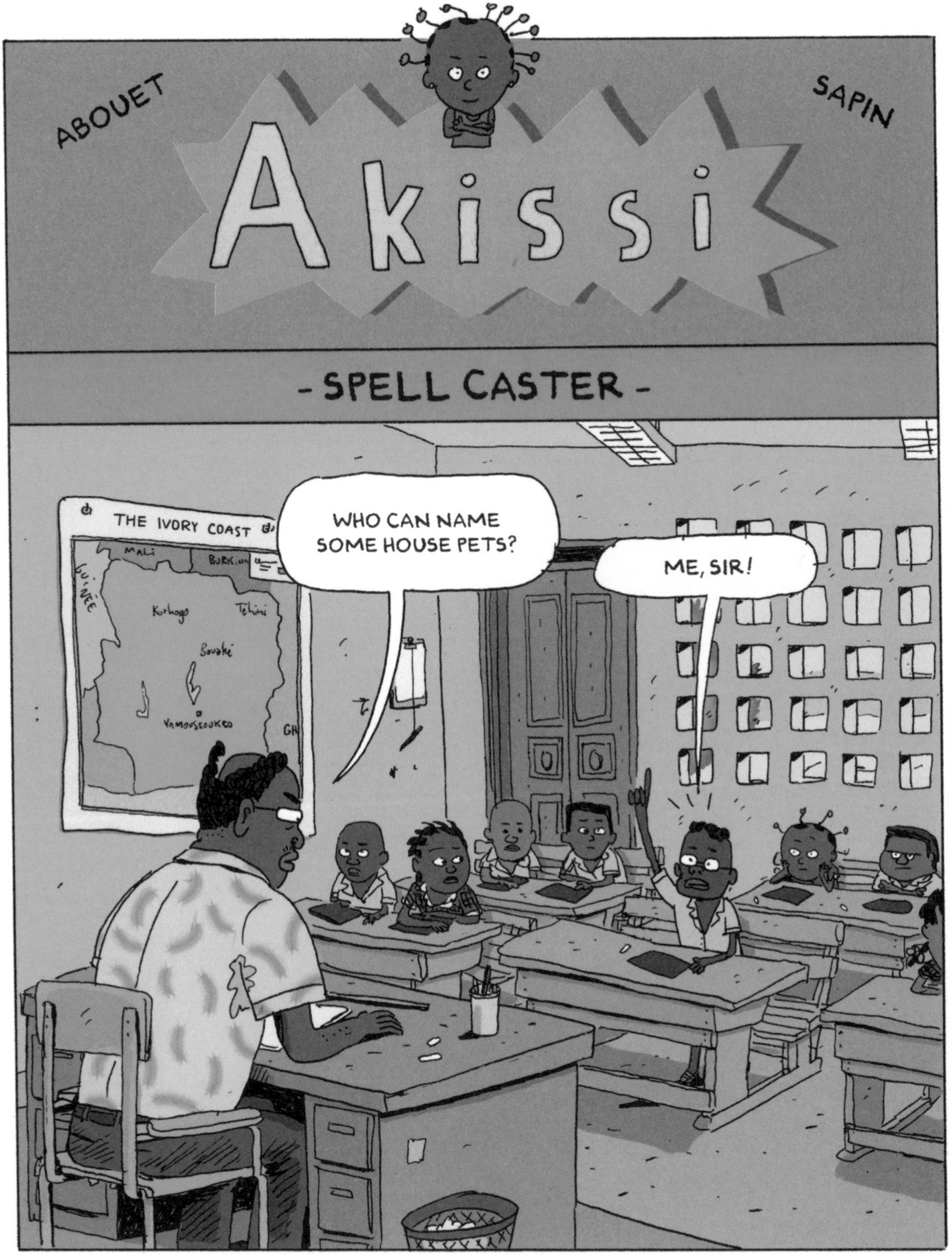
ABOUET
Akissi
SAPIN
- SPELL CASTER -
THE IVORY COAST
MALI
GUINÉE
Korhogo
Bouaké
YAMOUSSOUKRO
WHO CAN NAME SOME HOUSE PETS?
ME, SIR!

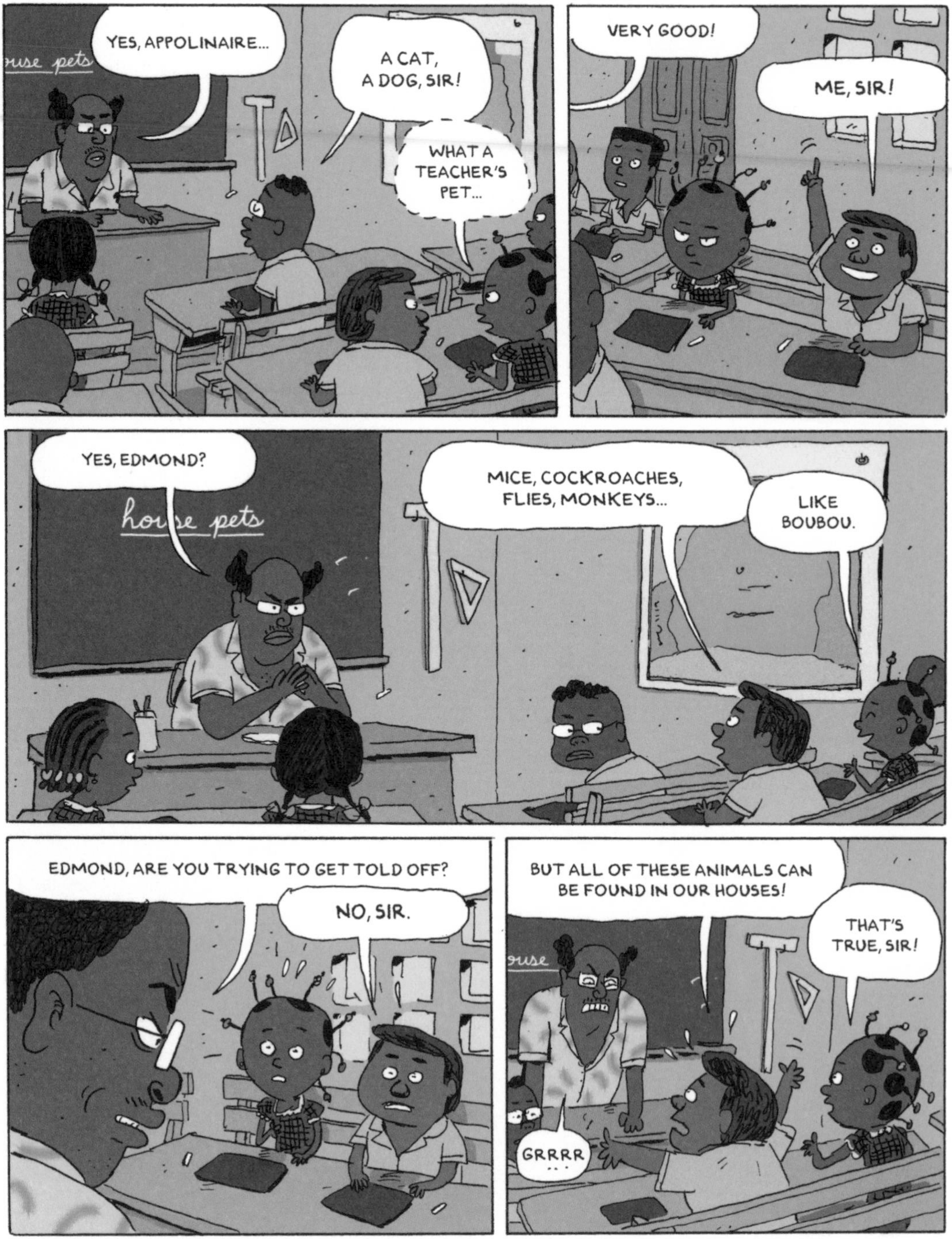
ouse pets
YES, APPOLINAIRE...
A CAT, A DOG, SIR!
WHAT A TEACHER'S PET...
VERY GOOD!
ME, SIR!
YES, EDMOND?
house pets
MICE, COCKROACHES, FLIES, MONKEYS...
LIKE BOUBOU.
EDMOND, ARE YOU TRYING TO GET TOLD OFF?
NO, SIR.
BUT ALL OF THESE ANIMALS CAN BE FOUND IN OUR HOUSES!
THAT'S TRUE, SIR!
ouse
GRRRR...

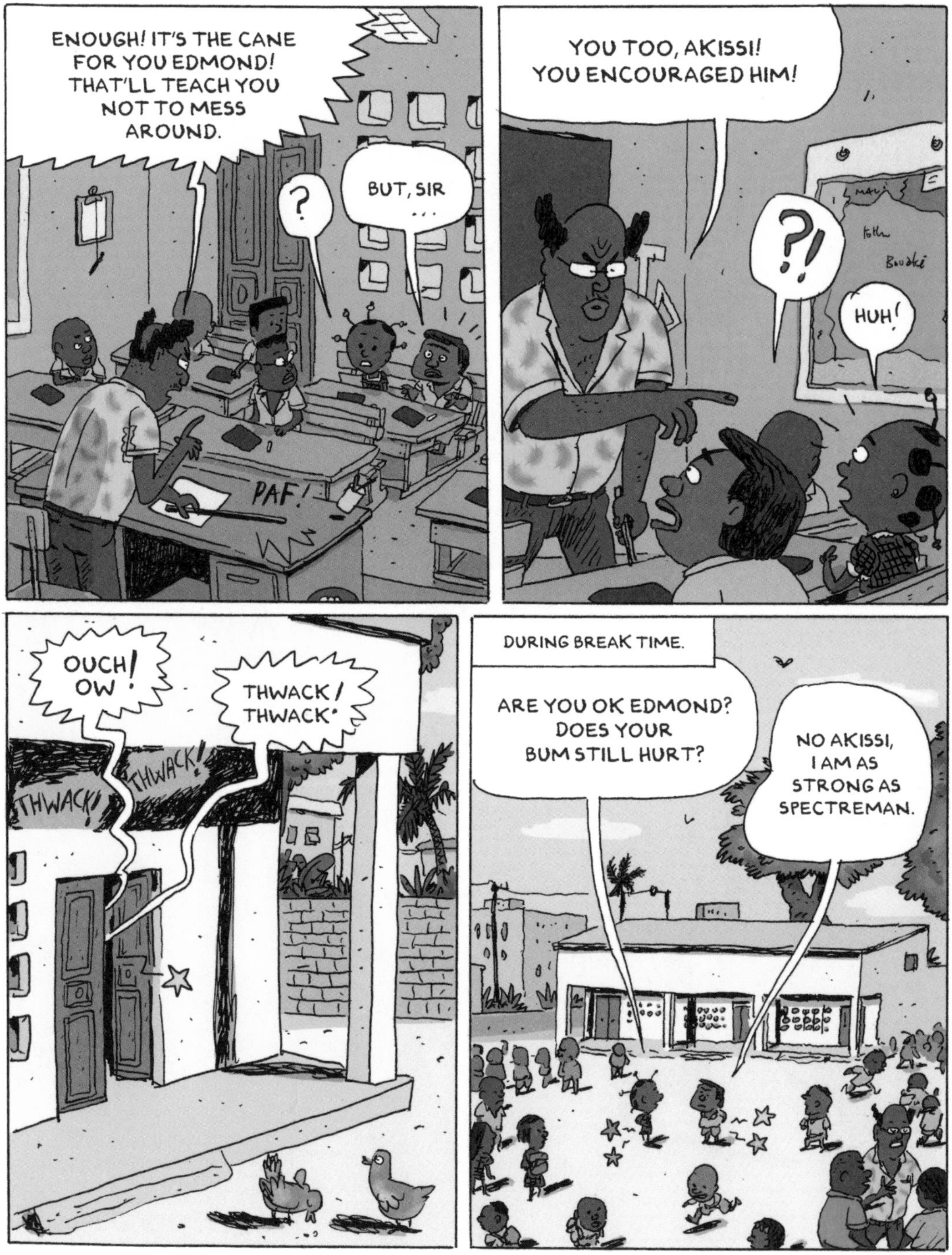

ENOUGH! IT'S THE CANE FOR YOU EDMOND! THAT'LL TEACH YOU NOT TO MESS AROUND.
?
BUT, SIR ...
PAF!
YOU TOO, AKISSI! YOU ENCOURAGED HIM!
?!
HUH!
OUCH! OW!
THWACK! THWACK!
THWACK!
THWACK!
DURING BREAK TIME.
ARE YOU OK EDMOND? DOES YOUR BUM STILL HURT?
NO AKISSI, I AM AS STRONG AS SPECTREMAN.

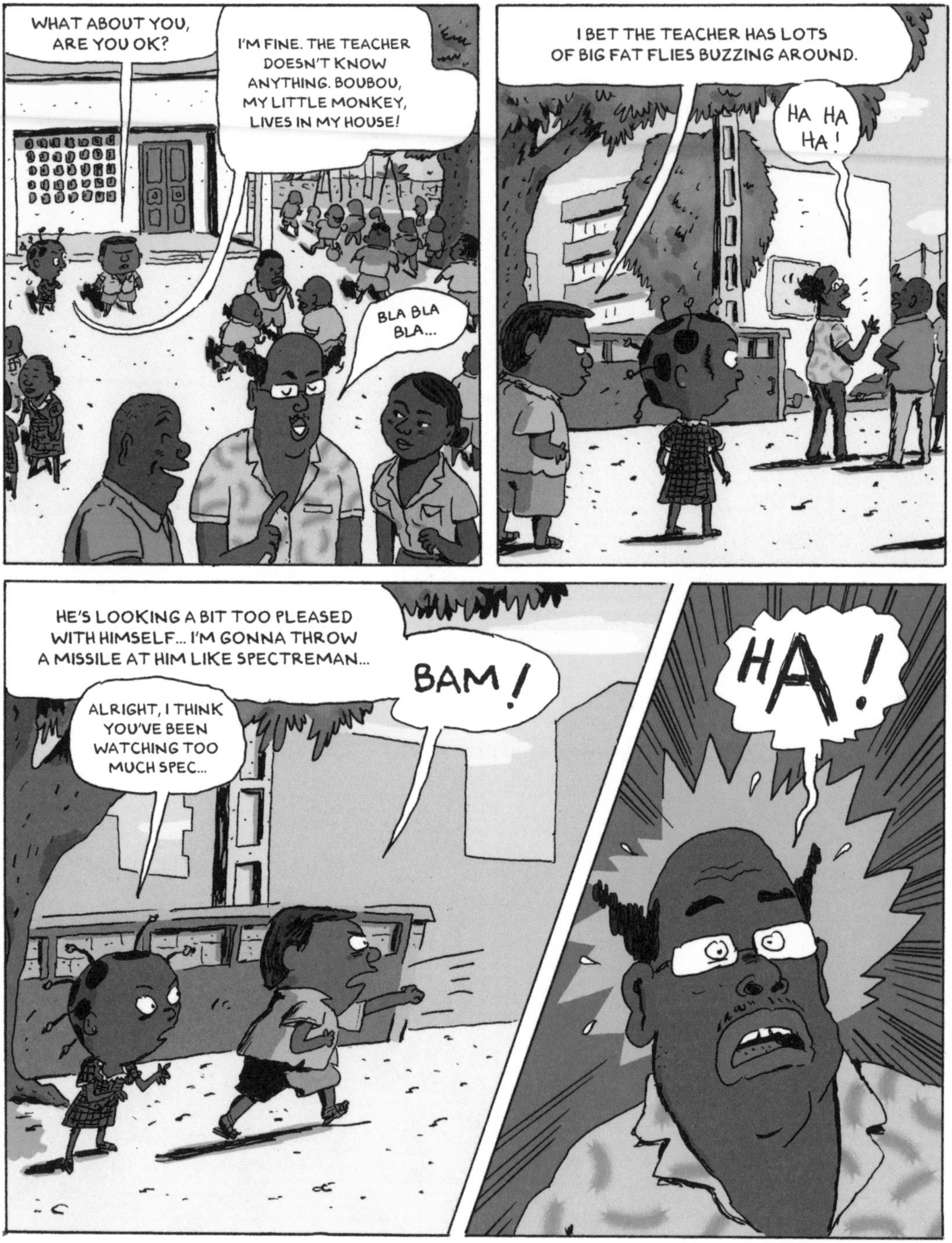
WHAT ABOUT YOU, ARE YOU OK?
I'M FINE. THE TEACHER DOESN'T KNOW ANYTHING. BOUBOU, MY LITTLE MONKEY, LIVES IN MY HOUSE!
BLA BLA BLA...
I BET THE TEACHER HAS LOTS OF BIG FAT FLIES BUZZING AROUND.
HA HA HA!
HE'S LOOKING A BIT TOO PLEASED WITH HIMSELF... I'M GONNA THROW A MISSILE AT HIM LIKE SPECTREMAN...
ALRIGHT, I THINK YOU'VE BEEN WATCHING TOO MUCH SPEC...
BAM!
HA!

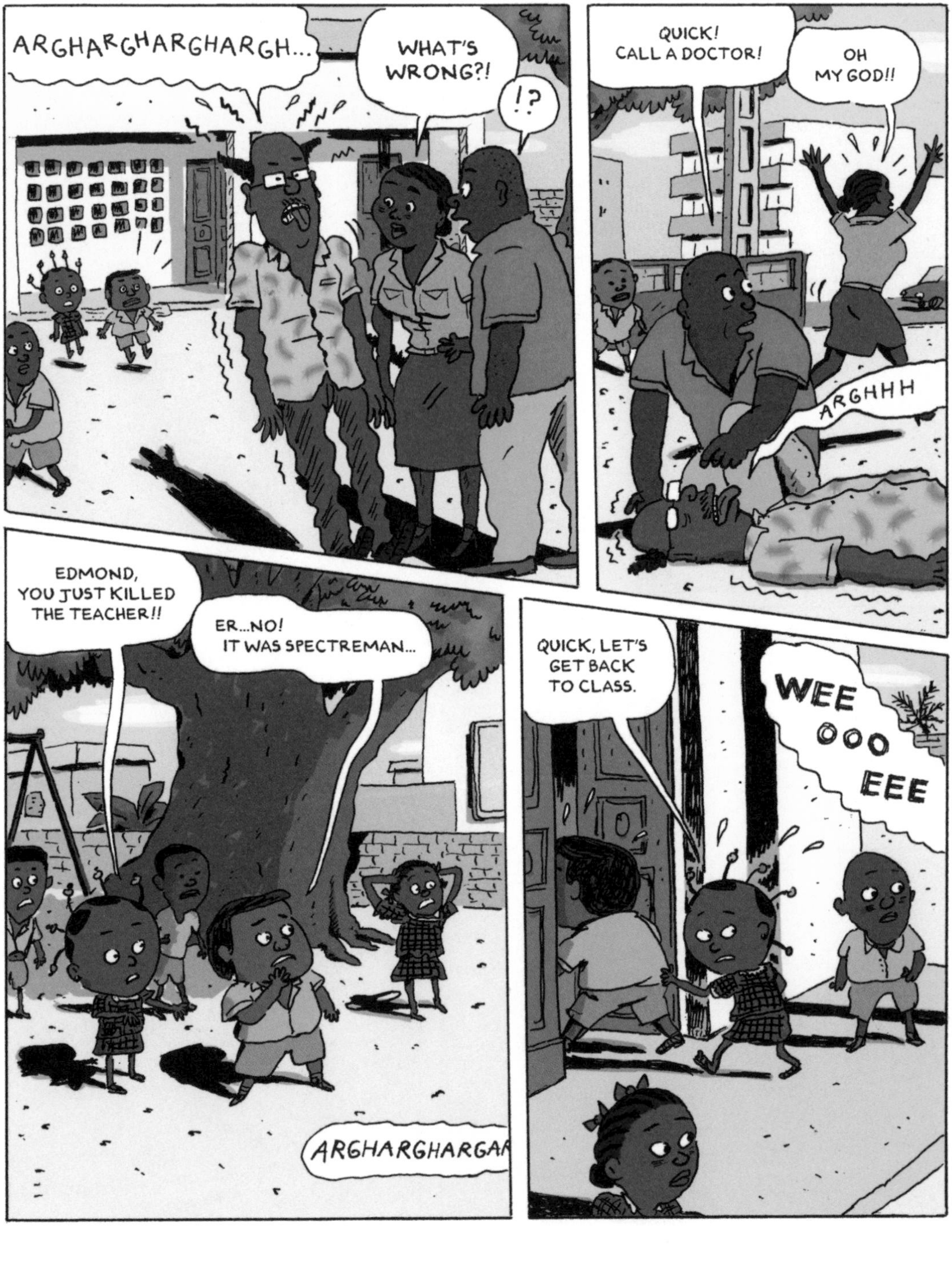
ARGHARGHARGHARGH...
WHAT'S WRONG?!
!?
QUICK! CALL A DOCTOR!
OH MY GOD!!
ARGHHH
EDMOND, YOU JUST KILLED THE TEACHER!!
ER...NO! IT WAS SPECTREMAN...
ARGHARGHARGAR
QUICK, LET'S GET BACK TO CLASS.
WEE OOO EEE

CHILDREN, YOUR TEACHER WILL BE OFF FOR THE REST OF THE WEEK...
HE HAD AN EPILEPTIC SEIZURE.
WOW, AKISSI! DID YOU HEAR?
MY MISSILE GAVE THE TEACHER A SEIZURE!
PFFF...WHAT A WIMP. IF THE REAL SPECTREMAN HAD LAUNCHED A MISSILE, THE TEACHER WOULD HAVE DISAPPEARED FOR EVER.
OH REALLY? HOW ABOUT I LAUNCH A SUPER MISSILE AT YOU, THEN LET'S SEE WHO'S THE WIMP!
?
NOOO, HELP!!
THE END

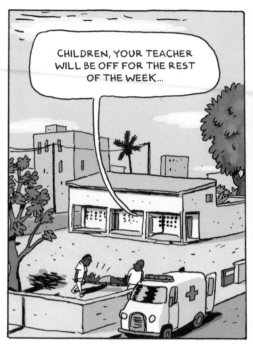

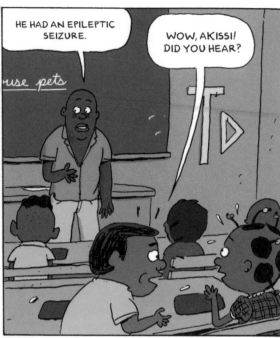

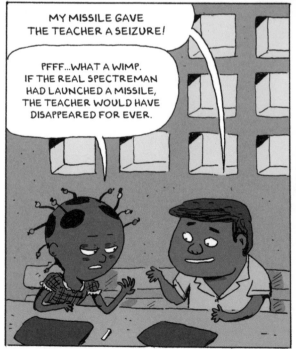

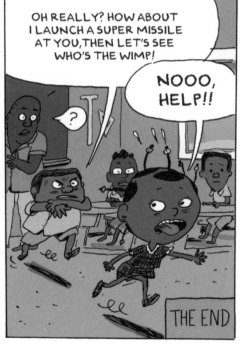

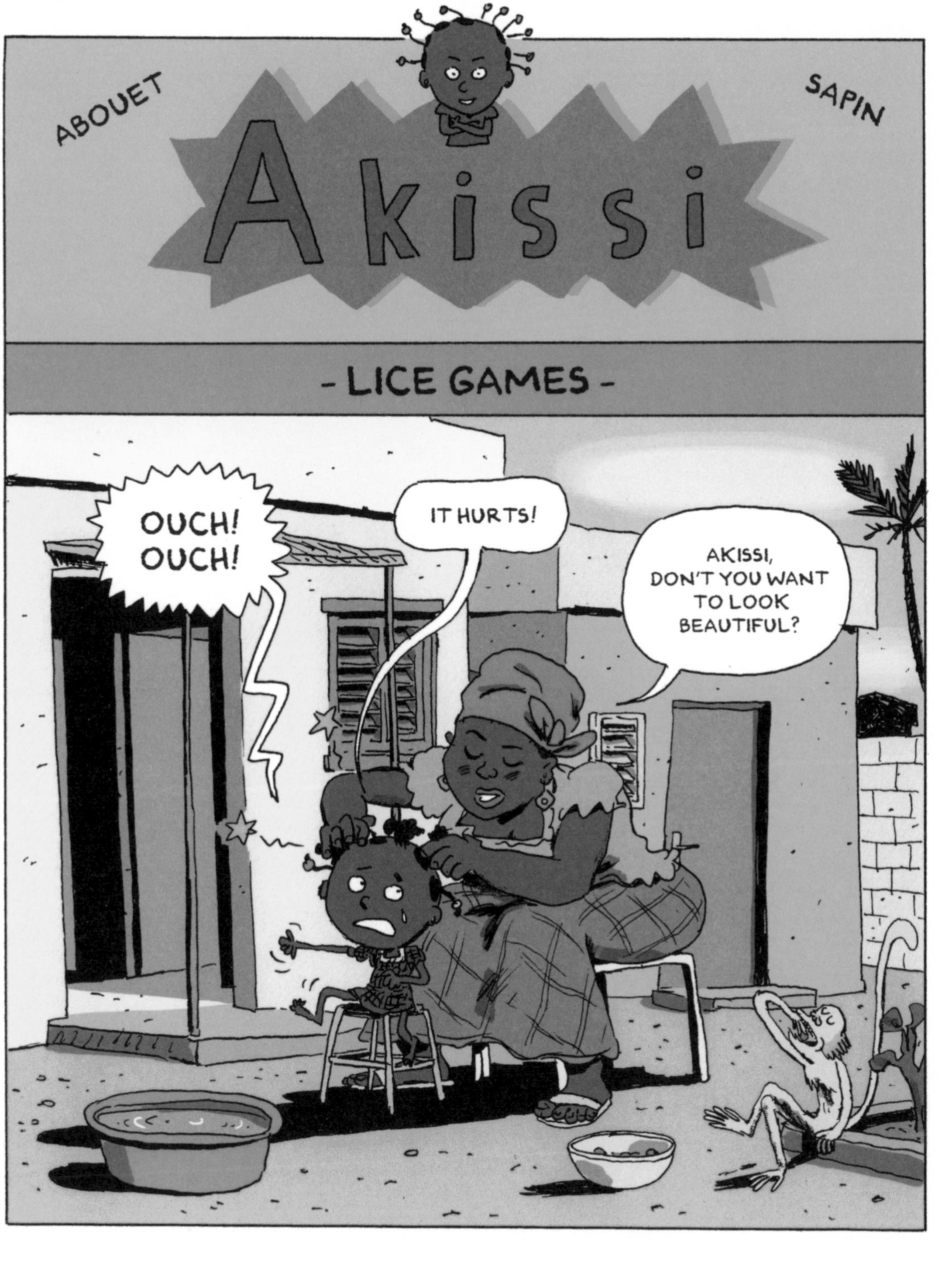
ABOUET
SAPIN
Akissi
- LICE GAMES -
OUCH! OUCH!
IT HURTS!
AKISSI, DON'T YOU WANT TO LOOK BEAUTIFUL?

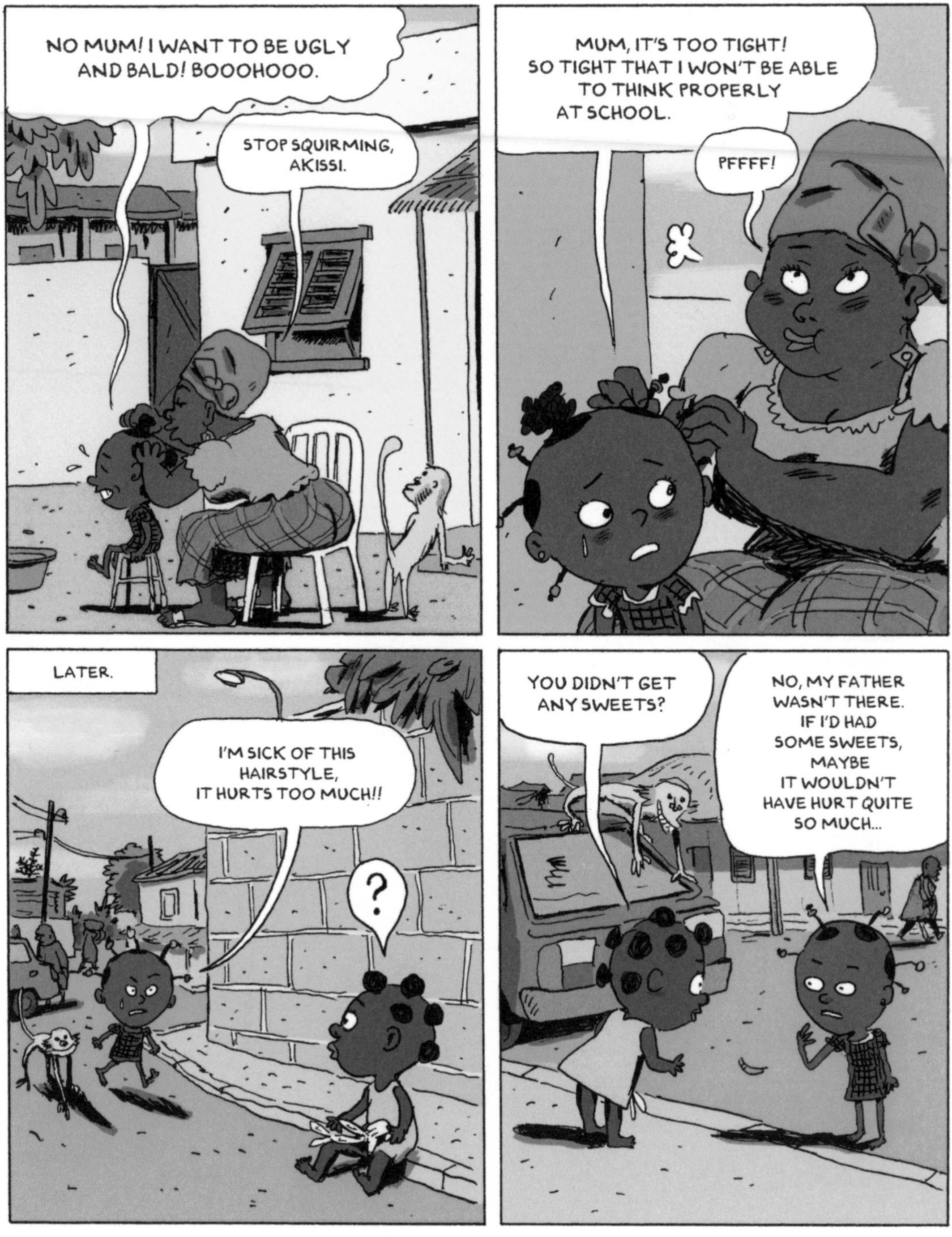
NO MUM! I WANT TO BE UGLY AND BALD! BOOOHOOO.
STOP SQUIRMING, AKISSI.
MUM, IT'S TOO TIGHT! SO TIGHT THAT I WON'T BE ABLE TO THINK PROPERLY AT SCHOOL.
PFFFF!
LATER.
I'M SICK OF THIS HAIRSTYLE, IT HURTS TOO MUCH!!
?
YOU DIDN'T GET ANY SWEETS?
NO, MY FATHER WASN'T THERE. IF I'D HAD SOME SWEETS, MAYBE IT WOULDN'T HAVE HURT QUITE SO MUCH...

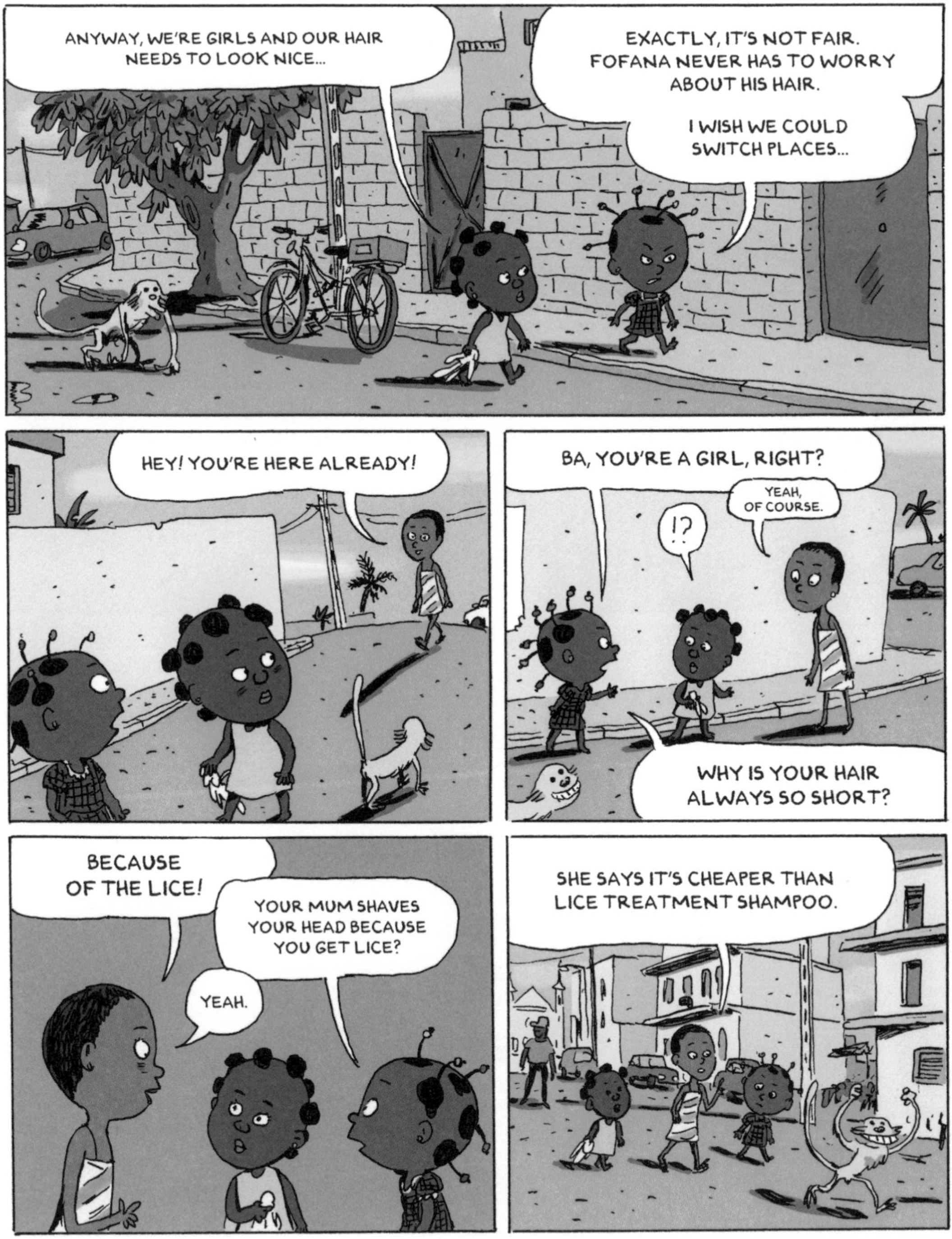
ANYWAY, WE'RE GIRLS AND OUR HAIR NEEDS TO LOOK NICE...
EXACTLY, IT'S NOT FAIR. FOFANA NEVER HAS TO WORRY ABOUT HIS HAIR.
I WISH WE COULD SWITCH PLACES...
HEY! YOU'RE HERE ALREADY!
BA, YOU'RE A GIRL, RIGHT?
!?
YEAH, OF COURSE.
WHY IS YOUR HAIR ALWAYS SO SHORT?
BECAUSE OF THE LICE!
YOUR MUM SHAVES YOUR HEAD BECAUSE YOU GET LICE?
YEAH.
SHE SAYS IT'S CHEAPER THAN LICE TREATMENT SHAMPOO.

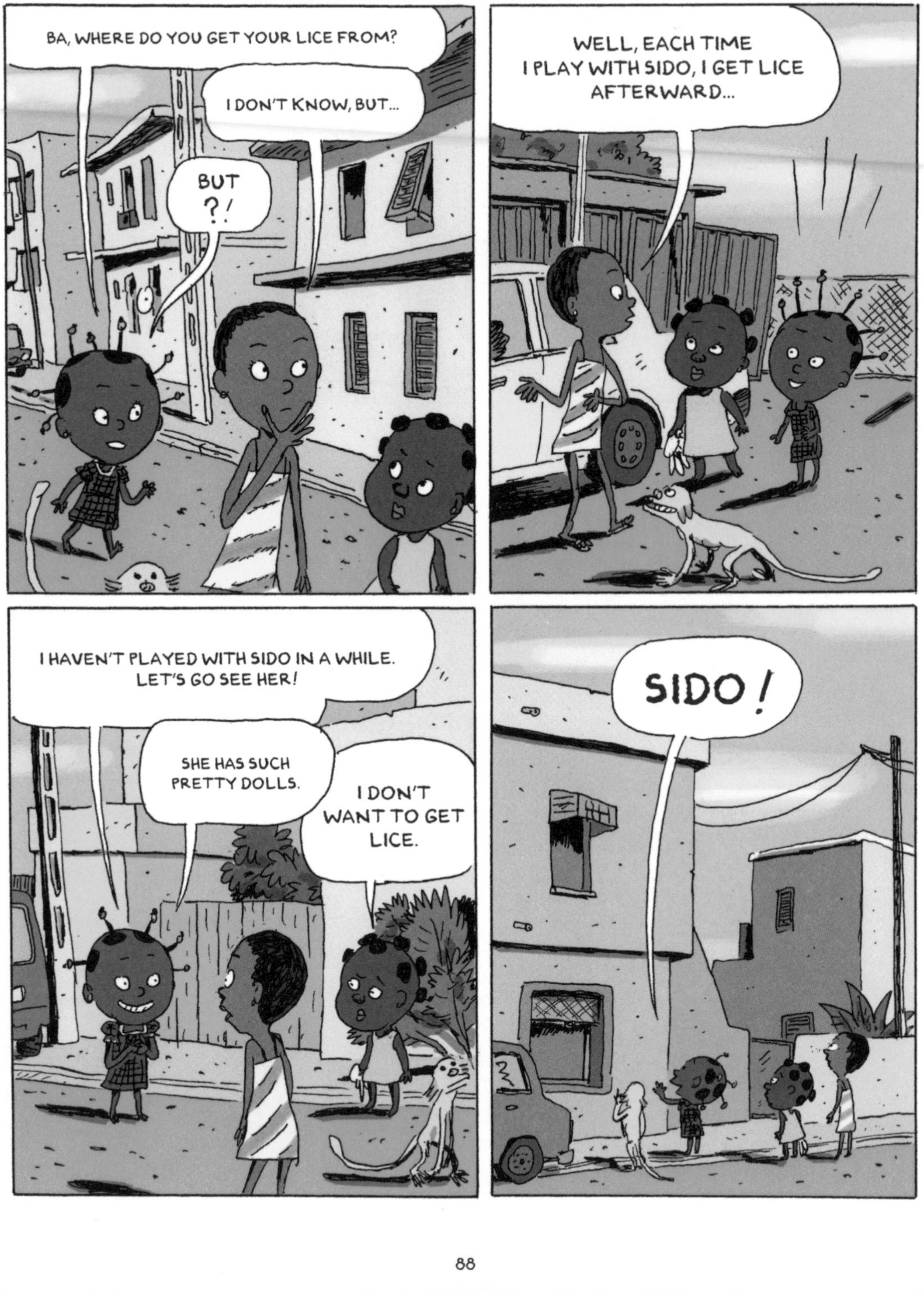

BA, WHERE DO YOU GET YOUR LICE FROM?
I DON'T KNOW, BUT...
BUT ?!
WELL, EACH TIME I PLAY WITH SIDO, I GET LICE AFTERWARD...
I HAVEN'T PLAYED WITH SIDO IN A WHILE. LET'S GO SEE HER!
SHE HAS SUCH PRETTY DOLLS.
I DON'T WANT TO GET LICE.
SIDO!

AKISSI?
WE'VE COME TO PLAY WITH YOU, SIDO!
?
SO NICE TO SEE YOU!!
WHAT DO YOU WANT TO PLAY?
LET'S PLAY HAIRDRESSER!
PLEASE HAVE A SEAT, MISS.
THANK YOU.
HOW DO YOU WANT YOUR HAIR?
ERRR...
EWW!
rub rub
AKISSI, WHAT ARE YOU DOING?
ME? NOTHING! NOTHING AT ALL!
?
RIGHT. IT'S LATE. I SHOULD GO HOME OR MY DAD WILL TELL ME OFF. SEE YA!

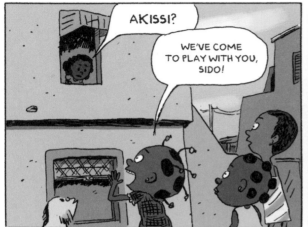

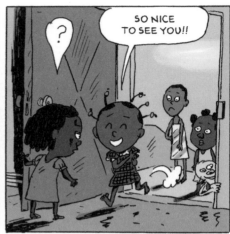

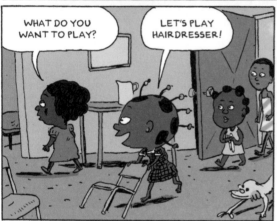

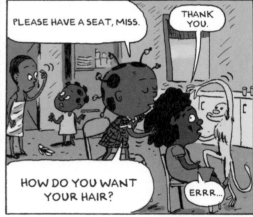

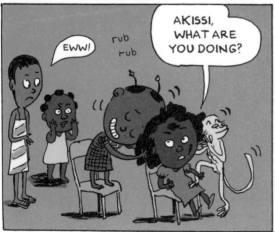

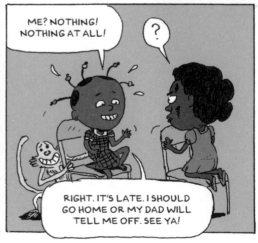

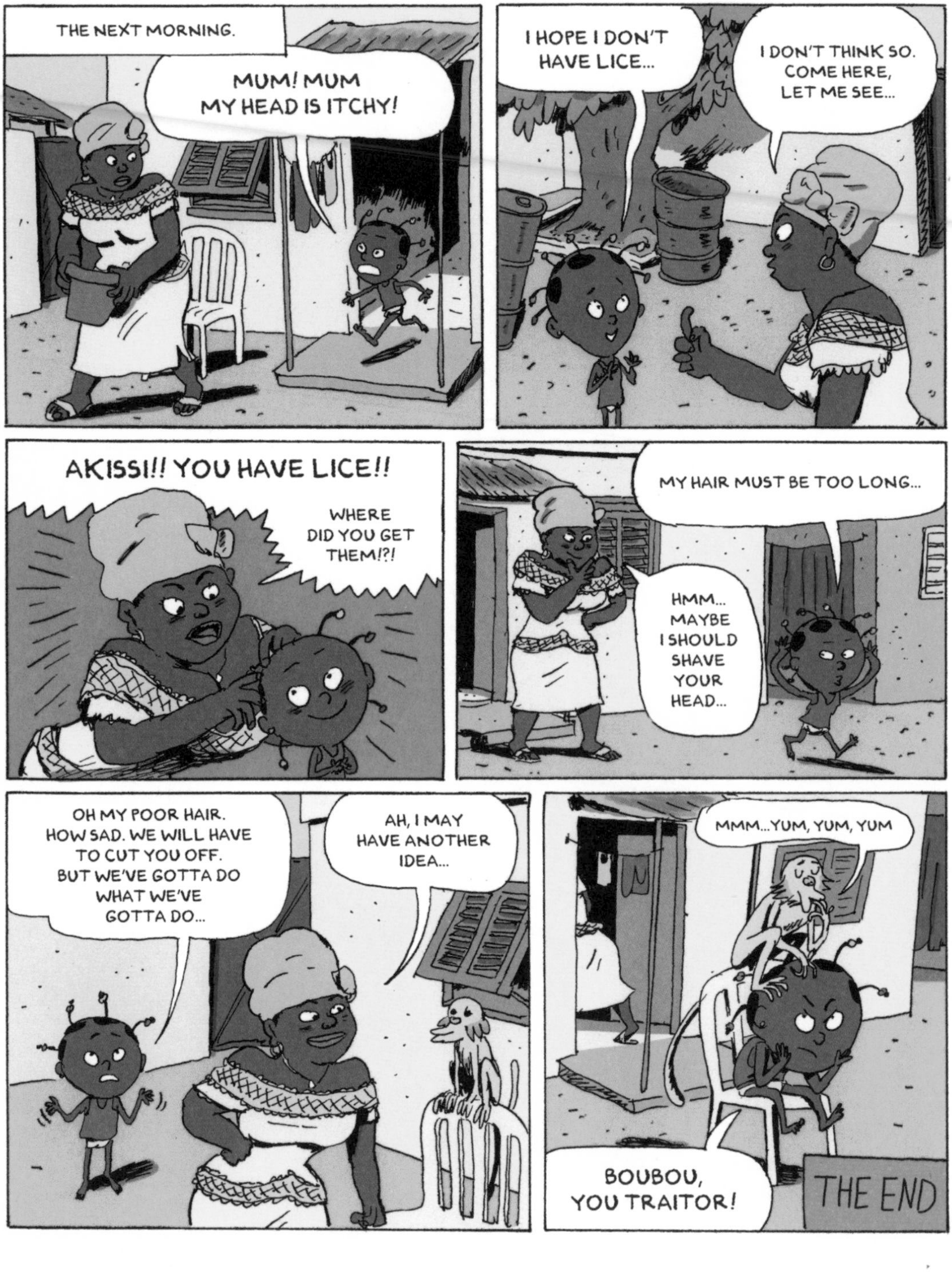
THE NEXT MORNING.
MUM! MUM
MY HEAD IS ITCHY!
I HOPE I DON'T HAVE LICE...
I DON'T THINK SO. COME HERE, LET ME SEE...
AKISSI!! YOU HAVE LICE!!
WHERE DID YOU GET THEM!?!
MY HAIR MUST BE TOO LONG...
HMM... MAYBE I SHOULD SHAVE YOUR HEAD...
OH MY POOR HAIR. HOW SAD. WE WILL HAVE TO CUT YOU OFF. BUT WE'VE GOTTA DO WHAT WE'VE GOTTA DO...
AH, I MAY HAVE ANOTHER IDEA...
MMM...YUM, YUM, YUM
BOUBOU, YOU TRAITOR!
THE END

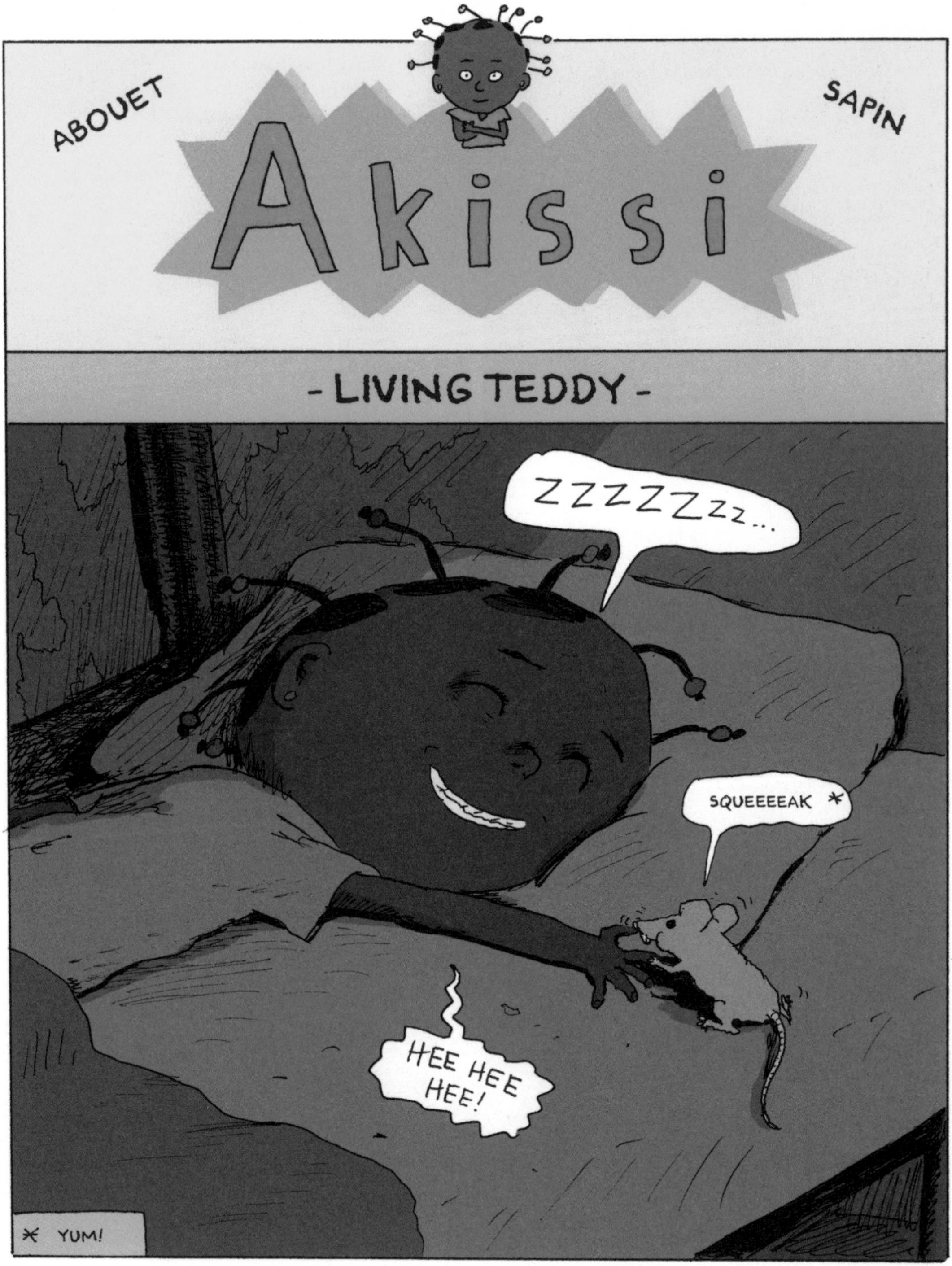
ABOUET
SAPIN
Akissi
- LIVING TEDDY -
ZZZZZZzz...
SQUEEEEAK *
HEE HEE HEE!
* YUM!

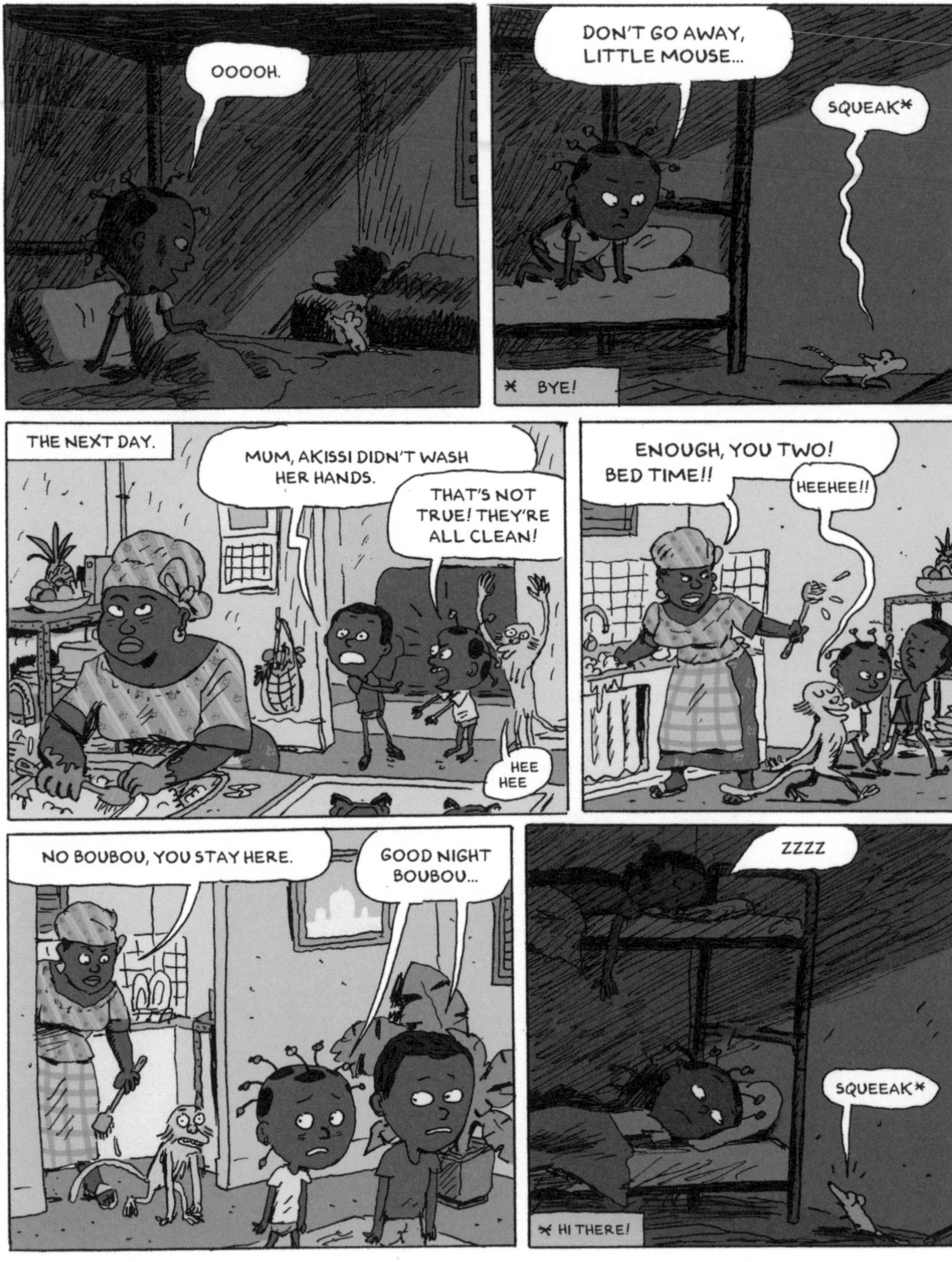
OOOOH.
DON'T GO AWAY, LITTLE MOUSE...
SQUEAK*
* BYE!
THE NEXT DAY.
MUM, AKISSI DIDN'T WASH HER HANDS.
THAT'S NOT TRUE! THEY'RE ALL CLEAN!
HEE HEE
ENOUGH, YOU TWO! BED TIME!!
HEEHEE!!
NO BOUBOU, YOU STAY HERE.
GOOD NIGHT BOUBOU...
ZZZZ
SQUEEAK*
* HI THERE!

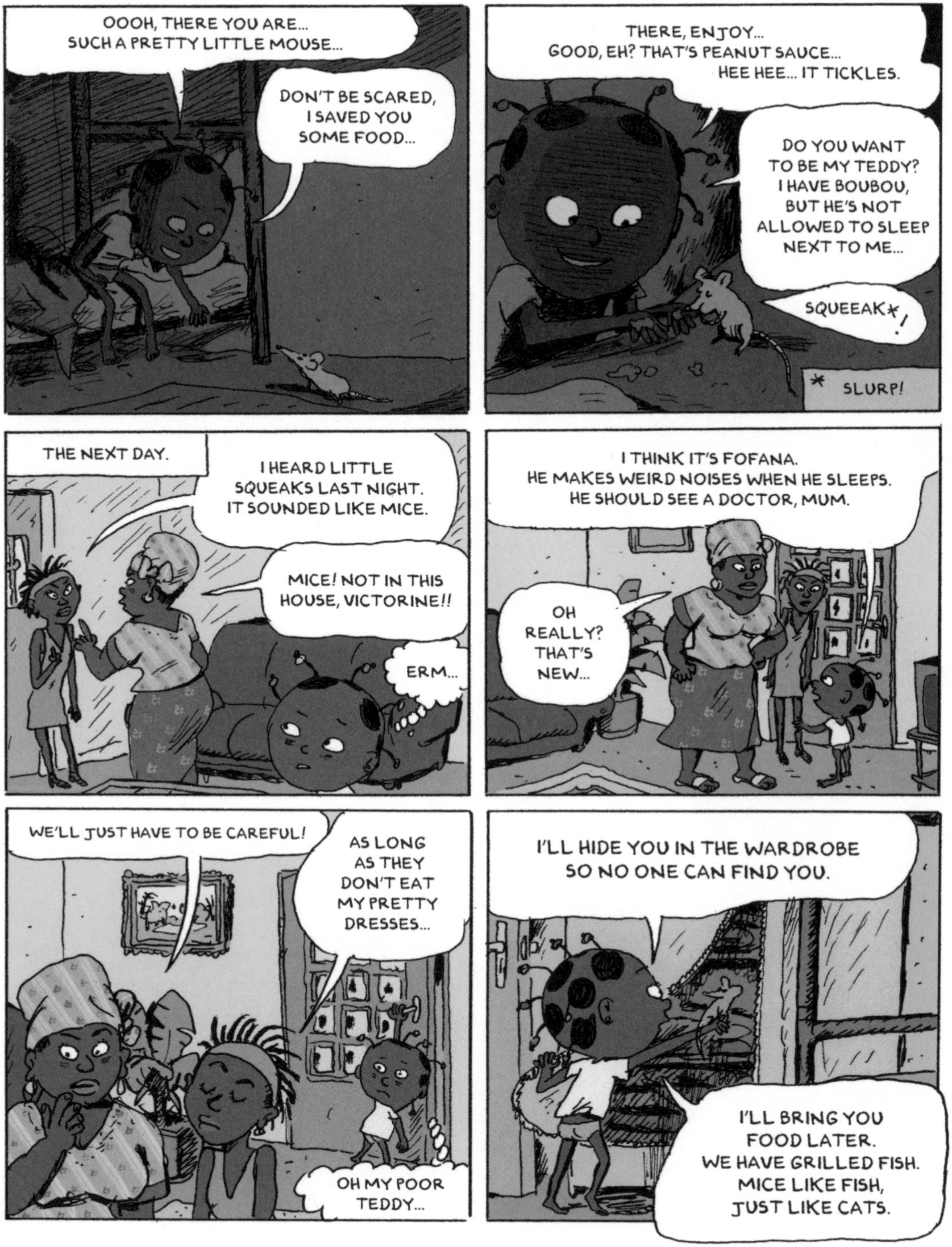
OOOH, THERE YOU ARE...
SUCH A PRETTY LITTLE MOUSE...
DON'T BE SCARED, I SAVED YOU SOME FOOD...
THERE, ENJOY...
GOOD, EH? THAT'S PEANUT SAUCE...
HEE HEE... IT TICKLES.
DO YOU WANT TO BE MY TEDDY? I HAVE BOUBOU, BUT HE'S NOT ALLOWED TO SLEEP NEXT TO ME...
SQUEEAK*!
* SLURP!
THE NEXT DAY.
I HEARD LITTLE SQUEAKS LAST NIGHT. IT SOUNDED LIKE MICE.
MICE! NOT IN THIS HOUSE, VICTORINE!!
ERM...
I THINK IT'S FOFANA.
HE MAKES WEIRD NOISES WHEN HE SLEEPS.
HE SHOULD SEE A DOCTOR, MUM.
OH REALLY? THAT'S NEW...
WE'LL JUST HAVE TO BE CAREFUL!
AS LONG AS THEY DON'T EAT MY PRETTY DRESSES...
OH MY POOR TEDDY...
I'LL HIDE YOU IN THE WARDROBE
SO NO ONE CAN FIND YOU.
I'LL BRING YOU FOOD LATER. WE HAVE GRILLED FISH. MICE LIKE FISH, JUST LIKE CATS.

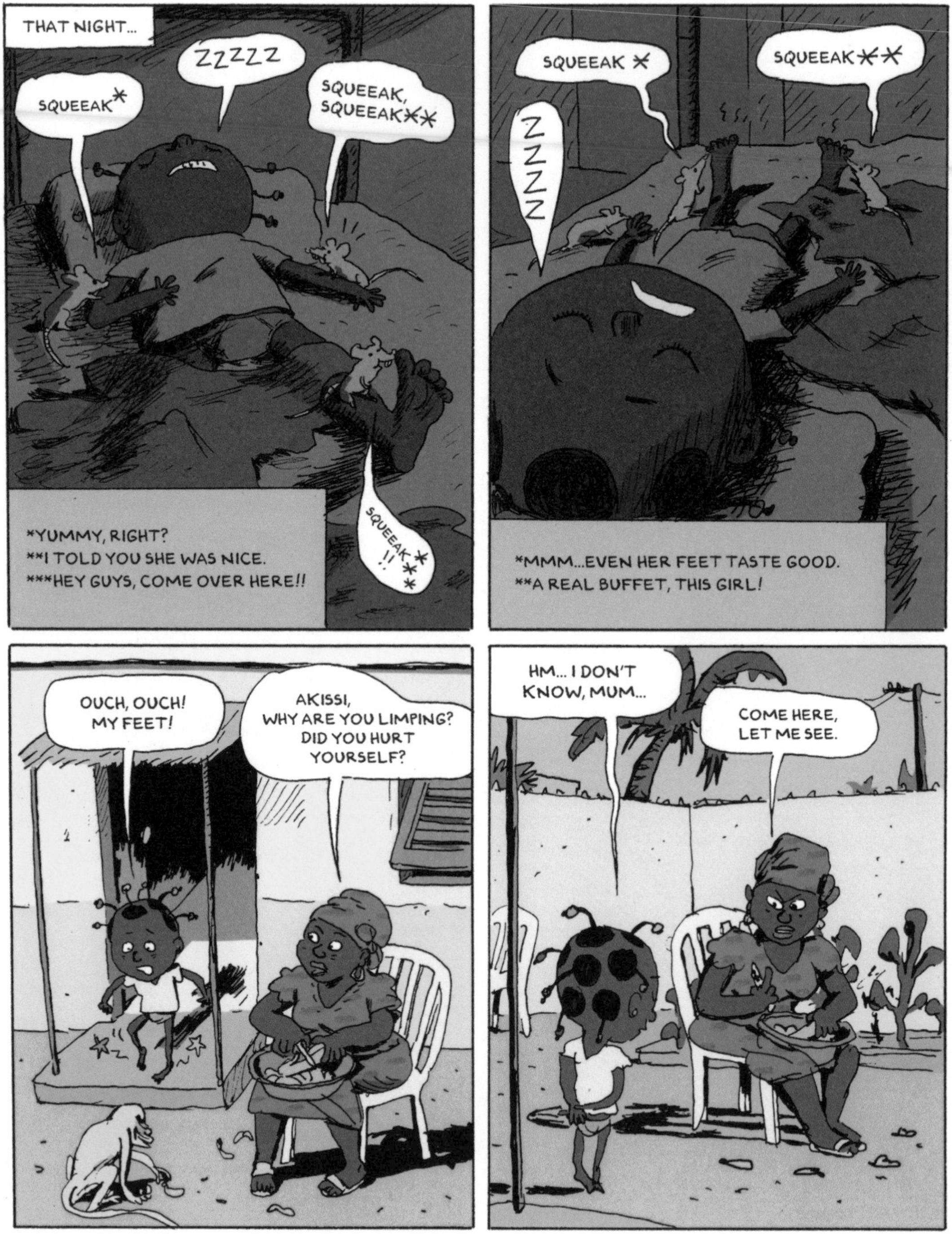
THAT NIGHT...
ZZZZZ
SQUEEAK*
SQUEEAK, SQUEEAK**
SQUEEAK***!!
*YUMMY, RIGHT?
**I TOLD YOU SHE WAS NICE.
***HEY GUYS, COME OVER HERE!!
ZZZZ
SQUEEAK *
SQUEEAK **
*MMM...EVEN HER FEET TASTE GOOD.
**A REAL BUFFET, THIS GIRL!
OUCH, OUCH! MY FEET!
AKISSI, WHY ARE YOU LIMPING? DID YOU HURT YOURSELF?
HM... I DON'T KNOW, MUM...
COME HERE, LET ME SEE.

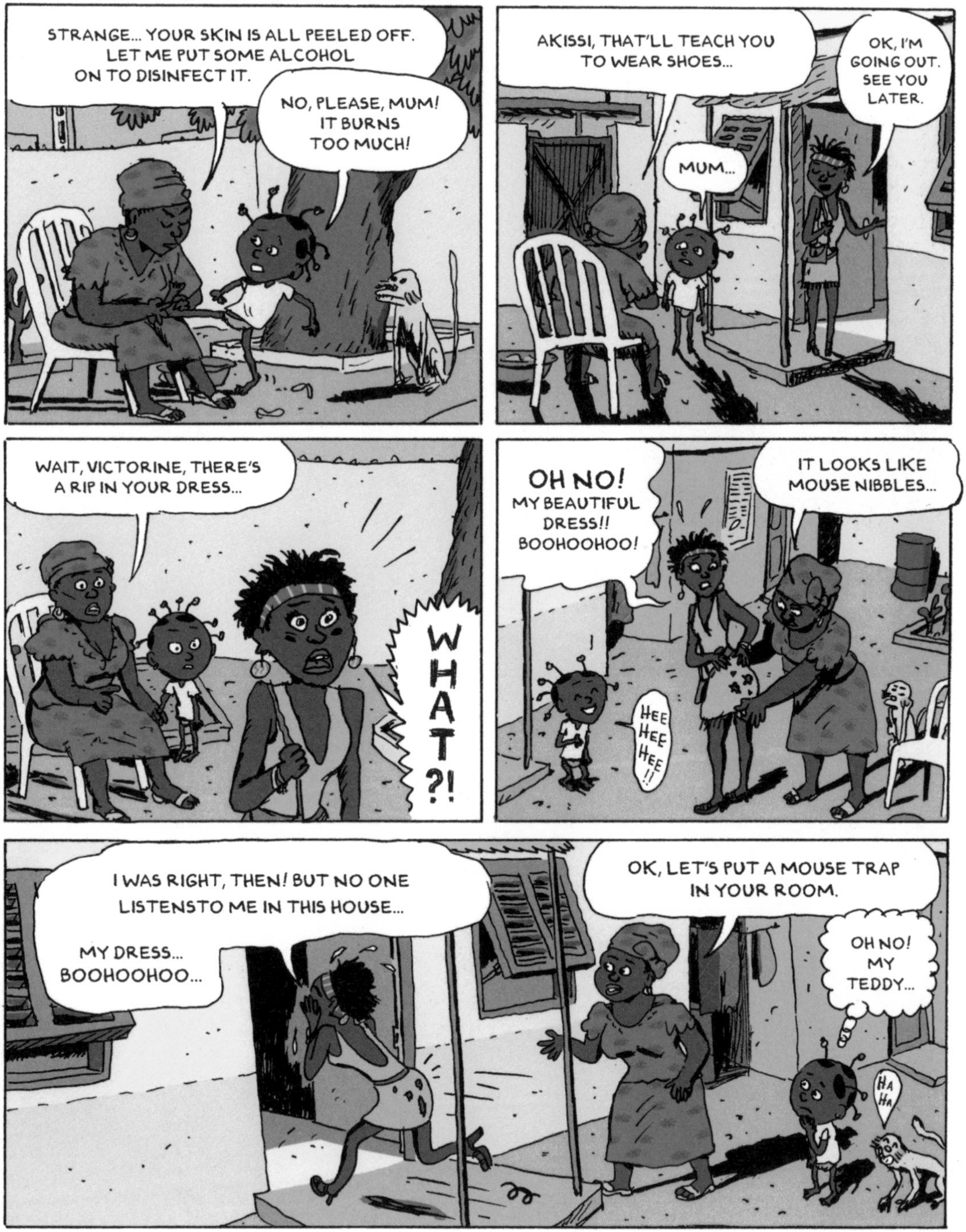
STRANGE... YOUR SKIN IS ALL PEELED OFF. LET ME PUT SOME ALCOHOL ON TO DISINFECT IT.
NO, PLEASE, MUM! IT BURNS TOO MUCH!
AKISSI, THAT'LL TEACH YOU TO WEAR SHOES...
OK, I'M GOING OUT. SEE YOU LATER.
MUM...
WAIT, VICTORINE, THERE'S A RIP IN YOUR DRESS...
WHAT?!
OH NO! MY BEAUTIFUL DRESS!! BOOHOOHOO!
IT LOOKS LIKE MOUSE NIBBLES...
HEE HEE HEE !!
I WAS RIGHT, THEN! BUT NO ONE LISTENSTO ME IN THIS HOUSE...
MY DRESS... BOOHOOHOO...
OK, LET'S PUT A MOUSE TRAP IN YOUR ROOM.
OH NO! MY TEDDY...
HA HA

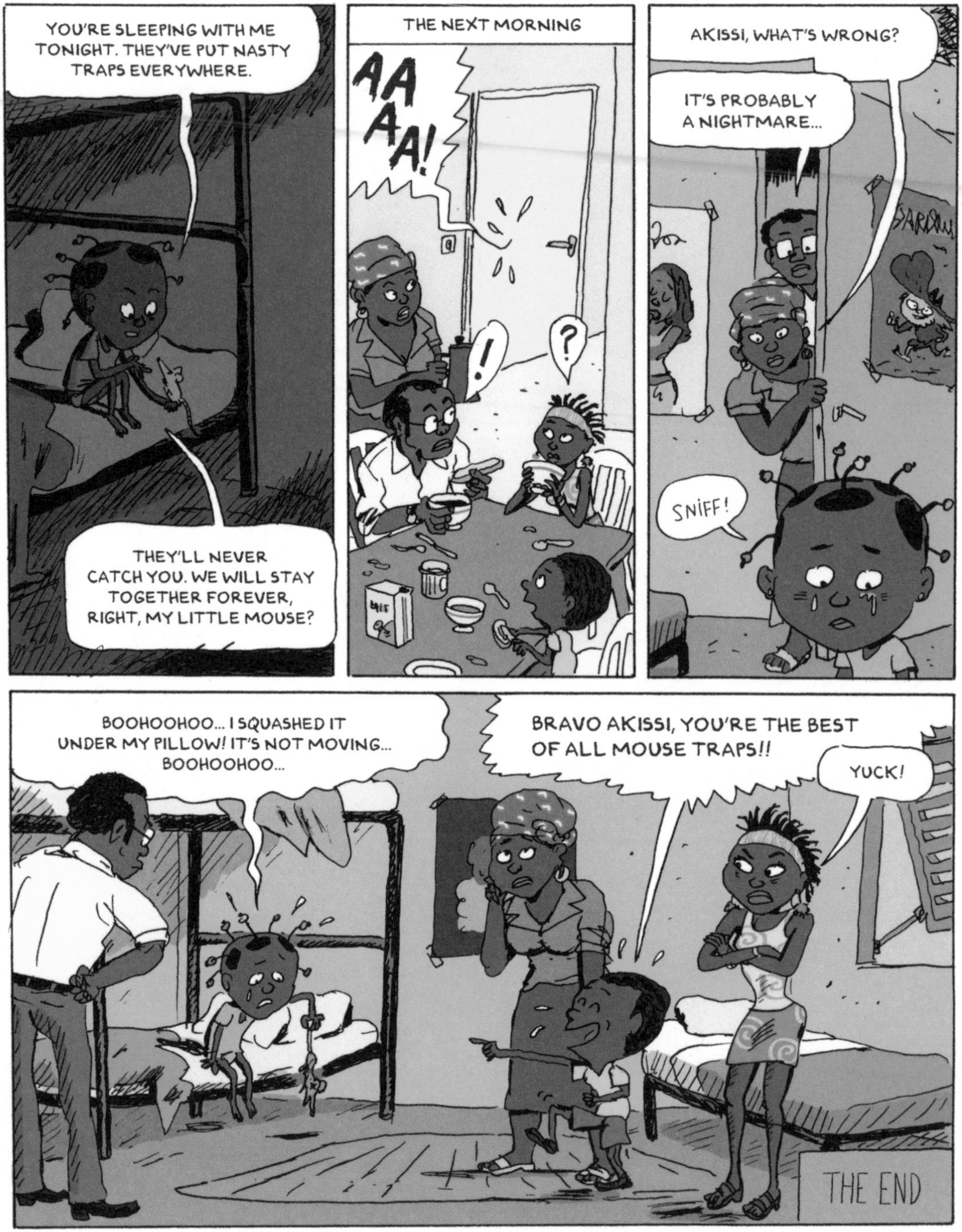

YOU'RE SLEEPING WITH ME TONIGHT. THEY'VE PUT NASTY TRAPS EVERYWHERE.
THEY'LL NEVER CATCH YOU. WE WILL STAY TOGETHER FOREVER, RIGHT, MY LITTLE MOUSE?
THE NEXT MORNING
AAAAA!
!
?
AKISSI, WHAT'S WRONG?
IT'S PROBABLY A NIGHTMARE...
SNIFF!
BOOHOOHOO... I SQUASHED IT UNDER MY PILLOW! IT'S NOT MOVING... BOOHOOHOO...
BRAVO AKISSI, YOU'RE THE BEST OF ALL MOUSE TRAPS!!
YUCK!
THE END

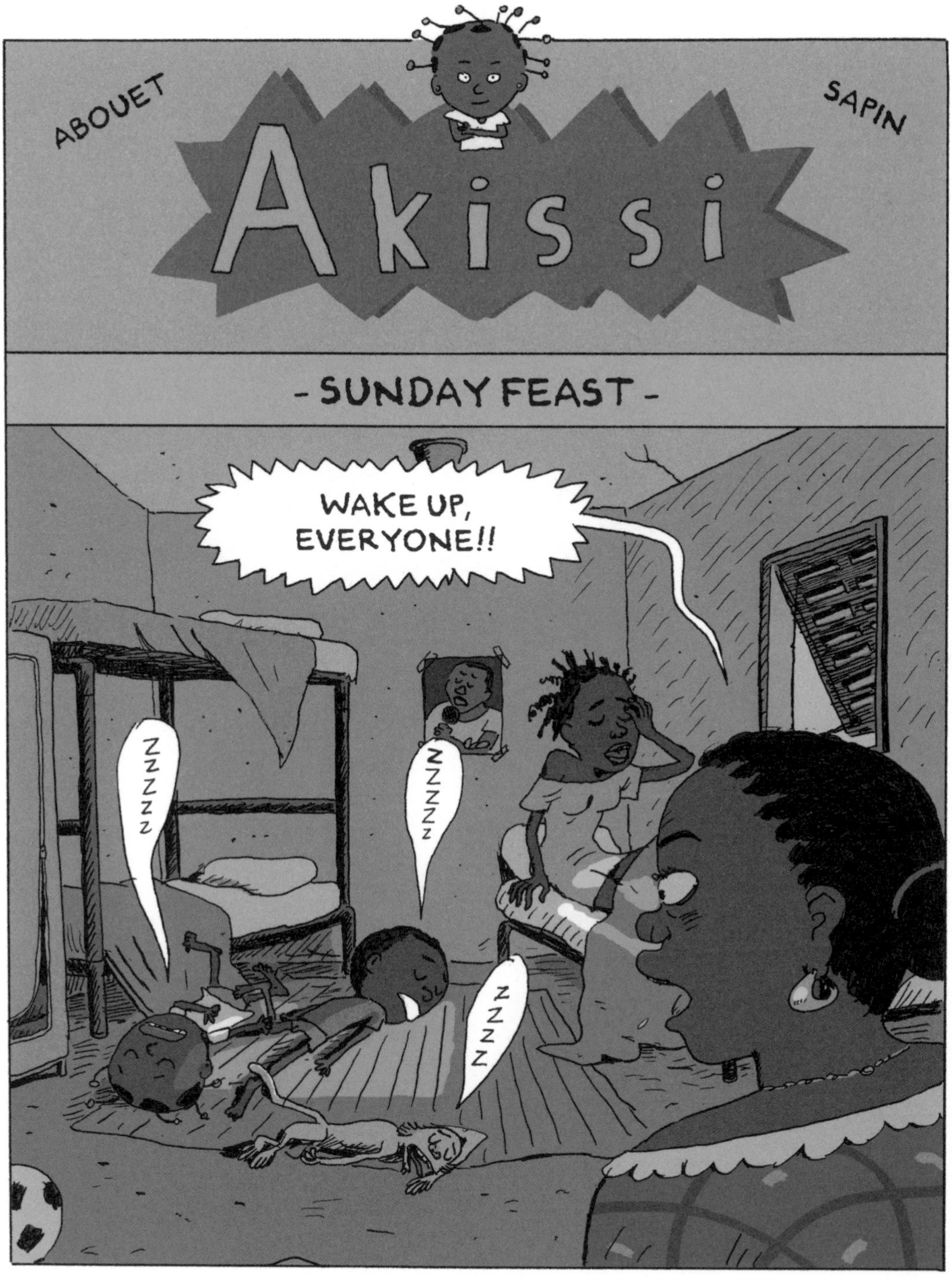
ABOUET
SAPIN
Akissi
- SUNDAY FEAST -
WAKE UP, EVERYONE!!
ZZZZZ
ZZZZZZ
ZZZZ

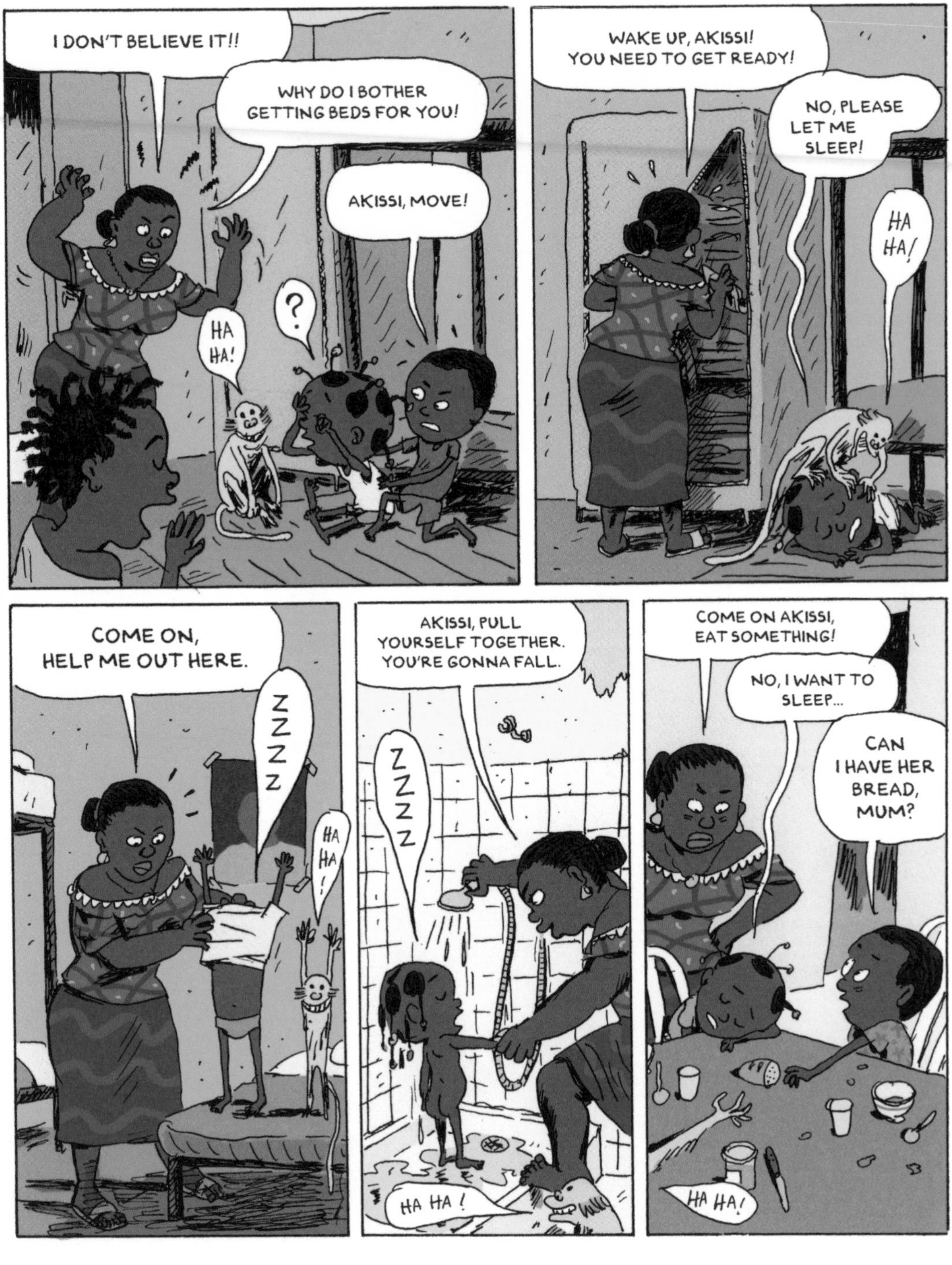
I DON'T BELIEVE IT!!
WHY DO I BOTHER GETTING BEDS FOR YOU!
AKISSI, MOVE!
?
HA HA!
WAKE UP, AKISSI! YOU NEED TO GET READY!
NO, PLEASE LET ME SLEEP!
HA HA!
COME ON, HELP ME OUT HERE.
ZZZZ
HA HA!
AKISSI, PULL YOURSELF TOGETHER. YOU'RE GONNA FALL.
ZZZZ
HA HA!
COME ON AKISSI, EAT SOMETHING!
NO, I WANT TO SLEEP...
CAN I HAVE HER BREAD, MUM?
HA HA!

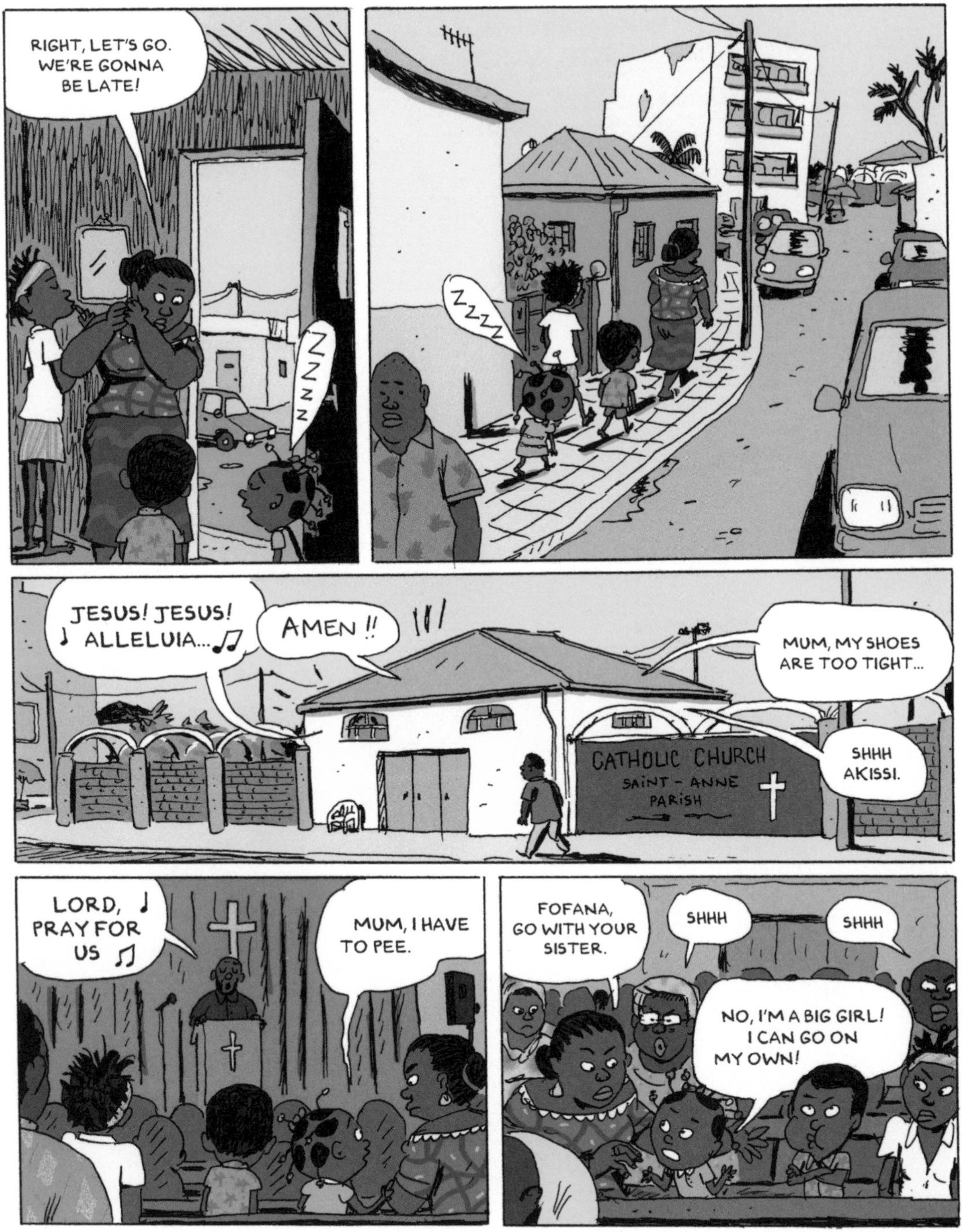
RIGHT, LET'S GO. WE'RE GONNA BE LATE!
ZZZZ
ZZZZ
JESUS! JESUS! ALLELUIA...
AMEN !!
MUM, MY SHOES ARE TOO TIGHT...
SHHH AKISSI.
CATHOLIC CHURCH
SAINT - ANNE PARISH
LORD, PRAY FOR US
MUM, I HAVE TO PEE.
FOFANA, GO WITH YOUR SISTER.
SHHH
SHHH
NO, I'M A BIG GIRL! I CAN GO ON MY OWN!

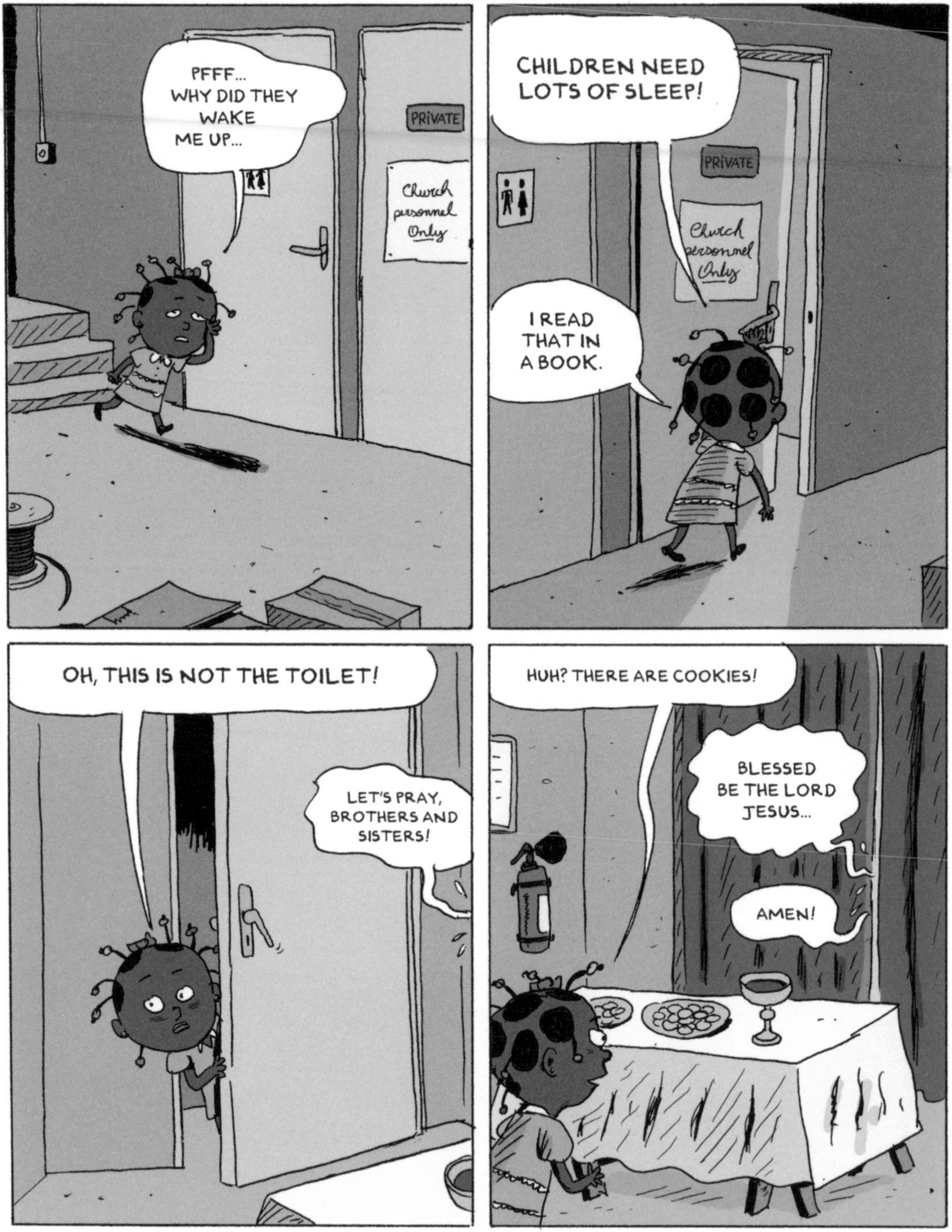
PFFF... WHY DID THEY WAKE ME UP...
PRIVATE
Church personnel Only
CHILDREN NEED LOTS OF SLEEP!
PRIVATE
Church personnel Only
I READ THAT IN A BOOK.
OH, THIS IS NOT THE TOILET!
LET'S PRAY, BROTHERS AND SISTERS!
HUH? THERE ARE COOKIES!
BLESSED BE THE LORD JESUS...
AMEN!

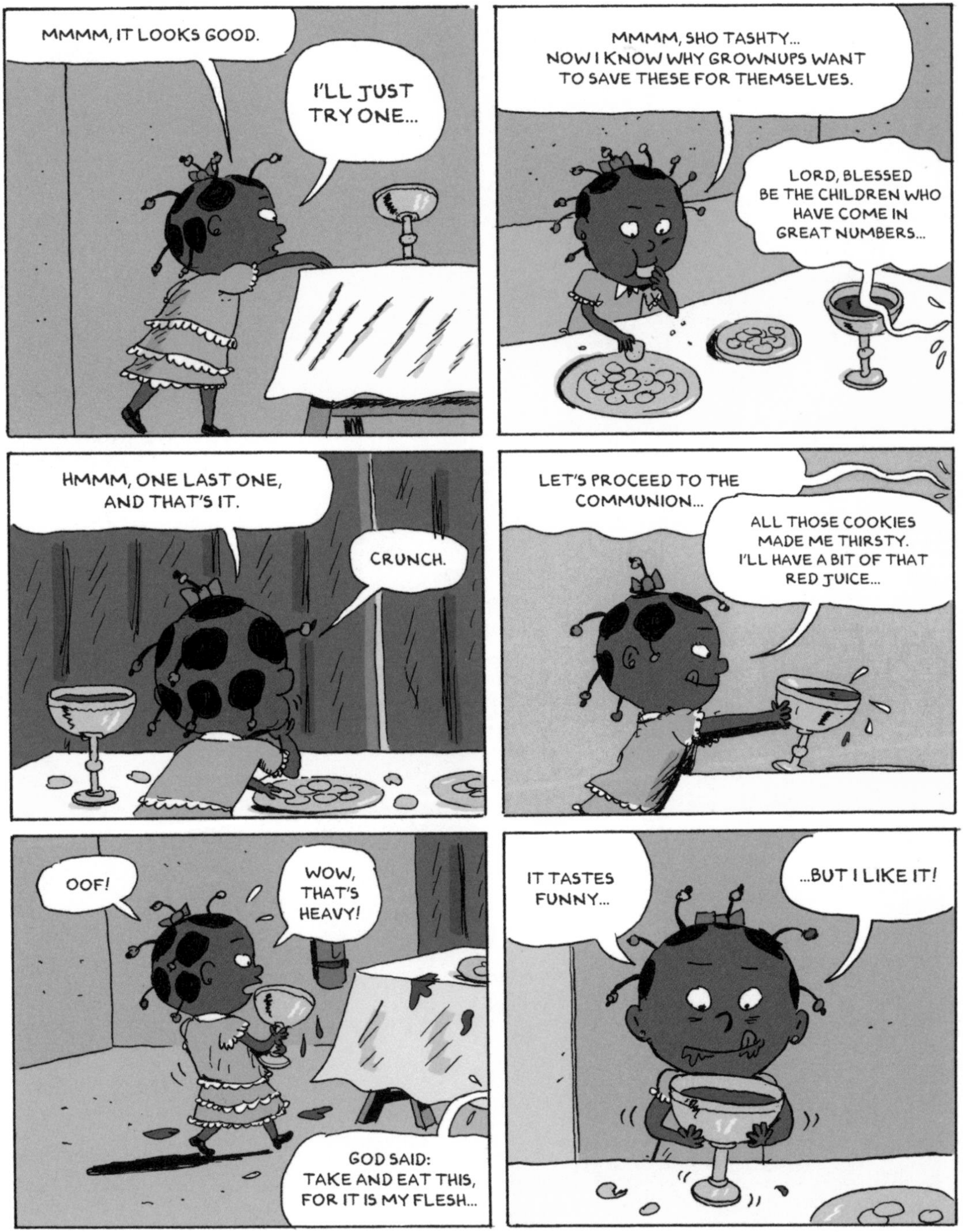
MMMM, IT LOOKS GOOD.
I'LL JUST TRY ONE...
MMMM, SHO TASHTY... NOW I KNOW WHY GROWNUPS WANT TO SAVE THESE FOR THEMSELVES.
LORD, BLESSED BE THE CHILDREN WHO HAVE COME IN GREAT NUMBERS...
HMMM, ONE LAST ONE, AND THAT'S IT.
CRUNCH.
LET'S PROCEED TO THE COMMUNION...
ALL THOSE COOKIES MADE ME THIRSTY. I'LL HAVE A BIT OF THAT RED JUICE...
OOF!
WOW, THAT'S HEAVY!
GOD SAID: TAKE AND EAT THIS, FOR IT IS MY FLESH...
IT TASTES FUNNY...
...BUT I LIKE IT!

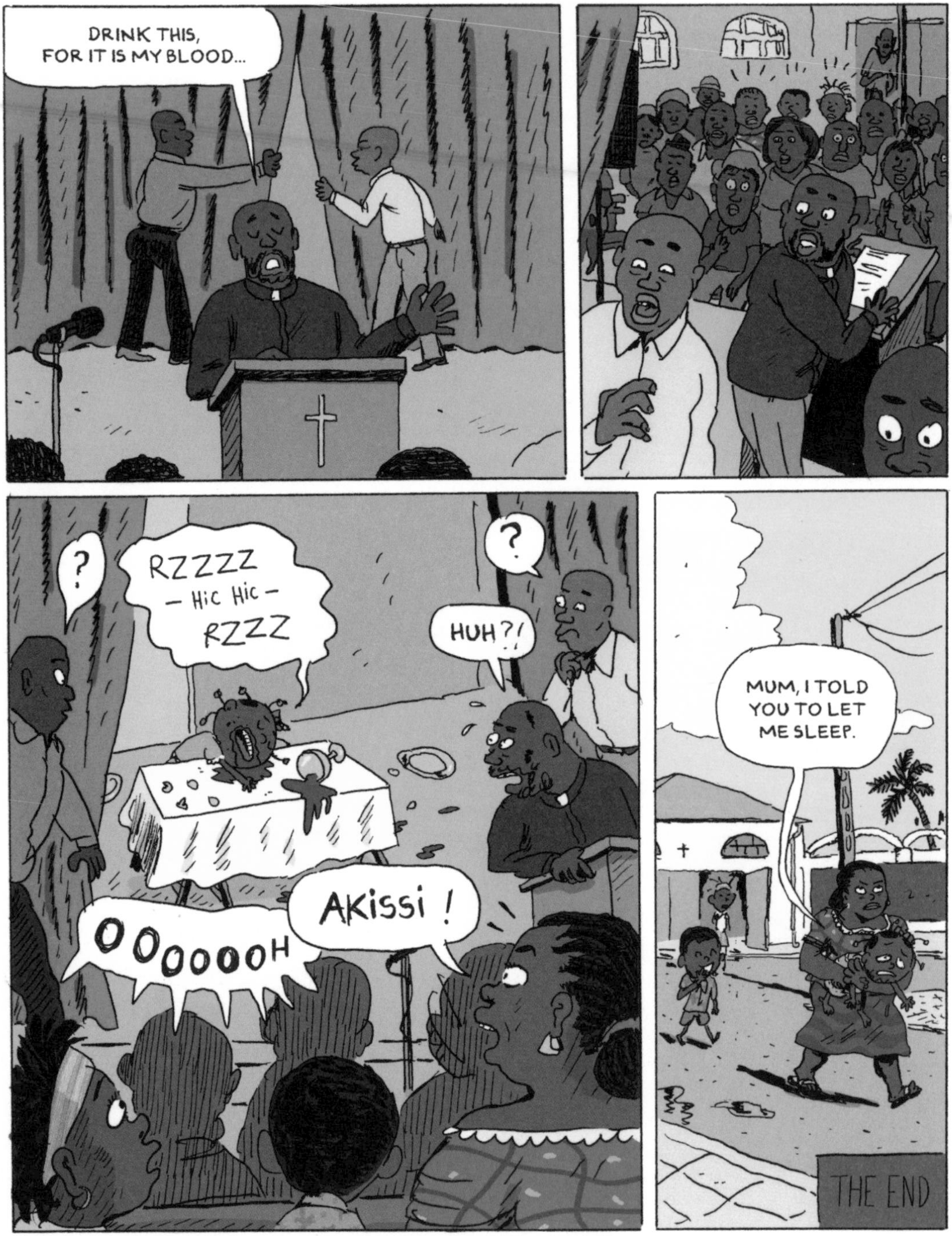

DRINK THIS, FOR IT IS MY BLOOD...
?
RZZZZ - Hic Hic - RZZZ
?
HUH?!
OOOOOOH
AKissi !
MUM, I TOLD YOU TO LET ME SLEEP.
THE END

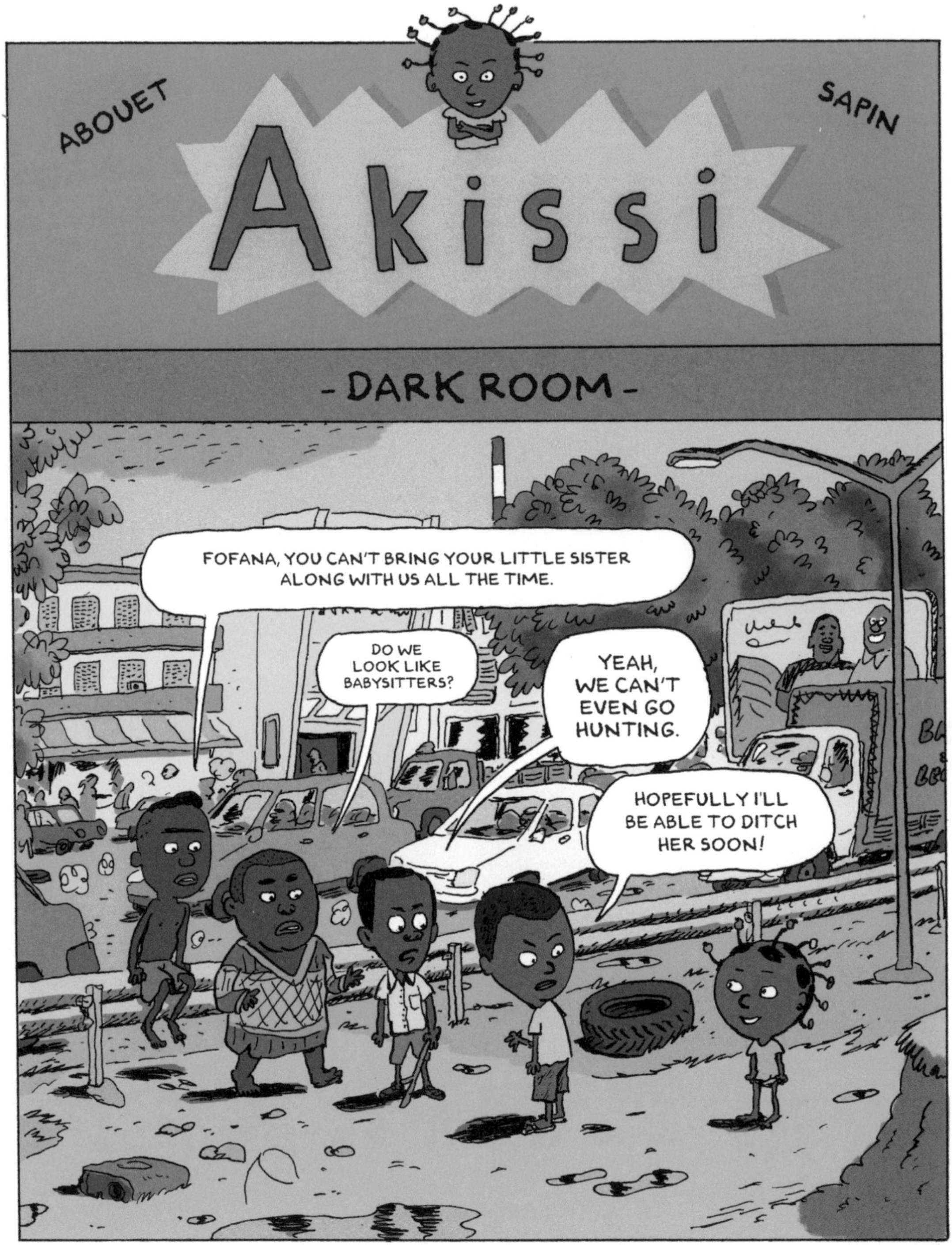
ABOUET
Akissi
SAPIN
- DARK ROOM -
FOFANA, YOU CAN'T BRING YOUR LITTLE SISTER ALONG WITH US ALL THE TIME.
DO WE LOOK LIKE BABYSITTERS?
YEAH, WE CAN'T EVEN GO HUNTING.
HOPEFULLY I'LL BE ABLE TO DITCH HER SOON!

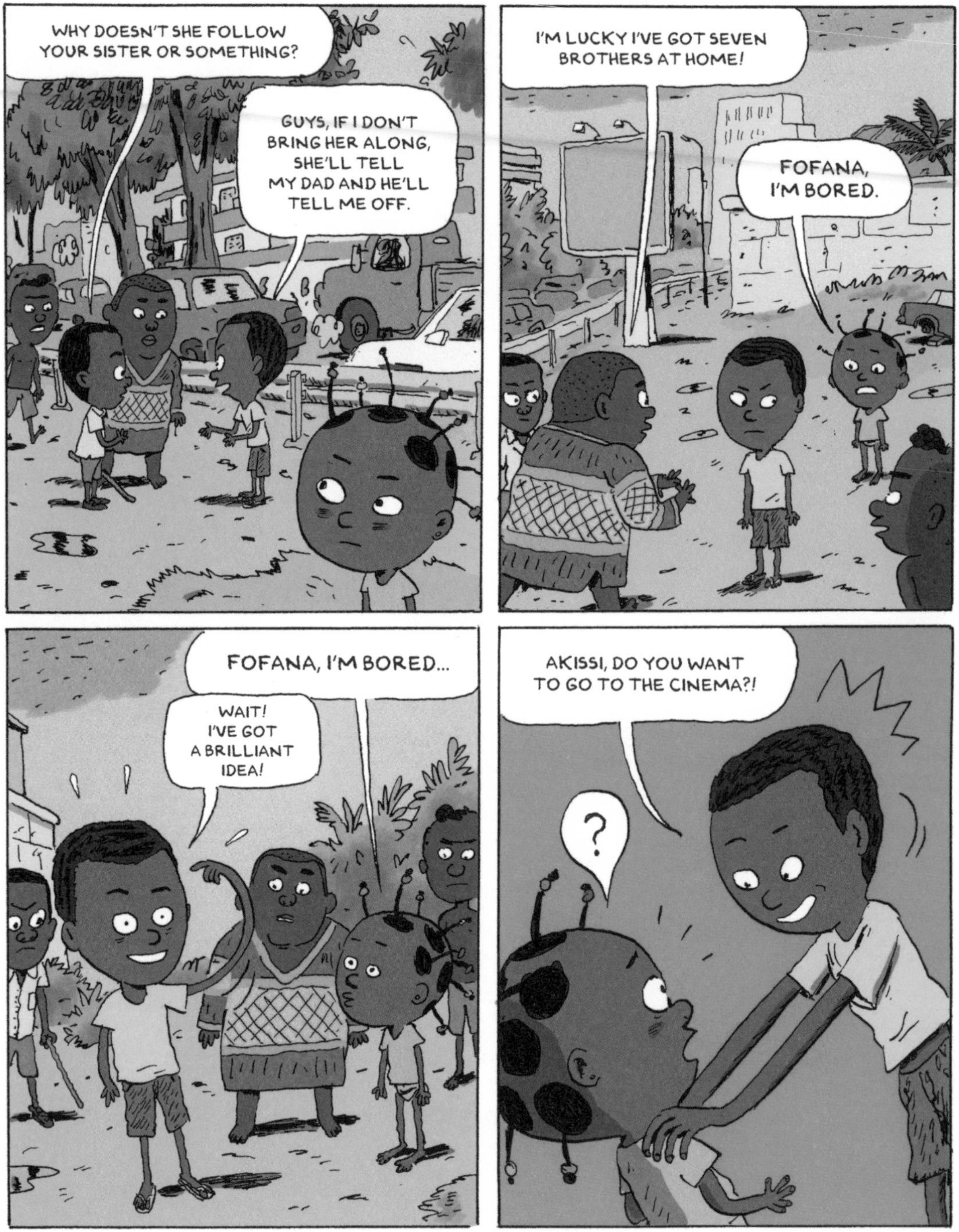
WHY DOESN'T SHE FOLLOW YOUR SISTER OR SOMETHING?
GUYS, IF I DON'T BRING HER ALONG, SHE'LL TELL MY DAD AND HE'LL TELL ME OFF.
I'M LUCKY I'VE GOT SEVEN BROTHERS AT HOME!
FOFANA, I'M BORED.
FOFANA, I'M BORED...
WAIT! I'VE GOT A BRILLIANT IDEA!
AKISSI, DO YOU WANT TO GO TO THE CINEMA?!
?

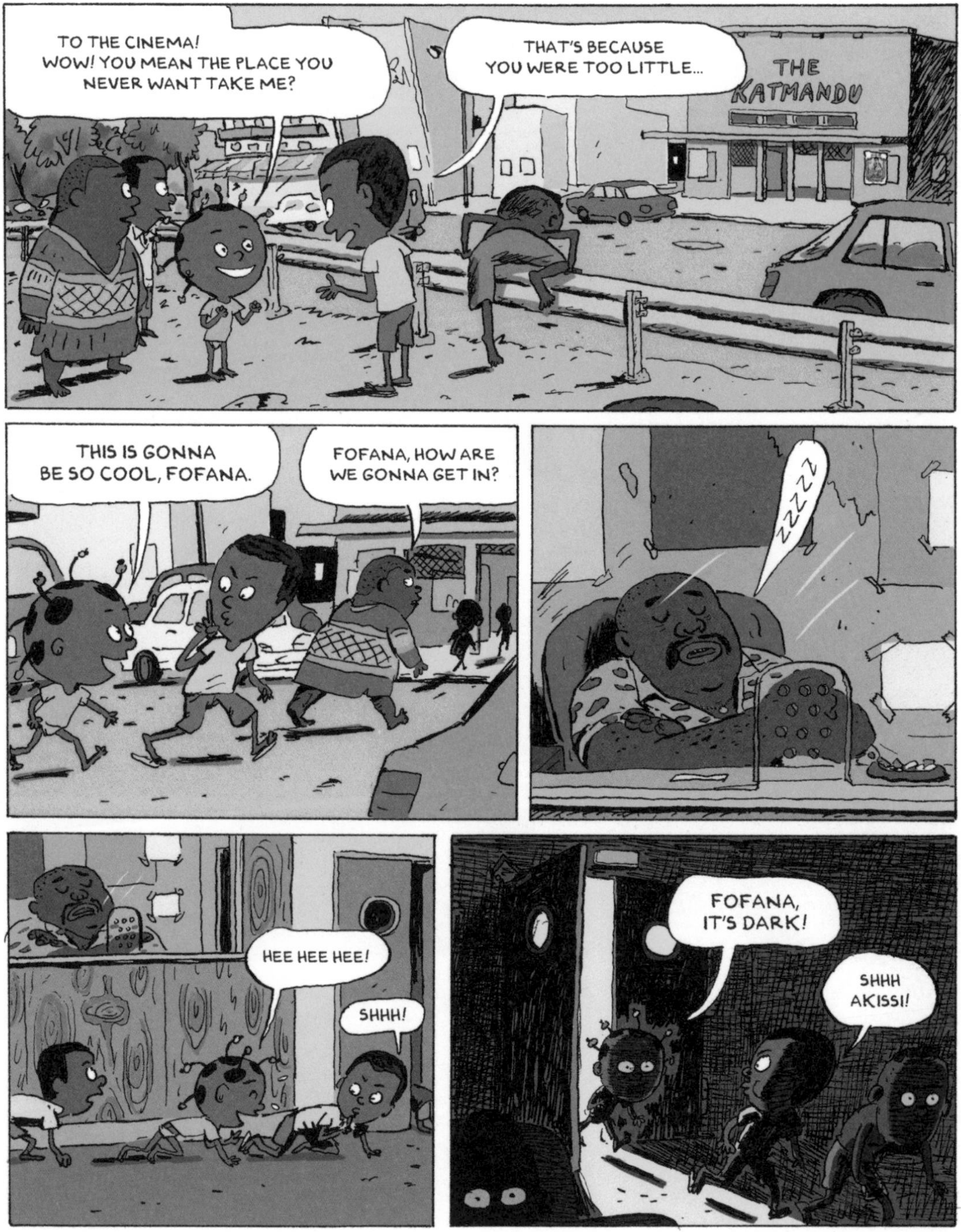
TO THE CINEMA!
WOW! YOU MEAN THE PLACE YOU NEVER WANT TAKE ME?
THAT'S BECAUSE YOU WERE TOO LITTLE...
THE KATMANDU
THIS IS GONNA BE SO COOL, FOFANA.
FOFANA, HOW ARE WE GONNA GET IN?
ZZZZZ
HEE HEE HEE!
SHHH!
FOFANA, IT'S DARK!
SHHH AKISSI!

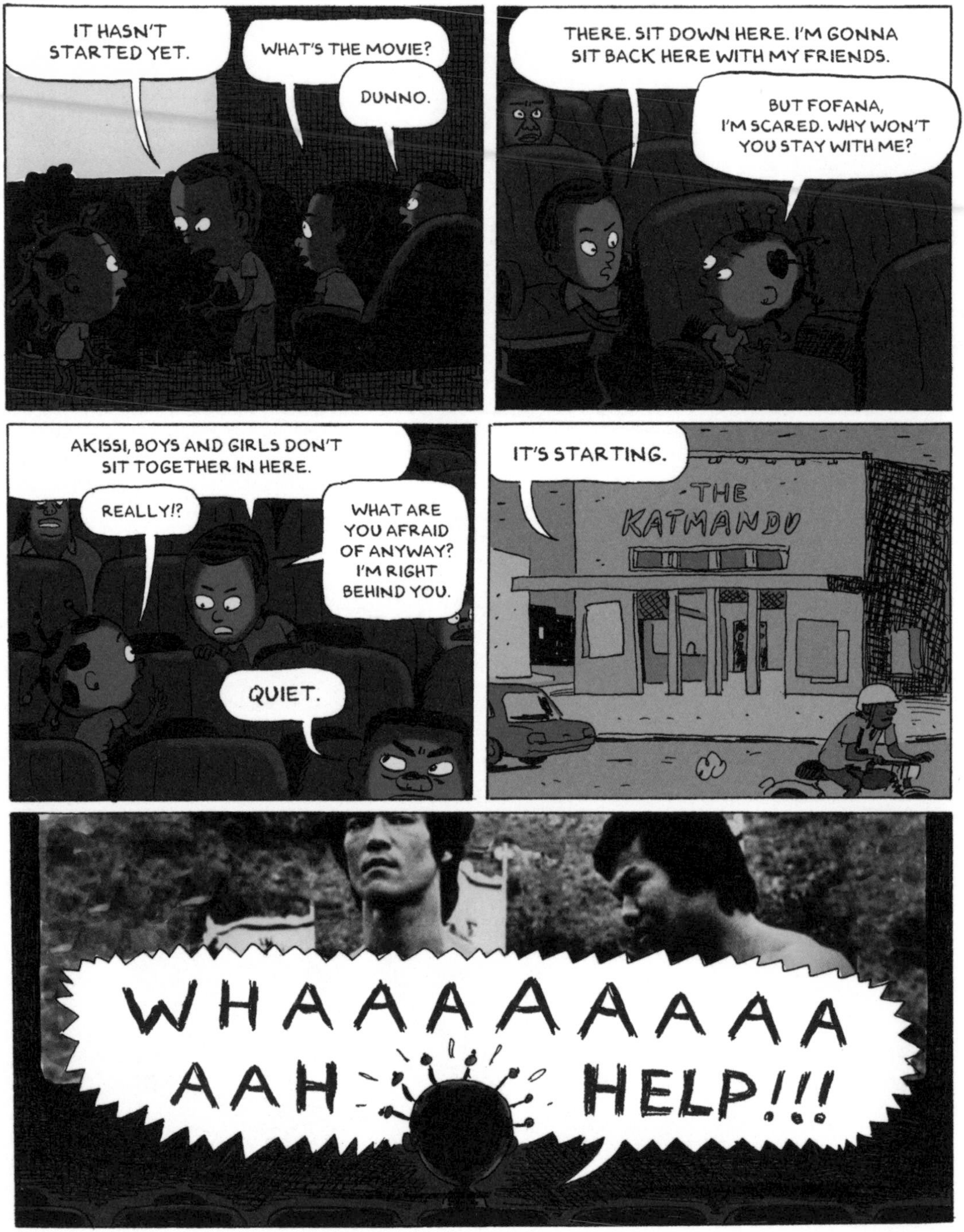
IT HASN'T STARTED YET.
WHAT'S THE MOVIE?
DUNNO.
THERE. SIT DOWN HERE. I'M GONNA SIT BACK HERE WITH MY FRIENDS.
BUT FOFANA, I'M SCARED. WHY WON'T YOU STAY WITH ME?
AKISSI, BOYS AND GIRLS DON'T SIT TOGETHER IN HERE.
REALLY!?
WHAT ARE YOU AFRAID OF ANYWAY? I'M RIGHT BEHIND YOU.
QUIET.
IT'S STARTING.
THE KATMANDU
WHAAAAAAAAAAAH HELP!!!

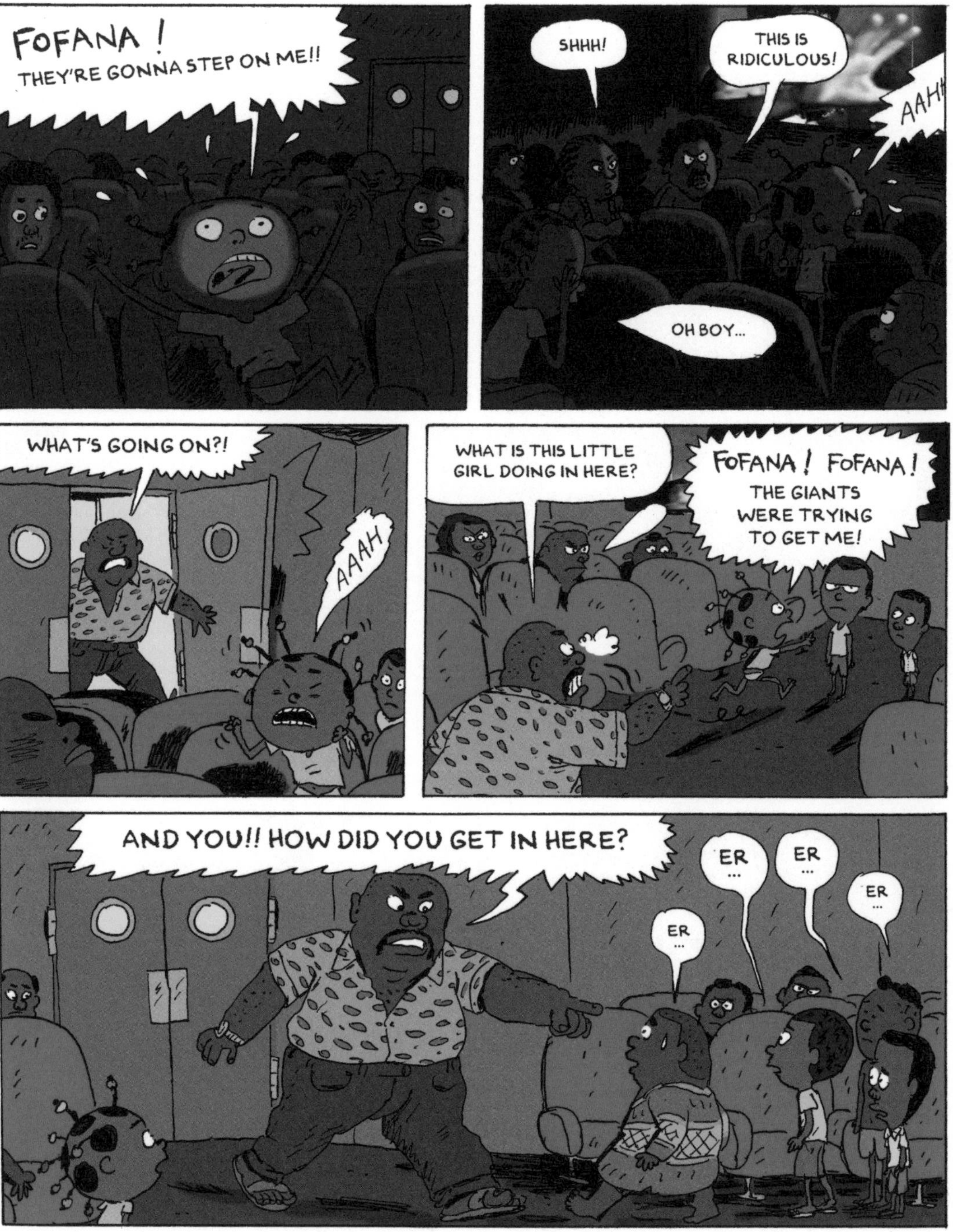
FOFANA! THEY'RE GONNA STEP ON ME!!
SHHH!
THIS IS RIDICULOUS!
AAH
OH BOY...
WHAT'S GOING ON?!
AAAH
WHAT IS THIS LITTLE GIRL DOING IN HERE?
FOFANA! FOFANA! THE GIANTS WERE TRYING TO GET ME!
AND YOU!! HOW DID YOU GET IN HERE?
ER ...
ER ...
ER ...
ER ...

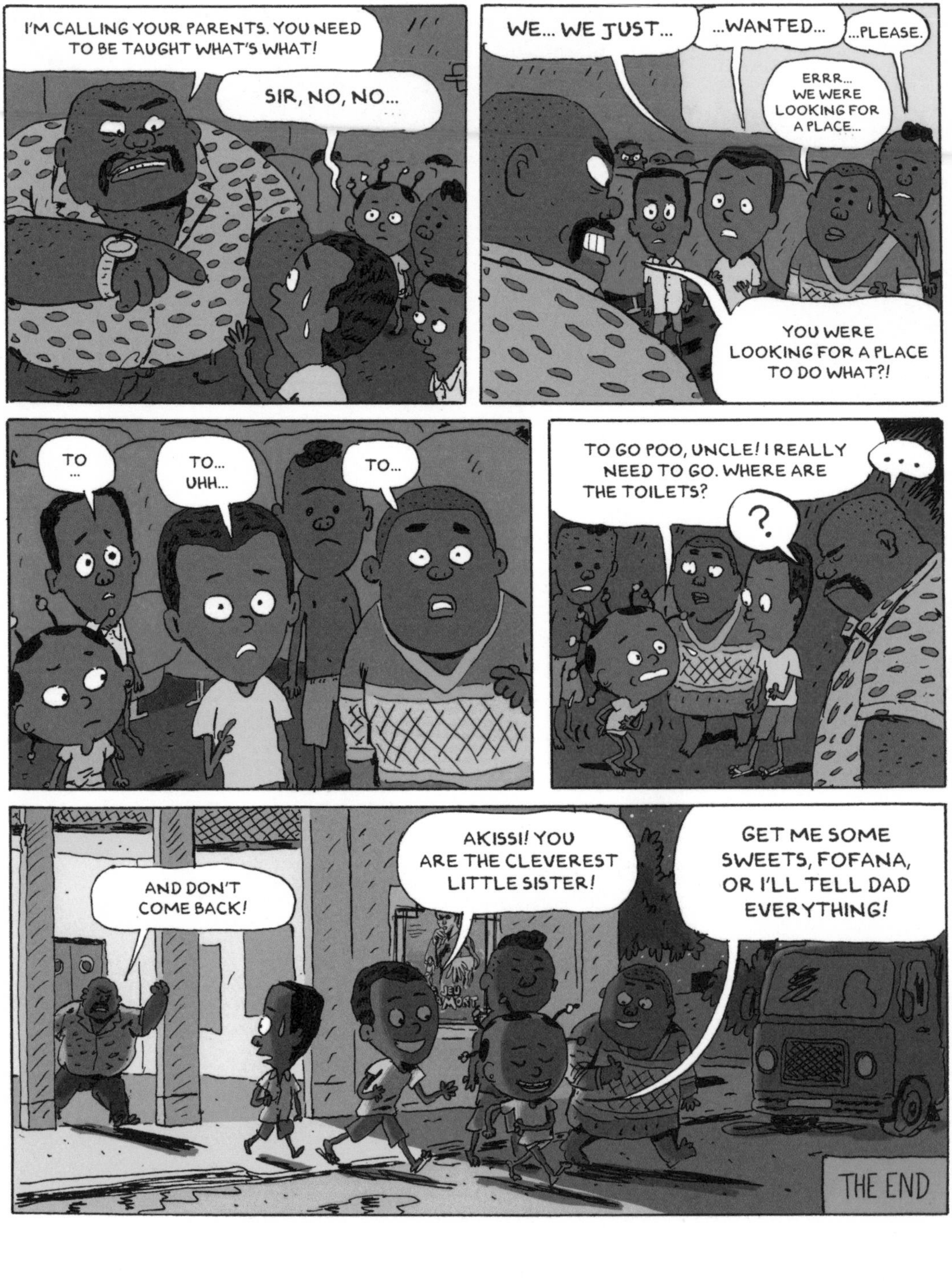
I'M CALLING YOUR PARENTS. YOU NEED TO BE TAUGHT WHAT'S WHAT!
SIR, NO, NO...
WE... WE JUST...
...WANTED...
...PLEASE.
ERRR... WE WERE LOOKING FOR A PLACE...
YOU WERE LOOKING FOR A PLACE TO DO WHAT?!
TO ...
TO... UHH...
TO...
TO GO POO, UNCLE! I REALLY NEED TO GO. WHERE ARE THE TOILETS?
...
?
AND DON'T COME BACK!
AKISSI! YOU ARE THE CLEVEREST LITTLE SISTER!
GET ME SOME SWEETS, FOFANA, OR I'LL TELL DAD EVERYTHING!
THE END

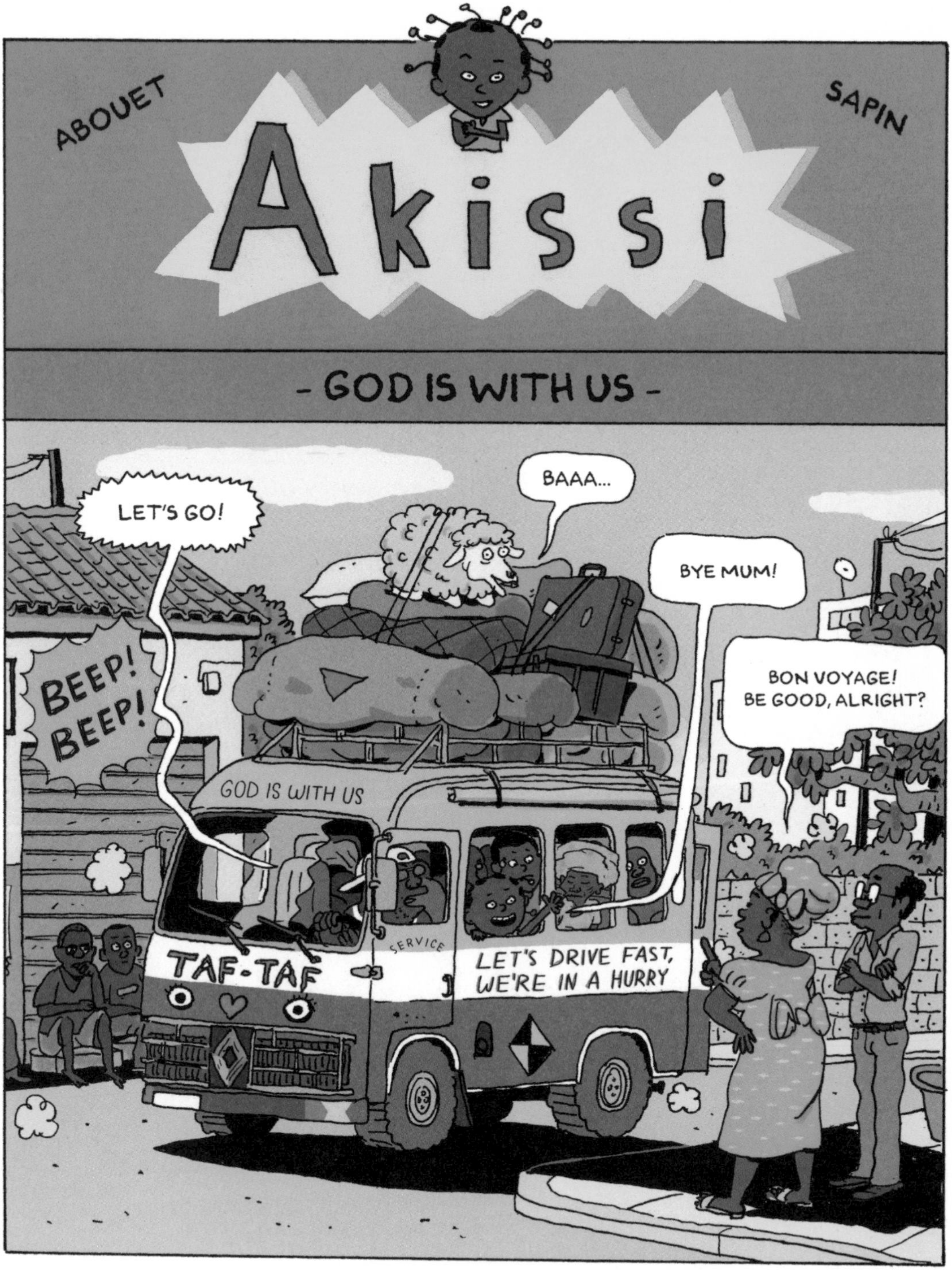
ABOUET
SAPIN
Akissi
- GOD IS WITH US -
LET'S GO!
BAAA...
BYE MUM!
BEEP! BEEP!
BON VOYAGE! BE GOOD, ALRIGHT?
GOD IS WITH US
SERVICE
TAF-TAF
LET'S DRIVE FAST, WE'RE IN A HURRY

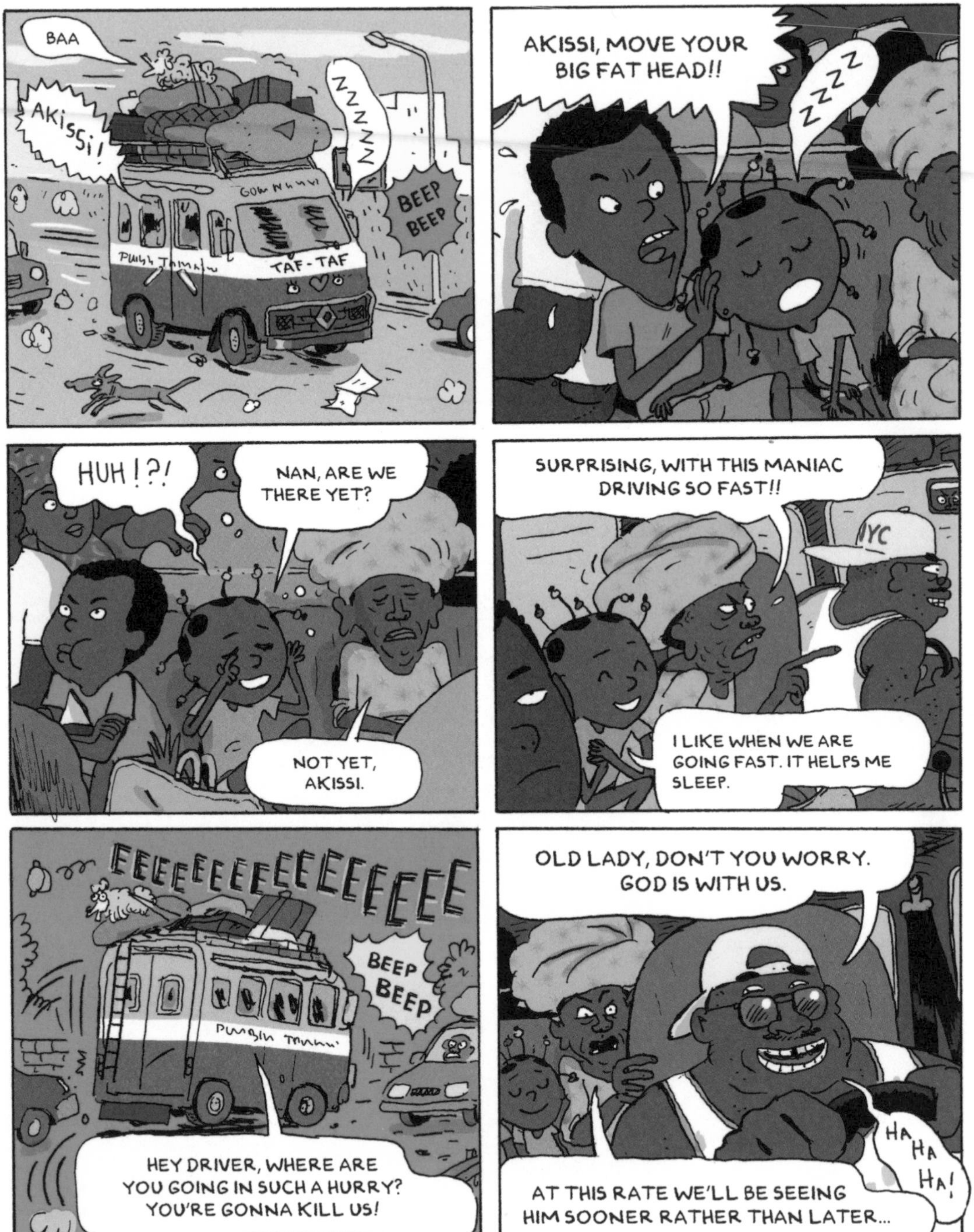
BAA
AKISSI!
ZZZZZ
TAF - TAF
BEEP BEEP
AKISSI, MOVE YOUR BIG FAT HEAD!!
ZZZZ
HUH!?!
NAN, ARE WE THERE YET?
NOT YET, AKISSI.
SURPRISING, WITH THIS MANIAC DRIVING SO FAST!!
NYC
I LIKE WHEN WE ARE GOING FAST. IT HELPS ME SLEEP.
EEEEEEEEEEEEEEEEEE
BEEP BEEP
HEY DRIVER, WHERE ARE YOU GOING IN SUCH A HURRY? YOU'RE GONNA KILL US!
OLD LADY, DON'T YOU WORRY. GOD IS WITH US.
HA HA HA!
AT THIS RATE WE'LL BE SEEING HIM SOONER RATHER THAN LATER...

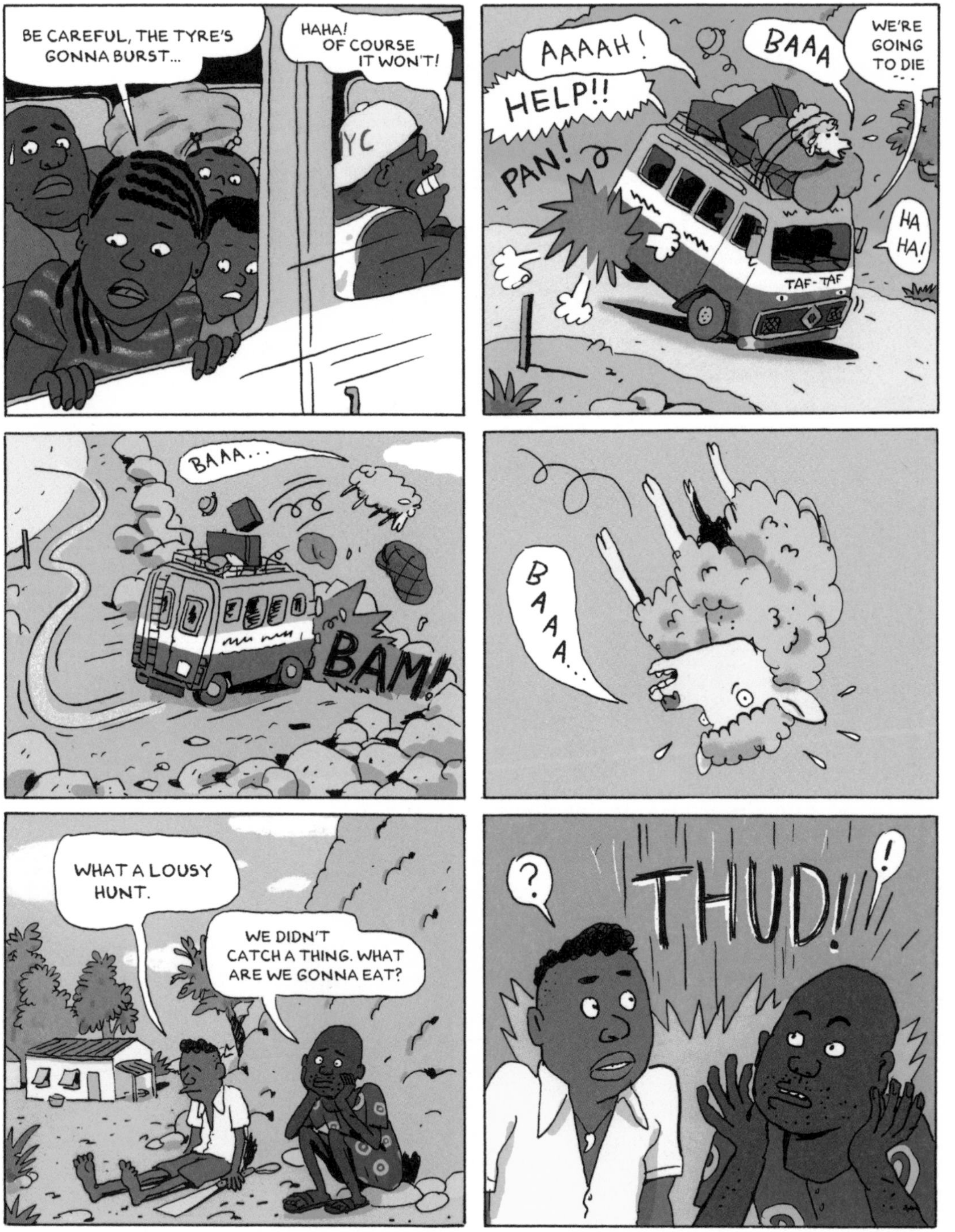
BE CAREFUL, THE TYRE'S GONNA BURST...
HAHA! OF COURSE IT WON'T!
NYC
AAAAH!
HELP!!
BAAA
WE'RE GOING TO DIE...
PAN!
HA HA!
TAF-TAF
BAAA...
BAM!
BAAA...
WHAT A LOUSY HUNT.
WE DIDN'T CATCH A THING. WHAT ARE WE GONNA EAT?
?
THUD!
!

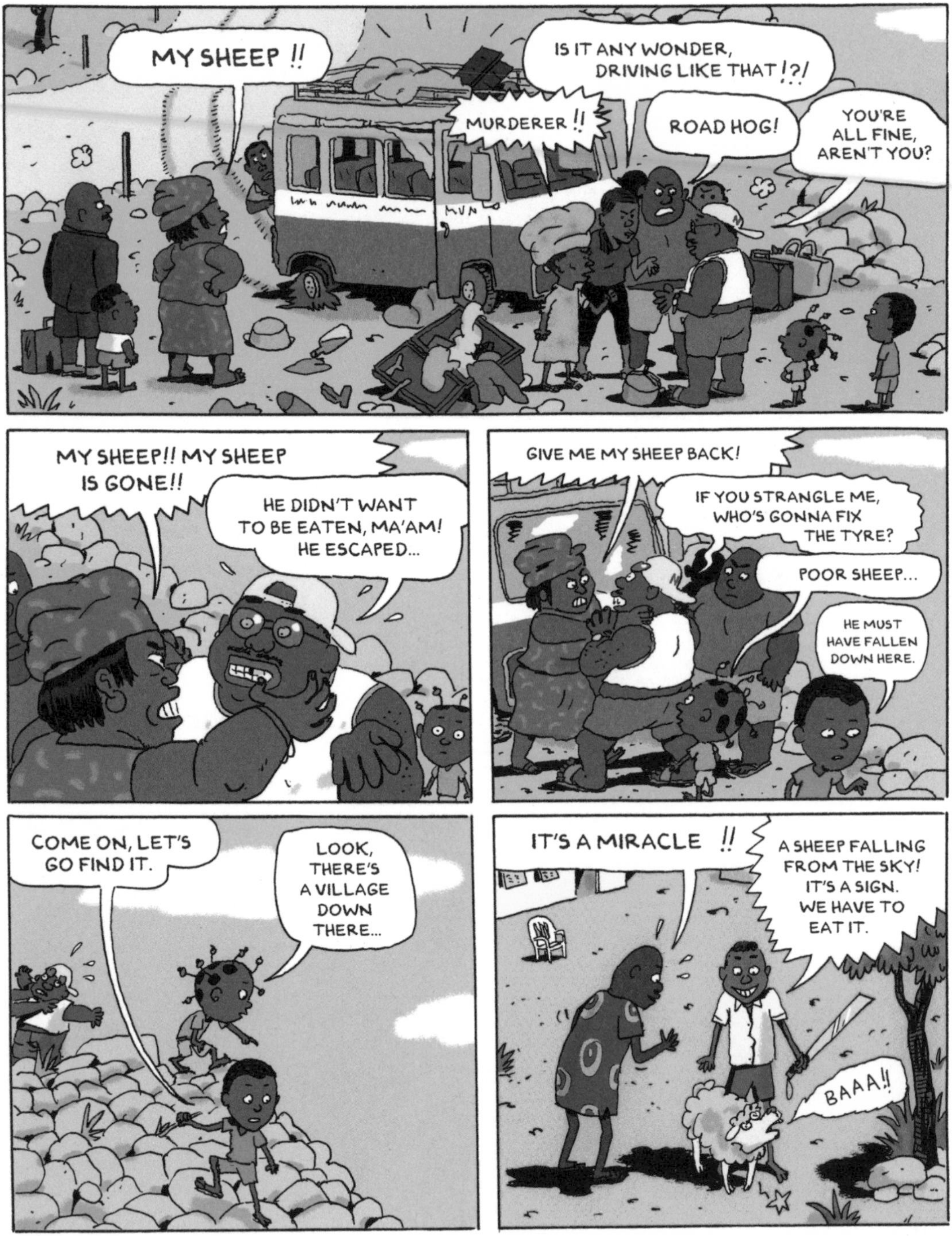
MY SHEEP !!
MURDERER !!
IS IT ANY WONDER, DRIVING LIKE THAT !?!
ROAD HOG!
YOU'RE ALL FINE, AREN'T YOU?
MY SHEEP!! MY SHEEP IS GONE!!
HE DIDN'T WANT TO BE EATEN, MA'AM! HE ESCAPED...
GIVE ME MY SHEEP BACK!
IF YOU STRANGLE ME, WHO'S GONNA FIX THE TYRE?
POOR SHEEP...
HE MUST HAVE FALLEN DOWN HERE.
COME ON, LET'S GO FIND IT.
LOOK, THERE'S A VILLAGE DOWN THERE...
IT'S A MIRACLE !!
A SHEEP FALLING FROM THE SKY! IT'S A SIGN. WE HAVE TO EAT IT.
BAAA!!

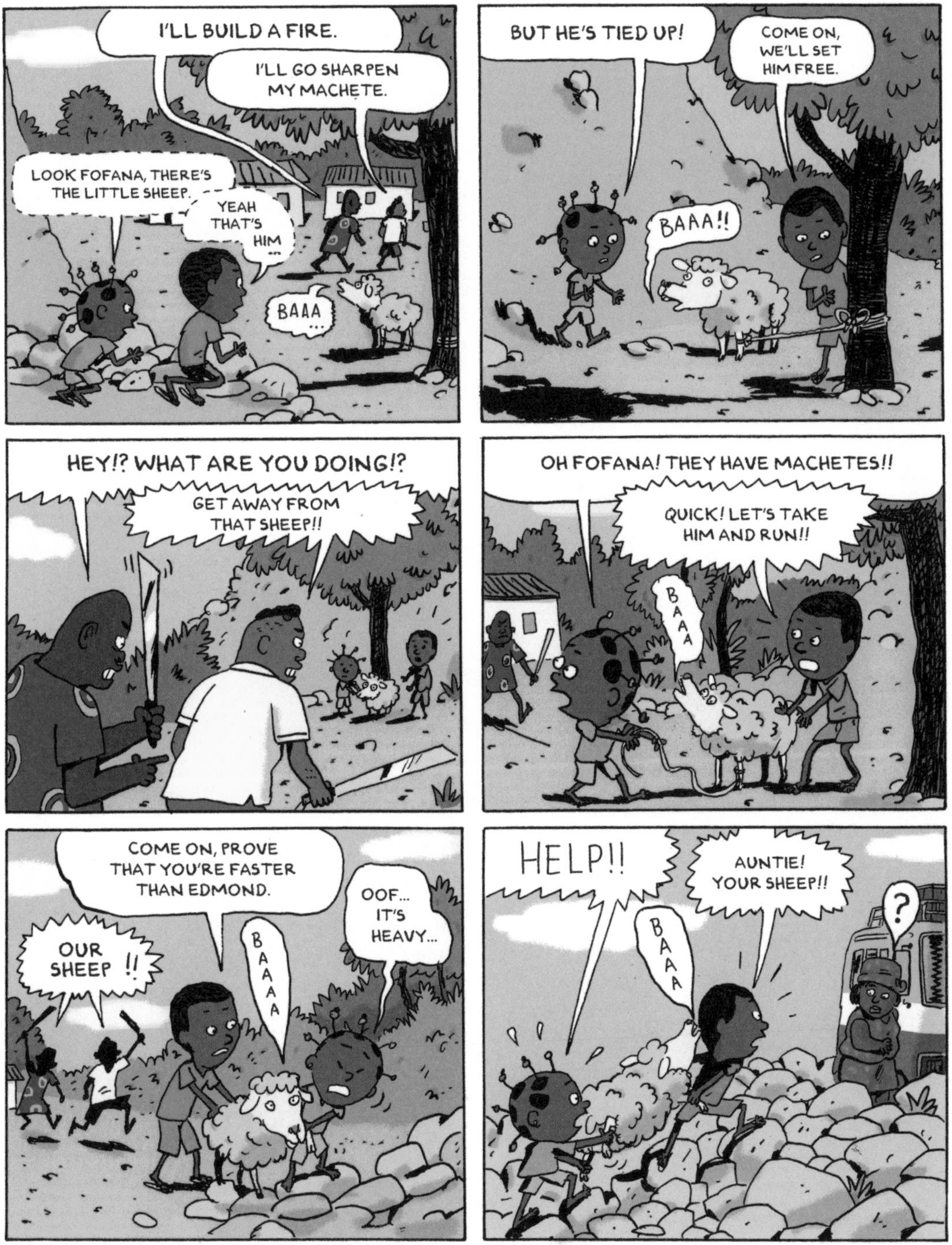
I'LL BUILD A FIRE.
I'LL GO SHARPEN MY MACHETE.
LOOK FOFANA, THERE'S THE LITTLE SHEEP.
YEAH THAT'S HIM ...
BAAA ...
BUT HE'S TIED UP!
COME ON, WE'LL SET HIM FREE.
BAAA!!
HEY!? WHAT ARE YOU DOING!?
GET AWAY FROM THAT SHEEP!!
OH FOFANA! THEY HAVE MACHETES!!
QUICK! LET'S TAKE HIM AND RUN!!
BAAA
COME ON, PROVE THAT YOU'RE FASTER THAN EDMOND.
OOF... IT'S HEAVY...
OUR SHEEP !!
BAAAA
HELP!!
AUNTIE! YOUR SHEEP!!
BAAA
?

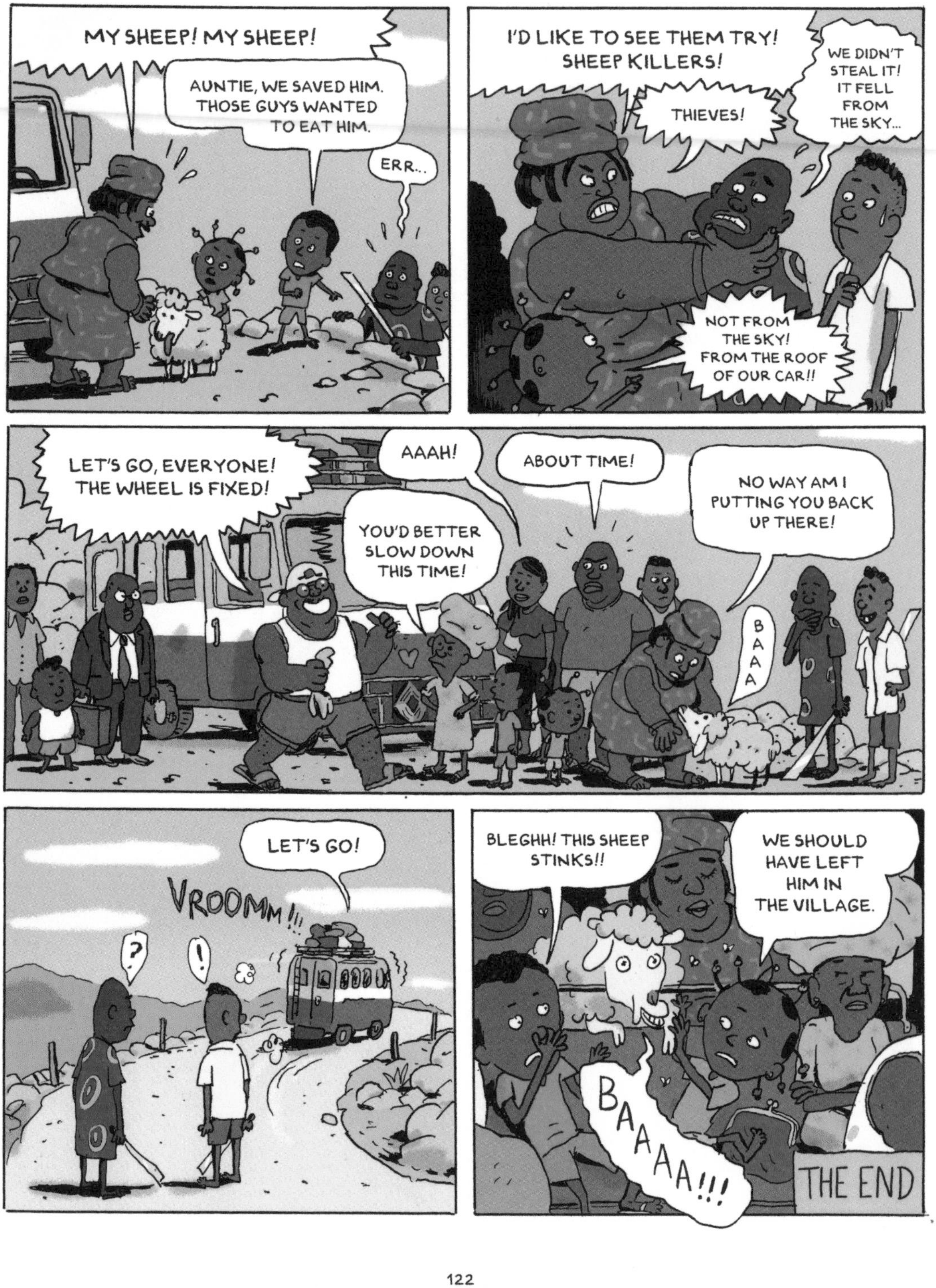
MY SHEEP! MY SHEEP!
AUNTIE, WE SAVED HIM. THOSE GUYS WANTED TO EAT HIM.
ERR...
I'D LIKE TO SEE THEM TRY! SHEEP KILLERS!
THIEVES!
WE DIDN'T STEAL IT! IT FELL FROM THE SKY...
NOT FROM THE SKY! FROM THE ROOF OF OUR CAR!!
LET'S GO, EVERYONE! THE WHEEL IS FIXED!
AAAH!
YOU'D BETTER SLOW DOWN THIS TIME!
ABOUT TIME!
NO WAY AM I PUTTING YOU BACK UP THERE!
BAAA
LET'S GO!
VROOMM!!!
?
!
BLEGHH! THIS SHEEP STINKS!!
WE SHOULD HAVE LEFT HIM IN THE VILLAGE.
BAAAAA!!!
THE END

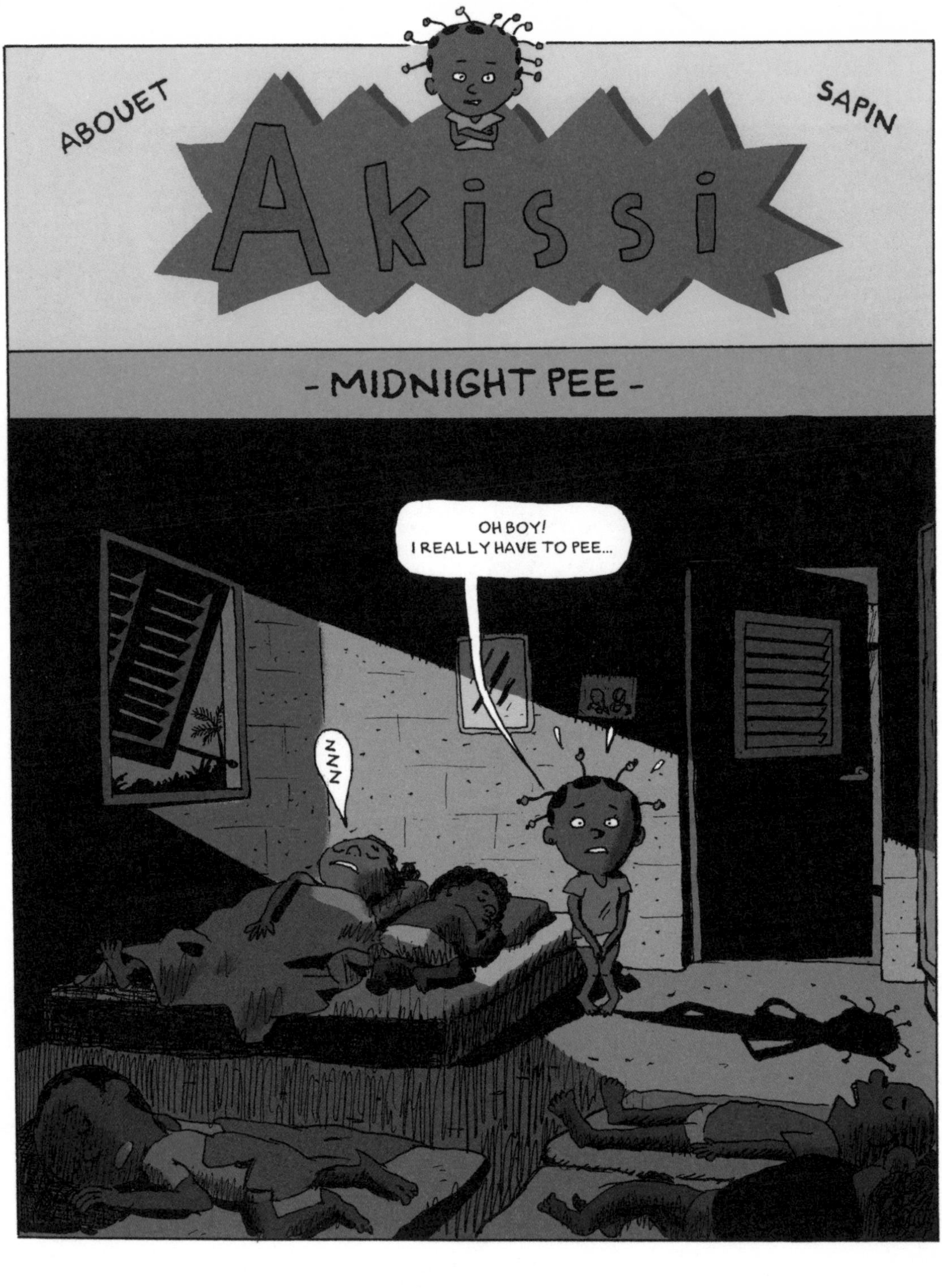
ABOUET
Akissi
SAPIN
- MIDNIGHT PEE -
OH BOY!
I REALLY HAVE TO PEE...
ZZZ

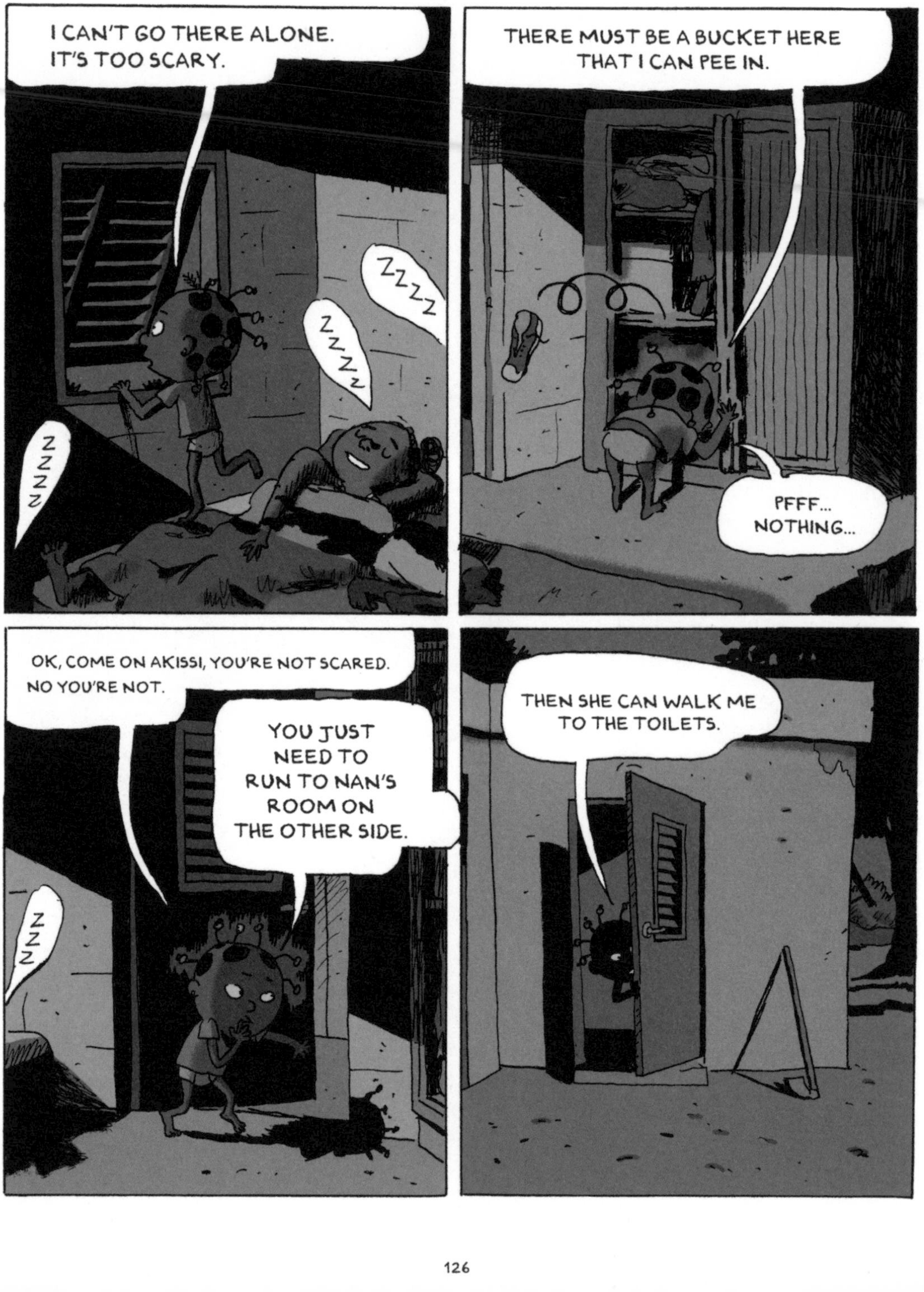
I CAN'T GO THERE ALONE. IT'S TOO SCARY.
ZZZZ
ZZZZ
ZZZZ
THERE MUST BE A BUCKET HERE THAT I CAN PEE IN.
PFFF... NOTHING...
OK, COME ON AKISSI, YOU'RE NOT SCARED. NO YOU'RE NOT.
YOU JUST NEED TO RUN TO NAN'S ROOM ON THE OTHER SIDE.
ZZZ
THEN SHE CAN WALK ME TO THE TOILETS.

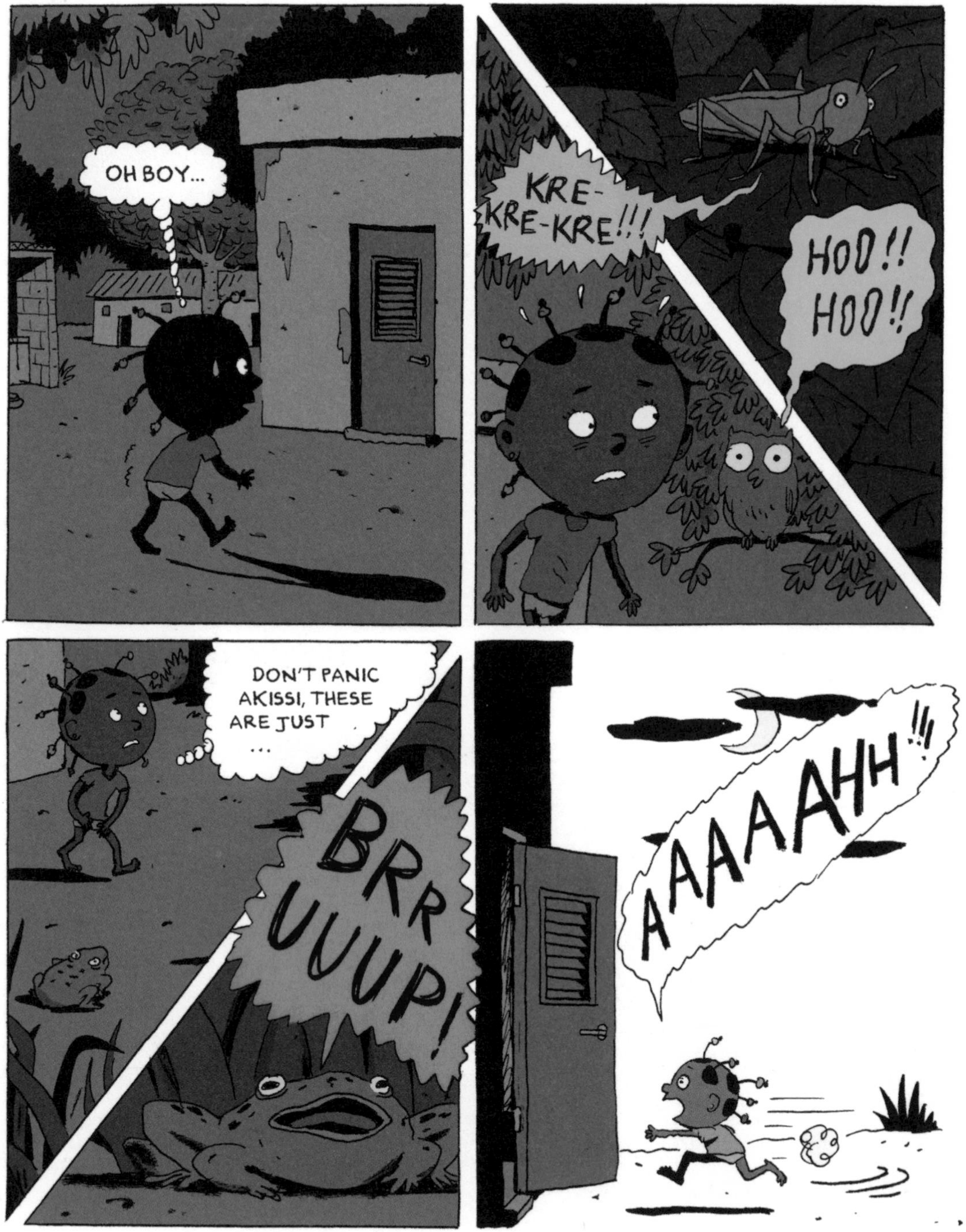
OH BOY...
KRE-KRE-KRE!!!
HOO!! HOO!!
DON'T PANIC AKISSI, THESE ARE JUST ...
BRRUUUP!
AAAAAHH!!!

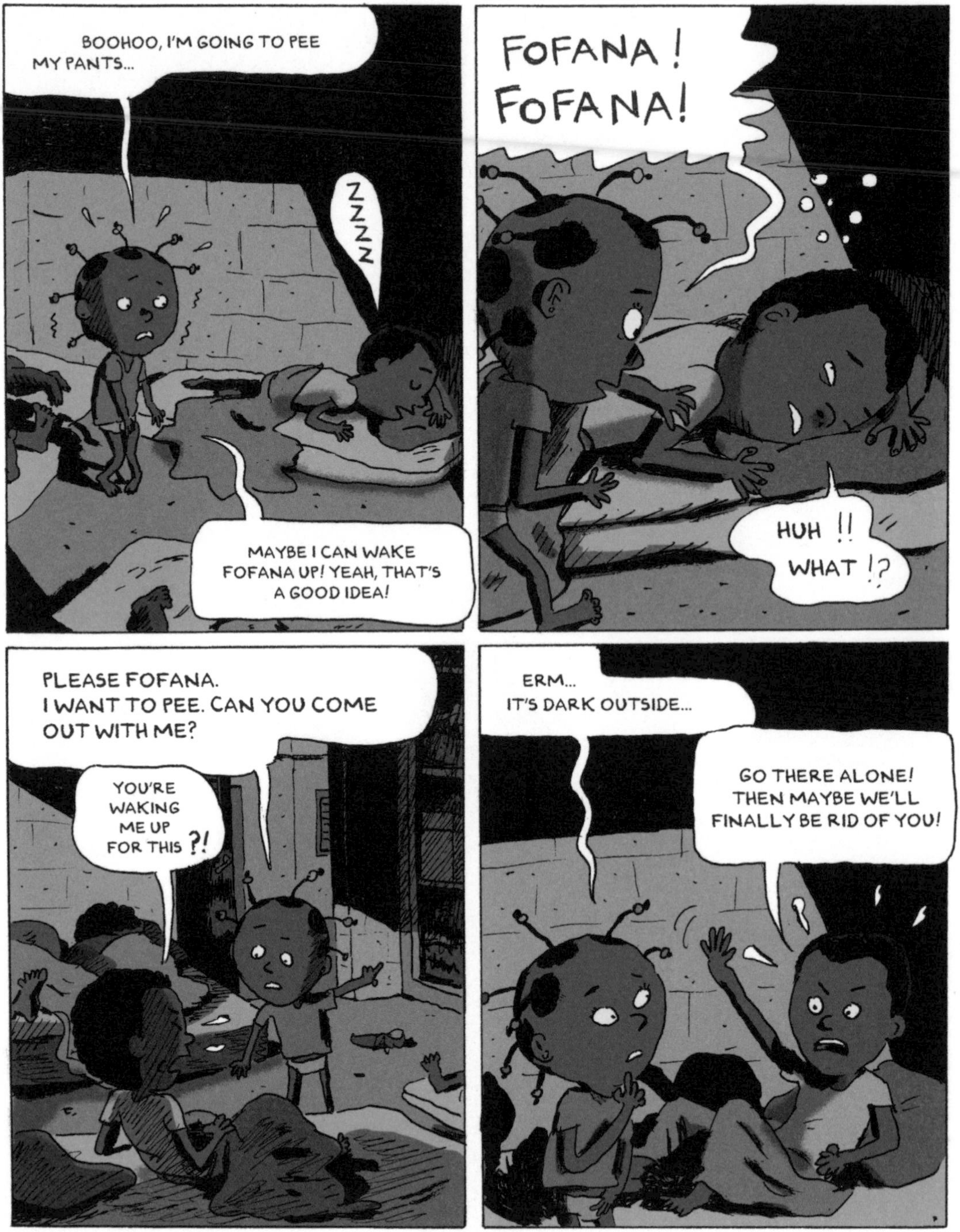
BOOHOO, I'M GOING TO PEE MY PANTS...
ZZZZ
MAYBE I CAN WAKE FOFANA UP! YEAH, THAT'S A GOOD IDEA!
FOFANA! FOFANA!
HUH !! WHAT !?
PLEASE FOFANA. I WANT TO PEE. CAN YOU COME OUT WITH ME?
YOU'RE WAKING ME UP FOR THIS ?!
ERM... IT'S DARK OUTSIDE...
GO THERE ALONE! THEN MAYBE WE'LL FINALLY BE RID OF YOU!

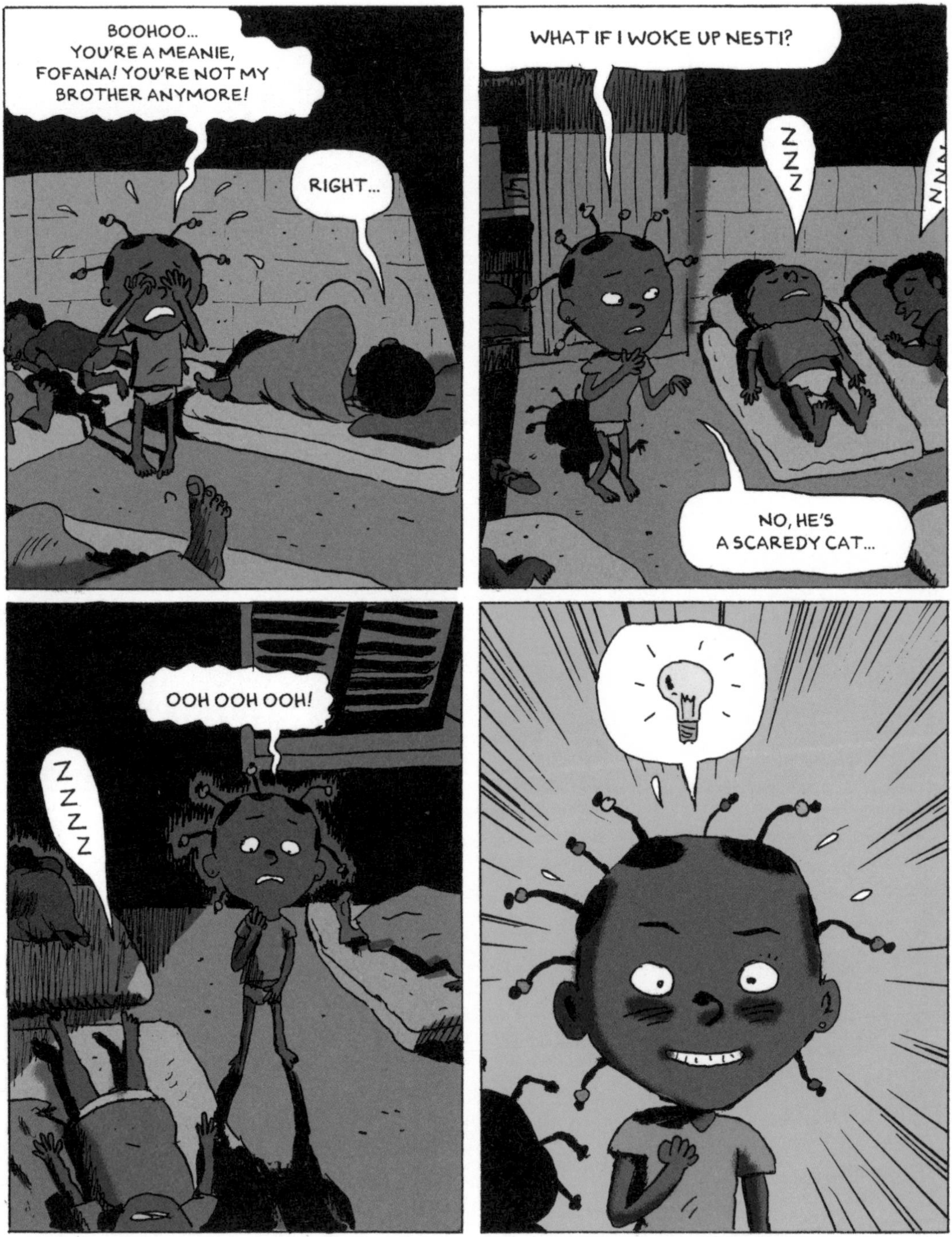
BOOHOO... YOU'RE A MEANIE, FOFANA! YOU'RE NOT MY BROTHER ANYMORE!
RIGHT...
WHAT IF I WOKE UP NESTI?
ZZZ
ZZZ
NO, HE'S A SCAREDY CAT...
OOH OOH OOH!
ZZZZ

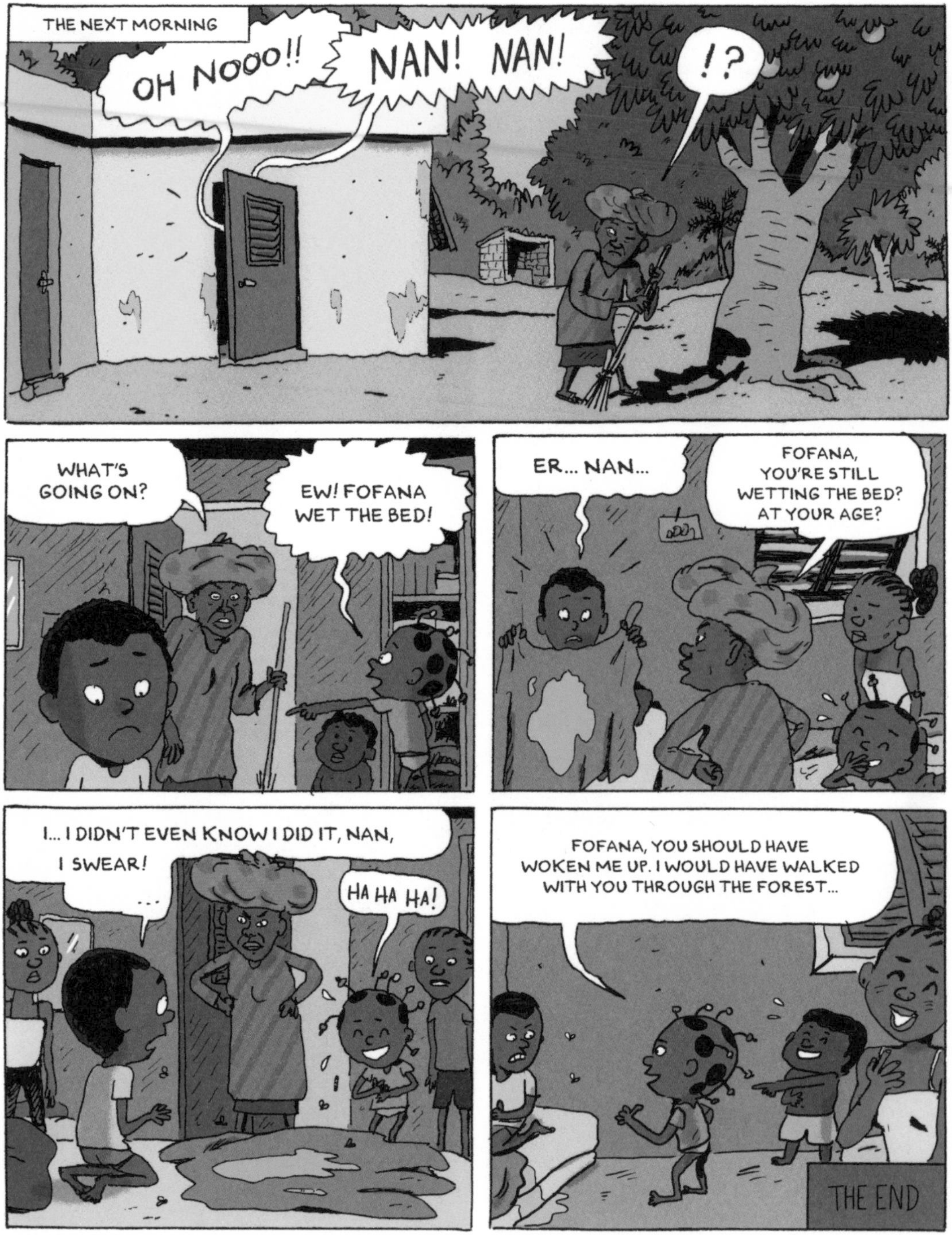
THE NEXT MORNING
OH NOOO!!
NAN! NAN!
!?
WHAT'S GOING ON?
EW! FOFANA WET THE BED!
ER... NAN...
FOFANA, YOU'RE STILL WETTING THE BED? AT YOUR AGE?
I... I DIDN'T EVEN KNOW I DID IT, NAN, I SWEAR!
...
HA HA HA!
FOFANA, YOU SHOULD HAVE WOKEN ME UP. I WOULD HAVE WALKED WITH YOU THROUGH THE FOREST...
THE END

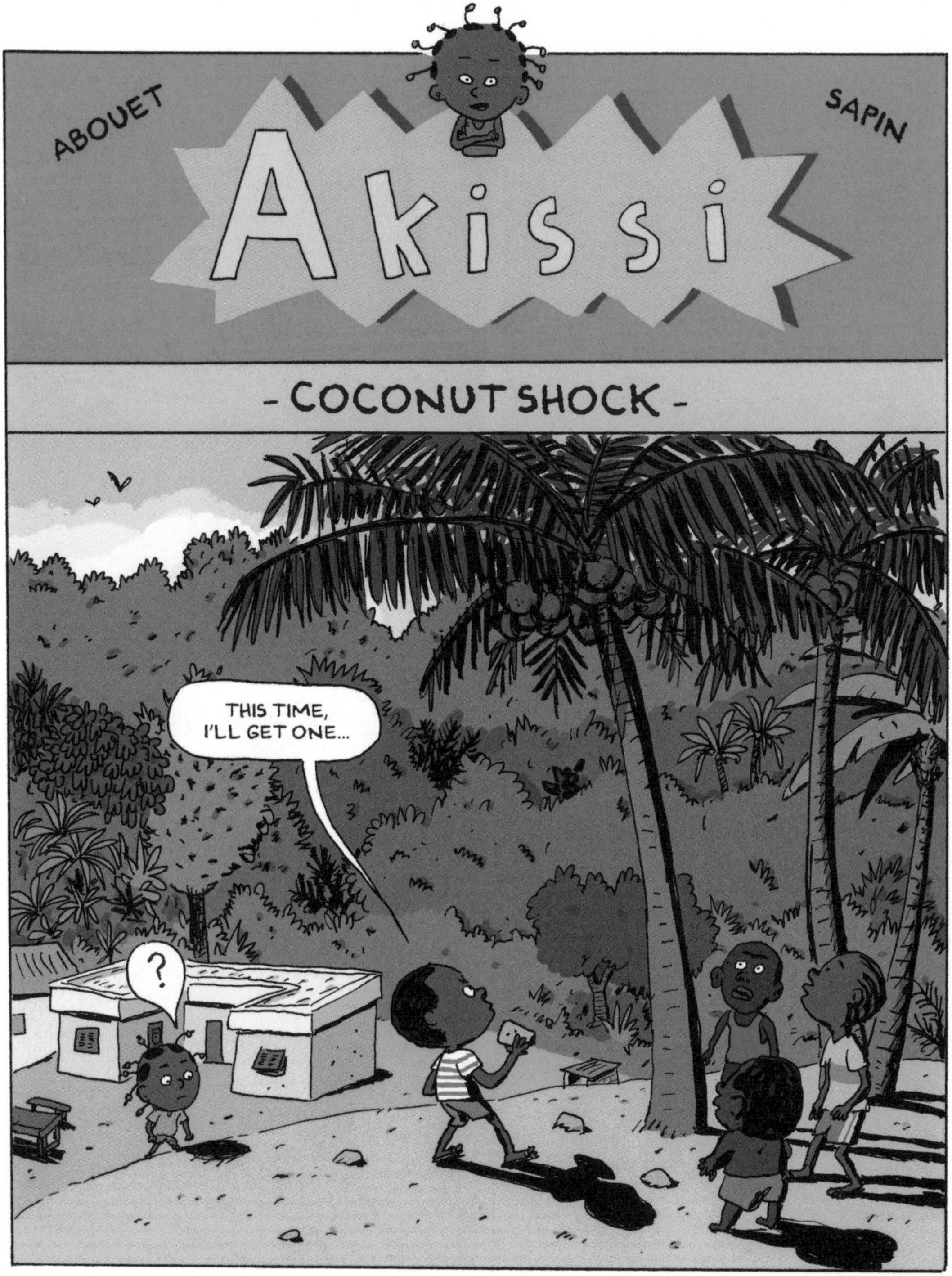
ABOUET
SAPIN
Akissi
- COCONUT SHOCK -
THIS TIME, I'LL GET ONE...
?

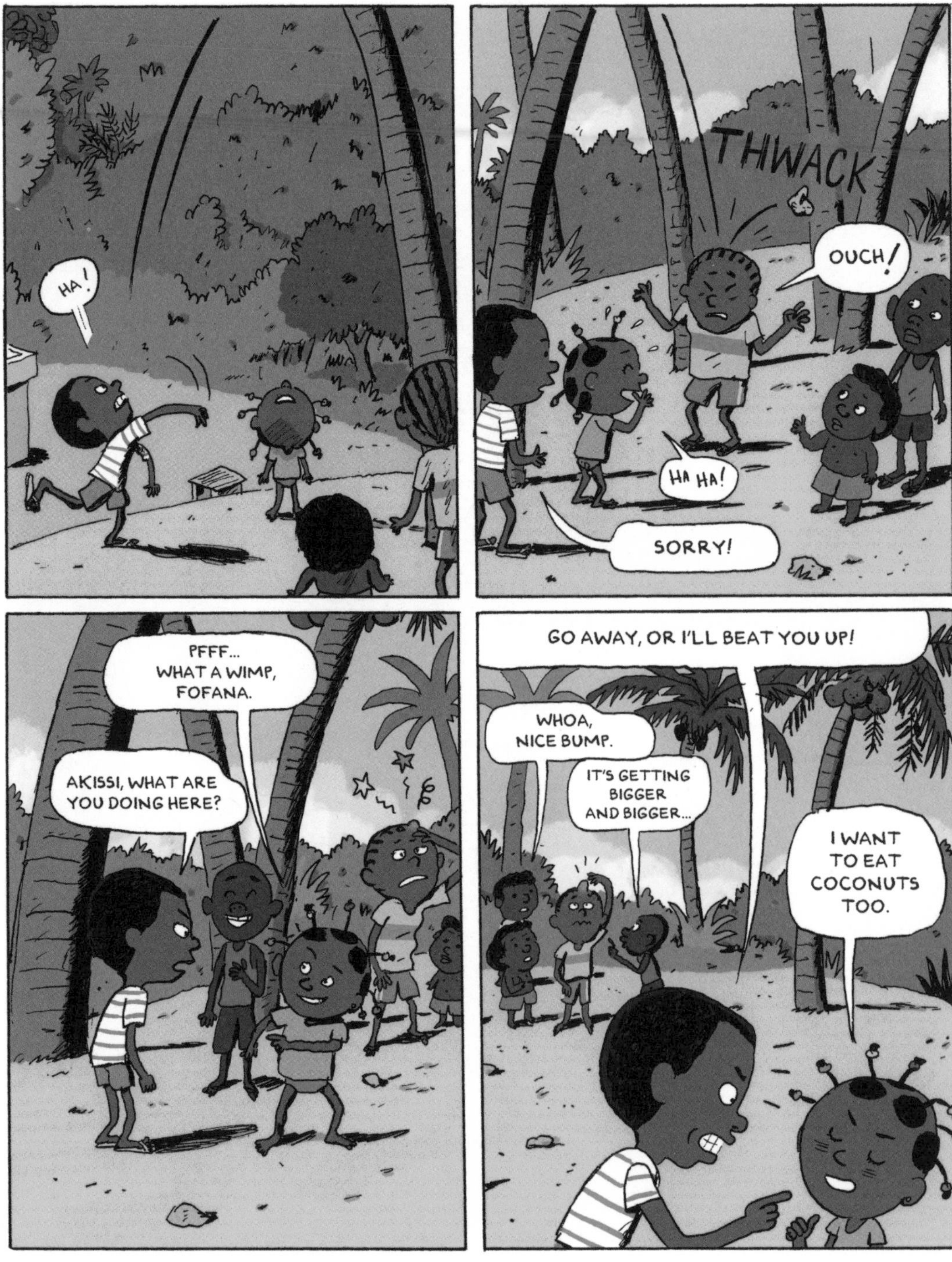

HA!
THWACK
OUCH!
HA HA!
SORRY!
PFFF... WHAT A WIMP, FOFANA.
AKISSI, WHAT ARE YOU DOING HERE?
GO AWAY, OR I'LL BEAT YOU UP!
WHOA, NICE BUMP.
IT'S GETTING BIGGER AND BIGGER...
I WANT TO EAT COCONUTS TOO.

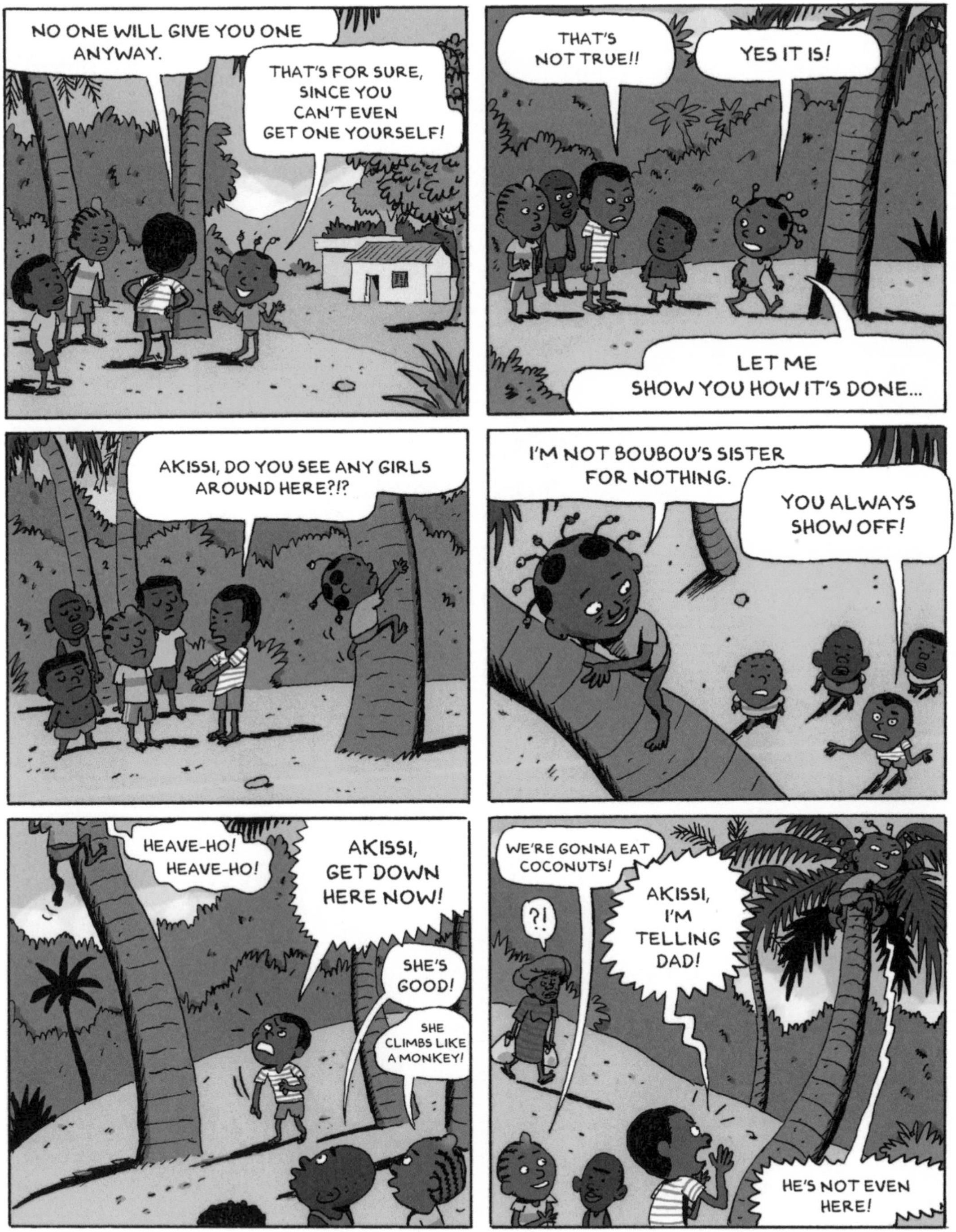
NO ONE WILL GIVE YOU ONE ANYWAY.
THAT'S FOR SURE, SINCE YOU CAN'T EVEN GET ONE YOURSELF!
THAT'S NOT TRUE!!
YES IT IS!
LET ME SHOW YOU HOW IT'S DONE...
AKISSI, DO YOU SEE ANY GIRLS AROUND HERE?!?
I'M NOT BOUBOU'S SISTER FOR NOTHING.
YOU ALWAYS SHOW OFF!
HEAVE-HO! HEAVE-HO!
AKISSI, GET DOWN HERE NOW!
SHE'S GOOD!
SHE CLIMBS LIKE A MONKEY!
WE'RE GONNA EAT COCONUTS!
?!
AKISSI, I'M TELLING DAD!
HE'S NOT EVEN HERE!

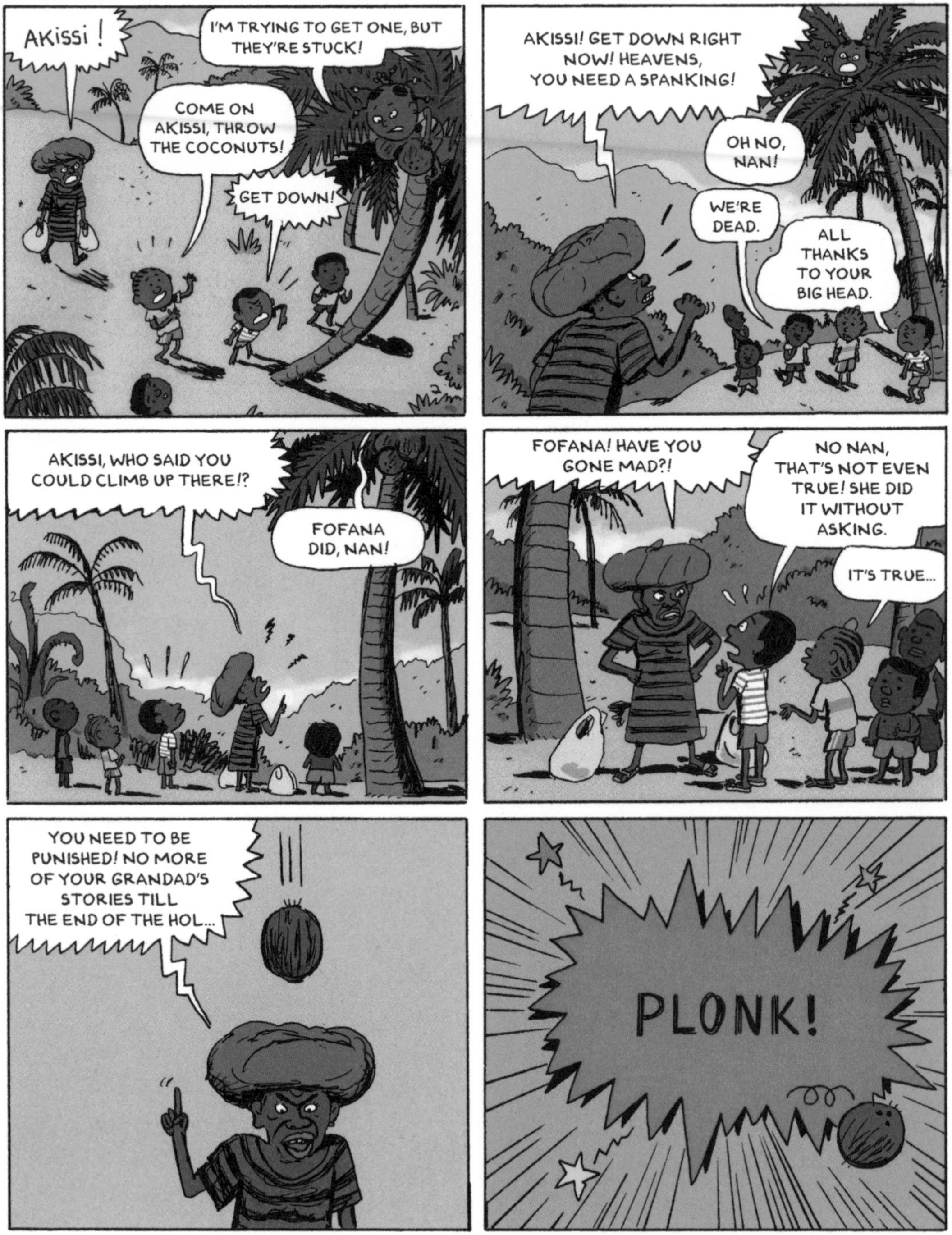
AKISSI!
I'M TRYING TO GET ONE, BUT THEY'RE STUCK!
COME ON AKISSI, THROW THE COCONUTS!
GET DOWN!
AKISSI! GET DOWN RIGHT NOW! HEAVENS, YOU NEED A SPANKING!
OH NO, NAN!
WE'RE DEAD.
ALL THANKS TO YOUR BIG HEAD.
AKISSI, WHO SAID YOU COULD CLIMB UP THERE!?
FOFANA DID, NAN!
FOFANA! HAVE YOU GONE MAD?!
NO NAN, THAT'S NOT EVEN TRUE! SHE DID IT WITHOUT ASKING.
IT'S TRUE...
YOU NEED TO BE PUNISHED! NO MORE OF YOUR GRANDAD'S STORIES TILL THE END OF THE HOL...
PLONK!

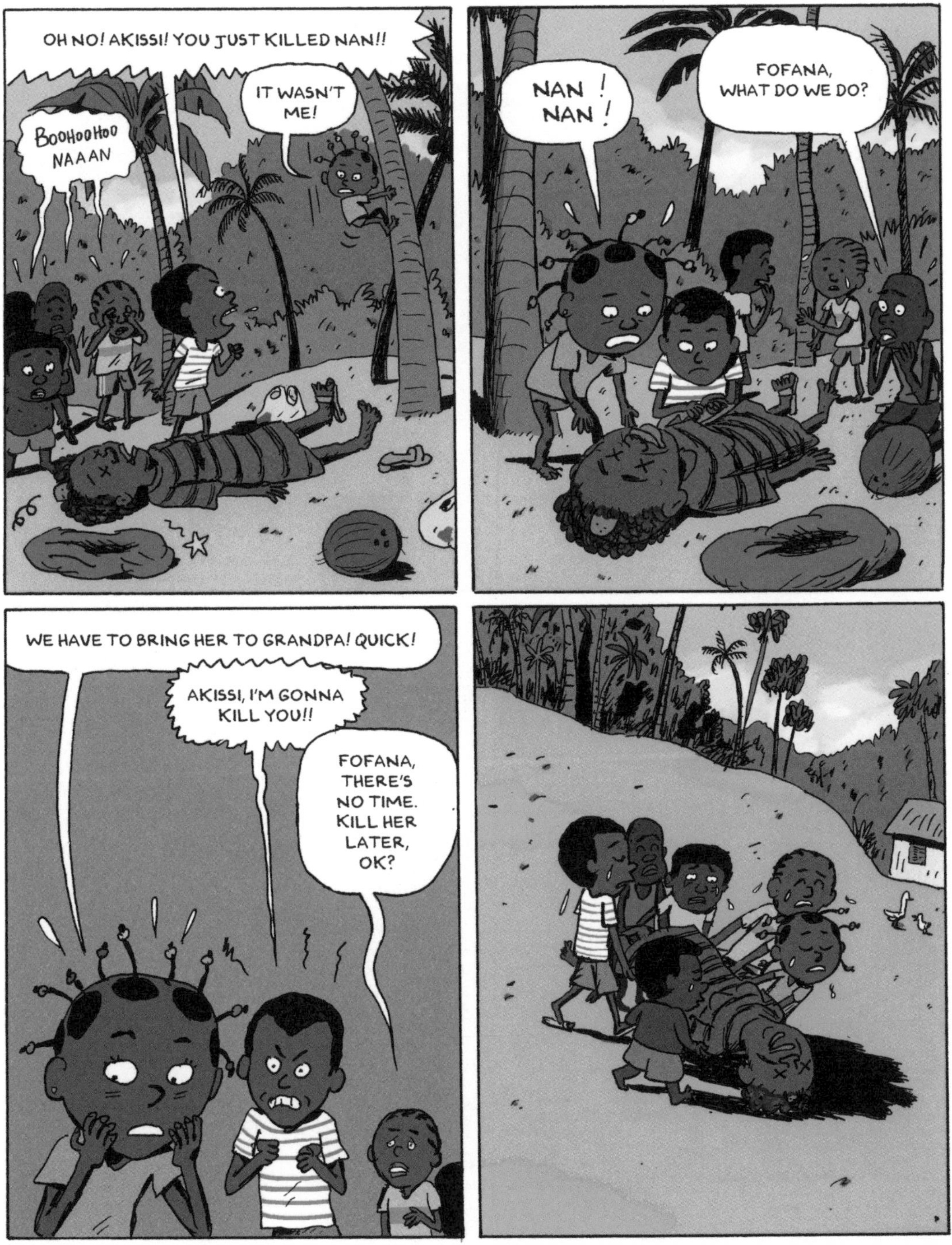
OH NO! AKISSI! YOU JUST KILLED NAN!!
BOOHOOHOO NAAAN
IT WASN'T ME!
NAN! NAN!
FOFANA, WHAT DO WE DO?
WE HAVE TO BRING HER TO GRANDPA! QUICK!
AKISSI, I'M GONNA KILL YOU!!
FOFANA, THERE'S NO TIME. KILL HER LATER, OK?

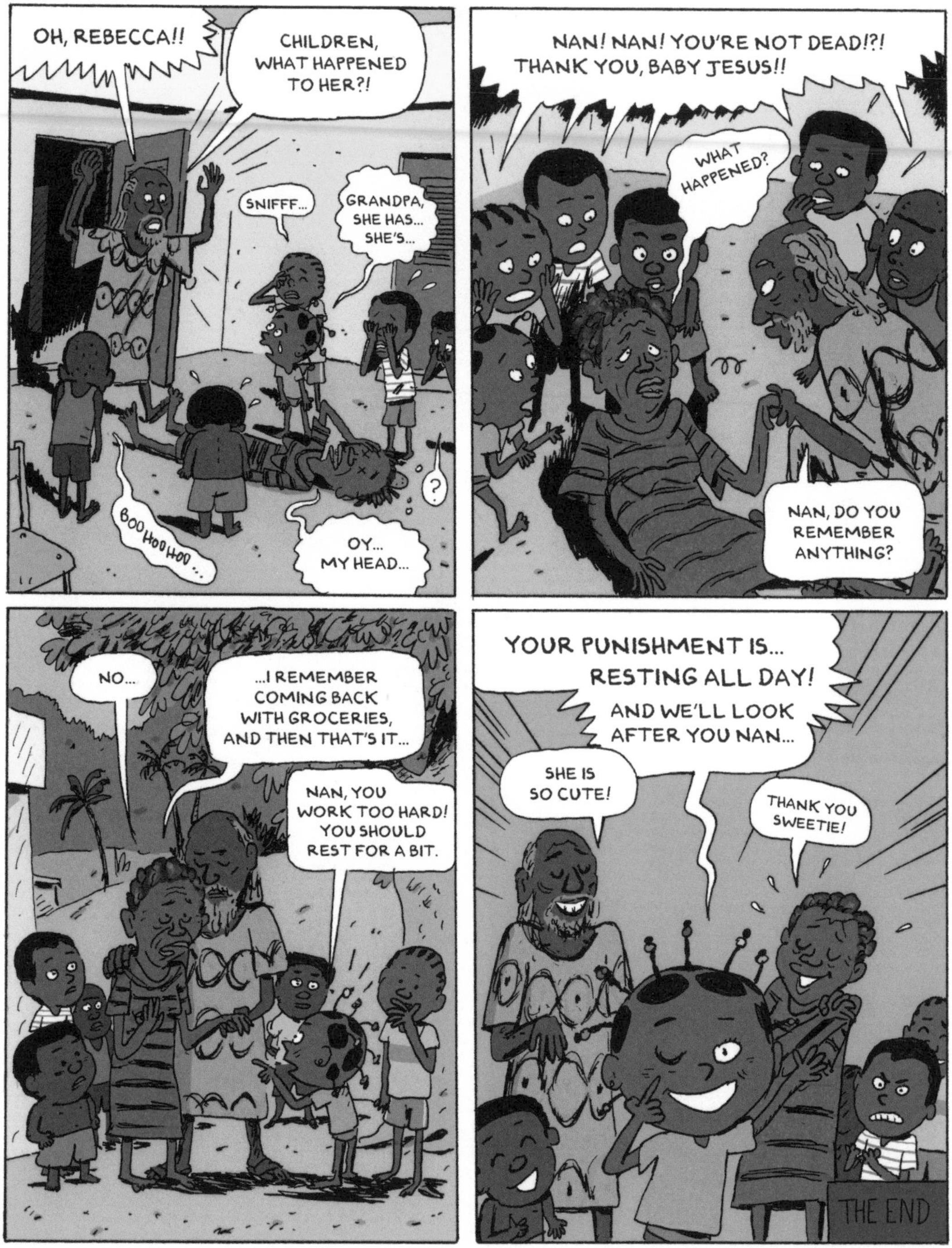
OH, REBECCA!!
CHILDREN, WHAT HAPPENED TO HER?!
SNIFFF...
GRANDPA, SHE HAS... SHE'S...
?
BOO HOO HOO...
OY... MY HEAD...
NAN! NAN! YOU'RE NOT DEAD!?! THANK YOU, BABY JESUS!!
WHAT HAPPENED?
NAN, DO YOU REMEMBER ANYTHING?
NO...
...I REMEMBER COMING BACK WITH GROCERIES, AND THEN THAT'S IT...
NAN, YOU WORK TOO HARD! YOU SHOULD REST FOR A BIT.
YOUR PUNISHMENT IS... RESTING ALL DAY!
AND WE'LL LOOK AFTER YOU NAN...
SHE IS SO CUTE!
THANK YOU SWEETIE!
THE END

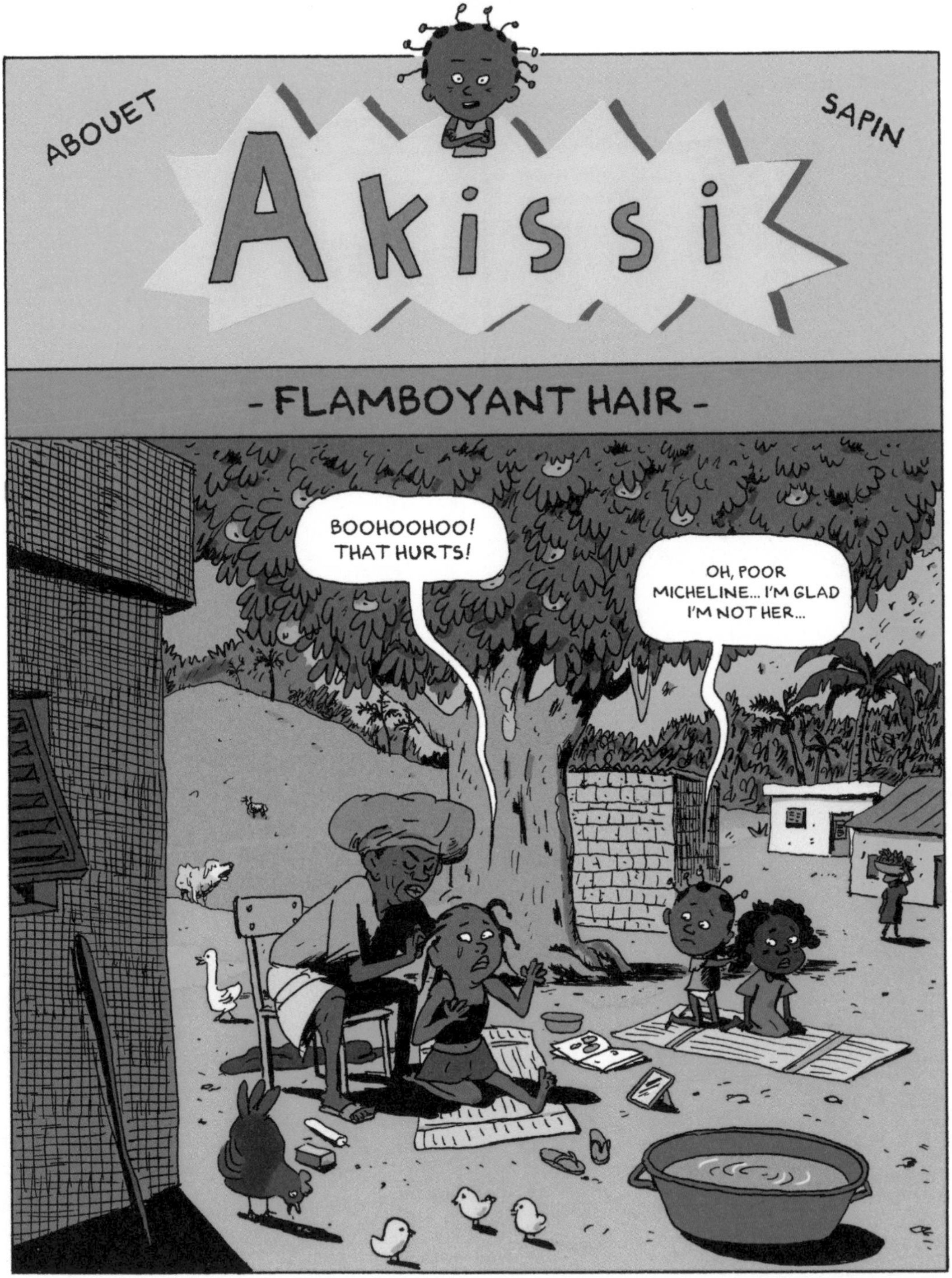
ABOUET
SAPIN
Akissi
- FLAMBOYANT HAIR -
BOOHOOHOO! THAT HURTS!
OH, POOR MICHELINE... I'M GLAD I'M NOT HER...

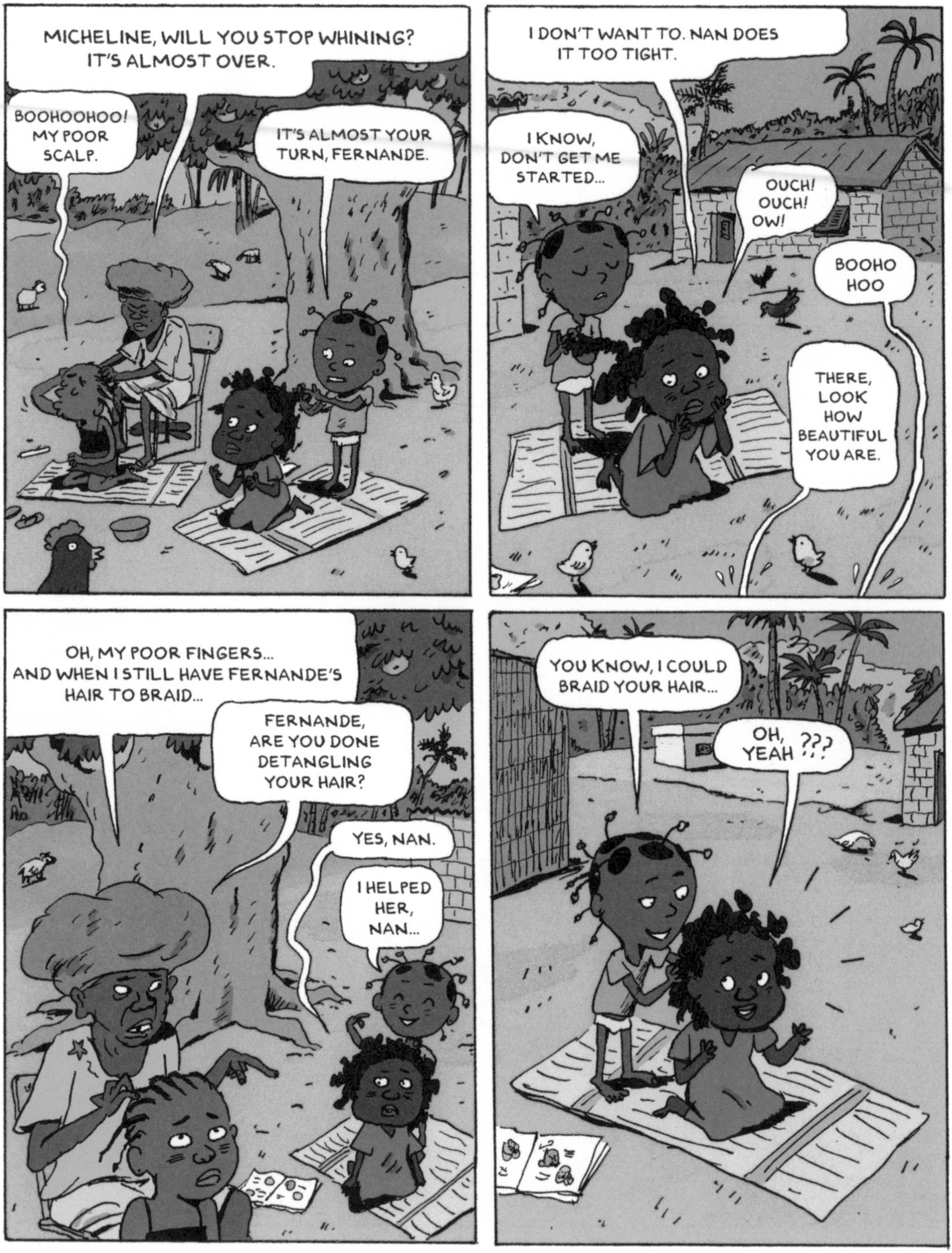
MICHELINE, WILL YOU STOP WHINING? IT'S ALMOST OVER.
BOOHOOHOO! MY POOR SCALP.
IT'S ALMOST YOUR TURN, FERNANDE.
I DON'T WANT TO. NAN DOES IT TOO TIGHT.
I KNOW, DON'T GET ME STARTED...
OUCH! OUCH! OW!
BOOHO HOO
THERE, LOOK HOW BEAUTIFUL YOU ARE.
OH, MY POOR FINGERS... AND WHEN I STILL HAVE FERNANDE'S HAIR TO BRAID...
FERNANDE, ARE YOU DONE DETANGLING YOUR HAIR?
YES, NAN.
I HELPED HER, NAN...
YOU KNOW, I COULD BRAID YOUR HAIR...
OH, YEAH ???

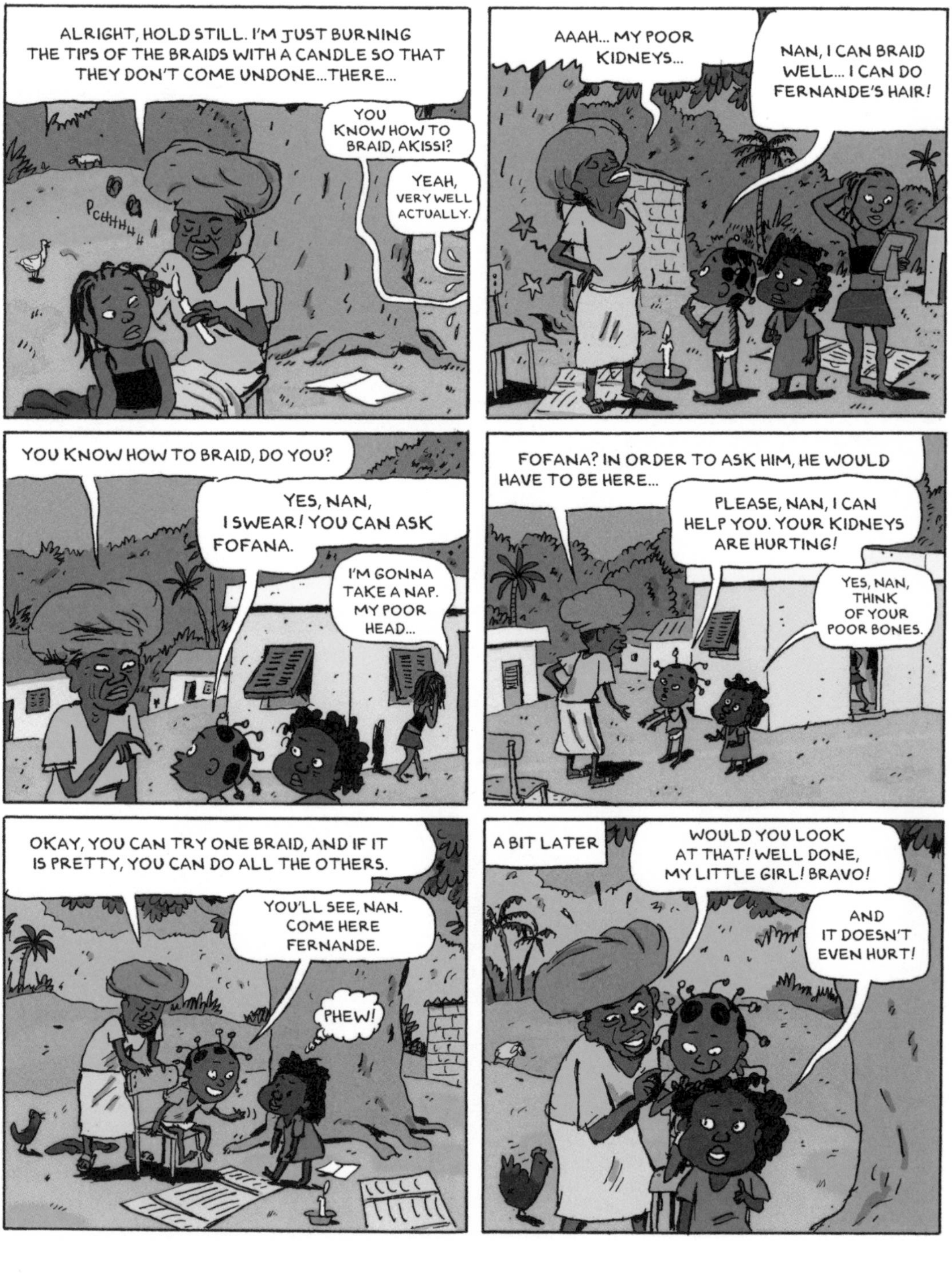
ALRIGHT, HOLD STILL. I'M JUST BURNING THE TIPS OF THE BRAIDS WITH A CANDLE SO THAT THEY DON'T COME UNDONE...THERE...
YOU KNOW HOW TO BRAID, AKISSI?
YEAH, VERY WELL ACTUALLY.
PCHHHHH
AAAH... MY POOR KIDNEYS...
NAN, I CAN BRAID WELL... I CAN DO FERNANDE'S HAIR!
YOU KNOW HOW TO BRAID, DO YOU?
YES, NAN, I SWEAR! YOU CAN ASK FOFANA.
I'M GONNA TAKE A NAP. MY POOR HEAD...
FOFANA? IN ORDER TO ASK HIM, HE WOULD HAVE TO BE HERE...
PLEASE, NAN, I CAN HELP YOU. YOUR KIDNEYS ARE HURTING!
YES, NAN, THINK OF YOUR POOR BONES.
OKAY, YOU CAN TRY ONE BRAID, AND IF IT IS PRETTY, YOU CAN DO ALL THE OTHERS.
YOU'LL SEE, NAN. COME HERE FERNANDE.
PHEW!
A BIT LATER
WOULD YOU LOOK AT THAT! WELL DONE, MY LITTLE GIRL! BRAVO!
AND IT DOESN'T EVEN HURT!

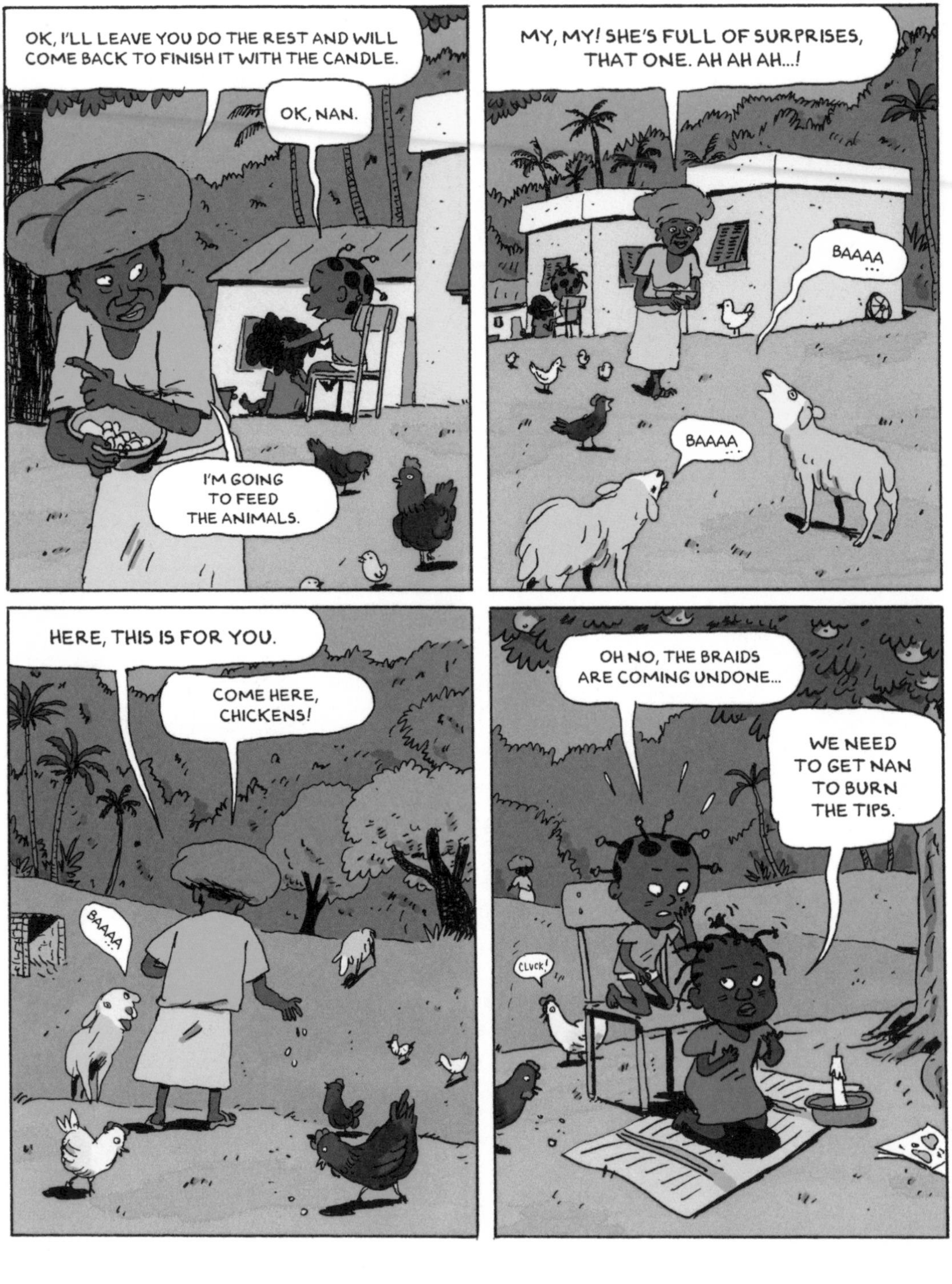
OK, I'LL LEAVE YOU DO THE REST AND WILL COME BACK TO FINISH IT WITH THE CANDLE.
OK, NAN.
I'M GOING TO FEED THE ANIMALS.
MY, MY! SHE'S FULL OF SURPRISES, THAT ONE. AH AH AH...!
BAAAA...
BAAAA...
HERE, THIS IS FOR YOU.
COME HERE, CHICKENS!
BAAAA...
OH NO, THE BRAIDS ARE COMING UNDONE...
WE NEED TO GET NAN TO BURN THE TIPS.
CLUCK!

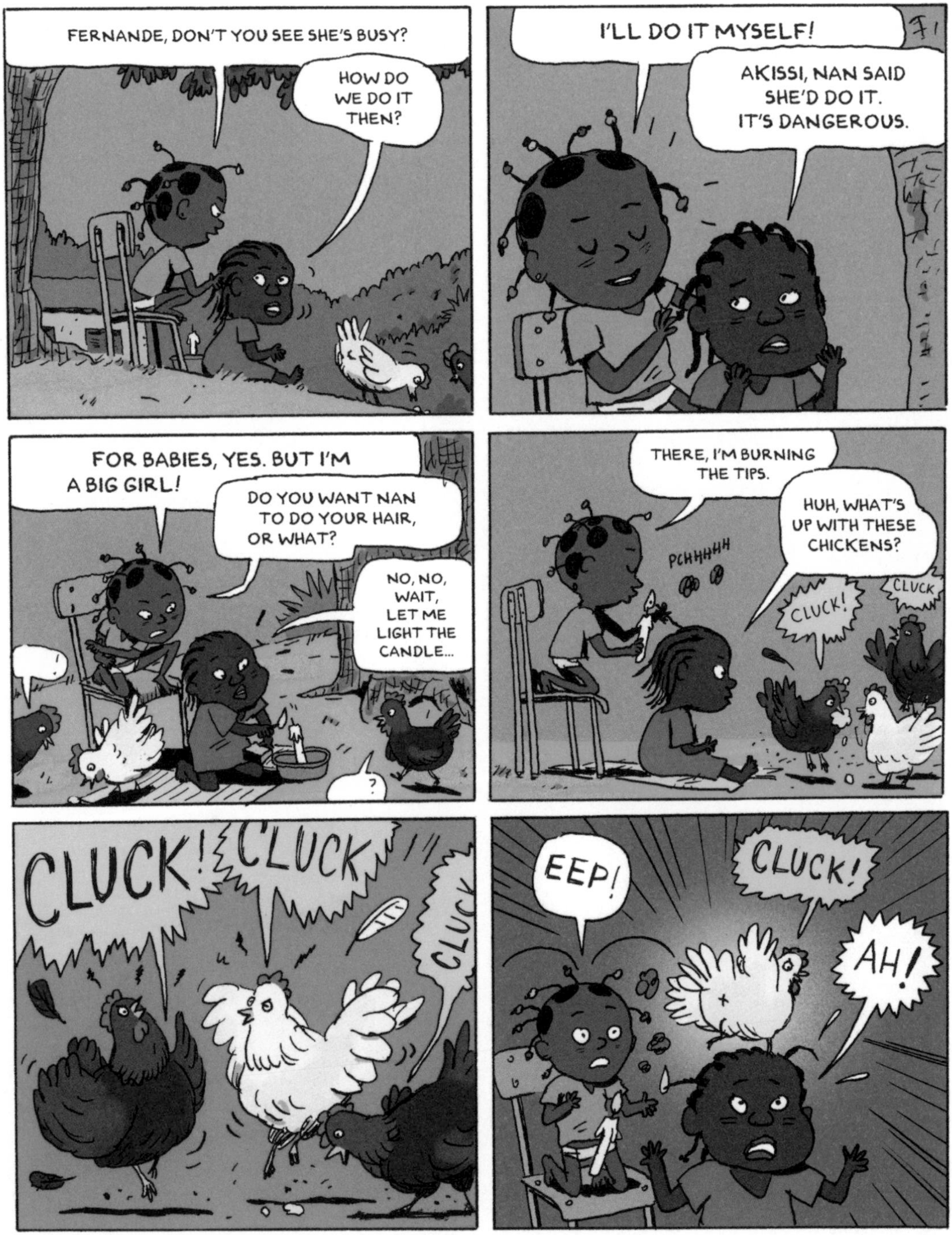
FERNANDE, DON'T YOU SEE SHE'S BUSY?
HOW DO WE DO IT THEN?
I'LL DO IT MYSELF!
AKISSI, NAN SAID SHE'D DO IT. IT'S DANGEROUS.
FOR BABIES, YES. BUT I'M A BIG GIRL!
DO YOU WANT NAN TO DO YOUR HAIR, OR WHAT?
NO, NO, WAIT, LET ME LIGHT THE CANDLE...
?
THERE, I'M BURNING THE TIPS.
PCHHHHH
HUH, WHAT'S UP WITH THESE CHICKENS?
CLUCK!
CLUCK
CLUCK!
CLUCK
CLUCK
EEP!
CLUCK!
AH!

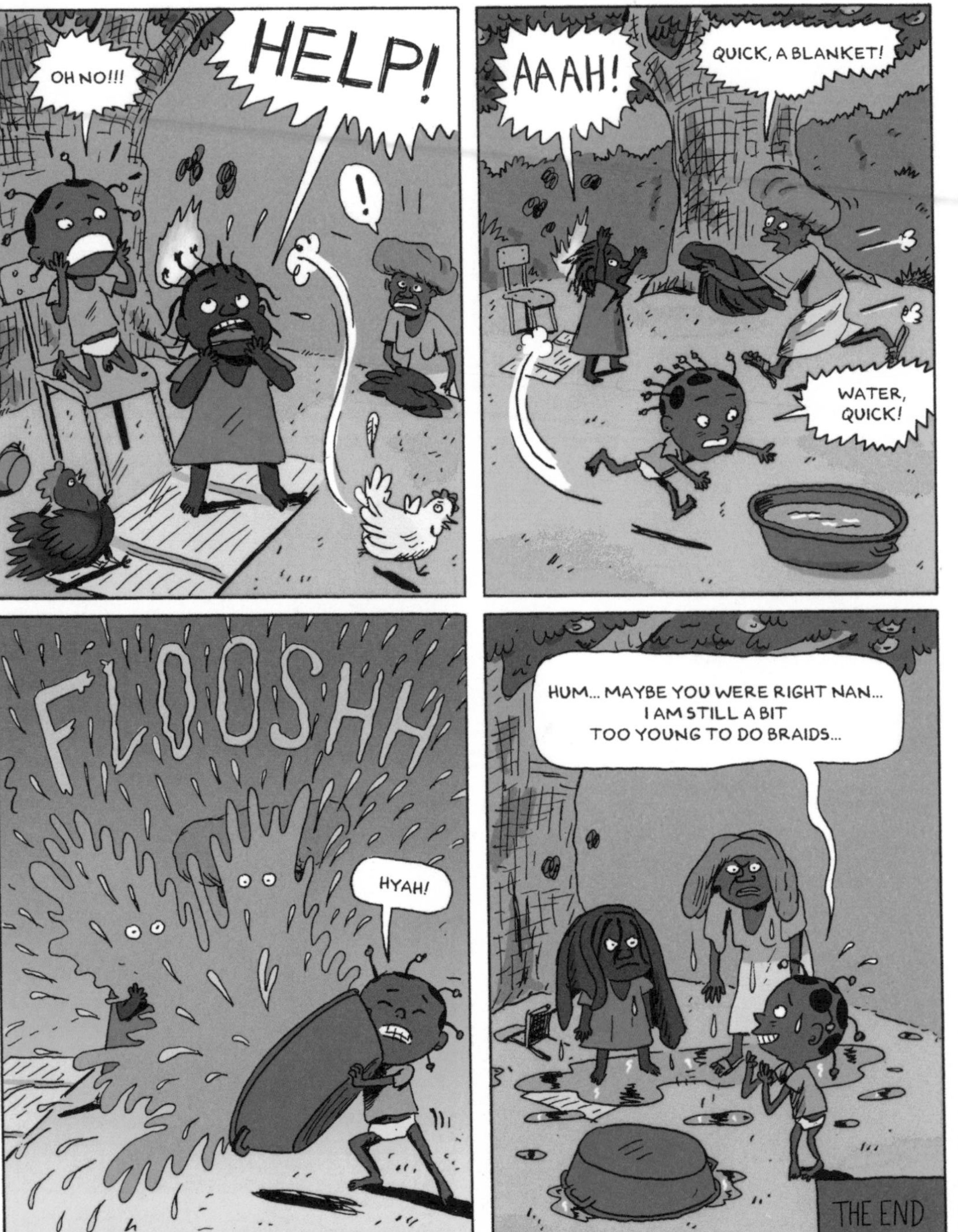
OH NO!!!
HELP!
!
AAAH!
QUICK, A BLANKET!
WATER, QUICK!
FLOOSHH
HYAH!
HUM... MAYBE YOU WERE RIGHT NAN... I AM STILL A BIT TOO YOUNG TO DO BRAIDS...
THE END

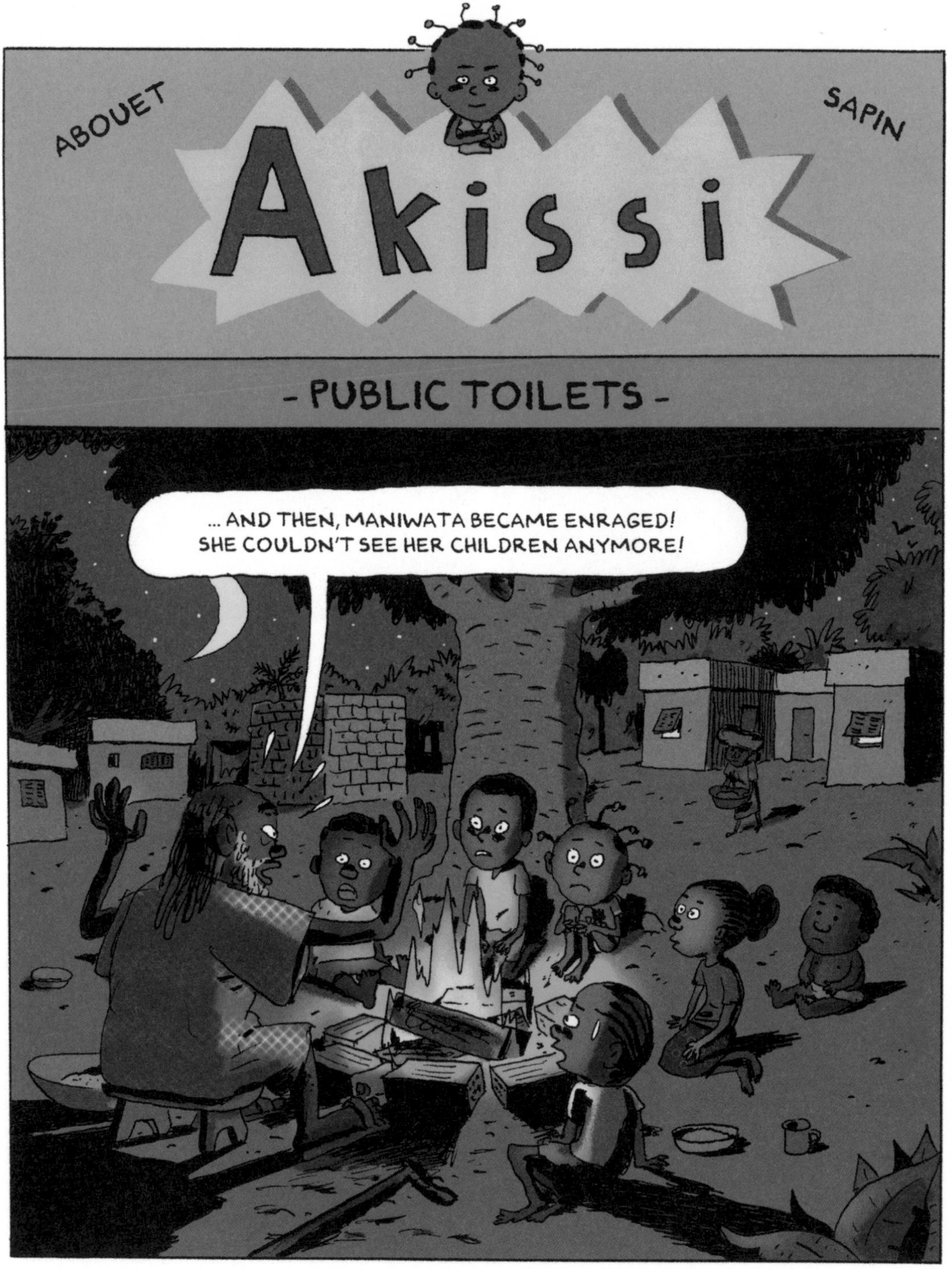
ABOUET
Akissi
SAPIN
- PUBLIC TOILETS -
... AND THEN, MANIWATA BECAME ENRAGED! SHE COULDN'T SEE HER CHILDREN ANYMORE!

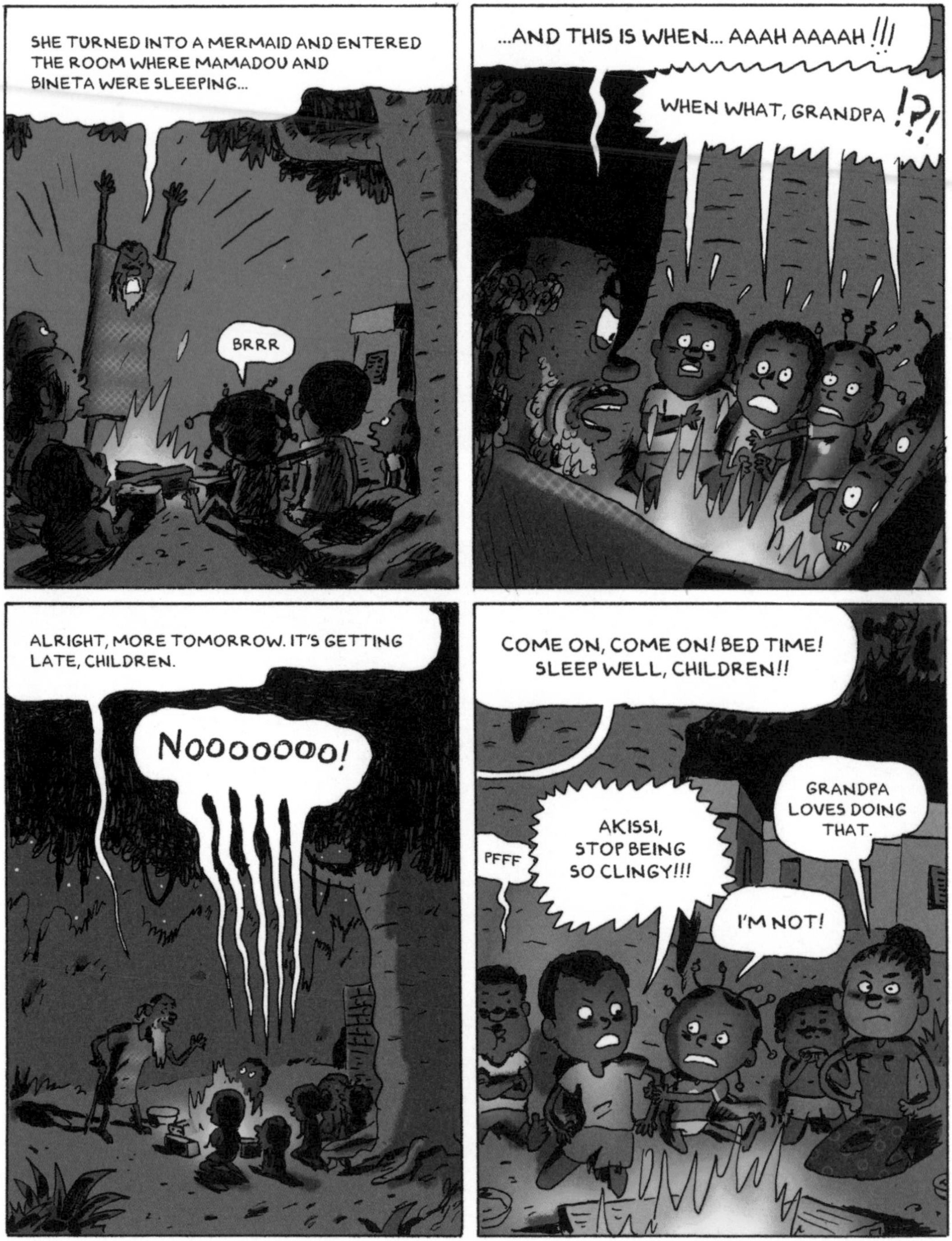
SHE TURNED INTO A MERMAID AND ENTERED THE ROOM WHERE MAMADOU AND BINETA WERE SLEEPING...
BRRR
...AND THIS IS WHEN... AAAH AAAAH !!!
WHEN WHAT, GRANDPA !?!
ALRIGHT, MORE TOMORROW. IT'S GETTING LATE, CHILDREN.
NOOOOOOO!
COME ON, COME ON! BED TIME! SLEEP WELL, CHILDREN!!
PFFF
AKISSI, STOP BEING SO CLINGY!!!
GRANDPA LOVES DOING THAT.
I'M NOT!

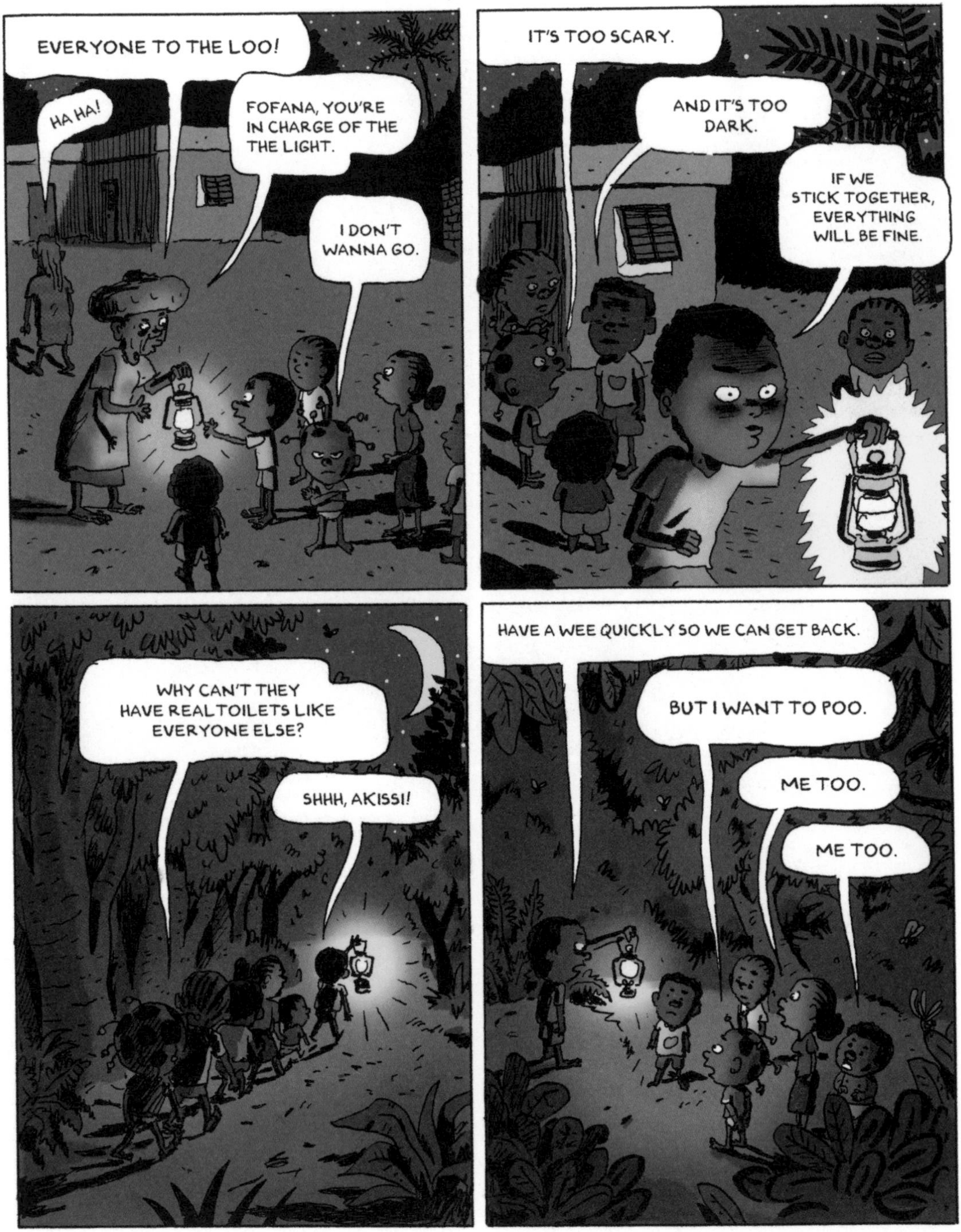
EVERYONE TO THE LOO!
HA HA!
FOFANA, YOU'RE IN CHARGE OF THE THE LIGHT.
I DON'T WANNA GO.
IT'S TOO SCARY.
AND IT'S TOO DARK.
IF WE STICK TOGETHER, EVERYTHING WILL BE FINE.
WHY CAN'T THEY HAVE REAL TOILETS LIKE EVERYONE ELSE?
SHHH, AKISSI!
HAVE A WEE QUICKLY SO WE CAN GET BACK.
BUT I WANT TO POO.
ME TOO.
ME TOO.

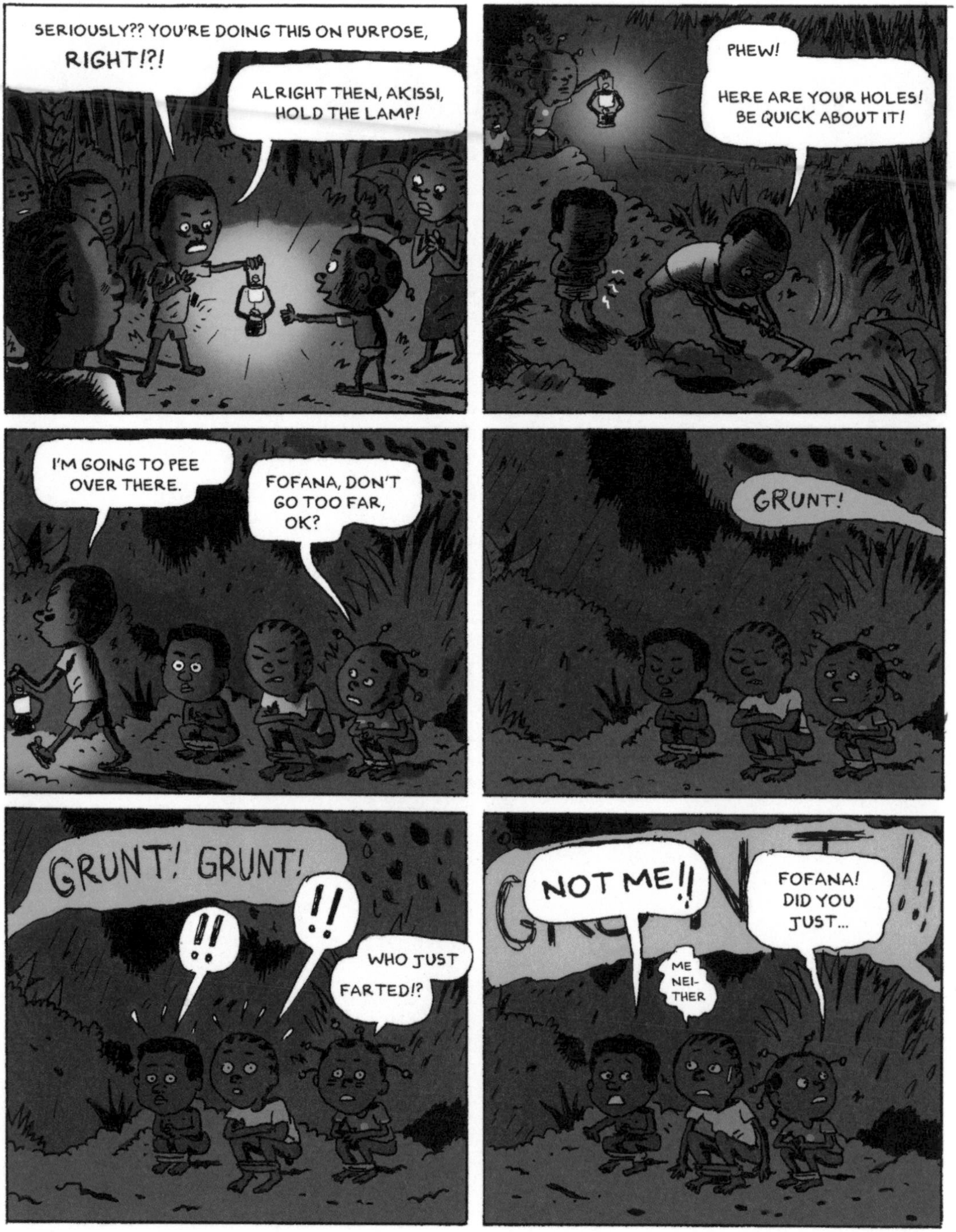
SERIOUSLY?? YOU'RE DOING THIS ON PURPOSE, RIGHT!?!
ALRIGHT THEN, AKISSI, HOLD THE LAMP!
PHEW!
HERE ARE YOUR HOLES! BE QUICK ABOUT IT!
I'M GOING TO PEE OVER THERE.
FOFANA, DON'T GO TOO FAR, OK?
GRUNT!
GRUNT! GRUNT!
!!
!!
WHO JUST FARTED!?
NOT ME!!
ME NEI-THER
FOFANA! DID YOU JUST...

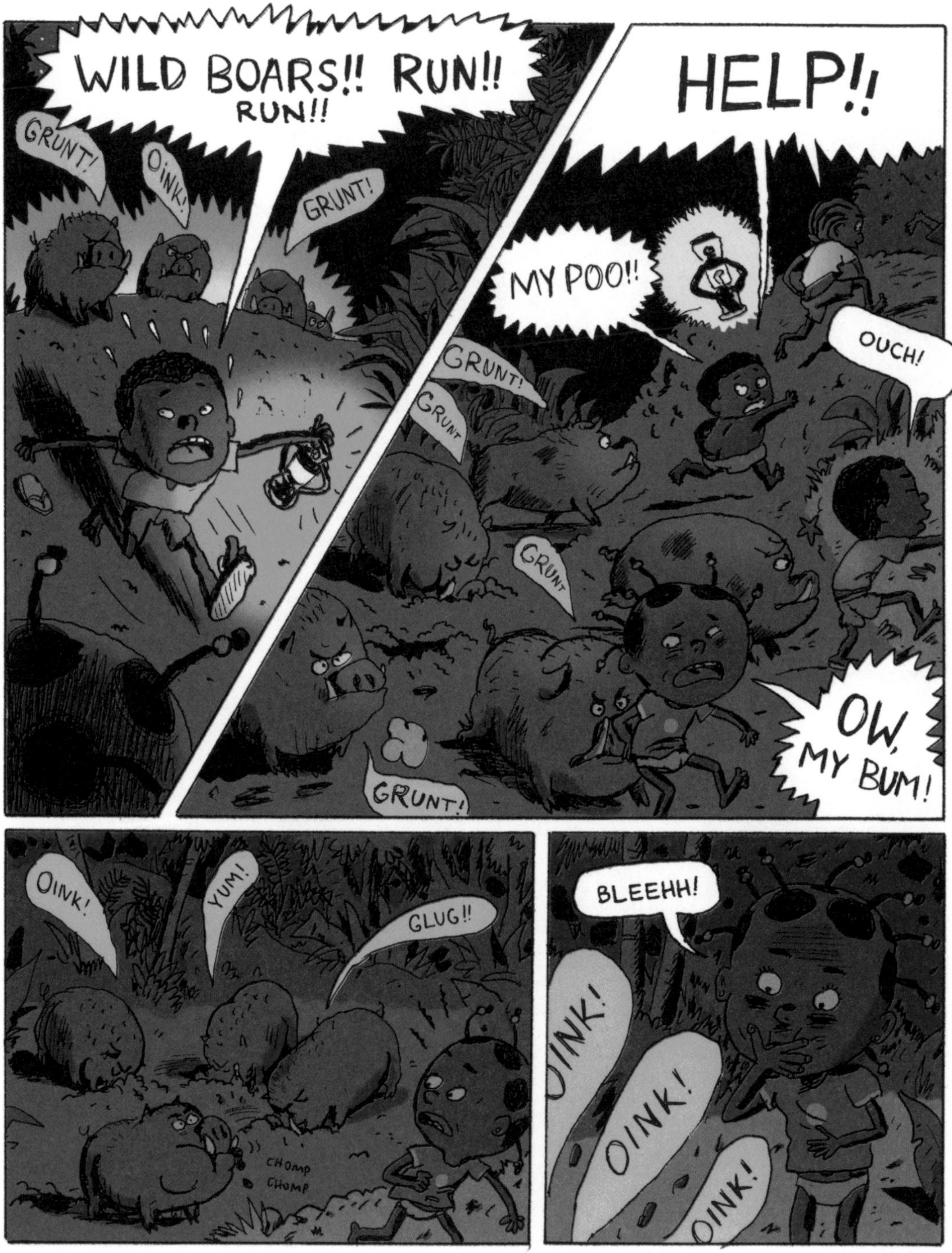
WILD BOARS!! RUN!!
RUN!!
GRUNT!
OINK!
GRUNT!
HELP!!
MY POO!!
GRUNT!
GRUNT
OUCH!
GRUNT
GRUNT!
OW, MY BUM!
OINK!
YUM!
GLUG!!
CHOMP CHOMP
BLEEHH!
OINK!
OINK!
OINK!

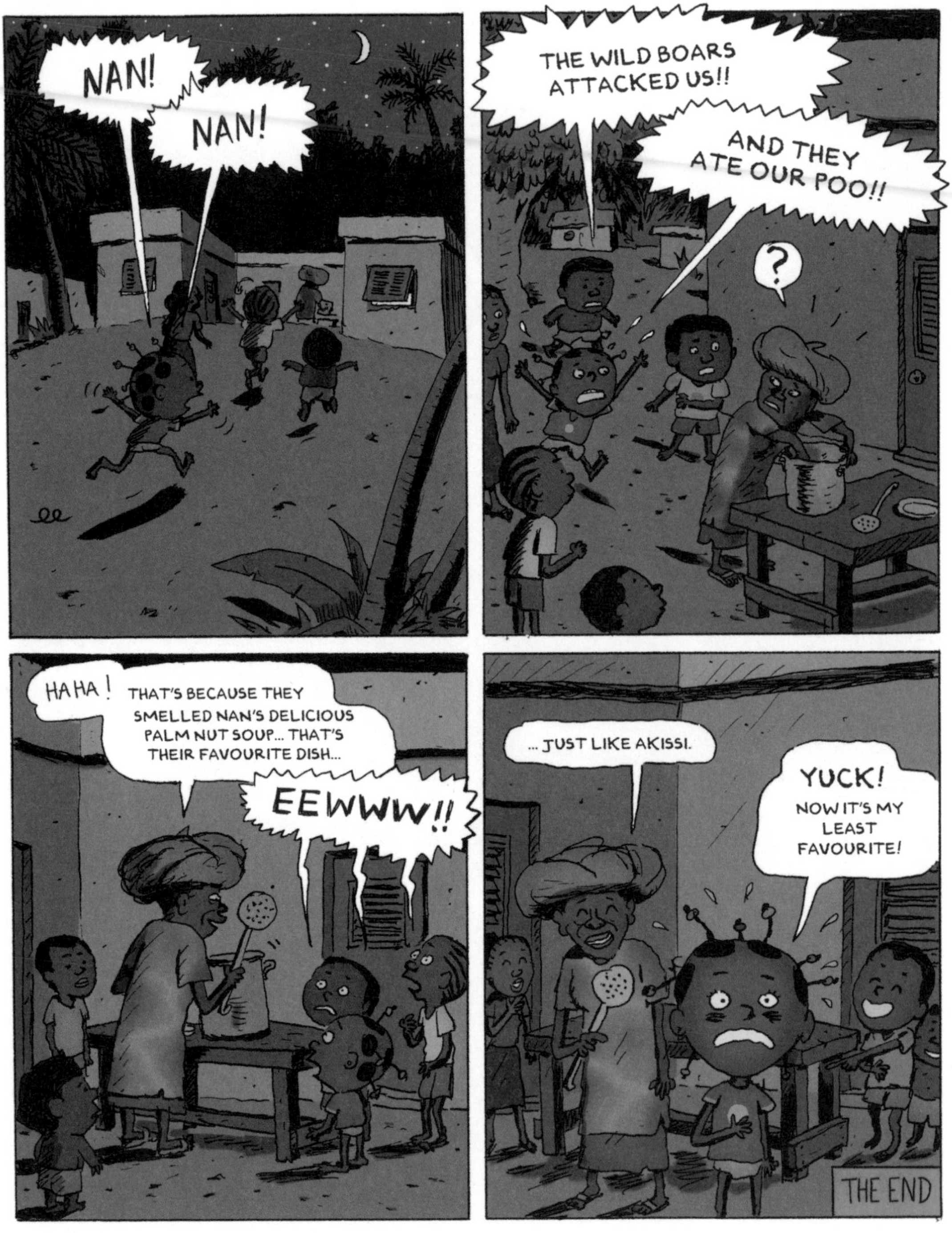
NAN!
NAN!
THE WILD BOARS ATTACKED US!!
AND THEY ATE OUR POO!!
?
HA HA! THAT'S BECAUSE THEY SMELLED NAN'S DELICIOUS PALM NUT SOUP... THAT'S THEIR FAVOURITE DISH...
EEWWW!!
... JUST LIKE AKISSI.
YUCK! NOW IT'S MY LEAST FAVOURITE!
THE END

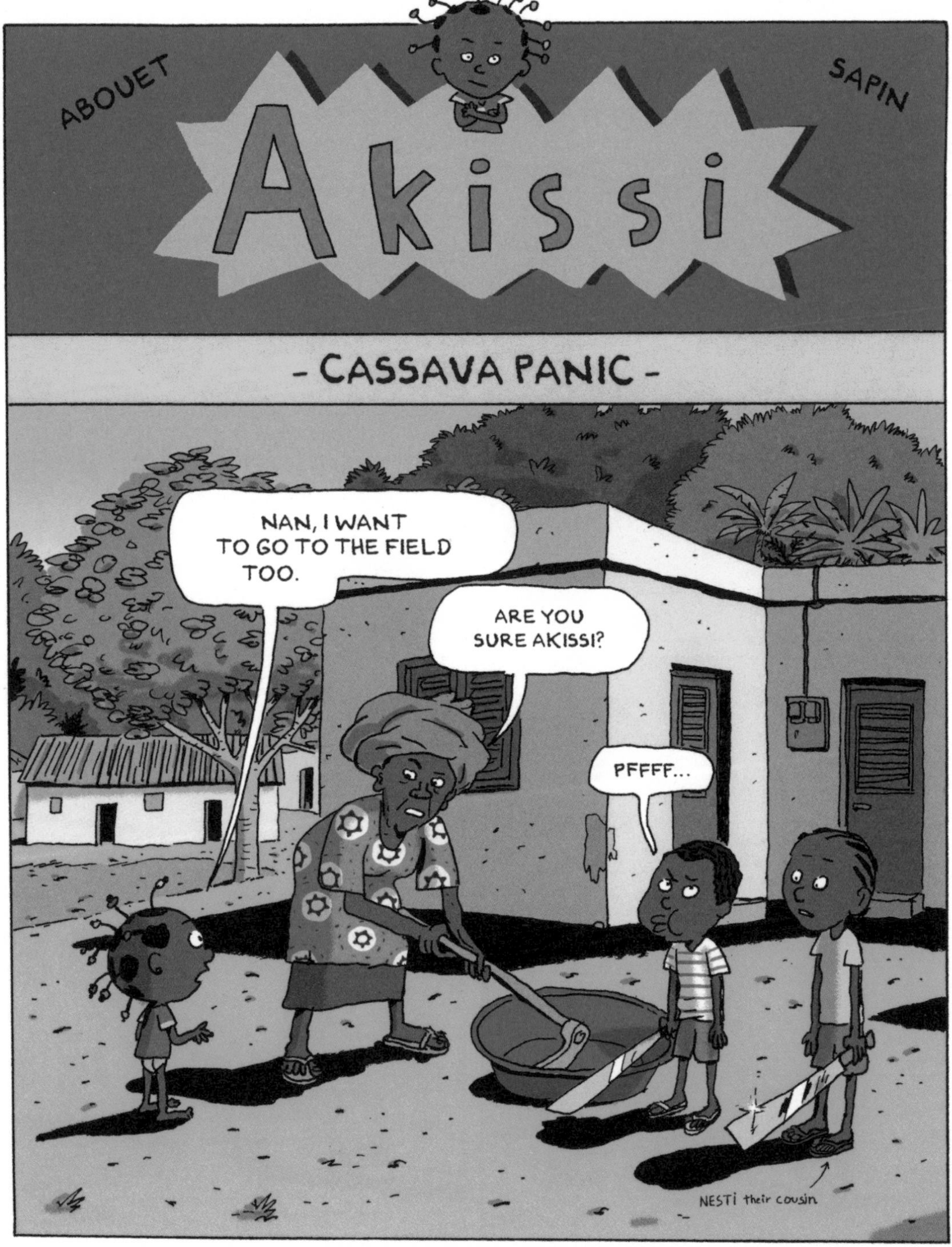
ABOUET
SAPIN
Akissi
- CASSAVA PANIC -
NAN, I WANT TO GO TO THE FIELD TOO.
ARE YOU SURE AKISSI?
PFFFF...
NESTI their cousin

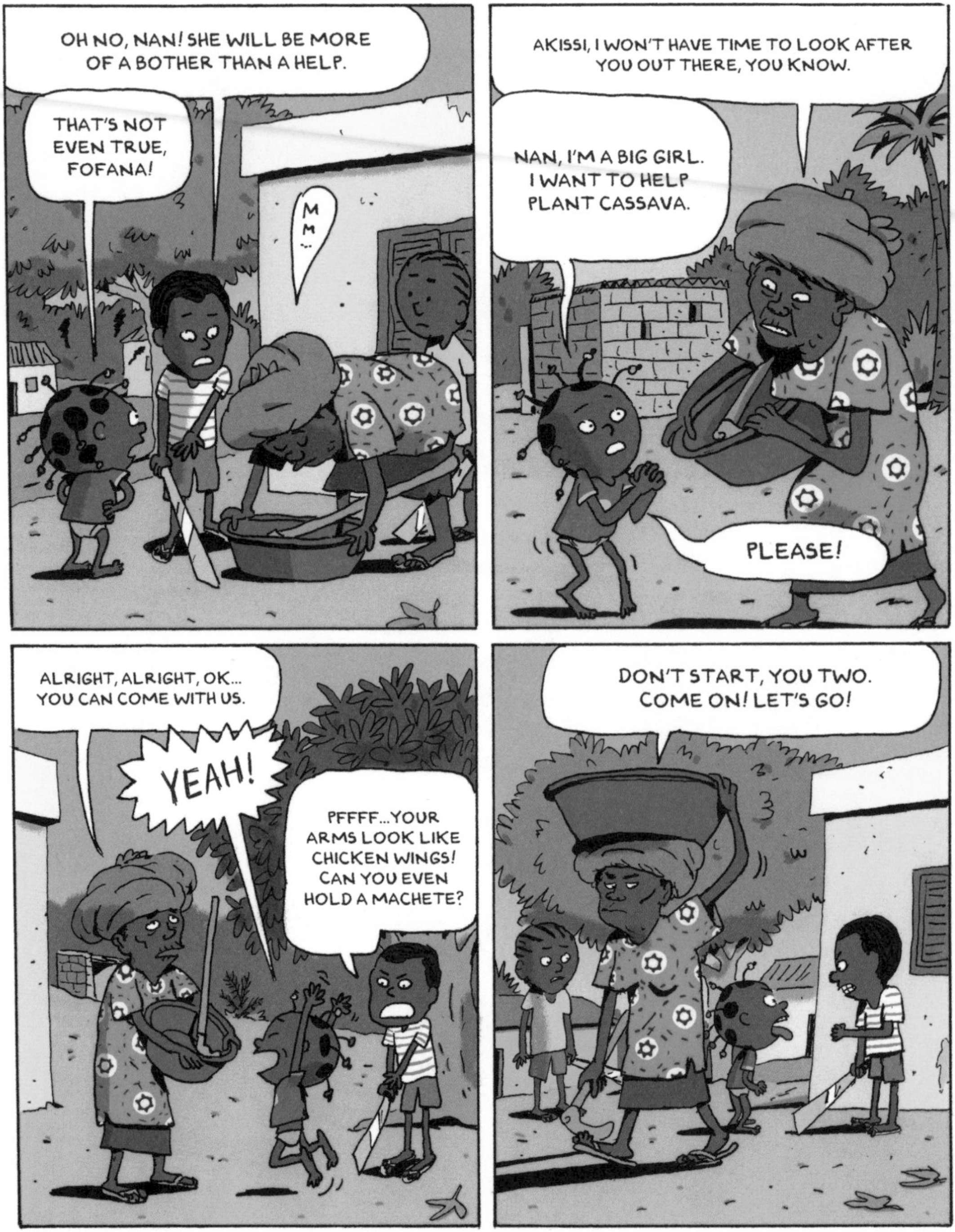
OH NO, NAN! SHE WILL BE MORE OF A BOTHER THAN A HELP.
THAT'S NOT EVEN TRUE, FOFANA!
MM...
AKISSI, I WON'T HAVE TIME TO LOOK AFTER YOU OUT THERE, YOU KNOW.
NAN, I'M A BIG GIRL. I WANT TO HELP PLANT CASSAVA.
PLEASE!
ALRIGHT, ALRIGHT, OK... YOU CAN COME WITH US.
YEAH!
PFFFF...YOUR ARMS LOOK LIKE CHICKEN WINGS! CAN YOU EVEN HOLD A MACHETE?
DON'T START, YOU TWO. COME ON! LET'S GO!

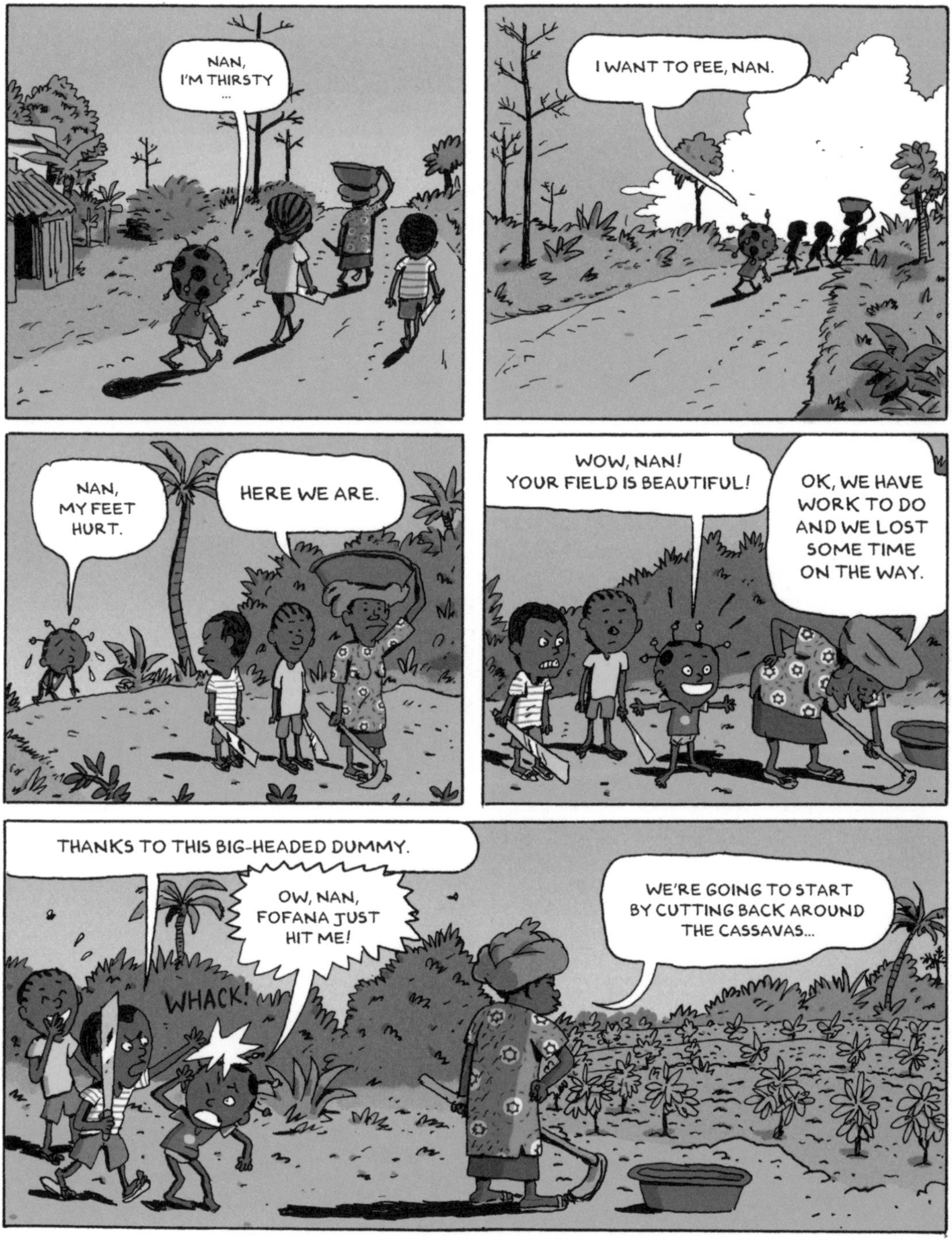
NAN, I'M THIRSTY ...
I WANT TO PEE, NAN.
NAN, MY FEET HURT.
HERE WE ARE.
WOW, NAN! YOUR FIELD IS BEAUTIFUL!
OK, WE HAVE WORK TO DO AND WE LOST SOME TIME ON THE WAY.
THANKS TO THIS BIG-HEADED DUMMY.
WHACK!
OW, NAN, FOFANA JUST HIT ME!
WE'RE GOING TO START BY CUTTING BACK AROUND THE CASSAVAS...

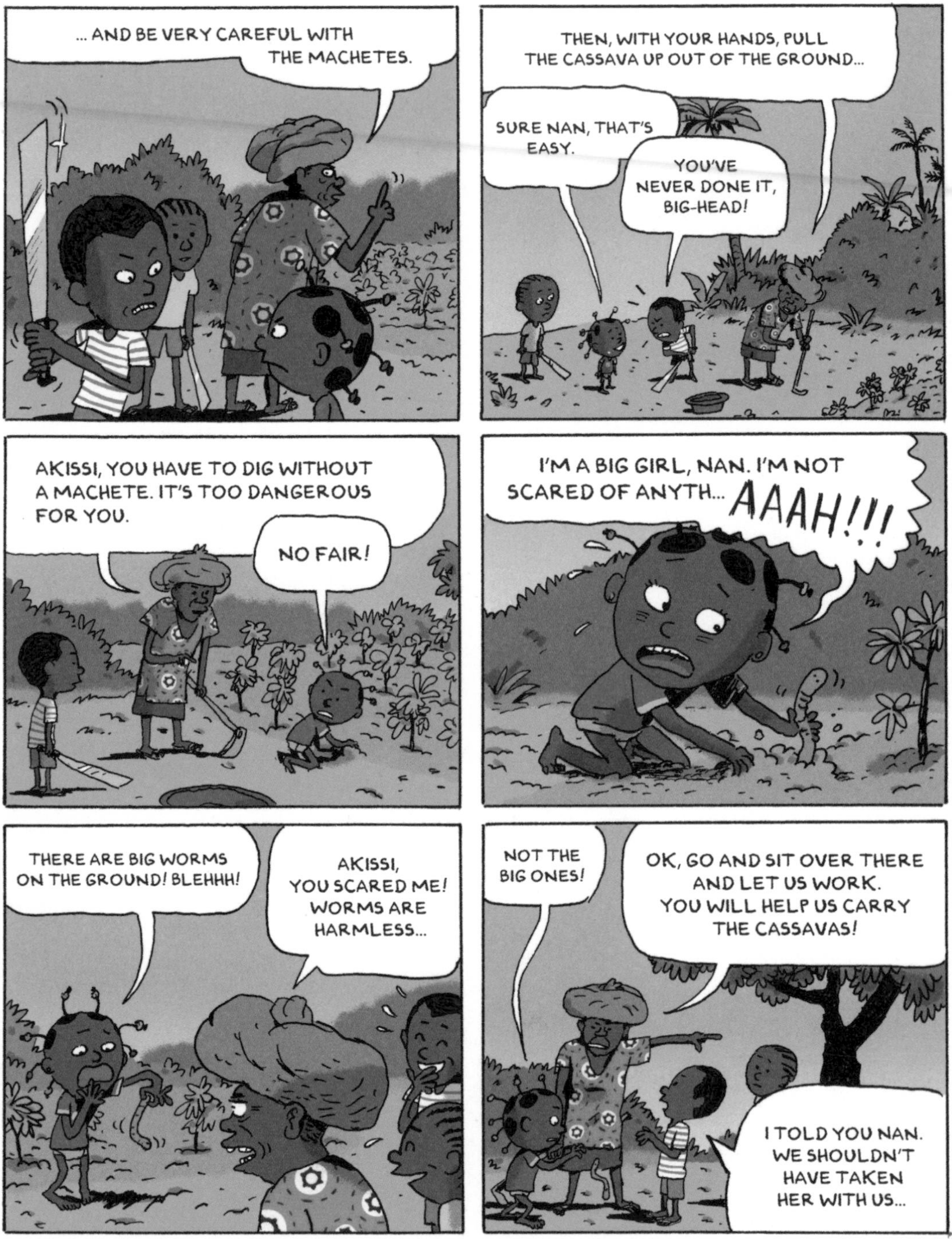
... AND BE VERY CAREFUL WITH THE MACHETES.
THEN, WITH YOUR HANDS, PULL THE CASSAVA UP OUT OF THE GROUND...
SURE NAN, THAT'S EASY.
YOU'VE NEVER DONE IT, BIG-HEAD!
AKISSI, YOU HAVE TO DIG WITHOUT A MACHETE. IT'S TOO DANGEROUS FOR YOU.
NO FAIR!
I'M A BIG GIRL, NAN. I'M NOT SCARED OF ANYTH... AAAH!!!
THERE ARE BIG WORMS ON THE GROUND! BLEHHH!
AKISSI, YOU SCARED ME! WORMS ARE HARMLESS...
NOT THE BIG ONES!
OK, GO AND SIT OVER THERE AND LET US WORK. YOU WILL HELP US CARRY THE CASSAVAS!
I TOLD YOU NAN. WE SHOULDN'T HAVE TAKEN HER WITH US...

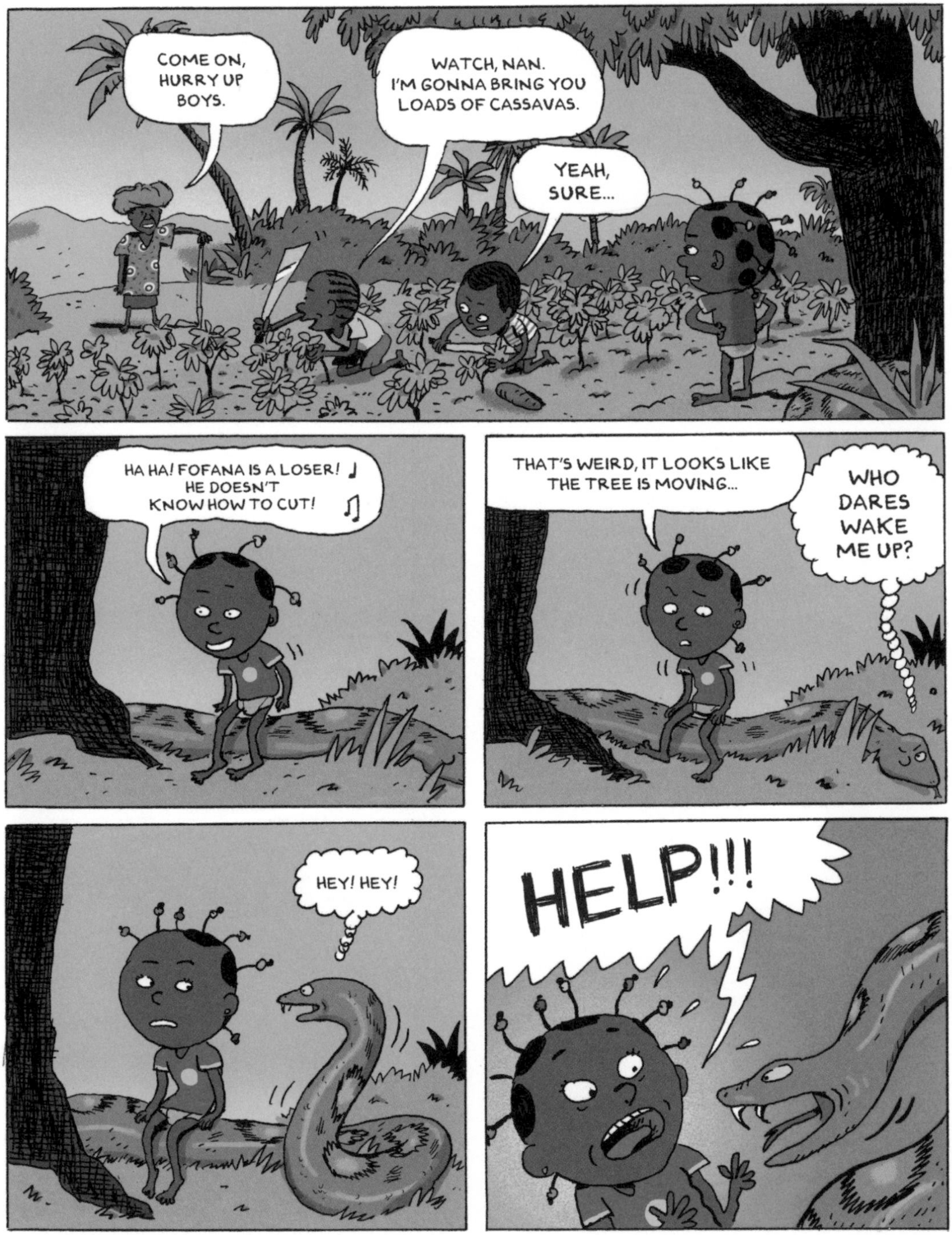
COME ON, HURRY UP BOYS.
WATCH, NAN. I'M GONNA BRING YOU LOADS OF CASSAVAS.
YEAH, SURE...
HA HA! FOFANA IS A LOSER! HE DOESN'T KNOW HOW TO CUT!
THAT'S WEIRD, IT LOOKS LIKE THE TREE IS MOVING...
WHO DARES WAKE ME UP?
HEY! HEY!
HELP!!!

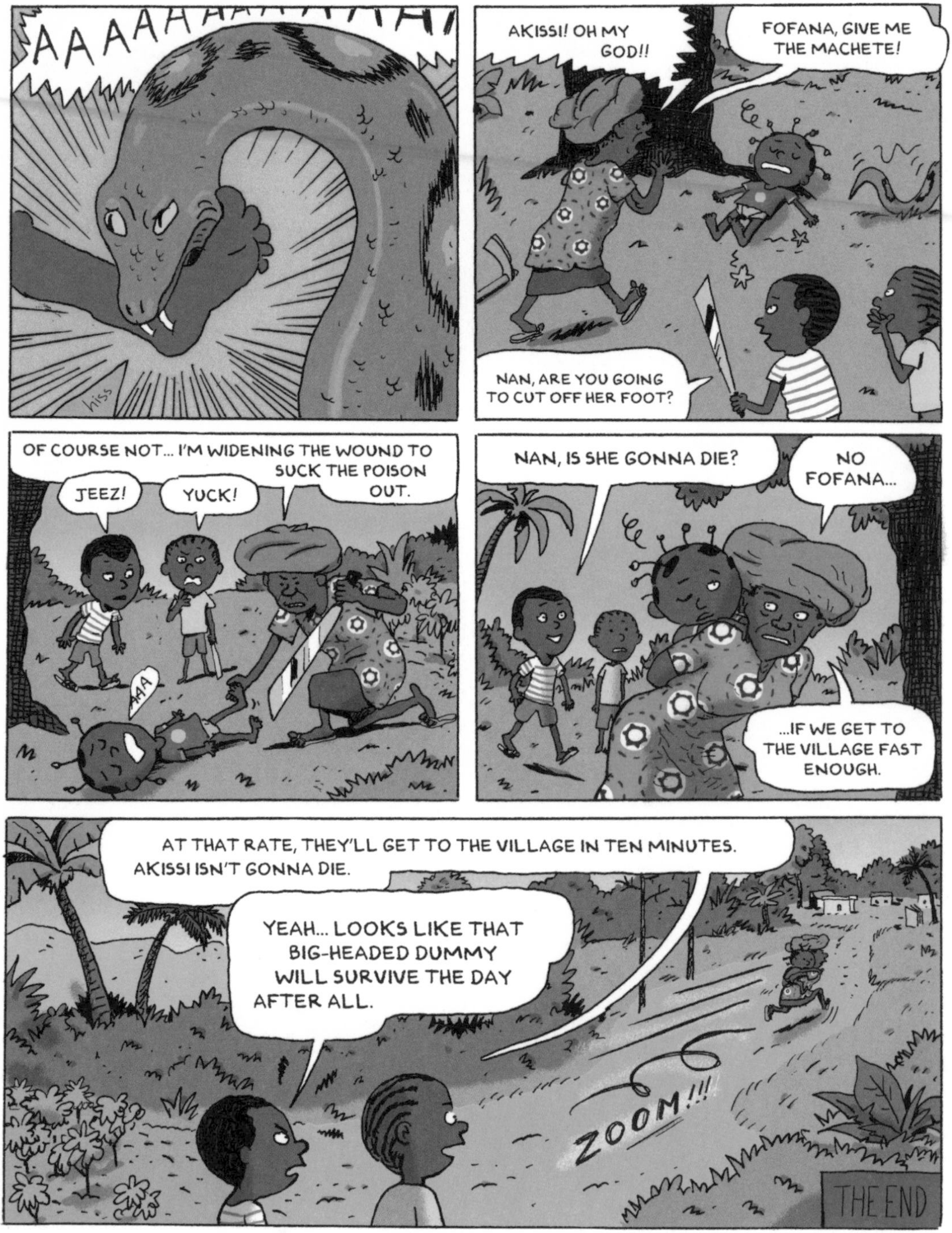
AAAAAAAAAAAH!
hiss
AKISSI! OH MY GOD!!
FOFANA, GIVE ME THE MACHETE!
NAN, ARE YOU GOING TO CUT OFF HER FOOT?
OF COURSE NOT... I'M WIDENING THE WOUND TO SUCK THE POISON OUT.
JEEZ!
YUCK!
AAA
NAN, IS SHE GONNA DIE?
NO FOFANA...
...IF WE GET TO THE VILLAGE FAST ENOUGH.
AT THAT RATE, THEY'LL GET TO THE VILLAGE IN TEN MINUTES. AKISSI ISN'T GONNA DIE.
YEAH... LOOKS LIKE THAT BIG-HEADED DUMMY WILL SURVIVE THE DAY AFTER ALL.
ZOOM!!!
THE END

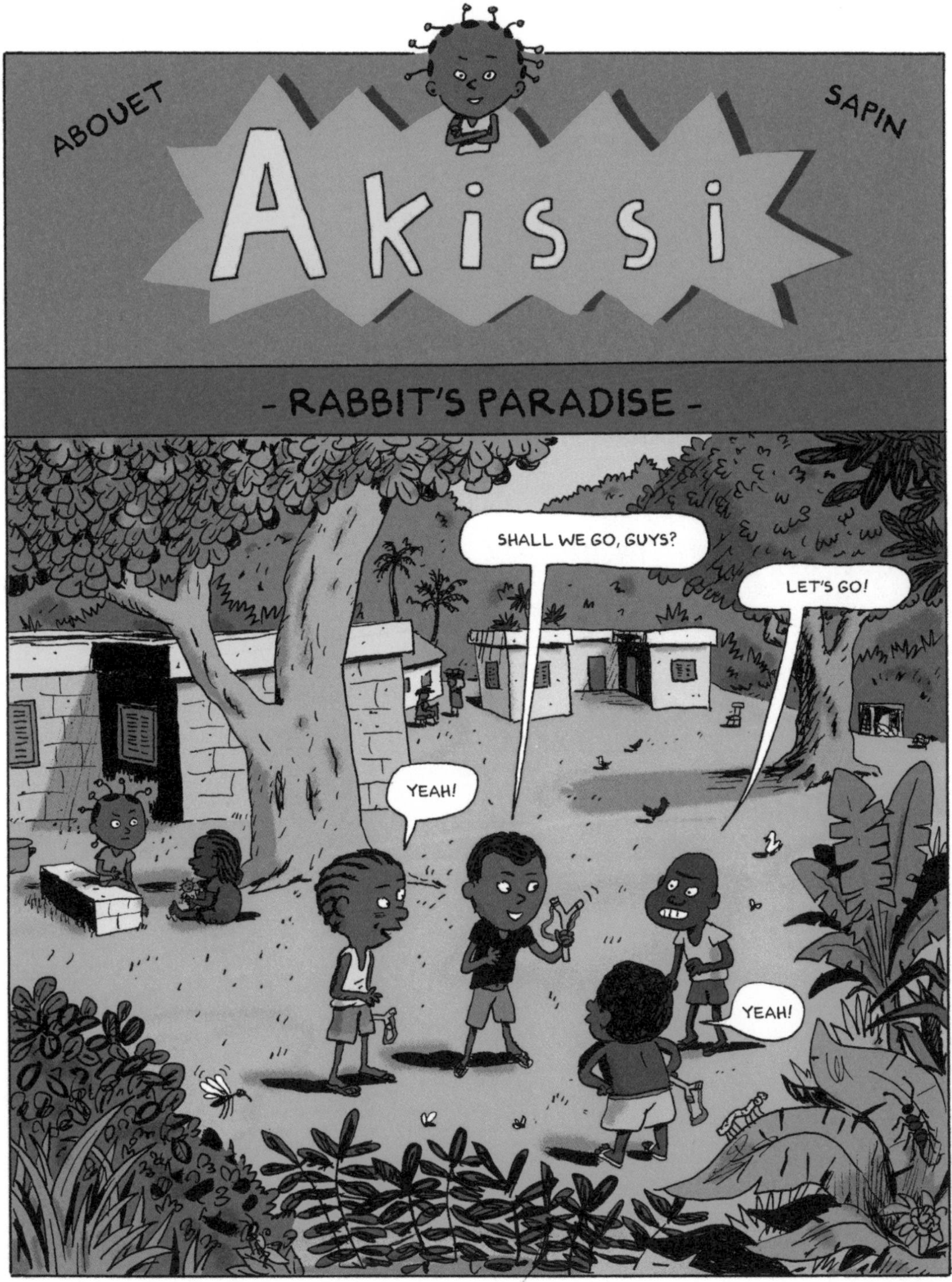
ABOUET
SAPIN
Akissi
- RABBIT'S PARADISE -
SHALL WE GO, GUYS?
YEAH!
LET'S GO!
YEAH!

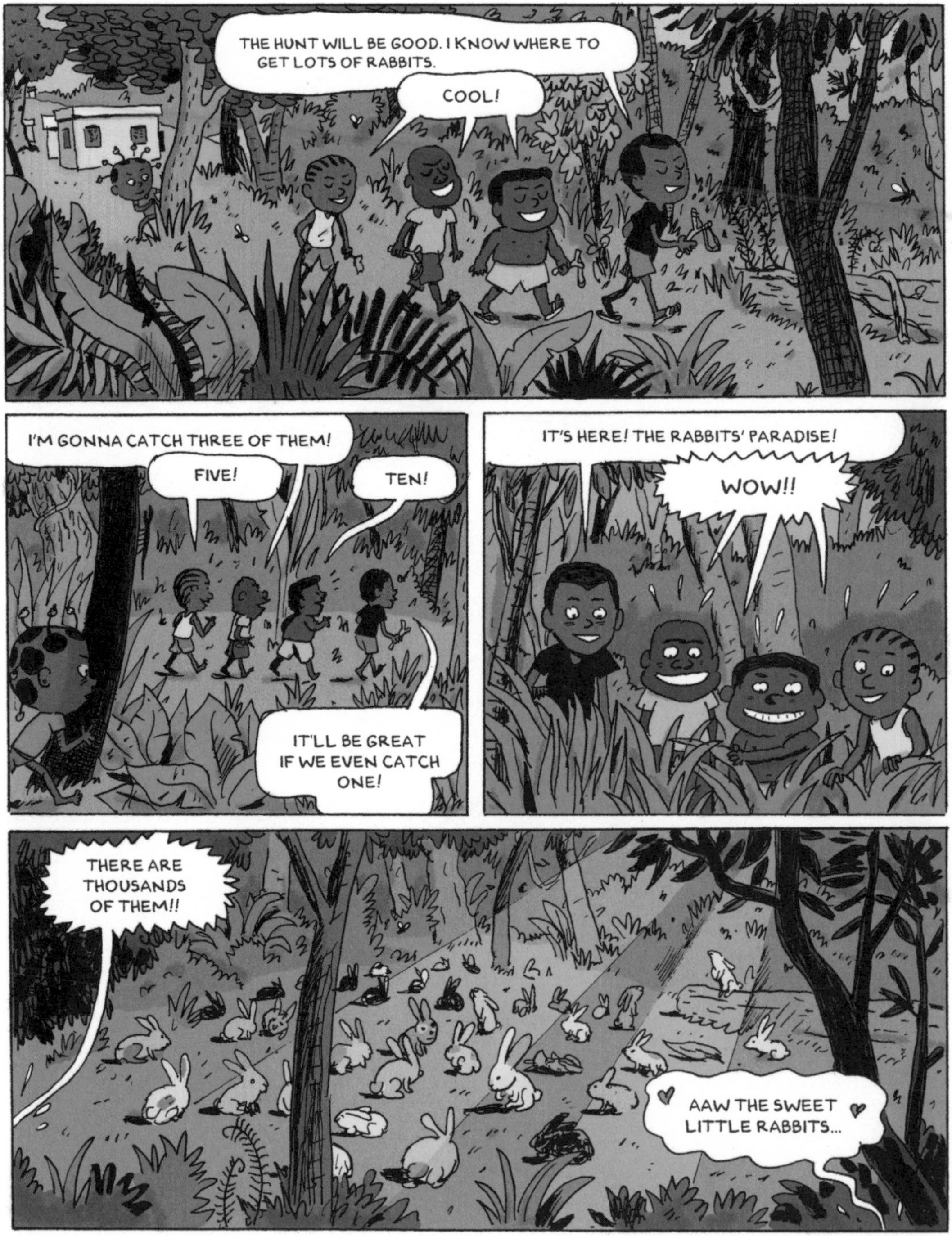
THE HUNT WILL BE GOOD. I KNOW WHERE TO GET LOTS OF RABBITS.
COOL!
I'M GONNA CATCH THREE OF THEM!
FIVE!
TEN!
IT'LL BE GREAT IF WE EVEN CATCH ONE!
IT'S HERE! THE RABBITS' PARADISE!
WOW!!
THERE ARE THOUSANDS OF THEM!!
AAW THE SWEET LITTLE RABBITS...

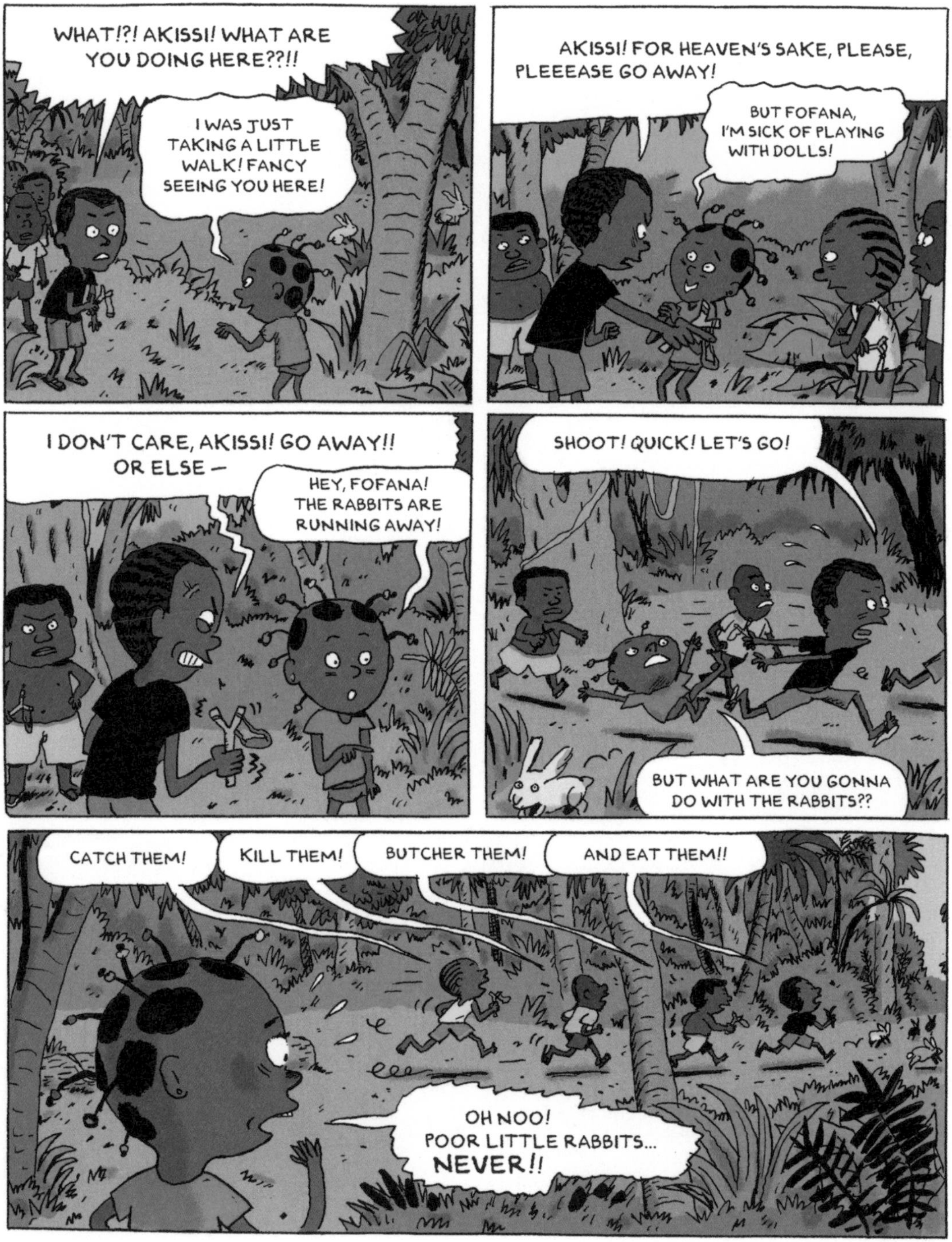
WHAT!?! AKISSI! WHAT ARE YOU DOING HERE??!!
I WAS JUST TAKING A LITTLE WALK! FANCY SEEING YOU HERE!
AKISSI! FOR HEAVEN'S SAKE, PLEASE, PLEEEASE GO AWAY!
BUT FOFANA, I'M SICK OF PLAYING WITH DOLLS!
I DON'T CARE, AKISSI! GO AWAY!! OR ELSE –
HEY, FOFANA! THE RABBITS ARE RUNNING AWAY!
SHOOT! QUICK! LET'S GO!
BUT WHAT ARE YOU GONNA DO WITH THE RABBITS??
CATCH THEM!
KILL THEM!
BUTCHER THEM!
AND EAT THEM!!
OH NOO! POOR LITTLE RABBITS... NEVER!!

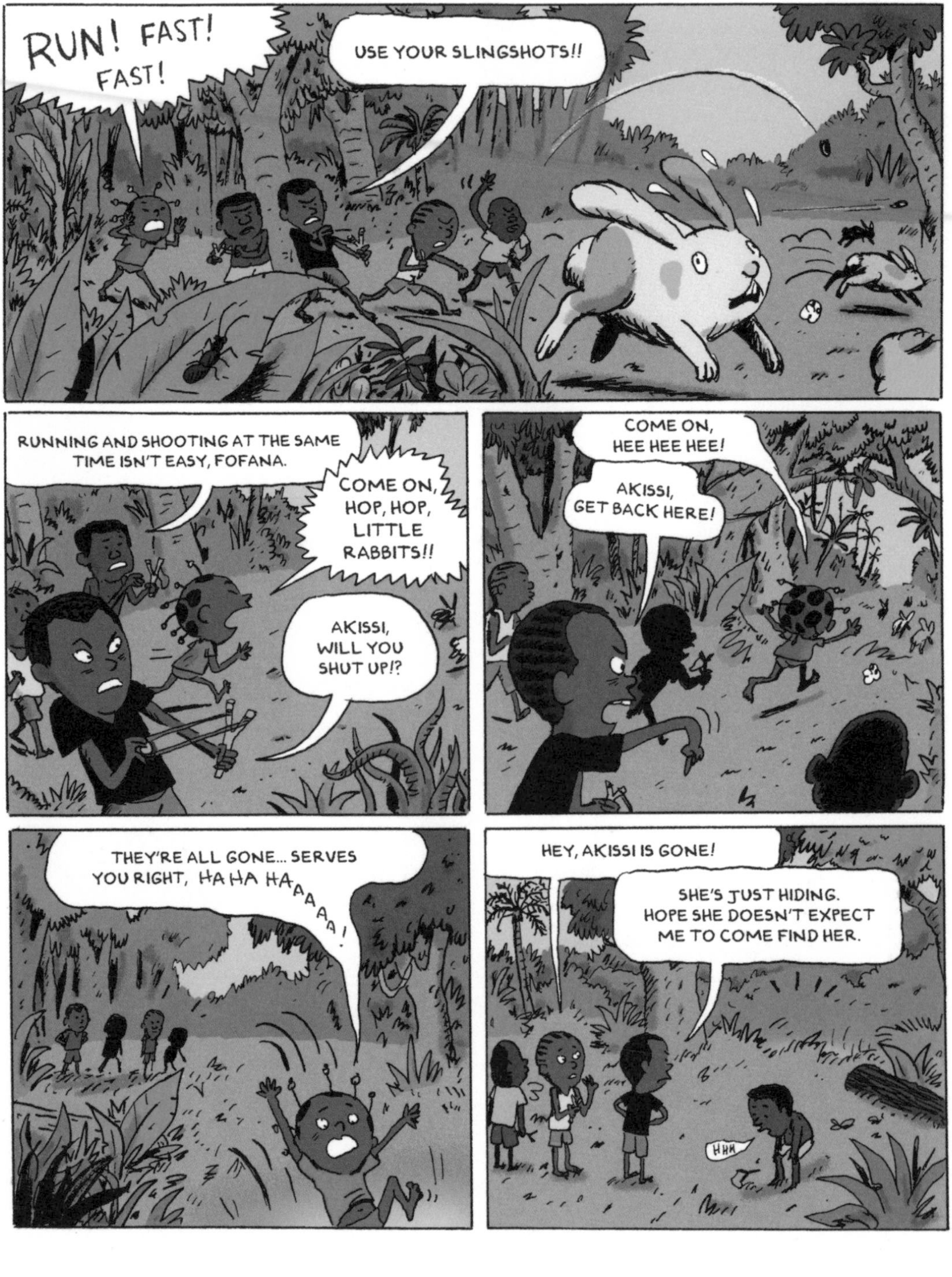
RUN! FAST! FAST!
USE YOUR SLINGSHOTS!!
RUNNING AND SHOOTING AT THE SAME TIME ISN'T EASY, FOFANA.
COME ON, HOP, HOP, LITTLE RABBITS!!
AKISSI, WILL YOU SHUT UP!?
COME ON, HEE HEE HEE!
AKISSI, GET BACK HERE!
THEY'RE ALL GONE... SERVES YOU RIGHT, HA HA HAAAAAA!
HEY, AKISSI IS GONE!
SHE'S JUST HIDING. HOPE SHE DOESN'T EXPECT ME TO COME FIND HER.
HHH

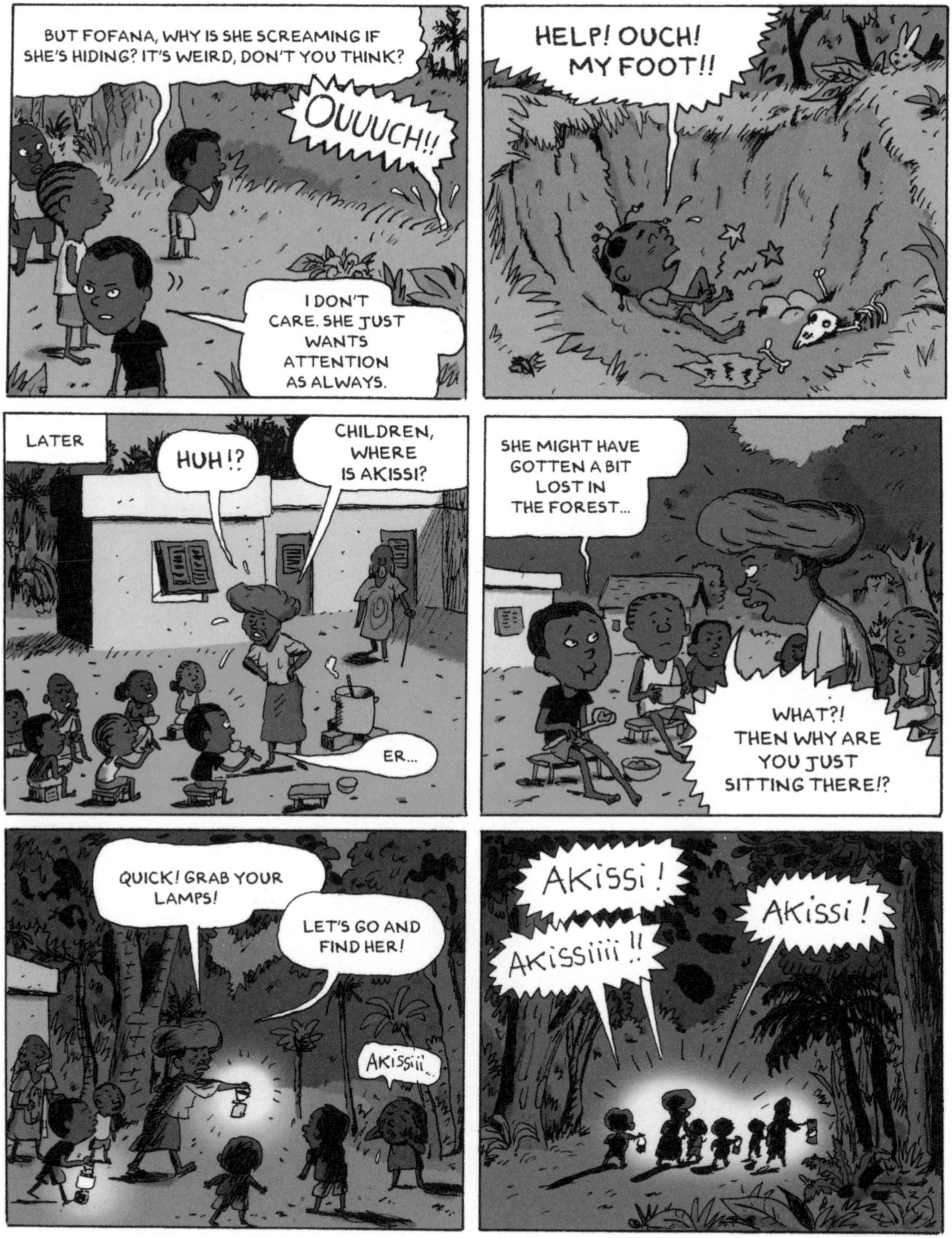
BUT FOFANA, WHY IS SHE SCREAMING IF SHE'S HIDING? IT'S WEIRD, DON'T YOU THINK?
OUUUCH!!
I DON'T CARE. SHE JUST WANTS ATTENTION AS ALWAYS.
HELP! OUCH! MY FOOT!!
LATER
HUH!?
CHILDREN, WHERE IS AKISSI?
ER...
SHE MIGHT HAVE GOTTEN A BIT LOST IN THE FOREST...
WHAT?! THEN WHY ARE YOU JUST SITTING THERE!?
QUICK! GRAB YOUR LAMPS!
LET'S GO AND FIND HER!
AKISSiii...
AKISSi!
AKISSiiii!!
AKISSi!

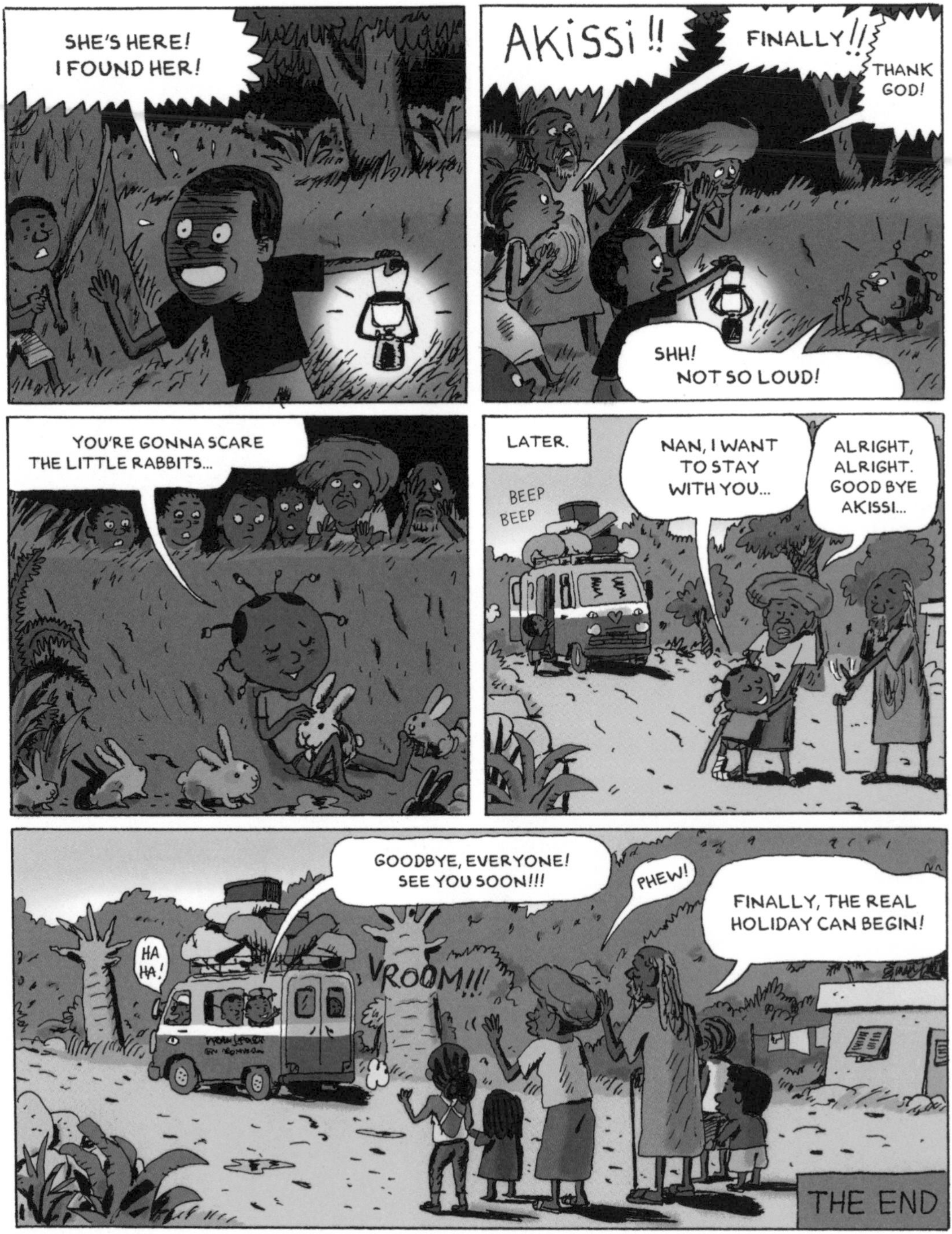

SHE'S HERE! I FOUND HER!
AKISSI!!
FINALLY!!
THANK GOD!
SHH! NOT SO LOUD!
YOU'RE GONNA SCARE THE LITTLE RABBITS...
LATER.
BEEP BEEP
NAN, I WANT TO STAY WITH YOU...
ALRIGHT, ALRIGHT. GOOD BYE AKISSI...
HA HA!
GOODBYE, EVERYONE! SEE YOU SOON!!!
VROOM!!!
PHEW!
FINALLY, THE REAL HOLIDAY CAN BEGIN!
THE END

BONUS

pages

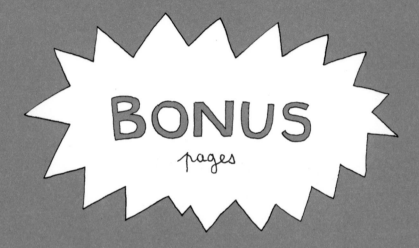

COCONUT MORSELS

for all my friends

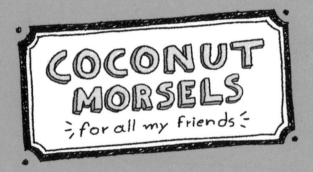

COCONUT MORSELS

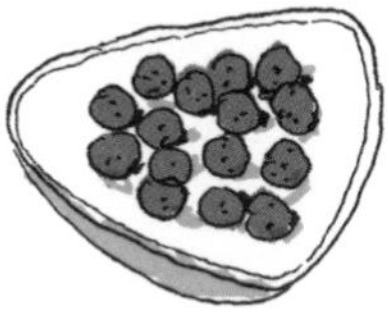

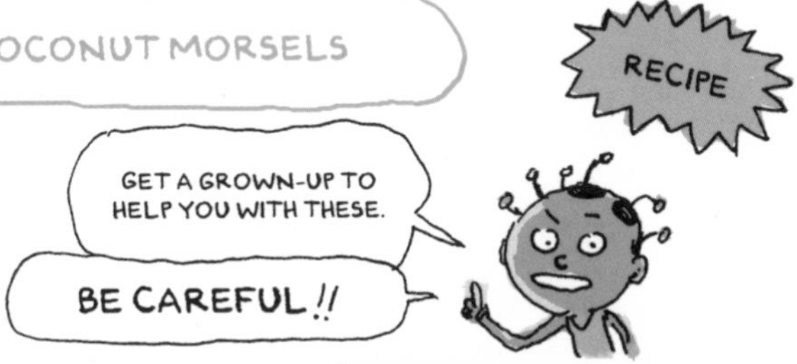
RECIPE
GET A GROWN-UP TO HELP YOU WITH THESE.
BE CAREFUL!!

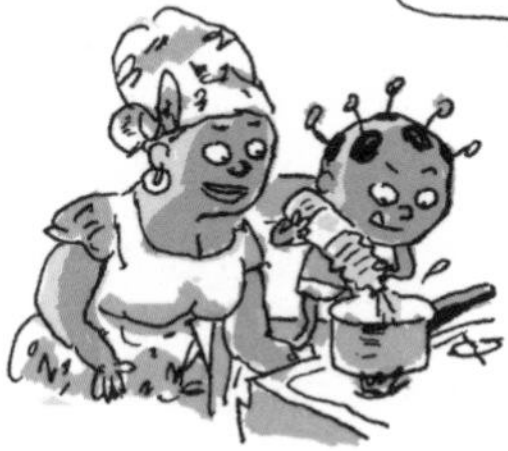

INGREDIENTS (SERVES 10 PEOPLE):

- ONE TIN OF SWEETENED CONDENSED MILK (397 GRAMS)
- 50 GRAMS OF SHREDDED COCONUT
- SUNFLOWER OIL (AS NEEDED)

PREP TIME: ABOUT TEN MINUTES

(1) FIRST, ASK A GROWN-UP TO GIVE YOU A HAND (TELL THEM YOU'LL SHARE SOME OF YOUR TREATS WITH THEM WHEN THEY'RE FINISHED).

(2) PUT TWO TABLESPOONS OF SUNFLOWER OIL IN A SAUCEPAN. HEAT THE OIL, THEN POUR IN THE SWEETENED CONDENSED MILK AND STIR FOR FIVE MINUTES.

(3) WHEN THE MIXTURE HAS STARTED TO TURN REDDISH, POUR IN THE SHREDDED COCONUT AND CONTINUE TO MIX FOR ANOTHER FIVE MINUTES, ALL THE WHILE TRYING NOT TO LET THE MIXTURE STICK TO THE BOTTOM OF THE SAUCEPAN.

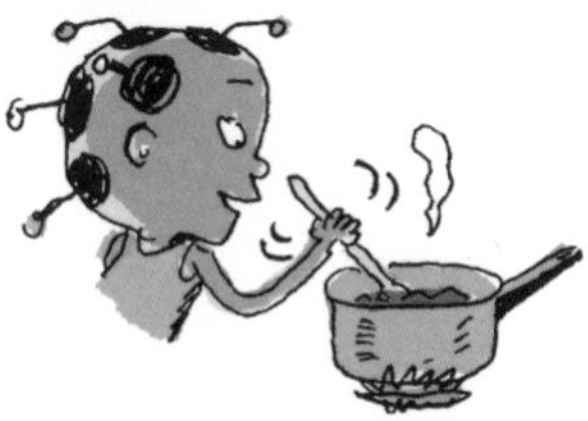

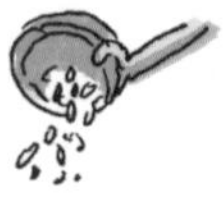

(4) WHEN THE MIXTURE BECOMES BROWN AND HAS A MOIST, DOUGHY TEXTURE (A BIT LIKE A THICK PUREE), SCOOP IT OUT OF THE SAUCEPAN AND INTO A DISH. MAKE LITTLE BALLS OUT OF THE DOUGH BY ROLLING PIECES OF IT BETWEEN YOUR HANDS. BE CAREFUL NOT TO BURN YOURSELF!

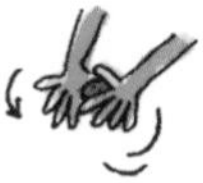

(5) AND THERE YOU HAVE IT! YOU CAN EAT THESE MORSELS WITH YOUR FRIENDS. WHEN THEY'RE WARMED UP THEY'RE SOFT, AND WHEN THEY'RE COLD, THEY HARDEN AND ARE VERY NICE!

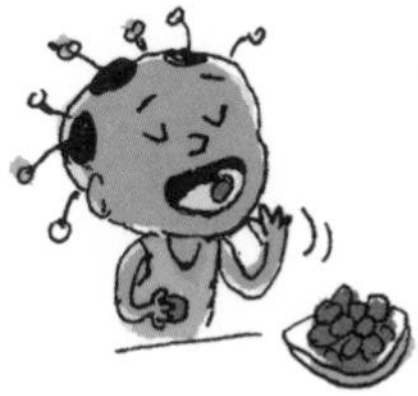

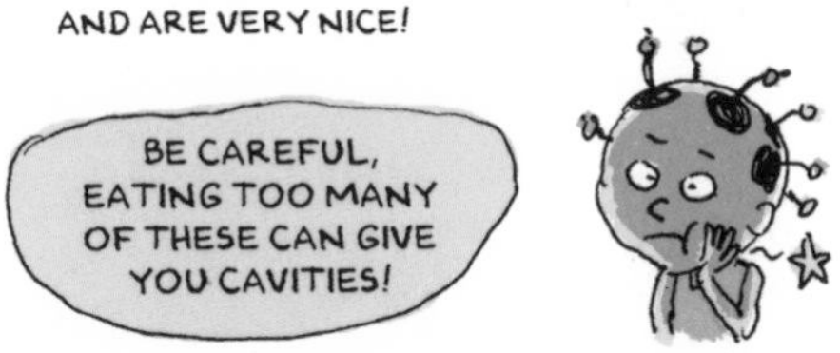
BE CAREFUL, EATING TOO MANY OF THESE CAN GIVE YOU CAVITIES!

Clé-Clé
or
CRUNCHY Jewels

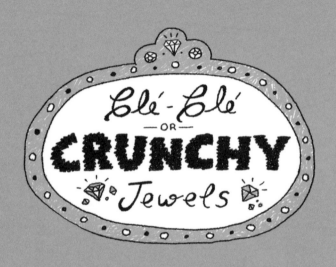

CLÉ-CLÉ   OR   CRUNCHY JEWELS

RECIPE

NORMALLY, THESE
ARE JUST FOR GIRLS, UNLESS
THE BOYS BEHAVE NICELY.

INGREDIENTS
(SERVES 4 FRIENDS)

- 200 GRAMS OF FLOUR
- 1/2 PACKET OF YEAST
  (OR ABOUT ONE HEAPING
  TABLESPOON)
- 3 TABLESPOONS OF SUGAR
- 1 PINCH OF SALT
- 100ML OF WATER
- SUNFLOWER OIL (AS NEEDED)

<u>CAREFUL!</u>
GET A GROWN-UP
TO HELP YOU WITH THIS RECIPE!

PREP TIME: ABOUT 15 MINUTES

(1) FIRST, ASK A GROWN-UP FOR
SOME HELP, TELLING THEM THEY WILL
BE ABLE TO HAVE A BITE TOO.

(2) WARM UP THE WATER
(DON'T LET IT BOIL)
AND ADD THE SUGAR AND SALT.

(3) IN A LARGE BOWL, MIX THE FLOUR
AND THE YEAST THOROUGHLY.

(4) ADD THE WATER
TO THIS MIX.
USE YOUR HANDS
TO MAKE IT INTO
A NICE DOUGH BALL.

(5) WITH THE DOUGH, YOU CAN
MAKE NECKLACES, RINGS,
BRACELETS AND EARRINGS.

(6) FRY THE JEWELS IN OIL
FOR SEVERAL MINUTES.

(7) VOILA! YOU CAN WEAR
YOUR BEAUTIFUL ACCESSORIES
NOW. AND DON'T FORGET
TO HAVE A BITE NOW AND THEN,
THEY TASTE SO GOOD!

CARAMELISED
PEANUTS

FOR CONSIDERATE
AND
OBEDIENT CHILDREN

CARAMELISED PEANUTS

RECIPE

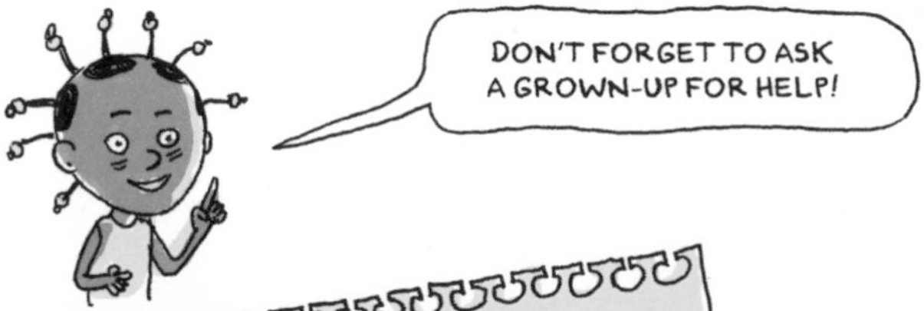
DON'T FORGET TO ASK
A GROWN-UP FOR HELP!

INGREDIENTS:

- 500 GRAMS OF CHOPPED PEANUTS
- 200 GRAMS OF SUGAR
- A SAUCEPAN
- A LARGE WOODEN SPOON
- A ROLLING PIN

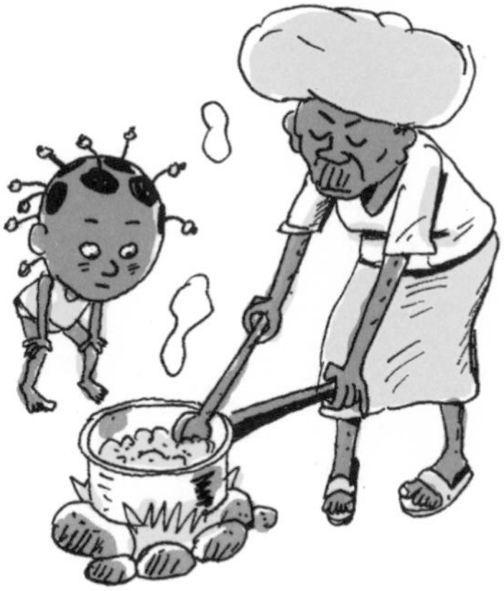

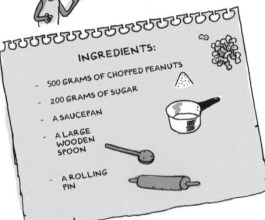

1. MELT THE SUGAR IN THE PAN, THEN ADD THE PEANUTS.

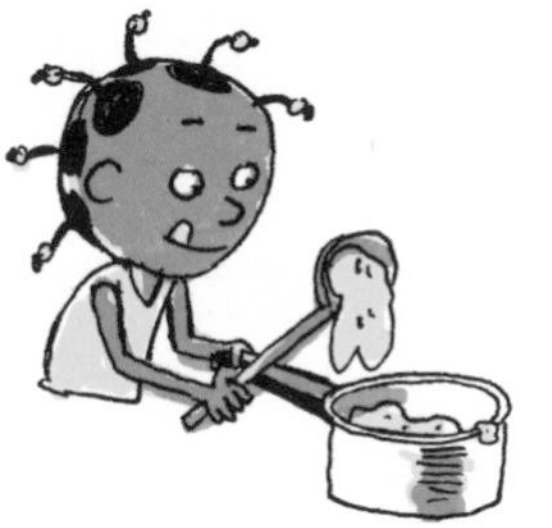

2. MIX THEM TOGETHER UNTIL YOU GET A DOUGH-LIKE TEXTURE.
3. AFTER 5 MINUTES, TAKE THE SAUCEPAN OFF THE HEAT, AS YOUR MIXTURE IS READY.
4. WITH YOUR ROLLING PIN, ROLL OUT THE "DOUGH" AND CUT IT IN ALL SORTS OF SHAPES (TRIANGLES, SQUARES, DIAMONDS). LET IT COOL AND HARDEN A BIT, THEN START MUNCHING!

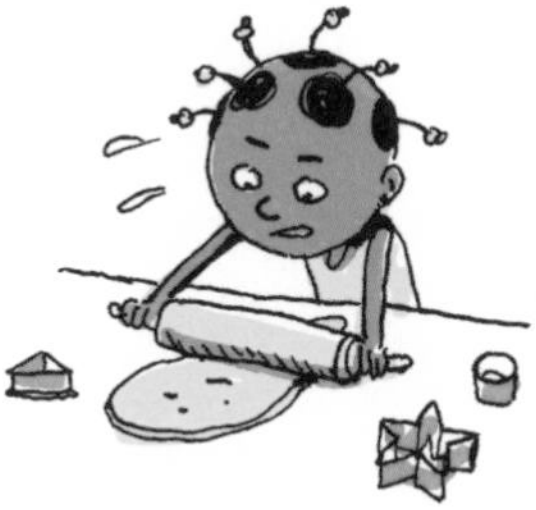

5. ENJOY!

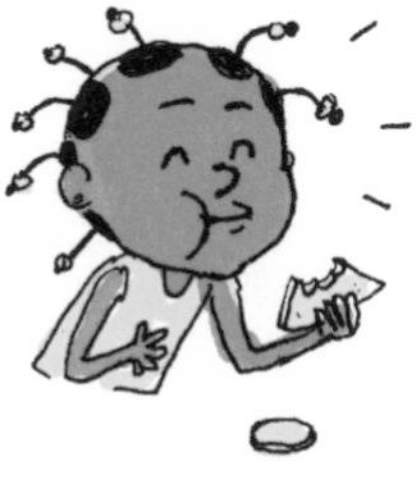

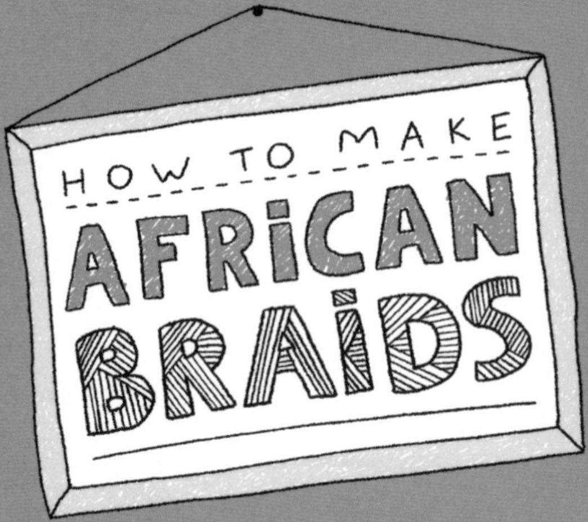
HOW TO MAKE
AFRICAN
BRAIDS

HOW TO MAKE AFRICAN BRAIDS

① TO START WITH, GO AND FIND A FRIEND WITH LONG HAIR (YOU CAN TRY IT ON YOURSELF, BUT IT WILL BE HARDER).

CAN I BRAID YOUR HAIR?

② TAKE A SECTION OF THE HAIR AND DIVIDE IT INTO THREE STRANDS.

③ PULL THE LEFT STRAND OVER AND INTO THE MIDDLE, BETWEEN THE TWO OTHERS.

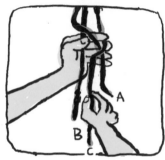

④ THEN PULL THE RIGHT STRAND OVER AND INTO THE MIDDLE.

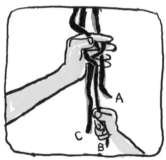

⑤ REPEAT UNTIL YOU GET TO THE TIPS OF THE HAIR.

⑥ WHEN THE BRAID IS DONE, YOU CAN SECURE THE END WITH A BEAD OR A HAIR TIE.

⑦ AND VOILÀ, NOW ALL YOU HAVE TO DO IS REPEAT FOR THE REST OF THE HAIR!

Marguerite Abouet was born in Abidjan, Ivory Coast, in the neighbourhood of Yopougon. At the age of 12, she moved to Paris, where she discovered wonderful libraries and developed a passion for books. After trying her hand at several different jobs, she became a legal assistant. In 2005, she published *Aya de Yopougon*, which won the Best Album prize at the Angoulême Comics Festival. The Ivorian series, drawn by Clément Oubrerie, comprises more than 700 pages that beautifully depict an authentic and seldom-seen side of Africa. The books are now translated into fifteen languages, and were adapted into a movie in 2013. In 2010, Abouet and illustrator Mathieu Sapin published the first volume of *Akissi*, a children's series inspired by her childhood memories. When she is not busy writing stories, Marguerite Abouet helps build libraries throughout Africa through her charity, Des Livres pour Tous (www.deslivrespourtous.org).

Mathieu Sapin was born in 1974. After attending the School of Decorative Arts in Strasbourg, he spent two years working at the International Center for Comic Strips and Images, where he illustrated children's literature for Nathan, Bayard Presse, Albin Michel, and Lito. In 2003 he began to devote himself entirely to making comics, namely the alcoholically adventurous series *Supermurgeman*. This series developed into a unique and quirky universe, rife with irony and absurdity. Today, his list of works includes over 30 titles, including the *Akissi* series, written by Marguerite Abouet.

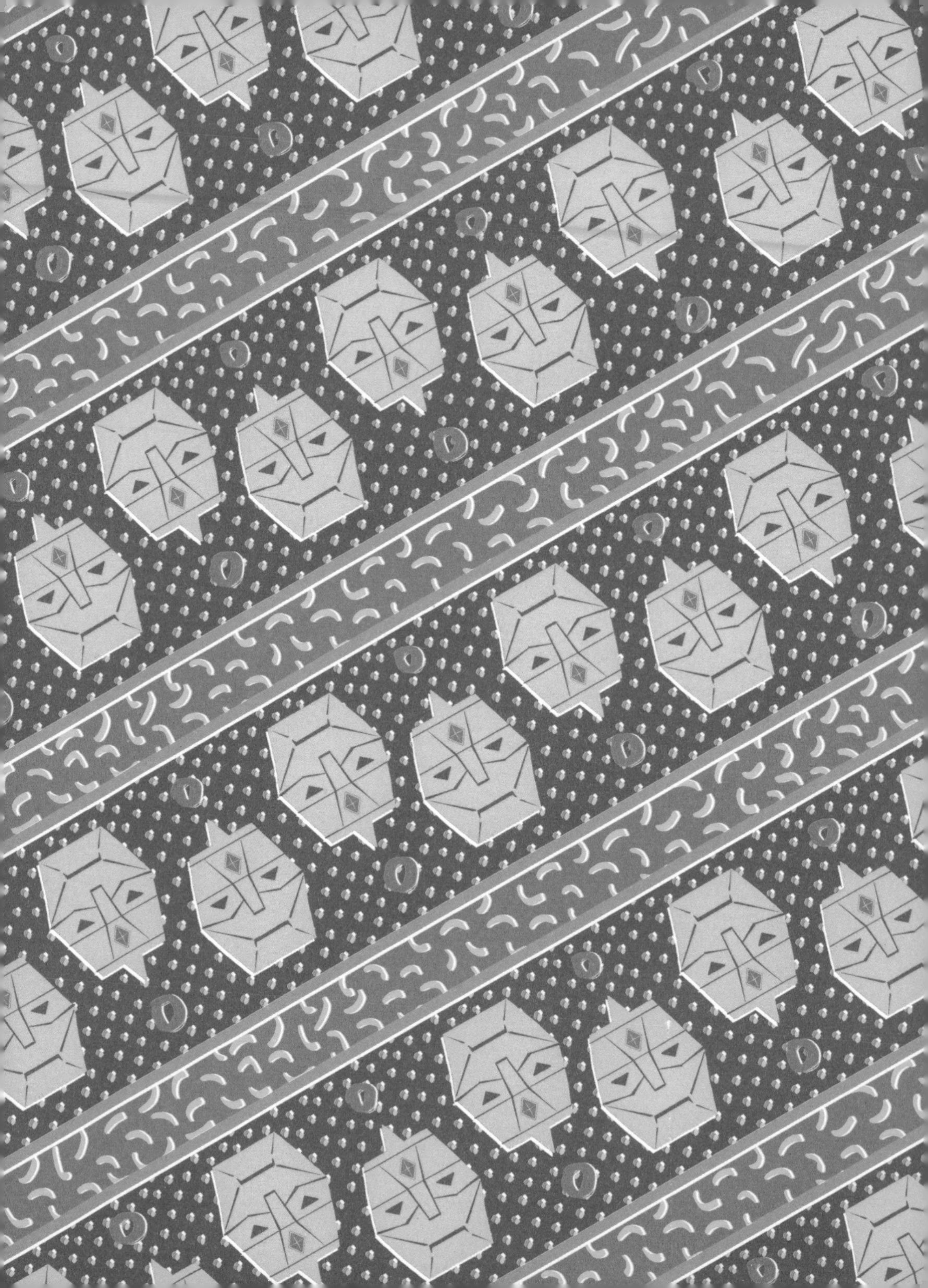